THE MOLECULE MAN

Martin

With Best Wishes

David Crisman

April 2008

Published by

Librario Publishing Ltd.

ISBN 10 : 1-904440-96-7
ISBN 13 : 978-1904440963

Copies can be ordered from :
www.librario.com

or

Brough House
Milton Brodie
Kinloss
Morayshire
IV36 2UA
Tel / Fax : 01343 850178

Printed in Times.

Typesetting and layout by Steven James
www.chimeracreations.co.uk

Printed and bound by
imprintdigital, Exeter

THE
MOLECULE
MAN

David Crigman

Librario

Also by David Crigman :

What's Truth Got To Do With It?
Librario, 2006

About the Author

A practising QC in criminal cases, David Crigman was educated at King Edward's School, Birmingham and the University of Leeds. Of indeterminate age. Married with one son. Frequently escapes the courtroom to travel to remote places but sometimes is not sure what to do when he gets there. Finds writing novels a great relaxation from court work and is currently working on his third, *In Death We Trust*.

The Molecule Man is the second novel in a trilogy featuring the character Naomi Nicholas following *What's Truth Got To Do With It?* which was published in 2006.

Prologue

As he spoke the old man carefully opened the lid of the case and lovingly removed the instrument from its red velvet bed. Immediately, the woman could see how his slender fingers curled around the precious fiddle, longing to make it sing, and she did not hesitate.

"Play it for us," she urged. "Please play it. Right now. And it must be music from Hungary. Music that tells us what it was like to have lived in Magyarovar."

In silence the stranger rose to his feet and turned to face them, placing the violin upon his shoulder in such a way that it appeared that his whole body had been constructed to bend around this frail instrument, his chin caressing its faded, varnished wood.

At first the arm moved slowly, as the bow gently encouraged the strings to communicate to the beautiful woman and the man at her side, the suffering he had endured but, as the music captivated them, the rhythm quickened and, beneath the hardship, they began to feel the joy and rejoicing in life that had enabled this unusual man to survive tyranny. Soon the stranger was stamping his heel into the ground and the volume of his wonderful music reached its piercing crescendo, before falling away as the last note, now mournful again and from a far off place and a far distant time, was carried away on the warm London breeze.

The stranger resumed his seat, his beloved instrument resting silent upon his knees. For a moment none of them spoke as the spell that had been cast continued to weave its magic, until the woman leaned across and took the musician's hand in her own.

"You took us to Magyarovar," she told him, "now we have been there too."

Chapter 1

"You'll use the Falcon Eye that came in last month from Damascus," breathed Abdelkarim Mohammed in that dark voice, now permanently hoarse, courtesy of the scar tissue on the vocal cords from one of the two Uzi bullets that had come within a millimetre of putting him in the ground. The second had carried away the lower part of his stomach.

"It's been anchored to the bed of the white Datsun pickup in the lock-up garage," the hoarse voice continued. *"There's a tarpaulin to cover it when you're on the road. Looks like you're just carrying a piece of machinery."*

"When do I learn the exact target?" demanded the younger voice of Fahid Yasin, unable to disguise his excitement at the prospect of real action after waiting so long for the orders to come.

"Meet Khalid in the garage at six o'clock this evening. He'll have the details. The type of aircraft and the expected time of approach. You already know where to strike from. The farmer isn't using that field this month and the dirt track leading to it from the road will be deserted. Go straight there with Khalid. Afterwards, do exactly as he says."

"It'll be dark by then. Is the nightscope equipment OK? You know what happened in Frankfurt, we don't want another night like that," Fahid Yasin enquired anxiously.

"Everything's been double-checked. It's top quality Surface-to-Air, with a high explosive warhead. Damascus got it direct from Cairo where they developed it. It's even better than the Stinger and it's brought down military jets, let alone lumbering commercial airliners. You'll have no problem, the plane'll be so low in its approach to the runway that you'll see the colour of the pilot's eyes," laughed Abdelkarim Mohammed. *"Your day has come. You have been chosen."*

"I pray to Allah that it will be an American target," intoned the younger voice. *"Make them suffer for Baghdad."*

"It won't be American this time. TransAtlantic flights arrive early morning. This is to be a European. One of the infidel's puppy dogs. You'll know soon enough."

As Ibrahim El-Hoorie carefully inched his way alongside the silver heating ducts and piping in the ceiling space above the Sunstream Internet Café on the outskirts of Manchester, he had been surprised to hear conversation in Arabic drifting up from below and passing with remarkable clarity through the false ceiling tiles into the grubby crawling space where, for nearly an hour, he had been searching for the electrical fault that had caused the heating to fail during the morning.

At first he had only picked up the occasional phrase, but sufficient to realise that this was not the Arabic of an immigrant family, touched by the inflection of the host country. This was the society Arabic of Riyadh or Jeddah. The older, hoarse voice in particular, had a purity of language that came only with education in high places and its tone conveyed authority and power.

At last he found the cause of the fault. Typically, the idle British workmen who had done the conversion work on the café had left chunks of rubble in the gaps between the wooden joists and, somehow, a large piece of brick must have shifted and fallen on to the electrical cable, stretching it and breaking the connection.

Crouching down in the restricted space and swinging his heavy tool bag into a position where he could extract the strippers that he would need to re-establish the connection, he moved a few feet further to his right, which must have brought him directly over the men, ignorant of his hidden presence above, speaking in their cultured Arabic in the café below. Their words stopped him dead in his tracks. They were so clear it was as if the men were talking directly to him and he froze in disbelief as, unwittingly, he found himself listening to invisible conspirators plotting death.

"You're to use the Falcon Eye that came in last month from Damascus."

"When do I learn the exact target?"

Undoubtedly two men, Ibrahim reasoned. The older voice in control, barking commands. Obvious blood-hunger in the younger voice. Ibrahim had no doubt that these were men in deadly earnest. Sweat poured from his brow and down his sides underneath his coarse work shirt as, crouched silently above, he tried to absorb every chilling word they spoke, whilst incredulity rapidly gave way to fear and horror. A sense of unreality made it difficult to decide what he should do. His calves were beginning to cramp from maintaining such an uncomfortable position and his neck ached as he held his head tilted to one side so as to pick up each exchange.

"Is the nightscope equipment OK? You know what happened in Frankfurt, we don't want another night like that."

"The plane'll be so low in its approach to the runway that you'll see the colour of the pilot's eyes."

When, in the early 1980s, his father and uncle had decided to buy up the commercial property leases in Harrow, Ibrahim had been too young to understand that this might mean that the family would remain indefinitely in Britain. Arabic tradition, religion, culture and language were as strictly applied in their luxurious Kensington flat as they had been in the Riyadh villa. The birth of his younger sister, deliberately timed to occur when his mother was on a visit to Riyadh, had re-enforced Ibrahim's expectation that sooner or later, the family would return to Saudi. But, as his father's property empire expanded and education at one of London's most fashionable schools exposed him to friendships and opportunities that the Middle East could never rival, he began to see his future as an Englishman, still an Arab, fluent in Arabic and faithful to their traditions, but also with an obligation to England and a sense of belonging to this tolerant, easy and hospitable society.

Eventually, he would be placed in a lucrative post within the family's commercial network but, having recently graduated with a degree in Electrical Engineering from Bristol University, he was currently spending six months at grass roots level in the variety of shops and buildings that the company now owned countrywide. Suddenly, in the dark, above the ceiling of a Manchester café, he found himself confronted with a situation which was beyond anything that he could ever have contemplated.

"I pray to Allah that it will be an American target . . . "

Backing awkwardly along the crawling space as fast as he could, Ibrahim realised that there was no choice to be made. By some grotesque quirk of fate he had listened to men plotting to bring terror and death to innocent people in a land which had offered his family and himself only kindness and opportunity. Arabs they may be, but *they* were criminals and murderers. He must get a description of these conspirators and then inform the Police.

Access to the roof space was through a trapdoor in the ceiling of the storage room and his feet soon located the top rung of the ladder that he had left in place. Within a minute he had scurried down the ladder into the storage room, out of the back door, up the side alley and on to the main road. Forcing himself to slow down to walking pace, he came to the large glass windows and front door of the café. There was a lot of traffic noise and some pedestrian activity, so lingering in the doorway would attract little if any attention. This was one of their larger Internet Cafés, containing eighty units set out in ten widely-spaced rows of eight, like library cubicles. Early afternoon was never busy and his eyes immediately told him that the place was empty except for the two men in the far corner, staring straight ahead at their computer screens but plainly engrossed in animated discussion. Neither of the two members of staff was in view, no doubt taking advantage of the slow time of day to get something to eat, in the kitchen behind the counter at the opposite end of the café from where the conspirators sat.

Even from this distance Ibrahim's vantage point afforded him a clear view of the left side of the face of the older man. Almost completely bald with a neatly trimmed grey beard. Bloated face with sallow, large-pored complexion. An unusual nose for an Arab, broad and flat. There seemed to be something odd about the neck but, denied a frontal view, Ibrahim couldn't be sure precisely what it was. The man was wearing a red lightweight sweater, his obviously expensive black overcoat lay draped neatly across the adjacent desk.

Seeing the men in the flesh, rather than listening to their disembodied voices floating through the ether, lent the scene a sense of cold reality which had been lacking as he had crouched in the roof space. Surprised at the calmness that had now descended upon him, Ibrahim pushed open the newly painted door, causing the automatic bleeper to sound as he walked inside, trying to appear casual and unconcerned. Studiously refusing to glance in the direction of the conspirators in the far corner, he could feel their eyes boring into his back as he made his way to the counter where the young girl had appeared on hearing his entrance. This was an inner-city suburb which had become predominantly non-white and Ibrahim was not over-concerned that his ethnic appearance would alarm the men. His grubby baseball cap was worn with the peak down low and his square-lensed prescription glasses rendered him anonymous amongst the myriad of mid-Eastern and Asian inhabitants that had made this sector of Manchester their home.

As the sullen girl operated the Gaggia Espresso machine to prepare his coffee, he selected a computer desk which would give him a clear frontal view of both men, whilst being far enough away from them not to unsettle them. The unsmiling girl with her straggly hair brought his coffee to the desk together with the password for half an hour's use of the computer. Only when she had walked away did he allow his eyes to lift and look in the direction of the far corner. Their conversation had ceased when he entered the café but there had been no sound from their direction indicating imminent departure and now, in more subdued tones, the talking had resumed, although he was no longer able to make out any of the words actually used.

The ugly deformity on the left lower neck of the older man was clearly visible from this angle. Running down towards the collar bone was a deep, puckered oval depression with pink ridges of healed flesh radiating from its centre. Heavy build. Too old for the front line now, probably in his mid-forties. Calm, solid and deliberate, whereas the younger man appeared more animated. Jet-black hair scraped flat and sideways across the scalp, narrow darting eyes, a prominent sharp nose which had clearly been broken more than once in its time, the bridge deviating sharply to the right with a distinctive, unsightly nodule of cartilage at the top. Customary moustache and beard. Well-built. Probably 15 stone. Muscular. Hard to judge the height but at least six feet. Mid-twenties.

Forcing himself to drink the coffee slowly, whilst surreptitiously absorbing every last detail of their appearance, Ibrahim used up sufficient of his computer time to prevent his departure arousing suspicion. As soon as he dared, he casually headed for the door, aware of the two heads looking up simultaneously at the sound of his departure, but still clearly engrossed in their desperate discussions. Within a dozen paces he was out of sight of the window and he could give vent to the pent-up anxiety that had beset him since the Arabic words had floated into earshot.

Dialling 999 was one option but the Police Station was less than five hundred yards up the road and the adrenalin made his legs pump, until the toe of his boot suddenly caught on the edge of a paving stone, sending him crashing into the gutter. A hole was ripped in the knee of his jeans, the scraped flesh beneath visibly bleeding through it, whilst his glasses were broken, cutting the bridge of his nose in the process. Undaunted, he picked himself up and hurried on as fast as he could, soon bursting through the doors into the reception foyer of the suburban Police Station.

Dressed in a floral sari that reached to the floor and jabbering in Urdu to a bemused and bored uniformed Desk Sergeant, the Pakistani woman made her unintelligible demands. They were the only two people present as Ibrahim arrived breathlessly at the counter.

"Help," he shouted, "I must have help immediately."

With his torn jeans, bleeding nose and hat knocked to a ridiculous angle, he looked like a wild man. Moreover, he suffered from a condition which meant that both of his eyes did not look in precisely the same direction, lending him a rather disturbed look, rendered even more noticeable by the loss of his glasses.

"Steady on, Sir. Steady on. I'm just arranging an interpreter for this lady. Her bag's been stolen . . . "

"Listen very carefully," declared Ibrahim, spitting the words out with intensity and leaning forward across the counter so that his peculiar eyes and bleeding nose were but a few inches from the Sergeant's fleshy face.

"I'm reporting a terrorist threat. You must get some officers to the Internet Café down the road. Now. Immediately. Two terrorists are in there and . . . "

The remainder of his sentence was drowned out as the Pakistani lady began to wail and shout in her language, seeking to push this rude and noisy youth away from the counter and stop him from queue-jumping in pursuit of the Sergeant's attention.

"Have you been drinking?" the Sergeant demanded, stepping back a pace from the wild youth. "You're behaving like you have and your nose is cut . . . "

"No, I bloody haven't," Ibrahim shouted angrily.

"Let me phone for the interpreter for this woman and then I'll listen to you," replied the Sergeant, placing his hand on the woman's arm in an effort to calm her. "She's very upset."

"I'm telling you this is an emergency. Lives are at stake. Get some officers in here immediately. I can identify the terrorists at the Café. Do it now or people may get killed, you incompetent idiot," screamed Ibrahim in frustration at this dullard's reaction.

"Don't start throwing your weight round in here. And don't scream at me.

"We get panic reports of terrorist threats all the time. They usually come to nothing. I'll get a couple of the PCs to come down from the canteen and take some details. Just be patient," he replied, picking up the internal phone to call for some men.

Nearly five frustrating minutes passed while the inept Sergeant phoned hither and thither within the Station, seeking available manpower as the Asian woman sat weeping and wailing in the corner of the reception foyer. Every time Ibrahim tried to instil some sense of urgency into the officer he was waved away by irritated gestures and shakes of the head. Pacing the floor in a state of extreme anger saw another two or three precious minutes evaporate until, eventually, two fresh-faced young constables, hatless and in shirtsleeves, emerged through the connecting security door, crudely wiping crumbs from their damp lips with the back of their hands, as evidence that their

17

refreshment break had been inconveniently interrupted.

Ibrahim failed to hear the Sergeant's aside to the young officers as they passed by him. "Completely barmy, I reckon. But check it out."

"What the hell took you so long," exploded Ibrahim. "There are two terrorists plotting to shoot down a plane. You've got to get down to the Internet Café now."

At last there was some action as the constables hurried Ibrahim back through the security door, along a corridor and out of a rear door into the yard behind the Station where the Police vehicles were parked. Barking a few questions at him, the officers headed for a white unmarked saloon, ushered Ibrahim into the back seat, jumped into the front and set off. It took less than thirty seconds to reach the front doors of the Café and the three men leaped from the vehicle and raced inside. The cupboard was bare. Where, but a few minutes ago, the two sinister Arabs had sat in earnest discussion about the Falcon Eye, there were two empty chairs. Not a soul was in the place except for the dim girl behind the counter, sitting on a high stool, staring vacantly into space and quite unable to give the Police any useful information. The conspirators had flown the coop.

"There are no terrorists here now," one of them observed to him cynically.

"Of course not," declared Ibrahim in a state of such anger that he didn't care how abusive he became. "While you sat finishing your bloody sandwiches and your idiot of a Sergeant hopped from one foot to the other, you've let two dangerous men get away. Lives are at risk. If they do what they threatened, you'll have a national disaster on your hands and, if you'd moved your lazy arses, you could have caught them."

"Just back off, mate. There's no one here. And terrorists are hardly likely to do their plotting in public. Most times, these kind of reports go nowhere. You may have misheard. They may have been a couple of jokers talking rubbish. We get a lot of it, sir," was the complacent offering of the tall, gangly constable who looked like he should still have been at school. "Don't get yourself into a lather. We'll take you back to the Station, get some details and put an extra couple of patrol cars on the airport runs tonight. Nothing'll come of it, mark my words."

"You haven't taken a blind bit of notice of me, have you? I'm not a fool. I know what I bloody heard, for God's sake."

The two officers looked at each other and raised their eyebrows. They had no doubt they had a nutcase on their hands.

"We've done what we could. We'll drive round the streets with you for a few minutes. See if you can spot 'em," offered the shorter red-haired officer. "Then, like my colleague says, we'll get some details off you back at the Station. People talk stupid all the time. But we'll inform the airport patrols."

Within the hour Ibrahim El-Hoorie's complaint had reached Inspector level at the Police Station. Fury and frustration had given way to complete despair, while the Inspector made it pretty clear that he was unimpressed by what he saw as the over-reaction of this scruffy youth with the torn jeans, bloodied face and half-deranged look. The exchanges were following the same pattern as before.

"You must understand, sir, that we get reports like this all the time. Bits of overheard conversation. But we've no intelligence of any terrorists planning anything up here. Obviously we'll run some checks but . . . "

"These men were terrorists," interrupted Ibrahim. "They meant what they said. They spoke in my language."

"My officers found no evidence of any Arabs having been there. Even if there were, you can't be sure what they said. You think you do. You think they meant what you think you heard. In Arabic through the ceiling. That's the reality of it. I've already assured you that we've alerted the airport patrols and I'll have a couple of extra crews check the perimeter of the airport throughout the evening. From what you've said to us I don't have sufficient material to close down the whole airport. You just misheard."

"I misheard nothing."

"Have you ever received any psychiatric treatment?" the Inspector asked.

"You've got a bloody nerve," Ibrahim shouted in a fury. "I'm a damned sight saner than you are."

"Do you have any idea what it costs to close an airport down, even for an hour? We don't overreact at the drop of a hat.

Encourages false reports. It's been referred to my Super and I've told you the steps we'll take," replied the Inspector rising from his seat so as to indicate that the conversation was over.

"I refuse to accept this," declared Ibrahim defiantly, banging his fist on the Inspector's desk. "I can identify these men. The older man was certainly a Saudi and it's a pound to a penny that he'll be known to your Intelligence Services. With a scar like that on his neck he's seen the Front Line. Don't you have a mug shot album? I can pick him out. You'd better do as I'm telling you or else . . . "

"Don't threaten me, Sir. I've already explained that there's no Intelligence of any imminent terrorist threat at the moment but we'll put extra cars out. Don't worry. We're on top of it. Good afternoon."

* * *

SPECIAL LATE EDITION

31 DIE AS JET DOWNED BY TERRORIST ROCKET

Remarkable skill of pilot saves countless lives. 2 suspected terrorists pursued by Police in death car chase. Prime Minister Denstone denounces attack as "cowardly atrocity"

[Associated Press. Manchester, England]

31 passengers were killed and over fifty seriously injured this evening when a TransEuropean Airbus was hit by an anti-Aircraft surface to air missile as the plane made its final approach to Manchester International Airport. At least one rocket, believed to be of Soviet design, ripped into the tail section of the aircraft when it was less than three miles from the runway at the Airport. According to first reports from aviation experts, only the skill of the pilot averted an even worse disaster as, despite massive damage to the tail section, he managed to bring the aircraft down on the main runway where emergency personnel extinguished flames which threatened to engulf the plane. Over 70 survivors were safely evacuated, although at least 50 were

seriously injured, of whom 11 are currently on the critical list. First reports suggest that the terrorists had launched the missile from a vehicle situated in a field under the flight path at a point where the aircraft was at very low altitude. Within minutes of the attack Police vehicles pursued a white Datsun pickup truck speeding away towards Sale and, after a ten mile chase, the Datsun careered over the central reservation of the main A56 and struck a telegraph pole, killing the driver and badly injuring the passenger. Both men were of Middle Eastern origin and, welded to the flatbed of the vehicle, was an Egyptian-modified Soviet anti-aircraft missile launcher, together with one unexploded missile. The surviving terrorist has been taken to an undisclosed military hospital. Police sources say no intelligence about an active Middle-Eastern terrorist cell in Lancashire had been received. Prime Minister Roger Denstone, who has only been in Downing Street for 9 months, denounced the attack as a "cowardly atrocity perpetrated by evil extremists who the British Government will pursue relentlessly until they are brought to justice".

[AP]

Chapter 2

On arriving home at the Kensington flat that evening Ibrahim El-Hoorie had immediately switched on the television to catch the early news, desperately hoping that there were no reports of any terrorist activity at Manchester Airport. He had kept his van radio tuned to Radio 4 all the way back down the Motorway and so far, to his enormous relief, it seemed that nothing had happened. His parents were in Paris for three days and his sister was away at boarding school in Sussex so the flat was strangely quiet and empty. There was nothing of interest on the news and as he relaxed, his anger and fear began to subside. It had been a long and difficult day.

Kicking his shoes off and stretching out on the deep-cushioned sofa, he must have fallen asleep almost immediately, because the next thing he knew was that the front door bell was ringing continuously and a glance at his wrist watch told him it was half past nine at night.

Security within their block of flats was very tight, but whoever was ringing the bell so aggressively had clearly gained admission through the street door and was actually outside on the landing.

"Who is it?" Ibrahim shouted through the front door. "And ease up on the bell," he added.

"Police. Open up. Now," came the ominous response.

Ibrahim felt his heart sink and a sense of nausea began to grip his stomach. There could only be one reason for the Police to come to his home tonight. The urgency in the ringing of the bell and the demand for entry without the doorman announcing their arrival both spelled out the same deadly message. Something must have happened connected to the men in the café. Hurriedly turning the Yale lock, Ibrahim pulled open the heavy oak door and stared directly into the grim faces of three overcoated men standing shoulder to shoulder on his doorstep.

"Are you Ibrahim El-Hoorie?" demanded the tallest of the three. Dark-haired with a noticeable five o'clock shadow, small eyes too close together, poor complexion and crooked teeth. Probably six four, but thin and stooped for a man only in his late-thirties, as if uncomfortable with his height.

"You've come about what I heard in the Manchester Café, haven't you?" asked Ibrahim, his voice shaking and his legs trembling, struggling to support his weight.

"I take it you've heard the news then, Mr El-Hoorie?" the same man asked in a flat and empty tone, whilst the other two stood immobile, deliberately blocking the doorway. "I'm Chief Superintendent Ray Leadbetter. Special Branch," he continued. brandishing his Warrant Card in its cheap imitation leather wallet, "You'll have to come with us. Is there anyone else at home?"

"I need to sit down for a moment. What's actually happened?" mumbled Ibrahim as he backed into the hallway of the flat and sat down heavily on the velvet upholstery of the Victorian love-seat his mother had bought in a Bath antique shop during the summer.

Only Leadbetter entered the flat while the other two remained guarding the front door. "We'll talk about it in our offices and it may take some time. Are you alone or not? I need to know."

"Everyone's away. Did a plane go down or is it something else? Your bloody Police Force. Didn't want to know. Am I under arrest or what?"

"Just get up and come with us. You won't be back for at least twenty-four hours. Let's go."

After a seemingly endless journey through the wet, depressing streets of South Eastern London they had eventually ended up in some anonymous office block a few miles off the old main road leading down to the Kent ports. Crammed in the back of the dark-windowed BMW between the two, surly un-introduced Officers, the long journey had passed in almost total silence. There was a driver with a totally shaved head who occasionally mumbled into a mobile phone and took infrequent instructions off the Chief Superintendent who sat hunched in the front passenger seat, his legs too long to allow him any comfort. Otherwise, there was no conversation between the hard-faced men, and any questions from Ibrahim had been met with hostile silence.

Once inside the building they had shepherded him into a linoleum-floored basement room without windows, lit by harsh overhead fluorescent tubes obviously controlled by switches outside the room. There was a grey metal desk without a phone, three cheap utilitarian chairs, a cracked wash basin, an electric kettle with old hardened sachets of coffee and a single bed made up with grubby sheets and blankets. His protests as they left him alone, locking the door behind them, were met with the same indifferent silence that he had encountered in the car, save that one of them tossed a late edition copy of the *Evening Standard* on to the desk as they departed. The horror of the attack and the deaths of 31 people brought back overpoweringly vivid images of those two Arabs in the Café and the outrageous ineptitude of the local Manchester Police. Yet, despite his anger, Ibrahim felt powerless to challenge these Special Branch Officers as their confidence in their own authority, their physical size and their sinister silence so overwhelmed him that he found himself cowed by their sense of control. Tired, hungry, still wearing the day's work clothes, he lay on the bed, in a state of fear, anger and complete bewilderment.

At just after one o'clock in the morning Leadbetter returned in the company of another, slender, silver-haired older man with eyes sunk deep into their sockets so as to be just slits, with lizard-like lids and hollow cheeks. Both men seated themselves on the far side of the desk, gesturing to Ibrahim that he was expected to take up the remaining chair alongside the yellowing wall.

"We regret the way we've had to treat you, Mr El-Hoorie, but we've reason to believe that you may hold vital information," began the older man in a cultured, condescending voice that echoed the days of the Empire. "We had to get you away before there was any chance of that information getting into the public domain and before you might carelessly have . . . "

"When I warned the Police in Manchester they treated me like a bloody fool," interrupted Ibrahim, refusing to be spoken to like a house-servant. "They made it quite clear that they thought I was some kind of nutter. Now I've been taken away from my flat by Special Branch, kept locked up, told nothing. I'm not a criminal. You've no right to treat me like this and when my father gets back you'll have him to answer to."

"It's better you understand the extent of our powers from the outset," snapped Leadbetter aggressively, staring intently into the frightened young face opposite him. "This gentleman is a Commander attached to National Security. His authority on matters affecting this country's security outranks that of any official except the Prime Minister. If he thinks it appropriate he can keep you here as long as he damn well chooses. We know who you are, who your father is, where you were born, how much money you owe on your credit cards, every number dialled on your mobile phone in the last twenty-four hours and where your sexual preferences lie. So don't start telling us what we can and can't do."

"All right, Ray. I think he's getting the message," continued the Commander in that distant voice, the hooded eyes still concealed so that the face appeared almost totally devoid of expression. "We know about the report you made to the Manchester Police. We now want every last detail. I mean everything. After that we'll show you some photographs to see if you can identify anyone. Then you'll be taken to a military hospital in Oxfordshire where you'll look at an injured man and see if you recognise him. You'll have to sign certain sections of the Official Secrets Act, which means that if you ever breathe a word to anyone other than us of what you saw today, or what's happening now, then you'll go to prison for a very long time and your family will be deported."

"But I'm a witness," protested Ibrahim in astonishment. "You can't just silence me. If the man in hospital is either of the men I saw in the Café then I'm the most important witness you're ever likely to find for goodness sake. What do you mean by threatening me and my family if I speak out. You'll need my evidence."

"That decision will be our decision. We'll cross that bridge if and when we come to it. For the moment you'll assist in our enquiries in the ways I've described and you'll keep your mouth shut. Firmly shut. You'll tell no one. Not even your family. And don't think we won't know, because we have the technology to know exactly what you're about. So let's get started. It's going to be a long night. Is the tape recorder ready, Ray?"

"Yes, sir."

"Very well, Mr El-Hoorie. From the beginning. Every single word you remember them saying. Every detail about the voices, the appearances, the plan. Everything."

For nearly two hours they relentlessly probed, questioned and double-checked the whole account. Finally, they appeared satisfied that there was no other information to glean, at which point Leadbetter shouted through the door for the albums to be brought in. Shortly afterwards, one of the officers who had been to the flat, struggled in with six foolscap albums which were placed on the desk. Some of the photographs were classic Police Station mug shots which were easy to see. Others were taken through a long-distance lens producing a grainy effect, diminishing the quality of the picture and obviously taken when the suspect was not in custody and was unaware that he was under surveillance.

It was at the beginning of the fourth book that Ibrahim saw the bloated face with the flat nose and the oval, depressed scarring down the left side of the neck. Pictured at a check-in desk at an airport. Slightly more hair and probably three or four years younger but, despite the distance he had been from the camera, it was undoubtedly the older man in the Internet Café.

"Abdelkarim Mohammed," declared Leadbetter and the Commander in unison as Ibrahim's finger came down decisively on the photograph.

"You were right about the dialect, he's a Saudi national," added Leadbetter. "Used to be a Professor of Mathematics in Riyadh. Useful for recruiting the radical students. Convicted last year in his absence of three murders in a car bomb incident in Stuttgart. Three life sentences hanging over his head if only they could catch him. Never been arrested. But he isn't either of the men in the Datsun truck. He'll have left the country before the missile was even launched, you can bet your bottom dollar on that. Probably back in Algeria by now, that's where we think this cell is based."

With customary bad grace they allowed him a couple of hours sleep after he had trawled through the rest of the albums without recognising the other suspect from the Café. At six in the morning Leadbetter came for him, bringing a mug of tea and a round of cold toast wrapped in a greasy piece of kitchen roll. There was no sign of the Commander and it was a different driver from the night before at the wheel of the black Range Rover as the silent trio headed north to the military hospital. Invisible from the road, tucked away in the depths of heavily wooded countryside, no signs or name boards, the hospital looked like a private country estate. The only indication that they were nearing their destination came when the driver got on his mobile phone and announced they were five minutes away and required admission, so that the heavy iron gates at the end of the drive were already swinging open as they turned off the road.

Ibrahim felt quite awful. His head ached, he was unshaven, unwashed and his mind was in turmoil. Before they had let him try to sleep they had sent for the Official Secrets Act papers, reading out the contents with the utmost care, coldly repeating that if he ever disclosed any part of his observations, his report to the Manchester Police or any of the dealings he'd had with Special Branch, then he'd be sent to prison for many years and his family would face immediate deportation. They had set out to terrify him and they had succeeded, emphasising that only with written Home Office approval could he ever be released from the obligation. Then they had told him to sign which, in a shaking hand, he had done.

Once an elegant country house, now converted into a small hospital, there seemed to be little activity. All the doors to the side rooms were closed so he could not see any of the patients as he was led along a flag-stoned corridor towards a dingy rear staircase. An occasional white uniformed male nurse was glimpsed at a distance but no acknowledgements were made or invited. At the bottom of the stairs a young man in a dark suit was seated on a chair observing their approach. Leadbetter produced his warrant card and some other paperwork which the man checked and signed before standing up to allow them to pass. After one flight of stairs they came to a locked steel gate running from ceiling to floor. Another man, indistinguishable in manner and greyness from his colleague a flight below, went through a similar silent routine before unlocking the gate and admitting them.

Outside the second door to the left a third guard was seated but his jacket was hanging on the back of his chair so that his shoulder holster, strapped across his chest, was freely visible. However, they walked straight past him before taking the next door to the left and entering a darkened room with a glass window running the length of its left hand wall.

"It's one-way," grunted Leadbetter. "He can't see you." Staring intently through the glass, Ibrahim saw a muscular young Arab in his twenties sitting upright in a hospital bed, his right hand manacled to the head of the iron bedstead, his left arm attached to a saline drip. The face was cut and bruised and the man was motionless with his eyes closed.

"Few broken ribs and a fractured patella. The bastard'll live, I'm sorry to say," Leadbetter volunteered. "Question is, do you recognise him?"

Ibrahim carefully studied the jet-black hair, scraped in that unusually flat way across the scalp, the ugly broken nose, the moustache and beard.

"That's the younger one in the Café. The hair, the nose. The size. That's him, all right."

"Fahid Yasin, another Saudi but with terrorist connections in Germany and Iraq. The Yanks want him but he'll stand trial here. We were already sure it was him from your description. We've got the body of the one that was killed in the morgue down below, but there's no point in you looking at that. Khalid Msalam. He was involved in the bombing of the Khobar Towers in Dhahran. So, we've got one dead and the one chained up next door. It's a start. We'll want a formal statement off you identifying him and then we'll take you home."

"Now you see the consequences of treating me like a madman . . . " Ibrahim began to respond.

"Shut it," Leadbetter interrupted aggressively. "Shut it now and shut it for the future. You're out of your league. Just keep that big mouth shut."

Three hours later when Ibrahim El-Hoorie let himself into his flat he was in a state of almost complete exhaustion. Warned that he could confide in no one and terrified of the information that he unwittingly possessed, he adopted the course of action that he sometimes turned to when he was troubled. He wrote everything down in the private journal that lay hidden beneath his clean underwear in the drawer of his bedside cabinet. Sooner or later, by some means or other, the public were going to learn that this massive disaster could have been avoided, but for the gross ineptitude of the Manchester Police.

Chapter 3

Once a radical student leader who had defiantly led the marches through the streets, brandishing the placards demanding more student grants, decrying American imperialist policy, calling for a lifting of all immigration controls and any other extremist left-wing rantings of the day, Will Templar was now a Minister of State, adorned by his red despatch boxes, Savile Row suits and Churchill shoes, chauffeur-driven limousine, an elegant Georgian town house in Chelsea and a thirty-acre estate in fashionable Sussex. It had been a volte-face of epic proportions, so brazen, hypocritical and unashamed that it engendered a perverse kind of respect from the media luvvies who now controlled, shaped and dictated public opinion. In fact, he'd never had a real job, passing seamlessly from student politics to Union politics to Parliament and into a Junior Ministerial position at the Treasury, which had been neatly engineered by his successful intervention in a strike in his constituency where he had been able to call in a few favours owed by his fellow militant Shop Stewards from his own Union days.

Always with an eye to the main chance, he had spotted the meteoric rise of the smooth Roger Denstone, who had landed his appointment as Minister of Europe while Templar was still at the Treasury. Discreetly insinuating himself into the same neo-political and social circles as Denstone, he had sought to attach himself firmly to the coat-tails of the high flyer, recognising the prizes that may come his way if, as seemed inevitable, Denstone could dispose of the unimaginative, dogma-ridden bureaucrat who then occupied the throne at Number 10.

Nevertheless, when the coup came, not even Denstone could have predicted its irony, for the boring, seemingly two-dimensional Premier, family man par excellence, turned out to have a surprising and rather shapely skeleton tucked away in his cupboard in the form of an actress-turned-MP. The end had been ruthless and swift. After a two year affair she had let a careless word slip and Fleet Street had done the rest. Denstone, oozing false sympathy at the fate of his leader, allowed his name to be put forward for the party ballot, nominating Templar to run his campaign, and then won by a landslide to become Prime Minister without ever facing the electorate.

Templar's reward was the Home Office but as Home Secretary he was proving a disaster. The prisons were overflowing, the plethora of Criminal Justice legislation he was implementing was all spin-orientated and of little substance, hampering the Judges and going down with the electorate like a lead balloon. His speech to the Annual Conference of Chief Constables claiming that burglars who sincerely apologised to their victims should receive only a community sentence had been dismissed as an absurdity. His immigration policies lay in tatters. But, by far the most damaging development, was his ineffectual and indecisive handling of outbreaks of severe racial rioting in several Northern towns, which had already prompted calls from the Parliamentary Opposition and the tabloids for his resignation.

Within a month of the riots, the TransEuropean Airbus had been shot down at Manchester Airport and his Department had come under siege, facing accusations that Home Office financial restraints had diminished security arrangements. Repeated public denials in the teeth of mounting evidence made his survival even more unlikely. Denstone, with predictable dexterity, was leaving the Minister to take the flak whilst skilfully allying himself with the public sense of distress. The saving grace, as Templar saw it, was that the Police had managed to catch the two terrorists, although it would have been far preferable if they had both been killed, thereby avoiding the trial of Fahid Yasin, due to start next week at the Old Bailey, with all of its attendant publicity.

However, Templar was desperately hoping that a successful conclusion to the trial might take some of the pressure off him and therefore it had come as a bombshell when, two days ago, Special Branch had despatched a top-security email to him, disclosing for the first time the existence of Ibrahim El-Hoorie and detailing the warning he had apparently tried to give to the Manchester Police, which had effectively been ignored.

Templar was mortified. If ever this got out in to the open, not only would he certainly fall as Home Secretary, but he might even take the entire Government with him. Thirty-one dead and dozens maimed when the whole catastrophe might have been averted by one phone call from the Police closing down the airport. The ramifications were so terrifying that he didn't know which way to turn, but two decisions made themselves.

Firstly, Denstone must not be told, for his immediate instincts would be to sacrifice Templar either forthwith or, even if the crisis were averted, then as soon as possible thereafter. Secondly, there was only one man who could possibly help. Euphemistically on the Home Office payroll as a Political Adviser, Lewis Barford was a lethal hatchet man, deeply feared within the Department because of his absolute ruthlessness, universally despised because of his control over Templar and with a network of influence whose tentacles extended from the gutter to the outer circles of the Royal Family.

Barford had responded to the revelation with the cold sense of control that Templar lacked, demanding the entire security file, which he had then devoured in one unbroken five-hour session, before advising that a meeting with the Commander and Leadbetter be arranged within twenty-four hours at a secret location well away from the Home Office or either of Templar's private residences.

Staring at himself in the reflection of the rain-spattered glass of the nondescript saloon car that Barford had insisted they use, the Home Secretary barely recognised the face that looked back at him. Where once the shock of black hair had stood proud, there were now long, thinning, white strands and the rebel student eyes had retreated into the skull where, haunted, they darted left and right, never still.

Meanwhile, Barford, intense as ever, was hunched over the wheel, picking his way through the heavy London West End post-theatre traffic, heading for Waterloo Bridge and the road South to the discreet rendezvous chosen by the Commander. Occasionally stealing glances at Barford, Templar acknowledged to himself just how much he hated the man, yet, at the same time recognising the terrifying extent to which he had come to depend on him.

The illegitimate son of a Liverpool docker and a Dutch Eurasian shopgirl, Norman Barford had been dragged up by his paternal grandparents on a decaying, crime-ridden council estate in Huyton. Inheriting his mother's dark sultry looks and his father's powerful physique had earned him early success with the opposite sex and, when only just sixteen, he had formed a relationship with Amanda Taylor, the promiscuous nineteen-year-old daughter of the local GP. While Amanda had introduced him to the world of sex and titillation in a bed with clean, soft sheets he had spent much of his energies observing, with undisguised envy, the trappings of middle-class luxury and grace in which she lived.

Naturally, Dr Taylor had detested him from the outset and, eventually, had persuaded his daughter to discard this ambitious ruffian from the gutter, but not before the Taylor family's material success had seduced Barford into a determination that he was going to break free from the social and economic constraints which had threatened to imprison him for ever. Abandoning the name Norman in favour of Lewis, he threw himself into his schoolwork at the run-down comprehensive, attracting scorn and derision from his fellow pupils and incredulity from his teachers. Three A's at Advanced Level gloriously carried him to Merton College, Oxford and opened the doors on a new, splendid world which had included, amongst others, the radical young Will Templar.

Swinging the car into a dark country lane to the east of Ashford, Barford strained his eyes to find the narrow dirt track that should lead them down to the canal and the isolated towpath where the barge was moored. Spotting the entrance to the track at the last moment, he jammed on the brakes and abruptly pulled the wheel over, provoking a sharp, disapproving intake of breath from his left.

"Not used to this kind of stuff are you Will?" he grunted.

"I know how to adapt."

"Like a chameleon?"

"No, Lewis. Like a survivor. We're going to survive this crisis," was the defiant response.

"Well, there she is," declared Barford as the car headlights picked out firstly the black saloon car parked on the grass and then the scrolled nameplate on the bow of a narrow boat moored at the side of the canal. "*Medici*. What kind of name is that?"

"The Medici family. They ruled Florence in its glory days in the fifteenth century," answered Templar.

"You would know all about ruling wouldn't you. It's been your life's work," grunted Barford, as he brought the car to a halt near to the plank that ran from the towpath on to the deck. "Come on. Let's see you use your authority on this pair."

Templar picked his way unsteadily down to the path, across the plank and on to the deck. He'd always been stiff and awkward in direct contrast to Barford's easy athleticism and now, on this moonless night, with so much at stake, the black, still water of the canal frightened him. No lights could be seen through the heavily draped portholes of the *Medici*, but Barford simply pushed the hatchway door open, squeezed himself through the opening and entered the gloomy cabin, where the two clandestine figures sat hunched over the fitted table anxiously awaiting the arrival of Barford and Templar.

Crammed in the saloon of the tired vessel, their overcoats thrown across the port bunk, the conversation began in earnest after perfunctory introductions. All four men were forced to crowd around the chart table on the hard wooden bench, constantly shifting their positions, particularly Leadbetter whose head, at six foot four, nearly touched the ceiling even when seated and whose legs would not fit properly beneath the table top.

Templar assimilated the pecking order in a single glance and, well aware of the weight of the Commander's authority, addressed his remarks to him.

"This trial starts next Monday, Commander. Who took the decision to withhold the El-Hoorie information from my Department until now?" was his opening gambit.

But the Commander, like Barford, intended to bide his time, test the atmosphere, feel out the true extent of the Home Secretary's fear before he spoke and it was Leadbetter who offered the reply.

"I advised it and the Commander authorised it. We knew immediately that it must never see the light of day. The damage to the Police would be serious enough, but the security and political implications would be catastrophic. We eliminated it from the equation."

"What about the Prosecuting authorities? The Attorney General, Counsel instructed in the trial – have they been told?" Templar barked.

"No, Sir. Absolutely not. Outside this room only the five officers at the Manchester Police Station, where the real mistakes were made, know about this. The three who actually dealt with El-Hoorie, their Inspector and his Super who originally phoned me with the information. You don't have to worry about any of them. They're the last people who ever want this out in the open."

"But how did you ever believe that you could keep it quiet?" demanded Templar angrily. "El-Hoorie would expect to be a witness at the trial."

"We thought we could handle that. He's only a youngster. Disciplined upbringing, accepts authority. So we closed him out on two fronts. Firstly, we made him sign an undertaking of silence under the Official Secrets Act. Complete and permanent silence unless called as a witness at the trial. Secondly, we compromised him so that there was never any risk that he would be called to give evidence at Court."

"What do you mean by compromised him?" Templar snapped.

"By ensuring that his evidence of identity would be legally useless. We took him to the military hospital and made him identify Fahid Yasin. There should have been proper Identification Procedures, subject to all of the rules and safeguards. We disregarded all of that."

"You deliberately broke all the procedural and statutory rules so as to render his evidence legally inadmissible?" exclaimed Templar in disbelief.

"Precisely, Home Secretary. Any lawyer, Prosecution or Defence, would see that we had committed a fundamental breach of the rules so that his identification of Yassin was worthless."

"And what about the course of justice in all of this? What about securing the convictions of terrorists who'd killed thirty-one innocent people? Didn't you give a damn about that?" raged Templar, his voice resonating eerily around the damp cabin, the air now heavy with sweat and the staleness of the mens' breath.

"We never put that at risk at all. We thought it through with great care. We picked him up from his flat at 9.30. Within 4 hours the Commander and I had reviewed all of the evidence, considered the political dynamite and reached a decision. El-Hoorie had to be silenced and compromised, but we still had to be seen putting these terrorists away. Our methods would achieve that."

"And what if El-Hoorie called your bluff? You couldn't keep him quiet indefinitely under the Official Secrets Act. He was bound to rumble that ploy."

"He was informed that if he breached the Act then he'd go to prison and thereafter the whole family would be deported. Whatever the niceties of the Act, we were confident that he wouldn't run the risk of the whole family being deported."

"That still doesn't answer my fundamental question. What about convicting the terrorists?"

"We weren't jeopardising that. Khalid Msalam, who we identified within the hour, was their weapons expert. We had an abundance of evidence linking him to the Khobar Towers outrage in Dahran. And he was killed in the crash. Within minutes of the plane being shot down, Fahid Yassin had been arrested in a pickup truck with a dead man who we could prove was an active terrorist. Welded to the bed of the truck was a Soviet-designed, Egyptian-modified, Surface to Air missile launcher, together with a rocket armed with a high explosive warhead of the exact specifications used in the attack on the plane. Forensic had confirmed that Yassin's clothing and hands were covered in explosives residue. No jury in the land would need any more than that. Yassin didn't have a feather to fly with," Leadbetter declared at length, in a tone which implied that he was talking not to a Government Minister but to a dullard.

"But what about the third man?" snapped the Home Secretary.

"It wasn't a problem," replied Leadbetter. "El-Hoorie's description of the other man in the Café could not possibly have fitted Khalid Msalam, who was only twenty-three. The man in the Café with Yasin was in his mid-forties, so he had to be someone other than Msalam. Once we'd studied the Interpol files and compared El-Hoorie's description of the other man, particularly the highly distinctive bullet scarring on the neck, we knew who it was."

"And once you knew it was Abdelkarim Mohammed you'd expect that he'd have got out of the country before the attack?" Templar asked.

"Of course. He's been on the run for years. He no longer runs any risk himself. He's just the brains, the organiser. We checked the flights and we're sure he was on the mid-afternoon flight out of Manchester to Paris and there was a connecting flight to Algiers. He would have been back in Algeria before the other two even pressed the button."

"But El-Hoorie was still a crucial witness against Mohammed, wasn't he?"

"More than that. El-Hoorie was the only witness against him. And we showed El-Hoorie albums of photographs of known terrorists including Abdelkarim Mohammed."

"So as to compromise the value of his evidence as against Mohammed?"

"To a lesser extent, yes. But, when we were sure it was Mohammed, it actually made our decision to keep El-Hoorie completely out of it much easier."

"Why?"

"Because Mohammed was not a problem. He'd already been convicted in his absence of three murders in Germany and sentenced to life imprisonment three times over, so we didn't need evidence against Mohammed to put him away for life. He's already nailed for that in spades. We just needed the body and we were sure he'd flown. Even if he's ever caught he'll never be tried for this attack – he'll just be extradited to Germany and locked up for the rest of his days or handed over to the Israelis."

"None of this explains why, with the trial of Yasin about to start, you suddenly decided to inform us about all of this. Cold feet?" enquired Templar disdainfully, looking directly at the Commander who had remained totally silent, staring straight ahead and absorbing every syllable, every nuance of these remarkable exchanges.

"Up until last week El-Hoorie had believed that he was possibly going to be a witness at the trial," Leadbetter continued, knowing instinctively that the Commander would not respond to the Minister's gibe. "Three days ago one of my men had the job of telling him that he wasn't."

"And?"

"He hit the roof. Accused the Police and the Government of suppressing the truth."

"And?"

"He was told that only Yasin was on trial and that we had overwhelming evidence against him. He would be found guilty. There was no question about it. There was no need to run any risk by him giving evidence. Yasin was dead and buried on what we had, without his evidence."

"So what was the problem?"

"He said we were frightened of people knowing that he warned the Police and was ignored. He was reminded that under the Official Secrets Act he must never speak of these events."

"But you're worried that he'll spill the beans?"

"Yes. It's now a real possibility. Apparently, he was getting very agitated. It has to be acknowledged that when the trial starts, there's a risk he'll talk."

"To whom?"

"To everyone. But most significantly to the Press. There's a Crime Reporter who writes under a pseudonym. I've written the name down on an envelope. I've got it here," Leadbetter declared, pulling a once-white, grubby envelope from his pocket and throwing it on to the chart table so that it fell face-up right under the Home Secretary's nose. Three words in black ink stared up.

"The Molecule Man" said Templar reading the name out loud without even needing to pick the envelope up. "Oh yes. We know him all right. Terminally dangerous."

"So that's why we're here," declared Leadbetter ominously.

Throughout these exchanges, Barford, like the Commander, had remained totally silent, his eyes never wavering from the grim, set face of the Chief Superintendent as Templar delivered his barrage of questions, eliciting answers that could bring down a Government. When Leadbetter mentioned the Press and then

"The Molecule Man", Barford turned his head sharply to study the Home Secretary's reaction and saw the beads of sweat across the thin upper lip and the tremor in the hand. For all his show of outrage and anger, the truth about Templar was that he was terrified by these deadly revelations. Not only would he be cast aside by his own party, but he would go down in history as the man who presided over the Department that destroyed the British Government. Having abandoned all of his principles in pursuit of power and influence, his excursion into High Office would end in humiliation, ignominy and disgrace. All of this was obvious to Barford and underlined by Templar's cowardly failure to ask the only question that now really mattered. So Barford asked it.

"What are you proposing to do about it then, Leadbetter?" growled Barford in his deep, gruff voice, heavily manicured but still leaking his Liverpool roots. "Your lot made the bloody mess. Your lot can clear it up."

"We're unsure what course to take. Obviously, we can't allow this information into the public domain, can we? That's why we contacted the Home Secretary."

"You're unsure what bloody course to take, are you?" snapped Barford with contempt. "You've sat on a piece of dynamite for over six months and then, days before a terrorist trial begins, you dump it in the Minister's lap."

"It seemed to be under control . . . "

"Control?" thundered Barford. "Completely out of bloody control more like. Now listen closely to me, Chief Superintendent and, I have to say, this also applies to you, Commander," he continued, his tone changing in an instant from anger to menace, as he rose from his seat, brandishing the thick Special Branch Security File and standing directly over the Commander, his head bowed in the confined space.

"Number one, you never communicated with the Home Secretary. The email has been deleted from our system and you'll do likewise in your system. Yourselves. Tonight. This meeting never took place. It never happened. You've never met the Home Secretary and you've never met me. Do you follow me so far?"

"No, I don't," came the startled reply. "I would ask you Home Secretary," Leadbetter continued, appealing to the now white-faced Templar who sat silently, pretending to be calm but unable to prevent his eyes from darting left and right and that damned tic in his left cheek from twitching, "to offer some advice and . . . "

"Don't involve the Minister," snarled Barford. "Like I said, you've never met him. Next. I'm returning the Security File you sent us. Now. Take it," he demanded, thrusting it at Leadbetter whose face displayed the shock he was feeling that this dangerous man, whose role he had never really understood, could behave so aggressively in the presence of a Government Minister. Not only did Templar obviously have no influence over him at all, the reality was that he didn't even try to pretend that he had.

"That's just about enough, Barford". The Commander's words crackled in the air like static electricity. Cultured, direct, authoritative and vicious, making Templar instinctively recoil backwards into the corner of his seat.

"We're not here to be rebuked like wayward children," the clipped voice continued. "If you've got a proposal, make it. Otherwise we'll just let El-Hoorie do his worst and you, for one, will be out on your peasant neck."

Barford, fists instinctively clenched at the wounding gibe about his antecedents, glared at the reptilian face, the eyes as invisible as the soul. After a moment of silence he slowly nodded his head, reluctantly acknowledging the power of the man.

"Very well, Commander. You've made your point," he eventually continued. "I see the way forward. I'm going to ask you and the Home Secretary to leave us. Perhaps you'd both wait in your cars. Leadbetter and I will sort this out without involving the Home Office. But, before you leave, all four of us must commit ourselves to the agreement that this meeting never took place. Commander, Leadbetter, I want your word on this. In the presence of the Home Secretary. This meeting never happened. Accepted?"

"What do I say, Home Secretary?" Leadbetter replied, appealing to Templar, in the forlorn hope that he could avoid being left alone with this bully boy.

"Mr Barford is right," came Templar's immediate, compliant response. "Security is the issue here. Sometimes security demands expediency and sometimes expediency calls for sacrifices from us all. We do require your word."

"You've got our word," interrupted the acid voice of the Commander, as he rose from his chair, picked up his coat and moved towards the door in one swift move. "I'll be in the car. Deal with it. The pair of you. Good night, Home Secretary."

As Templar followed the steps of the Commander along the saloon and through the hatchway, there was a palpable atmosphere of hostility and rancour between the remaining two men, both of them disliking each other intensely, but recognising that, by some joint illicit means, it was their exclusive duty to secure the silence of El-Hoorie.

Resuming his seat, Barford stared aggressively at the lean, angular figure opposite him. Achieving that high a rank in Special Branch before reaching forty would have called for some fairly tough decisions, he reflected. The unattractive, pallid complexion was accentuated by the poor light from the saloon ceiling bulbs and the small eyes flashed, displaying the bitter resentment that the officer plainly harboured at the manner in which he had been treated by these Government men who wielded such power, yet whose grip on that power was now under threat.

"Elimination from the equation. That was one of your expressions wasn't it, Leadbetter?" began Barford.

"I was referring to the information, not the man," Leadbetter retorted angrily.

"There's a difference is there? I'm buggered if I can see it. That Molecule Man is lethal. This material must not get into his hands at any price."

"We thought about using the Official Secrets Act . . . "

"That was bullshit and you knew it. How El-Hoorie was conned with that at all is a miracle."

"I'm just listing the alternatives."

"But you're not mentioning the alternative that prompted you to approach Templar with your problem, are you?"

"What do you mean by that?"

"You know damn well what I mean by that. You and your Commander thrashed about looking for a way out of the cock-up the Manchester Police and Special Branch had created. You realised there was only one way out of it and you wanted a Government seal of approval before you carried it out."

"I deny that."

"What precisely do you deny?"

"That we contemplated violence."

"More bullshit. You're Special Branch. You know, your Commander knows and I know that there are only three alternatives here."

"Namely?"

"The threat of violence. Actual violence. Fatal violence. Are we going to tiptoe round it all night or shall we come directly to the point?"

"We'd best come to the point."

"Exactly. At seven o'clock tomorrow night you'll meet me by the lake in Brockwell Park. You'll provide me with confirmation that El-Hoorie is still at the same address, when he's there alone, the security arrangements in the building. And you'll give me five thousand pounds in cash. In used ten pound notes so that there is no traceable link to the Home Office, to me or to this operation. That will conclude any dealings that you ever have with me. I shall then ensure that the matter is resolved. This meeting is over. It never happened. Tomorrow's meeting never happened. We've never met," Barford spat out, before abruptly getting to his feet signifying that there was no more to be said.

"Hang on a minute. How the hell am I meant to account internally for £5000?" demanded Leadbetter, badly shaken at the cold ruthlessness of Barford's commands, awkwardly grabbing his overcoat from the port bunk as he manoeuvred his long body into the narrow aisle.

"That's your bloody problem. Your lot and the idiots in Manchester are in deep shit. Frankly, I don't give a toss about that. But your monumental cock-up could do enormous damage to the Government. I'm going to make sure it doesn't. That's all you need to know," Barford replied, as Leadbetter rudely pushed ahead of him and headed for the hatchway.

"OK. I'll be there at seven o'clock," Leadbetter called back from the door, "Like you say, that's all I need to know."

"Brockwell Park. The east side of the lake," Barford shouted to the disappearing figure, while deftly snatching up the envelope which Leadbetter had previously tossed on to the chart table, thrusting it into his overcoat pocket and then heading for the car and the drive back to London with the quivering wimp who was the Nation's Home Secretary.

Chapter 4

Third side street on the left after the derelict Snooker Hall. Barford wore the old gabardine mackintosh that hadn't been out of the cupboard for the best part of a decade. Just off the Narborough Road heading in to Leicester. Predominantly Asian faces. Tired streets. Small shops dying. Terraced houses with rotting window frames. Rain beginning to spit from the leaden sky. Inside the betting shop the air was heavy with acrid tobacco smoke, blue filtered in the light from the bright tubes. Round formica-topped tables and straight-backed utilitarian chairs. Wall-to-wall televisions replaying the races; the greyhounds and the horses forever circling the same oval track as if trapped in an endless race to nowhere. Caged-in clerks behind their grills, awaiting the grubby, crumpled five-pound notes and the pink, carboned betting slips bearing the scrawled message of empty hope. As Barford eased himself into a chair at a corner table there was no sign of the Scotsman amidst the handful of punters, but it was a certainty that he would show.

Sierra Leone in the early nineties had been brutal. Hired on the International Mercenary market, the rewards had been staggering but the price had been the soul. After Oxford, the clandestine recruiting to the Eastern Bloc Department of the Foreign Office had delivered Barford to Helsinki, where Arctic training was followed by covert incursions into the frozen wastelands of the then-Soviet Union, but, after three hard years of operations, the Cold War began to fade and a new role had been identified. Planted by the Government into Central Africa as a mercenary for hire, he had been recruited by the South African sponsored assassin Colonel Merle and despatched to Sierra Leone to help suppress the violence, whether it came from the rebels or from the maverick government soldiers. Establishing some sense of authority and order in villages where half the population had been cut down in a killing frenzy and many of the survivors had had their hands, feet and genitals amputated, called for absolute determination and a strong stomach. Enrolment in Merle's Mercenary Brigade was available only to the toughest of the guns for hire. Which side of the Law you came from mattered not, so long as you knew how to kill, maim, gouge and still live with yourself thereafter.

The Scotsman had been well qualified for entry. Barford had met him on the border with Guinea where a rebel soldier, responsible for setting fire to a nearby village, had been in hiding until the Scotsman had found him and beheaded him. Violent, probably psychopathic, cunning, crooked but absolutely deadly. Definitely worth keeping on file. That had been Barford's assessment of Derek Lennox over the months they had been together until Lennox's contract had finished.

Back in the UK, before Barford's assignment at the Home Office, he had only used the Scotsman once, on an errand to issue an ultimatum to an Austrian businessman who was undermining a very important arms deal. Two broken legs had solved the problem. The upper leg, the Scotsman had explained. The femur. Harder to break because the bone is better covered with flesh than on the lower leg. Required several blows with a heavy iron pole but even more painful and taking far longer to mend. On three subsequent occasions, when he had tried to use Lennox again, he had been in prison. Yesterday's research had found him to be at liberty and living in Nottingham, so the betting shop in Leicester had seemed a suitable location for the meeting.

Slipping into the seat alongside him without a word, Lennox arrived. With his low centre of gravity he could move quietly and swiftly, despite his broad frame and that enormous head. Unshaven and unsmiling, the large aggressive jaw was thrust forward, demanding to know the reason behind the summons.

"You said five grand," he growled in that Glaswegian accent, thicker even than Barford remembered it.

Staring closely into those dead, grey eyes, Barford had little doubt that most men would do as they were told when under threat from this menacing psycho.

"If you can still hack it," challenged Barford. "You've been in the nick. Are you up to it?"

Lennox glared silently back across the table. No one spoke to him like that, but he wanted that five grand. The thin lips bared back on the yellow teeth, half-snarl, half-smile.

"Just spit it out, Barford. No crap. None of your fucking crap."

"OK. I'd reckon you can still do the business. A man I know wants a message delivering. Delivering very loud and very clear," he declared, leaning over the table and lowering his voice to a whisper. "You put the fear of God into this little shit. And I mean the fear of God. You terrify the bastard. But you control the violence. Slap him about a bit but we don't need any GBH. No need to go as far as you did with the Austrian. You get my meaning?"

"Will this geezer be tooled up? I need to know that?"

"I'll give you all the gen in a minute. Before I do, I want to know that we've got a deal. The job's in London. Must be done tomorrow night. The hit is just a kid. No tools. My man just wants him terrified. Told to keep his mouth shut. Are you on?"

"I'm on. Why else would I have come to this fucking dump of a town?"

"OK. I'm going to put a bet on. Make sure we blend in. Look like we're just a couple of punters. I suggest you do the same. Then I'll give you what you need," Barford announced.

Five minutes later the men had resumed their seats, two betting slips for the next race at Doncaster lying casually on the table in front of them.

"Right, Lennox," began Barford, looking anxiously about him at the few customers in the seedy shop as the 2.30 at Doncaster came under starter's orders and the volume of the commentary increased. "His name's El-Hoorie. Twenty-one. Arab but westernised. Flat 48, Delaney Mansions, Kensington. He'll be sleeping at home tomorrow night. Alone. Parents are out of town. Sister away. You'll get into the basement garage. It's a code on a keypad. 4976. Got all of that into your Scottish skull?"

"You've seen me operate. I only need telling once," snapped the Scotsman in reply.

"Fourth floor. You don't need me to tell you how to deal with the front door. It's a straight Yale lock. He only uses the mortise when he goes out, not when he's at home."

"Can he handle himself? Is he trained?" Lennox enquired, his great brow furrowed in concentration and the excitement already building.

"No. Ordinary upbringing. No military service. No martial arts. You'll have no problem," Barford responded. "His bedroom is the second on the left off the hall."

"And the message is?"

"The message is this. 'Mouth closed and no one gets hurt. Mouth open and you're all dead meat. The whole family. Sister raped and killed first. In front of the parents. Then the rest of 'em.' That's the message.

"Easy enough to remember. You can add your own bits to it, but that's the gist of it. And, like I said, smack him around enough to ram it home, but no need to get carried away. Just leave him terrified."

"Who's behind this then?" Lennox asked.

"It doesn't matter. You know the rules. No repetition of this anytime, anywhere. I'm giving you the five grand up front. Now. 'Cos I don't want to have to see you again for a long time. But if you don't do the job, then I'll come after you myself and you know what that means," Barford observed threateningly, as he slipped a fat wad of ten pound notes under the table into the Scot's large, calloused hand.

"Aye. I've seen what you can do," the Scotsman replied, swiftly tucking the wad into his side jacket pocket. "But once I accept a job you know I see it through."

"Remember. My man wants him shitting himself."

"Guaranteed. By the way, what was the name of the horse you put your money on?"

Barford picked up the betting slip off the table as he rose to leave. "Mad and Bad," he replied. "Why? Did it win?"

"No. Came last but one," Lennox answered, glancing at the screen.

"Odd that. It's got a winner's name," he laughed.

"You make sure you do the mad and bad business, Lennox," declared Barford, as he screwed the losing betting slip up in a ball, tossed it into the nearby waste bin and headed for the door. No doubt the villain would help himself to the odd item of the El-Hoorie household before he left, but that kid would have been given a warning he'd never forget. Lennox was a master at that.

As soon as Barford's back disappeared through the shop doorway, Lennox was out of his seat and his hand was diving into the waste bin to retrieve the tightly screwed-up losing betting slip. Just a touch of insurance. You always needed a touch of insurance, he thought to himself as he tucked it away in his trouser pocket.

Chapter 5

"You've got between four and six weeks left, Mr Lennox," the Doctor abruptly declared, making no attempt to package the chilling death sentence in soft words. "I've just received the biopsy report. There's no purpose in pretending. Your time has come."

"Is that your best bedside manner then?" Derek Lennox grunted sarcastically in his guttural Glaswegian accent. "Or do you get a kick out of it? Sending a con like me to hell?"

"What you've done wrong in your life will soon be a matter between you and your Maker. It's nothing to do with me," replied the Doctor coldly, making notes on the prisoner's records as he spoke. "I just tell you the medical facts. We have the drugs to make you comfortable. You may be transferred to the hospital in Durham towards the end. I'll be round again in the morning."

After the Doctor's brisk departure, Lennox lay back in his bed and tried to come to terms with the enormity of the Doctor's words. Pulling the thin, grey prison blanket over his head, he detached himself from the rest of the world. It was a device he had frequently deployed, enabling him to create a personal sanctuary where only he existed, where the rules were his rules and where, lurking in the dark recesses, self-justification for his lifetime of evil was occasionally found. This time, however, his sanctuary was inhabited by cold, unrelenting fear. Stark terror, of a kind he was accustomed to inflicting on his victims. Like a couple of years ago when he'd dealt with that Arab kid in London for Barford. Later that same year, when the Judge had sentenced him to twelve years' imprisonment for raping a schoolgirl on her way home from school on a dark winter's afternoon, he had sneered at the system. Derek Lennox knew how to serve his time, even with all the inmate hostility that existed towards sex offenders. In any event, this nick was full of nonces and Lennox knew every trick of survival. Working it out in his head, he had spent only six of the last twenty years at liberty.

Now forty-four, he would never see forty-five. Mother dead. Father unknown. Never married. Never had a relationship of any length with a woman. No children. No relatives. Other than six months as a doorman in a Glasgow pub and the year as a mercenary in Sierra Leone when he had hacked limbs off the rebels in exchange for diamonds under Barford's command, he had hardly done a day's work in his life. Now, suddenly, the day of reckoning was approaching and the grave beckoned. No one would be at his funeral. No one cared. No one would mourn his passing. He would be leaving the world without ever having given anything back. A parasite from beginning to end.

All of these desperate thoughts teemed through his diseased brain as he lay, shaking, under the coarse blanket. In the grim institutions and foster homes where his wretched childhood had passed, religion and God had been empty words. The philosophy had been simple to grasp. If there was a God, how could he allow any of his children to endure an upbringing such as that inflicted on Lennox? Now, for the first time, he found himself asking the question in reverse. If there was a God, how would he treat a man like Lennox, who had made others suffer so grievously? The next sentence was not twelve years, it was for eternity. Yet, even when confronted by the prospect of imminent death, the process of analysis remained self-absorbed, lacking in insight and devoid of feeling for those who had been his victims. All that mattered was Derek Lennox, but he had nothing left with which he could trade with any God. The account sheet was all red; there was not a single entry in black.

Facilities in the hospital wing of this prison were spartan. Four beds in the ward. One ill-qualified male nurse who was responsible for everything except the cleaning, which was the miserable job of a prisoner orderly. Meals were brought up on the grimy, steel trolley and were always cold by the time that they arrived. Twice a day the Doctor called in to check on any patients, before returning to his office on 'G' wing where he held what he euphemistically referred to as his 'surgeries', which, in reality, were an exercise in disposing of whingeing and malingering prisoners as rapidly as possible, so that he could resume his attack on the bottles of whisky that nestled in his desk drawer and which were the reason for his ending up on the medical scrap heap.

On this particular day Lennox was the only patient in the hospital wing and the other three beds lay empty. As in every other crisis of his life, Lennox was alone. Suddenly, beneath the blankets, the pain erupted again, deep within the centre of his head. There was no pattern or logic to its arrival, except that the time period between attacks was lessening. Once it started, his mind had no room left to think of anything else. Calling for the nurse in a thin, weak voice that he hardly recognised himself, he downed the painkillers in one gulp and surrendered to the torment, drifting in and out of sleep as another of his few remaining days ebbed meaninglessly away.

In the middle of the afternoon he awoke and, for those first few seconds of consciousness, failed to recall the message that the Doctor had delivered. Then, like a ton weight falling on him from the sky, the words returned. The pain had subsided and, with dread in his heart, he tried to face the question that, sooner or later, he knew he had to answer for, buried within his psyche, lay as dark a secret as any man could harbour. Did he take that secret with him to his grave or should he, as a final defiant act, disclose the truth? Any revelation would not be designed to persuade some deity that it represented the beginnings of self-redemption. All that mattered was that he could provoke national uproar and make them all suffer. The politicians, the lawyers, the authorities, the bureaucrats and the rest of the bastards responsible for destroying his life. He could strike back from the grave so that every one of them would come to curse the name of Derek Lennox. That was the prize.

"Crane," he called out gruffly towards the long, thin figure of the male nurse seated at the grey metal desk in the centre of the small ward. "Crane, get yourself over here."

Looking up from the well-thumbed paperback he was reading, Tom Crane peered in the direction of the sole patient in the ward, taking in the gaunt features and staring eyes, as the dying man struggled to sit upright in the bed.

"What the hell do you want now, Lennox?" he replied dismissively. "I'm busy."

"Get your arse over here, man. Now," he barked angrily. "I'm not dead yet. Not by a long chalk."

Pushing his hard, wooden chair back from the desk, Tom Crane wandered slowly over to the side of the bed and looked down contemptuously at the unshaven, mean face of the rapist.

"What is it then Lennox? What do you want?"

The arm snaked out so quickly that Crane was taken completely by surprise and, tightly grabbing his shirt front, Lennox pulled Crane down over the bed, momentarily displaying a strength that defied his disease. Thrusting his face close to Crane's, the prisoner spat out his demand.

"Listen, Crane. And listen good. There's a brief in Runcorn. Martin Smail. I want him up here. You'll get his number easy enough. Phone him tonight. You tell him Derek Lennox wants to see him. Urgent. Very urgent. Tell him he won't regret it."

Crane felt the strength ebbing away from the arm that clutched his shirt. Such was the proximity of their faces that he could smell the foulness of Lennox's breath, see the yellow of the skin and sense the touch of death upon him.

Wrenching the arm off his shirt and pulling himself up and away from Lennox's grasp, Crane took a step backwards away from the bed.

"Why should I bother, Lennox? There's nowt in it for me and your days of frightening people are over. You're finished. Write to him. You may get an answer before they carry you out in a body bag."

"Your choice, Crane," muttered Lennox menacingly. "Phone him tonight or it costs you an eye."

"What kind of threat is that, you bastard?" Crane replied with bravado in his voice, but fear stamped on his long, cadaverous face, as he stood staring at the wretched, but still deadly, creature on the bed.

"I know where to get hold of the hypodermics and I watch you falling asleep in that chair every afternoon. You can't help yourself. My chance'll come and I'll put the needle straight in your fucking eye. I'm dying, man, what they going to do to me? Send me to fucking Court? So, like I say, it's your choice. Martin Smail. Runcorn. Phone him tonight or I'll have your eye."

Lennox lay back in his bed and tried desperately to move his mind away from this hell-hole and the searing pain that he could feel building up again in the middle of his head. Crane would do his bidding and Smail would come running if he smelt money. Death may be near but he would leave a legacy that made the bastards remember the name of Derek Lennox all right.

Chapter 6

Despite setting off at five in the morning it had taken Martin Smail over three and half hours to drive from his neglected house on the outskirts of Runcorn to the forbidding edifice of Durham Gaol. Since his wife had left him for that anorak of a computer programmer, ordinary, everyday domestic tasks had become more and more demanding and his own appearance, like that of the former matrimonial home, had grown increasingly seedy. The cuffs of his shirts were frayed and the cheap suit had become shiny and worn. Both complexion and girth had suffered badly from subsisting on a fast-food diet, whilst his thinning hair was now seldom washed. Still only in his mid-forties, he could have passed for a man twenty years older with his patchy, red face and a stomach straining at every button of the cheap, nylon shirt.

Running a one-man firm on the High Street of a decaying suburb on the outskirts of a tired Northern town did not make for rich pickings. Over the years most of his clients had been at the bottom end of the market. Petty thieves, small-time cheats or Saturday night punch-up merchants. There had only ever been one truly evil, big-time villain that he had acted for and now nature was taking its revenge on Derek Lennox, reducing him to the emaciated living corpse that Smail had been listening to for the last three grim hours in that stinking Hospital Wing of Durham Gaol.

Now picking his way through the heavy traffic en route back to Runcorn, Smail leant back in the synthetic leather driving seat of the beaten-up Ford Granada that was reminiscent of a dustbin on wheels, reflecting ruefully on that Tuesday morning long ago when Derek Lennox had first walked into his dingy Runcorn office.

"Wanna make a name for yourself, pal?" he had demanded, bold as brass, in a Glaswegian accent so thick that Smail could almost smell the dank waters of the Clyde.

"What's the charge?" demanded Smail.

"No charge yet. That's why I'm bailed. They ain't got no evidence yet. But they'll charge me with attempted murder of a copper. Iron bar across his skull. From behind. So no ID. But they all knew I'd have the bastard one day."

"So what's the story?" asked Smail.

"The copper got smacked Sunday night. First thing Monday I heard on the grapevine they're after me so I took a quick trip to the shops. Got myself some top class gear. Then walked into the Cop Shop. They've been questioning me ever since. Seized all my gear. Sent it to forensics. Bailed me 'til next Wednesday. Then they'll have enough to charge me."

"Like what?"

"Fibres from my jacket. All over the copper."

"And?" demanded Smail.

"And it'll be a fucking plant, pal. They'll have taken fibres off the jacket before sending it to the lab and planted them on the copper's stuff. But every stitch of clothing the bastards took off me was bought after the attack. Got receipts for every fucking item. Timed to the minute. Individual stock numbers. And I dealt with the Manager. He'll remember me. You'd better get a statement off him today. Like I said, pal, do you want to make a name for yourself?"

Smail laughed to himself as he eventually turned on to the Motorway and headed South towards Runcorn. A lot of water had flowed under the bridge since that first fateful meeting. Just as Lennox had predicted the Police had charged him on planted forensic evidence and at trial the Defence had produced the receipts. Lennox had been acquitted and Smail's reputation amongst the criminal fraternity had soared. Since then Smail had acted for him on numerous occasions and had been obliged to visit him in most of the nation's high-security gaols. Twelve years for a brutal offence of rape had been but the latest chapter in an endless saga of violence.

And now, Lennox was bequeathing him the really big one. Smail had listened, initially with cynicism and then with rising excitement as, slowly and painfully, the prisoner had unlocked the spectacular secret. Fighting for every breath with which to tell his tale, Lennox had spelled out the facts until, eventually, he lay back on his pillow in total exhaustion.

Such had been the detail and the extent of the intrigue that Smail had no doubt as to the authenticity of the story. Moreover, the corroboration lay quietly in a safety deposit box in Barclays Bank in Preston to which Smail now had the coded access and, after one more visit to Durham Gaol, he would have Lennox's power of attorney and a repetition of the story on tape. Then, with the co-operation of that infamous hack *'The Molecule Man'*, he would prepare to detonate the explosive, ensuring his own pockets were lined to maximum effect. Contact with The Molecule Man would simply take one provocative telephone call to the Editor of that sensationalist tabloid promising them that his evil, dying client was about to unleash a national scandal. Here was a chance to rock the Establishment to its core, solve all of the lawyer's financial problems and, this time round, Martin Smail would be the Solicitor for the Righteous whilst his client, Derek Lennox, would be tucked away six feet under.

Chapter 7

The Molecule Man had always operated on three basic principles. Firstly, if you had any kind of skill then, somewhere, there was a niche in the marketplace where you could sell your expertise. Secondly, there was no substitute for absolute determination. Thirdly, it was essential to generate mystique and intrigue. It was this last principle that had proved most important in earning him success for no one, except the newspaper Editor, knew the true identity of the Molecule Man nor the secret of his double life.

As a Crime Reporter whose articles appeared in one of the country's best-selling tabloids, his stories could add hundreds of thousands to the daily circulation. In fact, he had remained freelance and fiercely independent, but the strength of the mutual trust between him and the Editor meant that his scoops always went to the same paper. Whenever the Molecule Man filed a report it would invariably make the front page headlines, as it would tell the savage, unvarnished truth at the heart of the story. Always meticulously researched, ruthlessly indifferent to any sensitive aspect of the story and, above all, completely accurate, he had played his part in the downfall of one Bishop, two Chairmen of Public Companies, one lesser politician, two television personalities and a rock star.

Still only young, he had established such a formidable network of contacts within the power structures of finance, politics and show-business that he could sniff out the truth at a hundred yards and still nobody knew his name. When face-to-face enquiries were required, he had a select team of hard-nosed, ambitious, young journalists at his disposal, all communication being made by telephone or email. The arrival of the mobile phone had made him an even more lethal force. No detail was ever missed. Nothing escaped his attention, however miniscule. Investigating every aspect of every player, the Molecule Man took his prey apart piece by piece, molecule by molecule, hence his name and hence his fearsome reputation.

Despite all of his success, one particular species of target had so far eluded him. The scalp of a Cabinet Minister. Always the ultimate prize, he yearned for the story that would bring down a member of this crony-ridden, manipulative and arrogant Government. Until yesterday morning when the Editor had telephoned to report a Runcorn solicitor's titillating promise of a story to topple a high-flier, he had never heard of either Martin Smail or Derek Lennox, but now they preoccupied every precious minute of the day and night. As he probed, dug and barked out his orders, the sweet stench of scandal filled the air.

Two days passed before he received the definitive phone call at just after six o'clock in the evening.

"Am I speaking to the Molecule Man?" enquired the male voice in its strong Lancashire accent.

"Yes, Mr Smail, you are. Before we continue I need the code-word I gave you when we spoke a couple of days ago?"

"Mesmeric," Smail snapped back without hesitation.

"Right. We can talk. What progress have you made?"

"Plenty. I've opened the Safety Deposit box in the Preston Bank. It's dynamite," came the triumphant reply. "Sheer, bloody dynamite."

"I need to see it then, don't I, Mr Smail? I can have it collected later tonight."

"Not bloody likely. That stuff's now been moved to another safe. You see nothing 'til we come to terms. Your Editor said once I'd got something concrete then we could talk turkey. Well, I've got something concrete all right, I can promise you that. So let's get down to business."

"I need to know this first," declared the Molecule Man. "Did you get a full written, signed statement from your client setting out every single detail?"

"Who's the bloody lawyer round here?" barked Smail. "Of course I did. And it's tape-recorded. And I had a witness with me. Another solicitor from a firm in Newcastle. I hired him. Paid him a handsome fee for his attendance. As such I am his client, so he's bound by legal privilege. He can't breathe a word of what he heard without my approval. And I've got the proof now from the Deposit box. So. How much?"

"I'll tell you the figures in a minute, but you need to understand a few things first. If the story isn't kosher then you don't get a bean.

Also, if you try to hawk the story round looking for a better offer, then don't waste your time coming back to me. We don't get into any bidding wars on the big political stories. It's 'take it or leave it' with me for one very good reason. If the outline you've given me is true, then you won't find any other paper that will run with this except the one where my stories appear. Denstone has his tentacles everywhere. He can silence all the other papers by one means or another. But he can't silence this paper and I can assure you that he tried when it exposed one of his knighted cronies a few months back. On this story he'll pull out all the stops. Do we understand each other, Mr Smail?"

"Aye. Right enough. You've spelt out your warnings so now spell out how deep your pockets are. You're not dealing with a mug. How much?"

"I want to read the statement you took and see the contents of the box. If I think they're crap you get nothing," began the journalist. "If I think there's something there then you get ten grand up front."

"Ten grand!" Smail spat down the phone. "Ten grand for the biggest story you've . . . "

"Just calm down, will you," came the interruption. "Calm down and listen. Once we decide there may be a story you get ten grand. If it leads to an article being published in our newspaper then you get seventy-five grand. If it leads to a prosecution, then you get a hundred and fifty. If it leads to a conviction, then you get quarter of a million."

"I want a hundred grand if the story gets published. Two hundred if we put a face in the dock and half a million if he's potted. Else I'll try another rag," Smail blustered in response.

"No deal. Once you walk away from this offer you'll likely end up without a cent. It's my offer or zip. You may know a bit about handling a criminal client but I can assure you the Editor and I know the realities of the Press and this control-crazy Government. So, like I said, take it or leave it."

There was a long pause as the small town solicitor pondered his options. This was the kind of opportunity that came only once in a lifetime to a man in his position, but there was no way he could handle this or take on the Establishment without the backing of someone with real clout. The Molecule Man had that clout and recent history suggested that Denstone could suppress virtually anything. Most, if not all, of the other papers would capitulate.

"It's a deal," grunted Smail eventually. "You can send your courier for the evidence to my office tomorrow at eleven o'clock sharp. And I'll want a copy of our financial arrangements in writing," he added.

"Nothing in writing. You'll get the appropriate cheque at the appropriate time. By then, we won't care about protecting our position. But until then it's on trust. I don't cheat. You know my reputation. The paper will pay the money. I call the shots. Do I send my man to your office tomorrow or not?"

There was a sharp intake of breath as Smail accepted the inevitable. You didn't negotiate with the Molecule Man. You did as he told you or you hawked your goods around Fleet Street. Probably unsuccessfully. The Runcorn solicitor had already decided that he would rather have this mysterious journalist on his side than look elsewhere.

"Eleven o'clock. I'll be waiting," he conceded.

"Phone me the day after tomorrow at six. I'll have a decision for you by then," came the satisfied reply. "New Codeword 'Dagger'. You got that?"

"Dagger," Smail repeated, now beginning to wallow in the intrigue. "Like a dagger in the heart of Government."

"No, Mr Smail. A dagger in the back. Far more effective because they don't see it coming. And far more satisfying," he added, as he clicked the mobile phone off.

Chapter 8

The black leather Manolo Blahnik stiletto with the three inch steel heel appeared first, before the long, shapely leg fully emerged from the driver's side of the metallic silver Mercedes CLK 320 and stepped directly into one of the numerous puddles of filthy, brown water that littered the bomb site of a car park alongside Bradford Crown Court. Naomi Nicholas cursed silently to herself as she felt the cold water flood into the outrageously expensive shoe, soaking the narrow, elegant foot within and creating a suction sensation between the sole of her foot and the bottom of the inner shoe. Easing herself out of the driver's seat, she gingerly manoeuvred away from the water-filled pothole and, leaning on the bonnet of her gleaming new car, removed the offending footwear and slowly poured the brown liquid out of it. Even in the midst of her irritation, the natural beauty of her face was clear to see, with those chiselled cheekbones and the high forehead, accentuated by the blonde hair brushed tightly back in anticipation of a day in Court spent under the weight of a barrister's horsehair wig.

For the first few months after Jack Farnham had walked out of her kitchen on that awful night, she had withdrawn into her work, caring little about disguising the despair that she had felt at the prospect of life without his strong, handsome presence always at her side. It had proved virtually impossible to stop thinking about him because his voice, picture and words were constantly on the sports channels as his television career expanded and his syndicated football analysis reports now appeared regularly in two broadsheet newspapers. Not a day went by without that dull ache starting, deep inside her body, as she battled to get her life back on course as a single woman and somehow to become whole again.

As she extracted her red bag containing her wig and robes from the boot and made her way towards the Court entrance, she reflected on her efforts of the last week, prompted by a chance meeting with Dickie Lampard in the case she was presently conducting at Bradford. Dickie was a genial fellow, always on the lookout for the latest gossip, deliciously indiscreet but with his heart in the right place. They had been Junior Counsel on opposite sides in the case that had led to the disaster with Jack and had not met since.

"Get yourself out again, girl," Dickie had urged her, shocked at the sadness he had espied in her eyes and her bearing. "Buy yourself a new outfit. Splash out. Lift the spirits. Let's see the old Naomi Nicholas, the most stunning female on the Northern Circuit."

The following weekend she had taken his advice and not only had she spent more on these designer shoes than she had ever spent on a pair of shoes in her life, but she had also traded in her run-of-the mill saloon for a Mercedes. Moreover, after six months of politely declining the constant social invitations from a stream of highly eligible men, who all viewed her as the most desirable but elusive woman that they had ever encountered, she had finally agreed to dine at Leeds' latest fashionable restaurant with the dashing young doctor from St James' Hospital who had been in anxious and relentless pursuit of her since Jack's departure.

Of course, it had all proved worthless. The doctor, pleasant though he was, had seemed like a fawning, one-dimensional youth when compared to Jack. He was the first man to have kissed her since Jack had gone and, as she closed her front door at the end of the evening on the disappearing and disappointed figure of the ardent suitor, she had, yet again, found herself weeping for Jack, her beautiful face pressing against the cold tiles of the kitchen table as the tears rolled down her cheeks, soaking the emerald green sleeves of the expensive dress that she had bought that day, while her sobbing was the only sound in that empty, sterile house. Nor had the new car or fancy shoes had the slightest impact upon her and, predictably, when she had finally got herself into Court this morning, the jury had convicted her client of the robbery with which he had been charged.

Her Honour Judge June Kensett had only been appointed as a Circuit Judge the previous Christmas and was keen to make her mark by imposing extremely heavy prison sentences on those souls unfortunate enough to appear before her. Invariably wearing heavy framed glasses which were far too big for her small, deeply lined and pinched face, she looked almost like a judicial caricature beneath her oversized, pristine Judge's wig. Lacking a sense of humour, devoid of compassion and having no sexual inclination of any kind, she had soon attracted the Robing Room sobriquet of "June the Prune" as, in her dry, clipped tones she meted out years of misery to the flotsam and jetsam in the dock.

Peering imperiously down from the Bench through those unfashionable glasses at the tall, elegant figure of Naomi Nicholas, the Judge seemed untouched by the plea for some degree of leniency in the sentence as the clear, alluring voice of the barrister tried to explain how life could be when you came from the very bottom of the pile.

"The jury have convicted my client of jumping over the counter at the newsagent's shop, pushing the shopkeeper to the ground and stealing two hundred pounds from the till," Naomi continued. "He's just twenty-one, has spent a childhood being shunted from one institution to another. Living rough on the streets, he became desperate. The shop was just closing, it was getting dark and he faced another night in the bitter cold on a Bradford pavement . . . "

Twiddling her highly sharpened, yellow pencil between her thumb and index finger, "The Prune" paid scant attention to the words of mitigation being advanced, but pondered over the injustice of nature that had made Naomi Nicholas everything that she was not. Tall, graceful, open-faced, sensual, desirable and quintessentially female, exuding style from every pore in stark contrast to the squat, unattractive and charmless figure seated in the ornate, red-leather chair on the Bench. Inequity was the name of the game, she thought to herself as she cruelly inserted the fateful number in her notes that would be the one word that the prisoner would be straining his ears to hear when her turn to pass sentence came in the next few minutes.

There was a long silence after Naomi had sat down. A deliberate silence, for the new Judge liked to build up the dramatic effect when she wielded the power invested in her by the State. Add to the suffering. Then, her hard voice boomed out across the Courtroom, castigating the white-faced inadequate standing in the dock, his head bowed in resigned despair. As she reached a crescendo, which culminated in the announcement of the figure she had pencilled in her notes a few minutes earlier, Naomi was filled with anger and contempt at the brutality of the sentence. The shocked, white face in the dock looked up and caught Naomi's eye as he was shepherded briskly away by the two warders towards the cells.

At the wheel of the car, heading back to her chambers in Leeds, she found herself, yet again, enduring a real crisis. When things had gone wrong before, there had always been Jack's unquestioning support. Now she was completely alone. None of the recent hollow trappings could make the slightest difference. Ten years that embittered woman had handed down to her client. Sitting in the claustrophobic cells after the sentence, Naomi had not minced her words in advising the bemused youth, huddled in hopelessness on the wooden slatted bench.

"We go to the Court of Appeal with this," she had declared emphatically. "Four years was the appropriate sentence, perhaps five at the very most. Ten years is an outrage. It'll take about six months to get the appeal heard but we are taking this to London. You have my word. This one goes all the way."

Back in chambers everyone made the right noises when she complained about the sentence but it was Friday and, in truth, all they were really interested in was getting home and starting the weekend. For Naomi the weekend held out only the prospect of emptiness. Depressed at the outcome of the case, no plans to go anywhere, no desire to make any arrangements, a deserted house, another brief to read for the following week and no Jack. Mercedes. Designer shoes. Money in her pocket. But no Jack. When would this sense of desolation ever end?

Chapter 9

Stretched out on the candy-striped sunlounger alongside the azure blue swimming pool, Douglas Curbishley QC imperiously snapped his long, elegant fingers with their manicured nails in the direction of the Embassy butler, signifying the latest demand for the immediate replenishment of his near-empty whisky glass. Throughout life he had cut a refined and graceful figure, thereby giving a false impression of authority and respectability. In truth, he had cheated in his final exams at Eton, bent the rules at Oxford so as to walk away with a second class Honours degree in Jurisprudence and had led a charmed life at the Bar for nearly thirty years.

When his equally devious brother recently manoeuvred his way, via the political cronies and chums' route, into the splendour of the British Embassy in Caracas, Venezuela as Ambassador, Curbishley had taken six weeks off to escape the worst of the English cold and gloom and live the life of Riley at the expense of the taxpayer. Neither his wife nor his Clerk in chambers had been sorry to see him go.

Sipping the Chivas Regal from the newly-filled cut glass tumbler, Curbishley watched the butler disappear slowly back into the house and reflected on the vagaries of life as the sun beat down from the cloudless sky. The family money had long since been dissipated and, if the truth be told, precious little work had been coming his way over the last few years. No civil briefs at all and only the odd criminal brief when none of the other three silks in chambers were available. Everybody recognised that he had only got silk by virtue of the Old Boys' network and wasn't really up to the job of conducting major trials in any field. Both of the murders in which he had appeared were returned to him at the last minute by other Counsel who had got themselves part heard in other cases and, in each case, he had made very serious errors of judgement leading to avoidable defeat. On the last occasion he had picked up the Prosecution brief and deliberately withheld some information from the Defence to which they were obviously entitled. Halfway through the trial a chance question by his opponent of the Senior Officer in the case had unearthed the deceit and undermined Curbishley's integrity in the eyes of the jury. They had duly acquitted.

His doleful reverie was interrupted by the approach of a young, sultry houseboy, dressed all in white, hurrying through the large French windows at the side of the house, carrying a portable telephone handset which he thrust into Curbishley's hands before turning away and returning to the house.

"Hello. Douglas Curbishley here," he articulated grandly into the mouthpiece.

"Good day, sir. It's Peter here. Senior Clerk from chambers. I've got an urgent message for you. A solicitor from the Director of Public Prosecutions' Office wants an Advice from you. Very important case apparently. They need Leading Counsel's Opinion as to whether they should prosecute or not," the cockney voice declared, his words spilling over each other as he urgently conveyed the message.

"Why me?" enquired the puzzled QC. "There's three other silks in chambers. The DPP never briefs me. Did you tell him I was visiting my brother in Venezuela?"

"I told him you were abroad, sir. He said it was your advice they wanted. No one else would do."

"Well, you'd better fax me the papers through on the Embassy Fax. I'll get you the number if you hold on a . . . "

"No, Sir," the Clerk interrupted. "You can't do it by fax. He explained all of that. This has to be done in conference in London. In person. And there's no papers yet neither. He wouldn't give me any more details but said he wanted to know by the end of today if you would handle it or not. I promised I'd speak to you on the phone."

"But I'm only halfway through my stay. I'd have to come home immediately," replied Curbishley, his tone betraying his bewilderment at why the DPP should be so anxious to instruct him when there were plenty of other silks about with far better reputations.

"Your choice, sir. But you must make a decision today. They want a conference next Monday at the crack of dawn."

"That only leaves me three days to get home," sighed Curbishley in exasperation.

"Exactly. One other thing of interest. The fee," added the Clerk.

"Yes?"

"They won't give you any paperwork so there's no preliminary reading to do. They'll spell out the facts at the meeting and want your advice in writing within twenty-four hours after that. They'll pay you ten thousand pounds for that and fly you home first class from wherever you are. Not a bad offer if I may so, sir."

"Ten thousand pounds! Too good to refuse, Peter, and who knows where it may lead," volunteered Curbishley immediately. "Tell them I'll be there."

As he pressed the disconnect button on the handset he felt his whole system shut down for a second, as if all the power had been momentarily turned off in his body before kicking in again. It had been happening quite frequently over the last couple of months. Anyway, better announce the news, phone home and start packing. Ten thousand quid! An important brief from the DPP. About bloody time as well.

* * *

British Airways. First Class. A wide seat that turned into a bed. Endless supplies of vintage Veuve Cliquot, a sensational chateaubriand and, far more important, the chance to feel important again. With the weekend to recover alone at home as his wife, despite the news of his sudden return to work, had made other arrangements which she assured him could not possibly be changed at the last minute without causing serious offence.

By the time that he strode into Lancaster Chambers on Monday morning, knowing that he was about to earn ten thousand pounds in the next twenty-four hours, plus whatever brief fee he may get if the case went to Court, he had convinced himself that he must have been chosen by the DPP because of his skill, experience and reputation.

"They're already here, Sir," announced Peter as he spotted the tall, haughty figure walking down the long book-lined chambers corridor. "I've shown them into your room as they said they would rather not sit in the Waiting Room on public display."

"Yes, of course. Very important case, so no doubt top level people. Quite right, Peter."

Just as his hand touched the brass handle of the door to his room at the end of the corridor he experienced that same judder within his body as if the system was shutting down, before it suddenly lurched back into action and he thrust open the door to discover what this mysterious case was all about.

"Good morning, gentlemen," he declared in a firm, authoritative voice as he espied the two suited men sitting on the brocade carvers that he kept on the client's side of his desk. "Douglas Curbishley QC. I don't believe we've met before."

The younger figure rose immediately to his feet, offering his hand in a limp handshake. Thin, short, in need of a haircut, weak face, no chin, cheap suit, no older than thirty.

"No, sir. We haven't. I'm Giles Brockley from the DPP's Office. I'm here as your instructing Solicitor. This is a National Security case so I have a Commander with me."

"How do you do, Commander," replied Curbishley to the older figure who made no offer to stand nor speak, merely presenting a cold hand to Curbishley in perfunctory greeting. "May I have your name, Commander?" he added.

"Just Commander," came the sharp reply. In uttering only two words he instantly established the hierarchy of power amongst the three men in that room. At that second Curbishley realised that he was about to be embroiled in something heavier than he had ever been exposed to before. The self-confidence that he had felt as he lay back in his First Class British Airways seat evaporated in the air. The DPP had obviously sent along a lackey as a façade, but the presence of a Commander made it clear that there had to be an agenda here which was out of his league. Why had they come to him? Why were they prepared to pay him ten thousand pounds just for a written Advice?

As Curbishley walked around the desk and adjusted his long body into the black leather chair, the Commander began to speak in a distant, metallic voice.

"We want your advice as to whether the DPP should instigate a criminal prosecution of a man named Lewis Barford."

"On what charge?" enquired Curbishley, trying to sound and appear as if he could remain in control of this meeting.

"Conspiracy to murder one Ibrahim-El-Hoorie. I have here three statements. One was made by a criminal. Name of Derek Lennox. The second is made by his solicitor in Runcorn and the third is from a Newcastle solicitor witnessing Lennox's statement. There are also copies of certain documents recovered from Lennox's Safety Deposit Box. We want you to read them. Now. In this room. In our presence. You will not be allowed to keep them, nor take any copies of them. As a QC you don't need me to tell you that, unless there is a prosecution, none of what you read or what we discuss can ever be repeated elsewhere."

Curbishley had stared in alarm and fascination at the reptilian features of the silver-haired man opposite as his words crackled through the air. The minion from the DPP's office sat with his head down, staring at the carpet, visibly squirming in discomfort at the charade he had been ordered to attend.

It had taken nearly an hour for Curbishley to read and digest the material that had been handed to him across his desk. It had made his blood run cold. Even a barrister of his poor judgement could have no difficulty in identifying the secret agenda that was really at work here. Any lawyer reading this material would know that there was a case for this man Barford to answer. The advice was simplicity itself. Prosecute. Charge him and prosecute.

For the entire time that it had taken the QC to read the statements the Commander and Brockley had sat in silence. When Curbishley eventually handed the papers back across the desk it was the Commander who broke the silence.

"You will appreciate from that material that Lennox was dying. He is now dead . . . " he began.

"But there are ways in which the Prosecution can seek to adduce the statement of someone deceased before a jury," Curbishley interrupted. "It is a certainty that we could get that statement read out in Court to the jury."

"You seem to be under a misapprehension, Mr. Curbishley, when you speak of "we". The "we" that matters in this case would not want a jury to hear that statement. Do I make myself clear?" announced the Commander.

There was along pause as Curbishley digested the full impact of this acid remark. It was a set-up. And he was the fall guy. But he'd get Governmental approval and a cheque for ten thousand.

"Oh, yes. I understand exactly," he eventually replied. "I now realise precisely the type of advice that you are looking for. But I am entitled to ask this question. Who supplied you with these statements? The test to be applied by the Crown, as to whether or not to prosecute, is based on whether the evidence provides a reasonable prospect of obtaining a conviction. If, by any chance, my advice was that you should not prosecute, how do you know that whoever supplied you with this material would not try to make a fuss? A pretty serious fuss at that. Claiming that there was clearly evidence providing a reasonable prospect of convicting Barford?" he demanded anxiously.

"These documents came from a particular member of the Press, no doubt via the solicitor Smail. If you advise that Barford should not be prosecuted, then we will use every means at our disposal to ensure that there is no publication of any of this material. But you should understand that we might fail. There still remains a small faction within Fleet Street that can be difficult to silence, even where National Security is involved. If we failed, then the DPP, and indeed any other National Agency potentially involved, would say that they had obtained a written, fully reasoned and detailed Opinion from a QC advising that we should not prosecute. I take it that your clerk informed you of the fee that we are paying for your Advice," came the devastating reply in that same cultured, clipped tone.

"It was mentioned."

"Well, I'm mentioning it again. I think you've made the connection. And on that note our discussions can come to an end. You have all the information that you require to come to your decision. My Department is powerful, Mr Curbishley. Better to have us as an ally than a foe," added the Commander, rising to his feet and heading towards the door in one swift move as the wimpish Brockley scuttled along behind him.

"We will expect your written Advice by ten o'clock tomorrow morning. Please don't use a typist. Your eyes only. It will be collected by hand."

After their departure Curbishley sat alone at his desk in a state of intense nervousness, playing the words of the Commander over and over again in his mind. Slowly, the various alternatives began to crystallise. Give the proper advice to prosecute and face a war with the Establishment which he could never win, whatever the outcome of any trial. Or, obey the tacit orders, advise against prosecution, pick up the ten thousand and pray that they kept this journalist and the Runcorn solicitor quiet. Or refuse to get involved by declining to advise and lose out on the ten thousand. The very process of clearly identifying the choices led him to his decision and he pulled open his desk drawer, produced a sheaf of paper and began drafting the Advice in longhand. He would perfect it and type it up at home later on his laptop.

R v Lewis Barford :

Advice of Douglas Arnold Curbishley QC

I have been instructed to advise on the merits of a possible prosecution of the above-named person on a charge of conspiracy to murder. I have read a variety of documents and discussed the matter in conference in my chambers with a representative of the Director of Public Prosecutions and a senior figure from the Security Services.

I set out in the following Paragraphs the detailed reasoning I have applied to my consideration of the issues raised but it will make a full understanding of my decision the easier to follow if I set out at this stage the conclusion to which I have finally come. This has proved to be a finely balanced exercise. The test to be applied by the Crown in such circumstances is whether or not there exists, on the likely available and admissible evidence, a reasonable prospect of securing a conviction. On analysing the many evidential and legal issues that these papers generate,

I have eventually concluded that this test cannot be satisfied.

Accordingly, it is my advice that there should not be a prosecution of Lewis Barford and that this matter should not proceed further . . .

* * *

An empty flat in Chiswick. Cold ham and salad for dinner with a whole bottle of Chablis to himself. Two hard hours on the laptop finalising and then printing out the Advice. Another of those disconcerting judderings of the system, like the petrol wasn't getting through the fuel pipe properly. Three large malt whiskies. Tired. Worried. And then the phone rang, startling him.

"Curbishley here."

"Is that Douglas Curbishley QC?" asked the male voice.

"Yes, who am I speaking to?"

"I'm a journalist."

"What's your name?"

"You don't need my name, but you do need to know that if you help them sit on this, then I'll destroy you."

"I've no idea what you're referring . . . "

"Don't feed me any bullshit, Mr Curbishley. Just listen. I know you've got a lousy practice, but at least you get by. It's because you've got a lousy practice that they chose you. They had good reason to believe that you'd do as you were told. But I'm telling you that if you let them buy you off, then you'll never get another case. Your name will be all over the paper as a sell-out merchant. You'll be ridiculed, despised and out of work."

"How dare you speak to me in these terms. I won't be bullied. I'll take this to your Editor, the Police and . . . "

"I told you not to give me any bullshit. I told you to listen. None of those threats is worth a bean. I'm suggesting that you give the advice that those statements demand. If you don't, you're finished. Have you got the message loud and clear?"

"I get the message that you're trying to blackmail me."

"Not blackmail. I'm recommending that you give honest advice.

Not to help suppress the truth. For thirty pieces of silver."

"What advice I give is a matter for my professional judgement and no damned business of yours."

"You're wrong on both counts. Your professional judgement will tell you there should be a prosecution, but you're under heavy pressure to go the other way. And it is my damned business because we shall run this story the day after tomorrow, whichever way you jump."

"So I get either you or them on my back. I can't win either way, can I?"

"Perhaps you can't win, but you can make sure that you don't lose. If there is a prosecution, my story will make no criticism of you. You won't feature. Leading Counsel will be deemed to have made the proper decision. The public will understand that. But if you sell out then you'll feature all right. Big time. Front page."

"Who the hell are you?"

"I'm known as the Molecule Man. I have the ammunition to take you apart. Molecule by molecule. In public. Your choice. Think about it. And while you're thinking, I'll be sharpening my pencil."

"When any article appears I shall know which rag you're from and then I can report your blackmail to your Editor and the Press Council."

"Of course you can. Most of my stories involve reports to the Editor. I specialise in exposing hypocrisy, treachery and cover-up. That's why I sell newspapers. The Editor would be disappointed if the complaints dried up. And my stories are always one hundred percent factually accurate, so the Press Council won't act. How the hell do you think I know that they came to you for an Opinion?"

"How do you know?"

"Because my sources are impeccable. And I know they came to you because they needed a written Opinion from a QC saying they shouldn't prosecute. An insurance policy if ever the story did get out. Most QCs are pretty clued up. They had to identify a weak one, short on integrity and compliant. They chose the right person, didn't they? But we still just about have a free Press. That's where I come in and hence this call. They'll try to shut me up. But now you've listened to me do you think I can be silenced? Like I said, your choice. Good night."

Chapter 10

The meeting had been arranged for midday in a room at the side of the Home Office which had its own private entrance, enabling visitors who wished to be discreet to arrive unobserved, as the car could draw up right to the side door. As the back doors of the Daimler swung open simultaneously, two figures, their faces grim and set, hurriedly emerged and headed directly into the building to keep their midday appointment with the Home Secretary. The Commander was carrying Curbishley's Advice in his briefcase whilst Barford strode along just behind, his broad shoulders held militarily erect, defiance etched in his expression and his dark eyes still displaying the anger he had just voiced on learning in the car of the Commander's failure to make Curbishley deliver.

Templar was waiting for them in the luxurious office that he had had redesigned and refurbished at vast public expense immediately after his appointment to the Home Office. Gesturing to the leather armchairs strategically placed near to the Edwardian antique desk at which he was already seated, he awaited the Commander's report, already aware from the mobile phone call made as the Commander had driven away from Curbishley's chambers that the news was bad.

"Leading Counsel's Opinion is that there is sufficient evidence to justify a criminal prosecution of Barford on the charge of conspiracy to murder," the Commander began solemnly. "I've already informed Barford."

"Why did Curbishley give that Advice? You assured me yesterday that he understood the position. He was chosen because he wouldn't resist. What went wrong?" asked Templar.

"He's not saying. His clerk said he wasn't in chambers. Called away to a meeting. He'd left the sealed envelope for me. Not answering his phone. Where's your money, Home Secretary?"

"The Molecule Man?" Templar suggested softly.

"Exactly."

"But are we necessarily bound by that Advice?" the Home Secretary enquired urgently.

"No. We're not. We can ignore it. But when we try to apply the pressure to that lunatic journalist and his Editor, they'll know that the Advice was to prosecute. We'll be left with no insurance policy."

"How will they know? They'll expect you to try to stop them publishing, whatever the advice."

"There are a number of reasons why they'll know. If we seek an injunction, then we'll have to declare whether we believe there is likely to be a criminal prosecution or not. If we don't seek an injunction they'll realise we're in trouble. If we apply more subtle pressure, which in reality is what we're going to have to do, then we're revealing that we haven't got any insurance. But the main reason they'll know is because that Molecule Man has got the best placed informants in London," the Commander explained in a tone of absolute frustration.

"So what do we do?" demanded Templar.

"We tell Special Branch to apply pressure to the Editor. I suspect they're intending to publish something in tomorrow's edition. If we manage to stop them tomorrow, then we've won an important victory and we'll have time to develop an alternative strategy. Once you halt their momentum the balance of power shifts. On the other hand, if we fail, then I can see no alternative to Barford being tried. The momentum will be unstoppable."

"I could make the bastard see sense," Barford spat out, tiring of listening to these two men debate his future like they were working on the Treasury budget."

"It's your methods of making people see sense that has got us into this mess in the first place," the Commander replied abruptly. "Anyway, you've no idea who he is. We've spent the last two days trying to get a name, but he's as elusive as the Scarlet Pimpernel."

"Don't talk about what you don't know, Commander," retorted Barford angrily. "You and the Minister were keen enough to hand the problem over to me on that barge. My instructions to Leadbetter and then to Lennox were not meant to . . . "

"Steady Lewis, steady," interrupted Templar. "We must keep calm. We've got to face the realities. If the paper publishes tomorrow then you probably will have to face a trial. We've got to start thinking along those lines and take steps to ensure that the verdict goes your way."

"My way?" exploded Barford. "Don't you mean our way? If I go down for this then you're done for as well, Minister. If you want to talk realities then let's spell them all out."

"I realise that there is a risk of serious consequences for us all, Lewis," Templar acknowledged with a conciliatory nod of his head. "But if the case against you is destroyed then at least we all have a chance of survival."

"Right," interjected the Commander decisively. "With your agreement, Home Secretary, I shall take the necessary steps. One of my most senior men will be despatched to the Editor's office this afternoon with authority to threaten the very existence of the newspaper and the liberty of the Editor and his madcap journalist if they publish. If there's nothing in tomorrow's edition, then we've won important breathing space. If they go to press then we must have the best legal team in London ready and in place to defend Barford."

"I've had those enquiries made already," declared Templar. "Curbishley will have the Prosecution brief. We know he's useless. Weak. Poor judgement. Slow. On our side we'll have the best in the business."

"And just who might that be?" Barford enquired urgently.

"There are two. The choice will be yours. Matthew Allendale QC. Rugby School. Oxford man, like you, Lewis. Christchurch. Double first in Jurisprudence and Chemistry. Amazing combination. Silver spoon in the mouth, but brilliant brain. Absolutely formidable in Court, but a complete gentleman. Wins by the book. Does high powered commercial work and crime. Will be on the High Court Bench within the year. Curbishley would be out of his depth."

"And the other one?" demanded Barford.

"A tough guy. Street fighter. Giant of a man. Trinity College, Dublin.

Sails close to the wind. A bully. Terrifying. Win at any price. Universally despised within the profession. Only does serious crime. Has hardly lost a case since he took silk and apparently he gets revenge with interest for his very occasional defeats."

"Name?" demanded Barford.

"Cadogan. Ronan Cadogan QC."

"There isn't really any choice, is there?" Barford spat out. "A toff with an intellect in the stratosphere or a ruthless bully boy. The question answers itself. Cadogan. Ronan Cadogan. Sounds like my kind of guy."

"Just what I thought you'd say, Lewis. The solicitors will be Matchley Bloom and Co. Best criminal solicitors in the City. Let's hope it never comes to it, but we'll have our team in place just in case."

"That concludes our discussions then I believe," announced the Commander. I have work to do. I want to brief the man sent to the Editor's Office myself. Immediately. Is there any other business before I go?"

"Yes. One last matter before you both leave," Templar responded. "We do have your assurance, don't we Lewis, that whatever happens you will keep the Commander, myself and the Department out of this."

"You think I may desert a sinking ship do you, Will?" replied Barford, instantly reverting to first names and abandoning all pretence at respectful formality as Templar's words revealed his true fears. "Worried I'll deploy the rat's charter. Well, let me tell you something. If they get me in the dock at the Old Bailey, my friend, the stakes will be as high for you as for me. How I play it will depend upon how much I can rely on your help. Your ghost will be sitting right next to me in that dock. On trial just like me. With a rope round your neck waiting to see if you drop."

DEATH BED CONFESSION ALLEGES MURDER TO SILENCE WITNESS WHO OVERHEARD TERRORIST PLOT

Terrorist rocket attack could have been averted but Police ignored warning. Was whistle-blower murdered to keep truth from the public? Did the Police know of intended target?

Were 31 lives lost through criminal negligence? Has murder been committed to suppress public outrage?

Crime Correspondent : 'The Molecule Man'

Once again 'The Molecule Man' has unearthed evidence of a major scandal which demands a criminal prosecution of those who may have ordered murder so that the public should never know that the Police had a detailed warning of the attack hours before it occurred. Who will ever forget the carnage at Manchester Airport 2 years ago when a terrorist rocket attack brought down an Airbus, killing 31 people and seriously injuring dozens of others? One terrorist was killed in a car crash during the ensuing Police chase but a second, Fahid Yasin, was later tried and convicted at the Old Bailey and sentenced to life imprisonment with a recommendation that he never be released. Now, according to information, supported by credible documentation, the Police had ample warning of the atrocity but failed to act.

A witness to the plot had reported the matter several hours before the terrorists struck but the Police paid scant regard to his report. On learning that he was not to be called for the Prosecution in the trial of Yasin, the witness threatened to release to the Press his account of overhearing the terrorists planning their attack. It was his belief that he was not being called so that the public would never learn that if the Police had acted on his information then the atrocity would have been averted. His threat of revelation was taken so seriously by the authorities that a decision was taken to pay a criminal hit man to eliminate him.

In a sensational death bed confession released exclusively to 'The Molecule Man' the hit man has told the whole story and documentary evidence has been supplied to support this account. This newspaper has released that material to the Prosecuting Authorities in the expectation of the arrest, charge and trial of at least one person closely connected to the Government. Once again, by maintaining his absolute anonymity, 'The Molecule Man' has provided the public with a means of striking back against suppression of the truth by the Establishment. Will they prosecute? Dare they not prosecute? Watch this space.

Chapter 11

Sitting alone in a soulless London hotel room on a Friday night with only a bottle of whisky as company, Jack Farnham found himself becoming morose. Having endured the crisis of watching helplessly as his football career was prematurely ended by a second rupture of the anterior cruciate ligaments and then suffering the indescribable pain of losing his wife in an accident caused by a drunk driver, he had somehow managed to pull himself up by his bootstraps. Writing his football column in the paper, expanding his broadcasting work, restoring his self-worth and gaining popularity in his new role, had given life some direction and purpose again. It had never occurred to him that he could ever be so lucky as to meet another woman who could mean as much to him as the wife who had been so cruelly taken away. And then he had stumbled across Naomi Nicholas, becoming completely captivated by her and the world had smiled again.

He had adored her and he had no doubt that she felt the same way about him. Their life together had been idyllic until that dreadful time at the end of the most important case she had ever been involved in and she had thrown him out. Of course he had let her down, but the dilemma with which he had been confronted was so awful that whatever he had done would have been wrong. There had been no right answer.

Nearly a year had passed since that fateful day, yet he could recall verbatim his own last words to her as he walked out of the kitchen, "Goodbye Naomi. I did love you and I still do. If ever you think that you may be able to give me another chance, then I hope that you will get in touch. I would never let you down again for as long as I live." From that day onwards he had never seen nor heard from her again. Following her career as a barrister in Leeds had been easy, because she was getting bigger and bigger cases, invariably reported in the Press and often on the local television. He knew that she had not moved because he often drove by her house near Roundhay Park and had seen her car parked in the drive, his heart always pounding in case he caught a glimpse of her or there was a strange car in the drive.

His own flat was not far away but he had consciously abandoned their old haunts and their paths had not crossed. Each day he had prayed that she might phone or even write, but as the months had dragged slowly by, he had come to realise that she was gone from his life forever. He knew that she would listen to his television commentaries and read his column and more than once he had deliberately slipped in a reference to a place they had visited together or a name that had a special meaning to them both. Nothing had provoked any response from her.

When the offer of the job as anchorman in the new Saturday night football discussion programme on the latest cable channel came his way, he had known that it would entail at least two nights a week in a London hotel, thereby further detaching himself from Leeds and any chance of a reconciliation. This was his second week on the programme and he'd booked a table for one in the hotel restaurant, lacking any desire to meet up with one of his football or broadcasting pals, preferring his own company. Now in his late thirties, solitude had become attractive. Controlling his drinking had not been easy, but he had refused to let it get out of hand and, as he looked at himself in the mirror, the jawline was still square, the face still handsome and the shoulders straight and broad, but there was a sadness now etched in the corners of the mouth that seemed unlikely ever to be erased.

Cable television companies were customarily generous with their expenses and the hotel was five star, on the river and a stone's throw from The Royal Courts of Justice. Wandering down to the restaurant the maitre d' had reserved him an excellent table right alongside the large picture window, looking out over the Embankment and the Thames beyond. It was already late for dinner but there were still quite a few customers left in the restaurant.

Heads turned as he took his seat and nudges of recognition passed between some of the diners. Occasionally, as he ate, someone would tentatively slip over to his table and politely ask for an autograph for a son or friend. It was his policy never to refuse, for these were the people who paid his wages and gave him a purpose in life, now that his playing days were over. There was a lot of traffic on the river tonight and he watched in fascination as the barges and the freighters bustled along the waterway with the small figures on the decks hauling ropes, shifting boxes or just leaning on the rails staring back at the city lights. As he finished his sea bass and put his knife and fork down, he became aware of a figure standing at the table and his hand instinctively went to his inside jacket pocket to pull out a pen to sign the autograph. But this time no piece of paper was thrust at him, for the person who stood motionless, staring down at him, was Naomi Nicholas, her face even more exquisite than in his memory. The pounding in his heart was so immediate and so intense that for several seconds he was in shock, before jumping to his feet and trying to speak, but her beautiful, clear voice cut across his strangled efforts.

"How are you, Jack?" she asked. "You look tired."

"Just working hard, Naomi. You know what it's like. Are you OK?"

"Surviving. Busier than ever. But so are you. I see you on the TV and still read the column."

"I'm glad that you do. Football had become important to you, there'd be no point in abandoning interest because of what happened between us."

"That's how I saw it."

"Will you sit down? Have a drink?"

"No, I won't stay, thank you. I've been in the Court of Appeal. Didn't finish until six and couldn't face the journey back to Leeds tonight so I checked in here. Just been out to dinner and heading for bed. As I passed the restaurant door I saw you. Alone. I walked on but stopped. You looked so . . . lonely . . . ," her voice began to tremble as she spoke and she hesitated, lowering her head for a second, before quickly regaining her composure.

"Please sit down, Naomi. Even if it's only for five minutes. Just have a glass of wine or a coffee. It's so good to see you and hear your voice."

Lifting her eyes she looked straight back into the face that had meant everything to her and, without answering, let him help her into a chair and call the waiter over. When his hand touched her arm, her whole body jumped involuntarily as if an electric shock was passing through her. It was obvious from his reaction that he had felt it too.

"A glass of red wine then," she said softly. "One rule though, Jack. No post-mortems."

"Understood. So tell me about the case today. Did you win?"

"Yes. An appeal against sentence for robbery. Female Judge sitting at Bradford gave him ten years. We call her 'The Prune'. Way over the top and the Court of Appeal reduced it to six, but not without a struggle."

"A good day's work then, in a manner of speaking. Four years lopped off."

"And you're thinking that means he'll be able to start robbing people again four years earlier then, aren't you?"

"Well, isn't that exactly what it does mean?" queried Jack.

"Probably," she replied mischievously, her face softening as she started to laugh.

How he had missed that laugh, he reflected to himself as the waiter arrived with a bottle of wine and two fresh glasses. Gradually the weight and tension eased as they both ensured that only small talk passed between them, never trespassing on to intimate territory, but once or twice Jack caught her staring intensely at him with a look of concern as she observed the sadness that lay beneath his smile. Yet, her own beauty was undiminished, as if the pain imposed by their parting had added even more grace and dignity to her bearing. By the time that the bottle was almost empty, most of the other diners had left and a silence fell across the table which neither seemed anxious to break. Naomi had realised when she saw him sitting alone at the single table in the window, seemingly so forlorn, that going over to him was likely to be extremely dangerous, for the last year without him had been empty and miserable. But nothing could have stopped her speaking to him. Cutting him out of her life by not phoning, writing or ever going where she was likely to see him was one thing. Walking past him and ignoring his presence was another. A magnetism more powerful than anything she could resist had drawn her into that restaurant and over to his table. Now the small talk was over. The bottle was empty. This silence was a defining moment in their lives. She knew that he was looking directly at her but she kept her face averted towards the window, the silhouette of her prominent cheekbones accentuating her classic beauty, staring out at the black river beyond, waiting for him to speak.

"I know it's late, Naomi. But it's a warm night and it's so wonderful to see you. Can we take a walk along the Embankment for a while?" he finally asked.

"Perhaps," she replied after a long pause, turning to look at him again as a smile of pleasure lit up her face. "All right. I'll go to my room and fetch a jacket."

It was after midnight as they strolled casually along the paved walkway that ran alongside the great river, enjoying the balmy night air, stimulated by the joy that each brought to the other, but both remaining frightened to cross that formidable barrier between small talk and intimacy. As they turned back towards the hotel, that special silence that falls over a big city as it snatches its brief nocturnal rest for those few hours between the last of the night revellers and the first of the day's workmen, began to descend.

Lights from the warehouse buildings and wharves on the far side of the river threw their eerie reflections upon the black surface of the water but, apart from the soft ripples of the ebbing tide there was no other sound, so that for those precious minutes Jack felt whole again, as if London belonged only to them.

At the next bridge they turned back towards the main thoroughfare, passing through a tiny, well kept public garden, illuminated by several flickering ornate lamp posts, which picked out the carefully tended flower beds and the occasional wooden bench along the path, inviting passers-by to rest awhile.

Seated upon one of these benches Jack observed the solitary figure of an old man in a dark, ill-fitting suit and a large black, felt hat, seemingly taking a few minutes rest as he, too, made his way homeward.

Instinctively, as they passed the bench, Jack nodded courteously to the oddly dressed stranger, who acknowledged the strikingly handsome man and the tall, elegant woman at his side.

"Good night, sir. And what a gentle London night it is," the old man said, spontaneously doffing the black hat as he spoke.

The deep, resonant voice was thick with an accent from Eastern Europe which Jack was unable to recognise and the use of the word "gentle" was such an odd choice of word that curiosity caused him to stop and turn towards the stranger. Despite being confined to the lower Divisions, Jack had played against a few of the lesser European teams but this accent was unfamiliar.

"That accent. I can't place it?"

The stranger laughed. It was a hollow laugh, not containing humour at all, but sounding as if a great sadness lay buried deep beneath.

"Hungary, sir. The cold open spaces of Hungary," he replied, "but that was long ago."

Steering Naomi to the bench, Jack sat down beside the old man and, from this closer position, he could see the evidence of hardship and pain that inhabited his eyes.

"You escaped during the 1956 Uprising, sir," he offered, more by way of a statement of fact than a question.

"My body escaped, but my soul remains in Magyarovar," he replied with a sigh. "You can never truly escape, for the demons are always with you."

Naomi well remembered that wherever Jack went, he would invariably strike up a conversation with those whose path he crossed but, she too, found herself intrigued by this sad Hungarian with his rich, expressive voice.

"I've never heard of Magyarovar," she declared, "how did you get out?"

"When it happened I ran to the Austrian border, maybe ten miles. Then I walked to Vienna, travelling only at night. Leaving eighty-two of my comrades in the ground. Students. Slaughtered by Soviet machineguns."

"How awful for you," breathed Naomi.

"And when I got to Vienna I couldn't find my way around. I'd never lived in a big city. I kept getting lost. I got a job and had to take a piece of tailor's chalk with me and mark the walls of the buildings between my room and my workplace so that I could find my way each day."

"What work did you find?" asked Jack.

The stranger leaned forward, reaching underneath the wooden bench upon which they sat and lifted up a battered black violin case from out of the shadows.

"The fiddle, sir, it earned me schillings which I sent back to Magyarovar. Later, I came to London and it earned me the money to stay here."

As he spoke he carefully opened the lid of the case and lovingly removed the instrument from its red velvet bed. Immediately, Naomi could see how his slender fingers curled around the precious fiddle, longing to make it sing and she did not hesitate.

"Play it for us," she urged. "Please play it. Right now. And it must be music from Hungary. Music that tells us what it was like to have lived in Magyarovar."

In silence the stranger rose to his feet and turned to face them, placing the violin upon his shoulder in such a way that it appeared that his whole body had been constructed to bend around this frail instrument, his chin caressing its faded, varnished wood.

At first the arm moved slowly, as the bow gently encouraged the strings to communicate to Naomi Nicholas and Jack Farnham the suffering he had endured but, as the music captivated them, the rhythm quickened and, beneath the hardship, they began to feel the joy and rejoicing in life that had enabled this unusual man to survive tyranny. Soon the stranger was stamping his heel into the ground and the volume of his wonderful music reached its piercing crescendo, before falling away as the last note, now mournful again and from a far off place and a far distant time, was carried away on the warm London breeze.

The stranger resumed his seat, his beloved instrument resting silent upon his knees. For a moment none of them spoke as the spell that had been cast continued to weave its magic, until Naomi leaned across and took the musician's hand in her own.

"You took us to Magyarovar," she told him, "now we have been there too."

"Then I shall play again for you," he replied, "and this time in a London garden you will hear the same music that has been heard in small Magyar villages over generations carrying a message which both of you will feel, for it is a melody understood only by those who are in love, as it is so obvious to me that you are."

Despite her efforts, his words and his perception made Naomi cry and she turned her head sharply away so that Jack would not see her tears as, for a second time, the musician got to his feet and the lines and angles of his body bent themselves to accommodate the treasured fiddle. Neither of them had ever heard such music before and, with a force of its own, the haunting melody brought Naomi into Jack's arms as, spontaneously, they rose from the bench and, in close embrace, danced to the Hungarian's mystical tune. After a year of desolation, once again Jack felt her warm breath upon his cheek and her body pressed urgently against his own and he knew that this chance meeting with a bizarre survivor from a strange, hard land was yet further confirmation that Naomi was destined to be part of his life.

The music made its own demands of how they should move, as its rhythm and pace controlled their feet and the sway of their bodies. In a dark London park, late at night, to the tune of an Eastern stranger, they danced an endless dance. Neither of them could ever remember how long it had lasted, or how it had begun or when it had ended. They were consumed by the music in its sadness and its joy and, through it, they tasted how love had once been in a small town for a lonely man who had walked to Vienna.

When it was over Naomi went up to the musician and kissed him tenderly upon the cheek.

"What happened to the woman you left in Magyarovar?" she asked gently, knowing from his music the agony of his loss.

"I kept writing. For a year. She never replied. One day I received a note from the old man who used to take the mail to our street. It just said 'Stop sending money, they shot her the day after you escaped'. That's when I decided to leave Vienna and come to London."

In his slow way he shuffled sadly back to the bench and carefully replaced his precious violin in its case. Jack walked across to him and offered him his large athlete's hand, which the stranger warmly received in his own.

"I have understood what you were telling us. It was fate that we met you. You can't realise how important it has been to us," Jack said to him.

"Then it was worthwhile," came the reply.

"Oh, yes, it was certainly worthwhile. We shall never forget the dance, nor your pain," added Naomi as the sad Hungarian musician eased away softly into the night and they were left alone.

Chapter 12

Standing 6 feet 5 inches in his stocking feet and weighing in at 18 stone, Ronan Cadogan took up a lot of courtroom space. A massive presence with a booming voice tinged with a Southern Irish lilt, he dominated any forum in which he appeared and he used his bulk and noise to maximum effect.

At school he had been a formidable second row forward and at Trinity College, Dublin he had represented the University in the heavyweight wrestling division for three of his four years as a student. Twenty odd years on, his frame had lost much of its shape but had retained and added to its bulk. Those who had known him as a boy, and later in adult life, would have all agreed that he had also retained one overriding characteristic. He was a monumental bully. Physically, verbally and emotionally, he threw his weight around until he got what he wanted.

Behind closed doors he was free with his fists and, by the time he became a QC, his wife despised him and his son felt only fear of him. There were times when the bully in him temporarily abated and he would charm and flatter and the house had a calmer atmosphere, but his mood could turn with the wind and the hectoring and tormenting would then begin anew.

In court, the witnesses, other barristers and even Judges would often wilt beneath the verbal assault, intimidated by the sheer size and volume of the man. Last year he had defended a man for murder at Leeds Crown Court and confronted Gordon Bertrand Haskitt QC, an adversary who had once cheated him in a case, and the titanic battle that ensued as Cadogan sought his revenge had provided macabre, yet gripping theatre for those who had observed the brutal spectacle. None had watched the unfolding drama with more horror and distaste than Cadogan's Junior, the stunningly beautiful Naomi Nicholas, who Cadogan had relished treating with complete contempt. That case had been paid for under the Legal Aid scheme and Cadogan had a Golden Rule that he would only accept Legal Aid cases if it was a very high profile murder or there was some other ingredient to spice the case up. Haskitt had been the spice on that occasion, but now Cadogan had been offered the Defence brief in a case which was just about as high profile as they could get and, it was privately paid as well. A further chance to make the national headlines and bolster the Cadogan coffers to the tune of a quarter of a million, for that was the figure that he had instructed his clerk, Arthur Halliwell, to demand from the Solicitors Matchley Bloom and Co., if they wanted Cadogan to accept the brief. Two hundred and fifty thousand on the brief and a further ten thousand a day for each day that the trial lasted.

"I doubt their client will have the funds to pay that kind of money, Sir," Arthur had gingerly suggested, ever fearful of any challenge to the QC's opinion, but anxious not to lose such a prestigious case out of chambers by pricing themselves out of the market.

Arthur had been a Barristers' clerk for forty-seven years in the same set of chambers, starting when he left school at fifteen and working his way up through the ranks. Over the years he'd had some top-notch Governors to work for, but things had changed for the worse and some of the new breed were quite unbearable, forever playing the high and mighty and treating the old school like Arthur as if they knew nothing. In Arthur's opinion the bully Cadogan had proved to be the most offensive of them all but, on the other hand, there was no doubt that he had a track record that was second to none.

"You heard my price, Arthur. It won't be Barford coughing up for this. The Government is in trouble on this one, mark my words. They'll pay the price if they think it will buy Barford's acquittal. You tell the solicitors my terms. They can take it or leave it and they'll take it all right. I want a conference in chambers with Barford next week. Conspiracy to murder charge and they've already got him out on bail. Don't tell me they aren't pulling out all the stops."

As usual, Cadogan had been proved right and Byron Bloom, one of the Senior partners at Matchley Bloom and Co. had agreed the fee without even a whimper of protest, arranging a conference in Counsel's Chambers at nine o'clock on the following Wednesday morning.

Manoeuvring his eighteen stone bulk into the high-backed ornate chair after the formal introductions, the QC was already studiously weighing up Lewis Barford, the Government hatchet man, seated awkwardly in the client's chair on the opposite side of the leather-topped desk sporting a charcoal grey Ralph Lauren suit and filling the air with his Nino Cerruti after-shave. Alongside Barford was the solicitor, Byron Bloom, one of the new breed of City whizz-kids, whose expertise embraced both high finance and Law. Bloom knew that in this case his principal role was simply to sit quietly, leaving the meter ticking at five hundred pounds an hour and let a QC of this calibre call all the shots. If something went wrong then, with a quarter of a million pounds on the brief, Cadogan could carry the can with the Home Office.

Looking directly at the small, narrowed eyes, Bloom instantly disliked what he saw. The corners of the mouth had been turned down so often, and for so long, that the deep lines had run into the heavy flesh of the jowls, lending Cadogan's natural expression a sourness and disdain which sat easily with his reputation as a cruel bully.

With customary arrogance Cadogan believed that he'd got the measure of Barford before he'd even asked him a question. Dark, brooding, and powerful but, above all else, always available for sale to the highest bidder, Cadogan concluded. Fitting that he should have played the role of mercenary in Sierra Leone and worked for a Government whose entire philosophy was based on control. In his college wrestling days Cadogan had fought one or two opponents like Barford. Tough and dirty. One of the prerequisites of survival when growing up on a Huyton council estate was an early abandonment of the Queensberry Rules. You didn't beat Barford's type by hurting them, as pain was viewed as an irrelevant, occupational hazard. You had to beat this kind of selfish brute in the mind. You made them realise that whilst you could match them physically, as Cadogan had no doubt that he still could, when it came to a clash of will and determination, then Cadogan would always be the victor. Having made his assessment, Cadogan immediately put his strategy into practice.

"You face an extremely grave charge, Mr. Barford. Conspiracy to murder will carry life imprisonment if you're convicted," he began heartlessly.

"To stand any chance in this trial I must receive very clear and very detailed instructions. So far, you've told your solicitor precious little and the Police even less."

"That's because I believe in biding my time, getting the lie of the land," Barford replied cautiously.

"Cards close to the chest, is it?" asked Cadogan.

"Not a bad tactic where lawyers are involved," came the glib response.

"In my experience where the tactics and the planning of a criminal trial are decided by the Defendant, then the verdict is usually easy to predict," was the immediate retort.

"I suppose by that you mean that the Defendant loses," grunted Barford.

"Exactly. Guilty. The Courtroom is the Gladiator's Arena. You don't know the rules. More importantly, you don't know which rules can be broken. Even more importantly you think you don't need to know."

"You make very quick judgements, Mr Cadogan."

"That's what I'm paid for. I've read the case papers and taken a hard look at you. Do you question my judgement?" Cadogan asked aggressively.

"Early days for me to answer that. Ask me when the verdict's in. For the moment I'm receiving your message loud and clear. You're talking guile, aren't you?"

"Guile, style and brute strength. I possess those qualities. So we all need to understand that if we're to fight this case as a team, then we can only afford to have one captain. Do I make myself clear, Mr. Barford?"

"Crystal clear."

"Very well. You need to understand how a Barrister has to work. You give me instructions. So long as you tell me that those are your instructions, however implausible they may sound, it is my duty to do my best with them. You may tell me that black is white. I will put that to the witnesses and the jury, regardless of its merits. Is any of that news to you?"

"Not really."

"But, if ever you tell me that your instructions are untrue, then I cannot advance what you tell me is a lie."

"In other words," replied Barford with a smile, "it's OK if I lie and arm you with lies for the jury, so long as I never tell you that I am lying."

"Now you have it, Mr Barford."

"I'm telling you that I'm not guilty."

"It may be that Mr Bloom has not had an opportunity to explain the full extent of the evidence against you, as some of the forensic test results only arrived a couple of days ago."

"I'm sure you'll cover it all," said Barford.

"Undoubtedly. After your arrest you were interviewed by the Police at Gloucester Rd. Police Station," Cadogan continued.

"In my presence," added Bloom, speaking for the first time since he had sat down.

"Indeed, Mr Bloom. The Police seemed very nervous at your presence. Their questions were completely inadequate. They were so ineffective and weak that one wonders what instructions they had received as to how vigorously they were to pursue Mr Barford . . . "

"I answered most of what they asked," Barford interrupted.

"Were all of those answers truthful then?" asked the QC.

"As far as I could remember the events I was questioned about."

"Did you know Derek Lennox?"

"I did. From Sierra Leone. He was one of the mercenaries hired by Colonel Merle. He worked for me once or twice. But only over a period of a few months."

"What kind of operations?"

"He was a mercenary soldier. Ostensibly so was I."

"What specifically can you remember Lennox doing?"

"He did one job I can vividly remember on the Guinea border. We sent him to locate a rebel who had set fire to a village, killing several women and children."

"Did Lennox find him?"

"Oh yes. He killed him. He beheaded him with a machete. Completely severed his head."

"How do you know?"

"Because he brought the head back to our camp with him."

"Had those been your orders?"

"No. My orders were to locate and capture. Alive if possible. But I had no control over how an armed and dangerous rebel may react. I don't know what Lennox was faced with. It wasn't a Cheltenham tea party."

"Did you tell the Police any of this?"

"They didn't ask. They just asked if I knew Lennox. I told them I'd met him in Sierra Leone doing mercenary operations and that was it. They didn't ask for the same detail that you're demanding."

"Did the Police ask if you'd seen him since Sierra Leone?"

"Yes, they asked that several times."

"Your answer?"

"I said that I hadn't seen him since Sierra Leone."

"I'm now asking you the same question. Had you ever seen or met with Derek Lennox after your return from Sierra Leone?"

"My instructions are that I had not seen him since my return."

"Did the Police ask you if you had met Lennox in a Betting Shop in Leicester the day before El-Hoorie was murdered?"

"They did. I denied meeting him in a Betting Shop in Leicester."

"I'm asking you again. Did you meet Derek Lennox in a Betting Shop in Leicester?"

"My instructions are that I didn't meet him."

"Do you bet on horses or dogs?"

"Very rarely. I'm not interested in that kind of stuff."

"Were you aware of any plan to kill El- Hoorie?"

"No."

"Are you aware of any connection between Lennox and El-Hoorie?"

"No."

"Had you been party to any discussion about El-Hoorie prior to his death?"

"None."

"This document," Cadogan explained as he produced a photocopied sheet of paper, "is a copy of a betting slip. The original will now be covered in a purple chemical called Ninhydrine. This is just a copy."

"Yes. The Police showed me the original in interview. In a transparent bag. With purple marks all over it like you say."

"Printed on the top of it are the details of a Betting Shop in Narborough Road, Leicester."

"So I understand."

"It also bears handwriting setting out a bet in the 2.30 at Doncaster on the day before El-Hoorie was murdered in his flat in London."

"I see."

"Have you ever placed a bet on a horse called 'Mad and Bad'?"

"Never."

"This slip was recovered from a deposit box in a Preston Bank which had been rented by Derek Lennox."

"Nothing to do with me."

"Really? When I pointed out that the original was covered in a purple chemical, I didn't explain that the chemical was applied by forensic scientists to look for fingerprints. Your fingerprints are all over that slip. The original had been crumpled at some stage but the experts had no difficulty in identifying prints that matched yours."

"Perhaps Lennox got me to touch a blank betting slip some time before. I wasn't in any Leicester Bookie's with him."

"When do you suggest he might have got you to touch a betting slip? In Sierra Leone? – You claim that you hadn't seen him since Sierra Leone."

"I've no idea."

"It's rubbish, isn't it."

"Perhaps I've bumped into him since we got back to England."

"And he's got you to handle a Betting Slip?"

"I don't remember."

"Another feature of the slip is that the handwriting that sets out the details of the bet has been sent to a handwriting expert for analysis. It's your writing. No doubt about it. And since I received the fingerprint and handwriting results I've had our own experts double-check the findings."

"And?"

"Your prints. Your writing. Your problem. Now, what are your instructions in the light of this information?"

There was a long silence. Cadogan watched the composure of the ruthless hatchet man beginning to disintegrate. Sweat had broken out across his brow as he nervously ran his finger around the inside of his expensive shirt collar. How Cadogan relished these moments when his words could make tough men squirm in their seats as he put them under pressure. It was just like the sensation of pinning the man face down on the mat, pressing the hold against the joint harder and harder until they were forced to beg him to release. The begging was always the time to press the hold still harder. It was satisfying enough in conference but even more gratifying when it happened on public display in the Courtroom when he could actually break lives on his wheel.

"You're in trouble, Mr Barford, aren't you? That betting slip will kill you."

"I'll have to think it through quietly on my own," observed Barford in a subdued tone.

"Of course. I know that you'll think of something. That's why I'm confronting you with the realities. It's only when you face them that you'll start giving me instructions that I can do something with. We haven't reached that stage yet, have we?"

"It would seem not."

"Well, here's another piece of evidence for you to think about. In Lennox's little box there were also two ten pound notes."

"The Police never mentioned those."

"No. When they interviewed you they didn't have the results of the fingerprint examinations. But in his deathbed statement Lennox alleged that these were the top and bottom notes of a wad of ten pound notes amounting to £5000 which you had handed to him in the Leicester Bookie's."

"He had no money from me."

"He says it was £5000. He spent it all but thought that the top and bottom tenners may be a good investment to keep in the box. These notes were used, so there were a number of prints on them, some were completely undecipherable or smudged, but some were clear and of considerable interest."

"And?"

"The bottom note had two very clear prints. One was Lennox's right middle finger. The other was equally clear but not attributable to anyone that has so far been identified. Belonged to someone as yet unknown. A third print had too few ridge characteristics to call a definite match."

"What does that mean?"

"Our fingerprints are made up of whorls and patterns. These are called ridge characteristics. No two prints are the same. Fingerprint experts will tell you that even four or five matching ridge characteristics are certain proof of identity. Nevertheless, Judges will not go that low. Eight, maybe seven, is probably the minimum to get the print in evidence. I've never known a Judge go lower than seven."

"Go on. What was the result on this third print?"

"Seven ridge characteristics were clear enough to identify. Each of the seven was a match for your right little finger. Whether the Judge will admit that evidence we'll have to see. Seven is a close call."

"Bad news then?"

"Not as bad as the top note. Again, some very clear prints. One of them matched the unknown print on the bottom note. Identity unknown but undoubtedly the same person who had handled the top note. Twenty ridge characteristics, so admissible and certain proof of identity but, so far, we don't know who it is."

"And the others?"

"One was conclusively Lennox's right ring finger. And the other was your right thumb print. Clear as a bell. Seventeen matching characteristics. You handled that tenner as sure as you're sitting in this room right now. So it's explanation time I believe."

"If I may interrupt, I think that Mr. Barford might appreciate a short break, Mr Cadogan, if that's all right with you. Perhaps he and I might have a short chat on our own," declared Byron Bloom as he watched Barford being forensically dissected.

"Of course, Mr Bloom. Good idea. I'll have some coffee sent in and leave you two alone for a while. Give our client a little break from the deadly purple chemical. No doubt you can use the time to give him the benefit of your experience," Cadogan responded, rising to his feet and moving his massive frame towards the door. "I'll be back to take further instructions in fifteen minutes. My absence may give you both the opportunity for some creative thinking."

Outside in the corridor the giant ordered Arthur to send in some coffee and then went and sat in another room, smiling to himself as he imagined the fevered discussions now going on in his room. Byron Bloom was no fool and Barford would soon be bending his tale in one way or another to meet the evidence that Cadogan had confronted them with. He only needed some half-decent instructions to swing a victory out of this blatant Government hush-up, because it was obvious that efforts were being made in very high places to scupper the case against Barford. There could be no more powerful proof of this than the fact they had instructed that insufferable old duffer Curbishley to prosecute. No doubt they had chosen him in the first place in the hope that they could wring advice out of him that rendered the Prosecution stillborn, but that deadly journalist had published his article with immaculate timing. More power to his elbow, for without him Cadogan would be a quarter of a million worse off. So it had to go to Court but, in the crucible of the Old Bailey, Curbishley would never be able to cope with Cadogan in full flight, so long as he could achieve some instructions from Barford that weren't quite as pathetic as his performance so far. Letting the fifteen minutes stretch nearer thirty, he eventually returned to his room to find the two men standing at his window, looking out over the Thames in silence.

"Very well, gentlemen," announced Cadogan as they all resumed their seats. "Time for the second half. Do we have a new game plan?"

"Mr Barford has a question," responded Bloom.

"More of a hypothetical question," Barford added hurriedly. "Suppose someone had hired a heavy to have a person threatened and just slapped around a little bit," Barford began hesitantly.

"Yes," replied Cadogan, "and then the heavy had gone too far and killed. Is that the hypothesis?"

"Exactly. I can see that the heavy would be guilty of murder but what about the hirer?"

"If the hirer genuinely believed that the heavy would do no more than cause minor injury at worst, then the hirer would not be guilty of conspiracy to murder."

"I see. Hypothetically speaking, could you work with instructions along those lines in this case?"

"There are problems. Firstly, the mainstay of this case is the deathbed confession of Lennox. I cannot cross-examine a ghost. There will be no Lennox for me to challenge. Just Prosecuting Counsel reading out his statement. Or actually playing the tape recording of his confession. So I can't put to Lennox that his instructions were merely to frighten and rough the fellow up a little bit and he went over the top."

"So where would that leave the hirer?"

"There would be no evidence that the hirer's instructions were limited to minor assault, unless and until the hirer went into the witness box and gave that evidence."

"I would have to say that?"

"Are you telling me that you were the hirer?"

"No. I am not giving you those instructions at present."

"The answer is that the hirer would have to give that evidence to provide any basis for such a defence. However, if your instructions were to be that you were the hirer, then you would still face considerable difficulties in being believed."

"Why?"

"Because £5000 is too much for a bit of roughing up. Because you would have lied to the Police and damaged your credibility. Because you knew Lennox and how violent he was. There are many reasons."

"So what do you suggest, Mr Cadogan?"

"I suggest nothing. I'm not allowed to make up defences for my clients. I explained matters carefully to you at the outset. I act on instructions," Cadogan snapped with false indignation, before pausing a moment and then continuing. "But I would have thought that there is a difference between being the hirer and being the message carrier."

"The message carrier who was in complete ignorance of the content of the message?" Barford enquired.

"Something along those lines."

"But Lennox's statement alleges that I gave him the instructions verbally in the Bookies. He claims that the instructions came from my lips."

"Like I said before, I cannot cross-examine a ghost. But nor can a ghost challenge evidence suggesting that you were an innocent message carrier."

"So I would have to go into the witness box and say that?"

"Perhaps. And be cross-examined on matters where you would still be extremely vulnerable."

"Why did you say perhaps?"

"Because we're talking hypothetically, aren't we?"

"Yes."

"Well, hypothetically, there may be someone else who could go into the witness box and suggest that you were an innocent message carrier."

"Who? There is no one who would do that."

"You know the personnel involved in this episode. I can only use my imagination. The question is not whether there is anyone who would do that willingly. The question is whether there is anyone who could do it. Not would do it. Willingly or unwillingly. Even if it was only to give me the chance to put it to them that you were the innocent message carrier."

"I will need time to consider that."

"Of course you will. As you said, we have simply considered a hypothesis. That's as far as we're likely to get today. You'll need more time to reflect. We'll arrange another conference for next Wednesday. But before you go I do have some encouraging news for you."

"Yes?"

"Prosecuting Counsel is Douglas Curbishley QC. It is my opinion that such a choice by the Prosecuting Authorities is indicative of a lack of enthusiasm for this case?"

"Not up to it you mean?"

"I didn't say that."

"Of course you didn't."

"But Curbishley has been known to take his eye off the ball, I will say that."

"Take his eye off the ball or have it taken off? I would think you're quite good at that."

"I have my moments, yes."

"I do have one final question of you, Mr Cadogan, before we finish."

"Yes?"

"Those other fingerprints on the money. The clear ones. On the top and bottom notes which were not attributable to any known person. Can you get me a copy of those prints?"

"Yes. Our fingerprint expert can be instructed to examine the originals, get a photograph of the prints and compare them to any we obtain or any on file. Why?"

"Just a thought. Instruct the expert to get a photograph of the prints and then, next time we meet, I might have something for him to compare it with. Just a thought. Very constructive meeting, Mr. Cadogan."

"Constructive and creative I suspect. Before we meet next week, Mr Bloom, it will be necessary for you to instruct Junior Counsel to assist me. I always need a runner."

"As you know, Leading Counsel is now allowed to appear without a Junior," replied Bloom anxiously. "Your fee was fixed at such a level that we had hoped the extra expense of instructing Junior Counsel could be avoided on this occasion. Particularly as your reputation is that you always do all of the work yourself."

"No. I must insist on a Junior. Image and convenience, you know. Speak to Arthur on your way out. He'll find you someone suitable but make sure it's not a female. They're invading the Bar like flies. Dithering about in the Robing Rooms. All dressed in black trousers trying to behave like men. Frightened to make decisions in Court."

"Very politically correct if I may say so," Barford interjected sarcastically.

"I don't do political correctness. I don't do niceties. I don't do the gentleman. That's why I have clients queuing up for my services."

"What do you do then?" asked Barford.

"I do success. I do winning. And I do the 'grind them into the dust' kind of winning. Far more satisfying than political correctness, I find.

Don't forget to see Arthur on your way out. One Junior. Male, heterosexual and ready to carry my bags and my messages. This case looks like it's going to be all about carrying messages, don't you think? Good day to you both."

Chapter 13

Over a month had passed since their fateful meeting with the old Hungarian musician and, for every one of those days, Jack Farnham felt as if a suffocating blackness had been lifted, leaving him bathed in sunshine and hope. Faithfully honouring Naomi's stricture in the London Hotel restaurant that there should be no post-mortems, neither of them had breathed one word about the traumatic circumstances of their parting but, apart from Fridays and Saturdays when Jack left Leeds for London to do the television programme, they had seen each other every day. On several nights Jack had stayed at her home on the edge of Roundhay Park and had given the house, which had been like a mausoleum since his departure, an atmosphere of vitality and fun. Resolutely avoiding any talk of love, they had become lovers again.

At ten o' clock exactly she switched to the cable channel to watch his programme go out live. Dressed in the light green Amani cashmere jacket that she had bought for him last week, he looked more handsome than ever. Whether it was the skill of the make-up staff or whether it was the effect of the resumption of their relationship, those thin lines of despair at the corners of his mouth had faded and, as his voice filled her living room, she longed for his return tomorrow, knowing that nothing could ever take him away from her again.

As the programme moved on to an analysis of the game between Arsenal and Liverpool, Naomi's mind wandered away from football to her own career. When fortune had led her to that London Hotel and the chance meeting with Jack, she had not told him the whole purpose of her visit to London that day.

Whilst it was absolutely true that she had been engaged in a case in the Court of Appeal, she had also had a lunch meeting with the Head of Lancaster Chambers, to ask whether they would offer her a door tenancy in those chambers, in the event of her application to take silk proving successful. In years gone by, if a practitioner from the provinces took silk and became a QC, then they had to move to London chambers. Nowadays, it was permissible to retain one's provincial base and not establish any London connection at all, but the risk was that you might miss out on some of the really big London cases. Naomi's attitude to London had been severely damaged during her pupillage days by a disastrous sexual assault and she had no appetite to return there permanently. However, a door tenancy in London, whereby she would continue to live in Leeds and practise from her Leeds chambers, but at the same time have a professional base in London through which any London work could be clerked, was the perfect compromise. Moreover, with Jack down in London two nights a week, they might even consider buying a small flat.

All of this she had decided to keep secret from Jack while they gradually re-established the terms of their relationship. The physical side, inevitably, had an intensity to it that reflected a year's separation and, emotionally, they were both having to make major adjustments. In her mind therefore, it was essential not to submerge him under the weight of important decisions about their future. Letting things take their natural course was the sensible approach and, just as importantly, it was most unlikely that she would get silk first time round. Very few barristers became QCs at the first time of asking. The awarding of silk occurred only after the most meticulous assessment of the application. Only the very best barristers applied and the failure rate was high. Being a woman didn't increase her chances any and being from the Provinces reduced them still further. Still only in her mid-thirties, the chances of success became even more remote but she had, nonetheless, put in her application, deriving some satisfaction from the Head of Lancaster Chambers' promise that, in the event of her application succeeding, he would definitely offer her a door tenancy, although he gently pointed out that they had never had anyone get silk who was under forty, so not to build her hopes up too much.

These were good, albeit not outstanding, London Common Law chambers, enjoying close connections with the Northern Circuit to which Naomi belonged, and three previous Leeds barristers who had taken silk had moved to London and practised from those chambers. Two of those had subsequently gone on to the Circuit Bench and one was still in practice. There were three other silks in the chambers including the Head, so there was sufficient number to bring in a fair quantity of Leading work, although one of the silks had proved to be an exception to the rule of excellence and added nothing to the work supply. With twenty-three Junior Counsel in the set, Naomi would be very happy to establish a London base there and, in the early days of silk, when she would be dependent upon the returned briefs of other silks who were double booked, the Head had assured her that some of this work would trickle through to her.

An hour later, just as she was about to go to bed, the phone rang and she knew it would be Jack.

"Did you watch?" he asked.

"Of course. I'm missing you, Jack."

"Likewise."

"Two nights a week without you isn't easy."

"You could come down to London with me."

"Perhaps next week I will."

"This show looks like running right through the year. We'll have to come up with a plan."

"I may have one," she found herself saying, suddenly deciding that this was a good opportunity to break the news.

"What?"

"I've applied for silk, Jack. Probably won't get it. But if I do, I should get some London work. We'd hardly be apart at all."

"You mean you'd move to London?" he asked.

"No, no. We'd stay in Leeds but I'd have my name up in a London set. Get the odd case down there. Come down on Fridays with you and do some work in those chambers when I wasn't in Court."

"Why didn't you tell me before?"

"One step at a time. One step at a time. The chances of me getting it first time are poor, so don't get too excited."

"When will you know?"

"Very soon now. If you've made it they send you a big fat envelope full of information on what you then have to do. If you've failed you receive a small, thin brown envelope with a slip of paper inside saying you've missed out. So you know the result the moment the envelope drops through the door."

"Good job you've got such a big letter box at home then, isn't it? You're the best Junior at the Leeds Bar. You deserve it. My money's on you. Got to go now. Back in the morning. Good night, Naomi Nicholas QC.

Hey, that's got a ring to it, hasn't it?"

Chapter 14

Each day as the trial approached Douglas Curbishley QC had made his way into chambers and worked assiduously on the only brief he had. It had taken a while to dismiss from his mind the extremely unpleasant telephone call he had received from that aggressive journalist but, after succumbing to the man's threats, he had started to relish the attention that he was suddenly receiving from other members of chambers and from many of the barristers around the Temple. Once the word was out that he had landed such a high profile prosecution, he easily misinterpreted the looks of incredulity that the DPP had chosen him, for looks of admiration and respect.

Lancaster Chambers was down a narrow alley at the Eastern end of The Temple and one had to travel the length of Chancery Lane and across High Holborn to reach Grays' Inn, which was Curbishley's Inn of Court. Taxis were usually impossible to find during the busy lunchtime period and so, despite the effort involved, he had developed the daily habit of walking up Chancery Lane to take lunch in the magnificent Dining Hall at Gray's, dominated by the timbers taken from *The Golden Hind* once captained by Sir Francis Drake. The effort proved to be more than worthwhile as he would be seen by many of his contemporaries who had dismissed his elevation to silk as a product of nepotism and the Old Boys' Network. Several times he caught them whispering behind his back and casting what he took to be envious looks in his direction. Three or four of the more ambitious Juniors had jockeyed for a position near him so as to win a tilt at the Junior brief and last week one of the High Court Judges had been in for lunch and had actually wandered over and chatted to him about his trip to Venezuela.

Meals at Gray's Inn were taken on long narrow tables that ran almost the full length of the Hall and today at lunch a most engaging fellow had taken the seat opposite. Cambridge man, appearances in the Footlights Revues, a cricket blue and possessing a fund of stories about the Judges, all delivered in brilliant mimicry of their voices, causing great hilarity in their little dining group. No mean lawyer either as apparently he'd written several articles for the Criminal Law Review. When Curbishley had regaled him with details of the very important case he was soon to prosecute at the Bailey this fellow, Mike Myott, had seemed to have heard nothing about it, but had simply pressed on with his latest snippet of judicial gossip. It was only in passing, as they happened to walk out of the Dining Hall together, that Mynott had mentioned his latest treatise for the Criminal Review which was currently receiving its final touches. An analysis of the current law on the evidence of dead witnesses.

Curbishley's ears had immediately pricked up but, in a trice, Myott had changed the subject and was doing a faultless impersonation of the Lord Chief Justice, before suddenly darting off with a cheery farewell as he dodged the heavy High Holborn traffic and disappeared from view.

What an excellent fellow. And what a difference one good case could make, Curbishley thought to himself as the self-confidence returned and there was a spring in his step as he strode purposefully back to chambers, the furled umbrella now shouldered like a General's baton. Climbing the twisting wooden staircase up to the second floor in chambers he experienced one of those system shut-downs again which were becoming most irritating, but it passed in a second.

Of course, there were some problems with the case but he refused to let them get him down. Since he had advised the authorities to prosecute, after the call from that journalist, it had proved the devils' own job to get any co-operation from them at all. His phone calls were seldom returned and, apart from the delivery of the brief itself, he had received precious little response to the requests for further evidence that he had made. While he had never expected to see the Commander again, after going against his wishes, it was Giles Brockley's duty to keep him informed of any developments and arrange further conferences, but the lack of enthusiasm from that quarter was obvious. It was absolutely essential that he had a Junior to assist at the trial, preferably one who knew what he was about, as there seemed to be several rather tricky points of Law lurking about in the case papers which Curbishley didn't too much fancy without a guiding hand, but any phone calls by Peter, his clerk, to that

Brockley fellow to suggest a Junior, had hitherto met the same fate as his own calls. It would be a great bonus to have a Junior who was a dab hand on declarations from the deathbed like that Myott fellow, he reflected. Picking up the phone he dialled Brockley's direct line and, to his amazement, the call was answered on the first ring.

"Giles Brockley."

"Good afternoon, Brockley, Curbishley here. Been after you several times but always missed you."

"Oh, yes, Mr Curbishley. I've been out of the office a lot, I'm afraid. We're understaffed. You know the score."

"I'd like a conference. Not long to go before the trial. I've been asking for additional evidence to be prepared and served. Number of things to discuss."

"I'll fix a date with your clerk. One day early next week."

"Right. Much better, much better. One matter cannot wait, though. A Junior. Must have a Junior. This is a big case, lot of work, lot of research into the Law. I have written and phoned about this."

"Of course. I do have authority to instruct a Junior now. The powers that be have given me a couple of names. I'll get right on to it. Instruct him in time for our next conference."

"Matter of fact I have a name for you. I don't know if he's available but I'd like you to try. Mike Myott. Don't know if you've come across him. Tall chap. Skinny. Early thirties, untidy dark hair, rimless glasses, long face. No idea which chambers he's in. Bright, bit of an academic, bit of a card."

"I've never heard of him. Have you worked with him before?"

"No, but I think he'd be a useful chap to have in the team. See if you can get him."

"I'd have to get him approved by the powers behind me, if you understand. If they approve, I'll track down which chambers he's in and see if we can instruct him."

"Excellent. I'll transfer you to Peter then to fix the con. So glad we spoke. Myott. Mike Myott. Good afternoon."

Chapter 15

On the day the QC appointments were to be announced Jack Farnham, by a combination of willpower and sacrificed sleep, managed to wake himself up at five o'clock in the morning and slip out of bed without an alarm and without disturbing Naomi. A shaft of light was already filtering through the pale blue curtains so that he could see her thick, golden hair lying across the pillow, the perfectly carved contours of her cheekbones and the full, pink lips outlined against the whiteness of the sheets. Her body lay in an abandoned position with her right arm stretched across to his side of the bed where she had held him so tightly during the night, never wanting to let him go. So vulnerable, so soft but, when the chips were down, as tough as teak. Silently pulling on the tracksuit and running shoes that he had deliberately placed on the floor by the bed last night, Jack noiselessly slipped out of the bedroom, downstairs and out of the house.

Even while they had been apart, Jack and Naomi had independently enforced their own strict athletic regimes and both were as fit and strong as before, so that a two mile run across the park and down to the newsagents only took Jack a touch over ten minutes. This morning the adrenalin was pumping hard and he raced like the wind, for he was on a mission. Normally, the envelope would have arrived before any Press announcement but Naomi had heard nothing. Apparently, there had been three other applicants for silk in Leeds that year and each of them had received their envelopes yesterday. Thin little brown envelopes carrying the poisonous words of rejection.

Today the names were due to be published in *The Times*, not set out alphabetically but in order of seniority, together with their Inn of Court. Nodding a nervous greeting to the young Asian girl working the unwelcome shift, Jack thrust the coins into her hand and left the shop with his copy of *The Times* tucked under his arm. Standing near the illuminated shop window he unfolded the paper, his heart pounding as if his very life depended on it. Under the contents index on the front page he saw the entry that the names of the new QCs appeared on page 33. As he fumbled awkwardly with the broadsheet in the early light of a Leeds morning, his strong hands actually trembling with tension, Jack Farnham's gentle eyes brimmed with tears as he experienced a surge of pride that made his heart feel as if it might burst with joy. Her name was the very last name. She was the youngest. And one of only four women. The girl from the pit village who'd had a dream was on her way to a ceremony in the House of Lords.

How Jack ran. He flew across the park. He scored the winning goal at Wembley every hundred yards. He leaped in the air. He was eighteen again. Throwing the front door wide open he began bounding up the stairs, shouting her name, the now-mangled paper hanging from his hand.

She appeared at the bedroom door in her nightgown, her beautiful hair tousled and unbrushed, her exquisite face still half-bathed in sleep and her blue eyes bemused and wondering.

"You've got it," he shouted, gasping for breath. "You've got it, you've got it. I went for a paper. Here. Look for yourself. Page 33," he exclaimed.

Whether it was because she was still not fully awake or whether it was because in that moment, seeing his unbridled joy for her, she came to realise just how much she loved him, Naomi remained composed and quiet.

"So I'm to receive the fat envelope," she finally remarked after studying the full list of names. "No one else from Leeds and only four women. Amazing."

"How can you stay so calm?" Jack laughed, slowly regaining his breath.

"Because in my mind it meant so much and was so important," she began, "and then I looked at your face and realised that, without you, it had no worth at all."

Taking her in his arms at the bedroom door he held her tightly. Again he heard the haunting melody of the Hungarian musician and his eyes were moist. They had found each other and, for that moment, everything in the world was right.

Chapter 16

So severe were the blockages in the carotid arteries that several of the associated vessels ruptured simultaneously and the supply of blood to the brain was immediately halted. Perhaps if the recurring transient ischaemic attacks had been diagnosed earlier, then the massive stroke might have been avoided. There had been a second of numbness when the left side of the face seemed to lose all sensation, the left leg suddenly dragging uselessly on the ground and then he fell, crashing on to the Fleet Street pavement in a heap, his long body stretched across the flagstones and his umbrella in the gutter, its handle still clutched between the elegant fingers with their manicured nails.

The conference had been a success and they had even agreed to instruct Myott, having secretly satisfied themselves beforehand that he didn't appear to have much of a practice, was seldom in Court and seemingly had but an academic interest in the Law. They had eventually furnished Curbishley with the extra information he had been demanding for so long and that morning, in his chambers, they had selected those parts that they intended to serve as additional evidence before the trial. Myott had sat quietly throughout the various exchanges and accepted with enthusiasm his delegated task of ensuring that they were fully prepared to meet any argument from the Defence that Lennox's statement was inadmissible in Law.

Flushed with his sense of self-importance and buoyed by the prospect of having a Junior who could be saddled with some of the more intellectually challenging aspects of the case, Curbishley had called the conference to an end, donned his Crombie overcoat and set off for the bank. Surprisingly, on his arrival at chambers that morning, he had discovered to his delight, that his ten thousand pound cheque for the Advice had arrived. Normally not due until the case was over, he had nagged Peter incessantly to press them to pay it up front, so as to ease the old cash flow problem, and now it was folded neatly in his pigskin wallet, soon to inflate the current account to a level it had not seen for years.

Turning left out of the Temple he had been within a hundred yards of the doors of the bank when the vessels in the neck ruptured, the brain became starved and the heart gave in. 'DOA' said the Ambulance Report. Dead on arrival. "Dead before he even hit the ground, more like", observed the Hospital pathologist as he authorised that the body could be released for burial as soon as the Coroner had signed on the dotted line.

Chapter 17

A long line of black Daimler limousines filed slowly though the imposing gates of the Courtyard in front of the House of Lords and disgorged each of the new silks, formally dressed in full-bottomed wigs, frilled jabots, frock court coats, lace ruffs, silk breeches, black tights and patent leather silver-buckled shoes. Proud relatives filled the public gallery whilst the chosen took their seats centre stage in the massive hall, surrounded by magnificent paintings of historical battles awaiting the Lord Chancellor's call to recite the oath to the Sovereign. Jack Farnham, sitting in the front row of the public section, had eyes only for the last in line and later, when they sat at a small corner table at San Lorenzo's having lunch, he opened the red leather case containing the Letters Patent and read them to himself over and over again.

Custom required that the new appointments spent the afternoon shuffling round the Royal Courts of Justice, queuing to get into the main Courtrooms where they engaged in a series of bowing charades. Naomi had opted to give this pantomime a miss and so it was, within two hours of swearing her allegiance to the Queen in the House of Lords, that she landed her first case as a QC. And what a case it threatened to be. Her mobile phone had rung whilst she was sipping her third cup of San Lorenzo's Irish coffee.

"Miss Nicholas?" said the Cockney voice.

"Yes."

"It's Peter. Your clerk from your new London chambers."

"Oh, yes, Peter. Sorry, I'll have to get used to having two sets of chambers now, won't I?" she laughed.

"I need to know if I can put your name forward, Miss. For a Prosecution. Very important case indeed."

"What is it?"

"Conspiracy to murder. Victim was some geezer who overheard a terrorist plot. Government took him out. That's what's alleged any rate."

"It's been all over the news. It's a major case. Why are they likely to show any interest in briefing me? I haven't been in silk two minutes."

"Not as simple as that, Miss. We had the Prosecution brief in these chambers. Bit of a coup for us, as you'll understand. Normally it would go to Treasury Counsel at the Bailey. But, some kind of shenannigans going on I reckon and I had to drag our Mr. Curbishley back from Venezuela. They insisted on him."

"Well why are you phoning me then, Peter?"

"'Cos Mr. Curbishley won't be doing the case, Miss. Won't be doing any case. He's dead. Dropped dead in the street yesterday."

"That's awful."

"It's awful all right, but life goes on. We want to keep the case in chambers. Do us a power of good if we can. But seeing as the trial starts in less than two weeks, all of our other silks are tied up. Every one of 'em has a fixture that they can't possibly get out off. You're the only silk I can offer."

"They'll never accept me. A brand new silk. In a case of national importance. I'm afraid you'll be wasting your time even putting my name forward."

"You're probably right, Miss. But you're the only silk I can offer and I don't want to let the brief go without a fight. Besides, it may not be impossible."

"Why do you say that?"

"Because choosing Mr. Curbishley in the first place was a very odd choice. Not meaning to speak ill of him, you understand. But he wasn't exactly a high flier. In fact, truth be told, he hadn't had a brief in his own name for as long as I can remember. Like I said, perhaps some kind of shenanigans. Anyway, all I need to know is if I can suggest your name, then see what they say."

"All right, Peter. I'm on. I doubt they'll have me, but see what you can do. What's the name of the case?"

"Barford, Miss. I'll enjoy having you in our chambers. I can tell you're game before we've even met. There's a Junior, so, if you do get it, he can fill you in and save you some time. Name of Myott. Not from these chambers."

"Never heard of him I'm afraid. Keep me posted. Goodbye."

Whilst Jack and Naomi lingered over the Irish coffees before moving on to port, the telephone traffic in the Legal Mile reached fever pitch. As soon as Peter had ended the call to Naomi he had contacted Giles Brockley and offered her name as a substitute for the late Curbishley.

Brockley had made five calls before, eventually, he had located the Commander who, as was to be expected, quickly became rude and aggressive but nevertheless promised to give Brockley a decision within the hour. The Commander had located Templar within five minutes and they had immediately resolved the issue. The person now best qualified to decide whether or not to offer Naomi Nicholas the Prosecution brief was Ronan Cadogan QC. Not only could the powers that be ensure that there was complete inequality of arms working in Barford's favour, but they could also give Defending Counsel the veto on who he had for an opponent.

The Commander telephoned Barford with the instruction to by-pass Bloom and get Cadogan's opinion directly as a matter of urgency. Barford's call to Cadogan's chambers came just as the QC walked through the door, after taking a few days off to go shooting.

"Mr Cadogan, this is Lewis Barford. I was told to speak to you directly, rather than through Mr Bloom."

"Why?"

"Curbishley is dead."

"What a loss to mankind."

"In one sense it is."

"To your chances, you mean?"

"From what you said about him."

"Have they got a substitute? A Junior can't do a case of this magnitude."

"No. They're shopping around now for a suitable QC."

"We'll know soon enough when they find one. They can't go lower than Curbishley – he was as useless as they get. Should never have got silk."

"They're hawking a name around. I've been asked to get your view."

"What's the point of asking my view. We'll get who they choose," snapped Cadogan impatiently.

"Nicholas. Naomi Nicholas QC," Barford persisted.

"The woman from Leeds?"

"That's the one."

"But she's only just taken silk. This time around. It would be her first case in silk."

"That's the name. Do you know her?"

"Oh, yes. I know her. I led her a while back in a murder in Leeds. Shrewd. Pretty. Tough. And she hates my guts. I can't see them letting a first-time silk loose on this."

"But what would you say if they chose her."

"I'd say Curbishley was a gift, but he's gone. Nearly all the other QCs are on the ball. So I'd say let's take the new one. First case in silk. Female. I know how she thinks and I know her weaknesses. I'd reckon to have her for breakfast. Regrettably though, it's not my choice and it's certainly not yours."

"Thank you, Mr Cadogan," replied Barford, thereafter immediately telephoning the Commander with the news. From the Commander to Brockley to Peter at Lancaster Chambers to the San Lorenzo Restaurant took ninety seconds. The die was cast. The puppets had taken their places upon the stage. The time to start pulling the strings was near.

Chapter 18

Nowadays the cleaners had vacuum cleaners to sweep away the daily grime and dust but on the same site, long ago, men had been incarcerated in filth and squalor before being marched to the gallows to confront the baying crowds, the Public Executioner and their Maker. Built on the foundations of the former dreaded Newgate Prison, the Central Criminal Court had staged some of the most gruesome and fascinating trials of the twentieth century. Commonly referred to as the Old Bailey, a name taken from the street where the new building had been erected in 1907, many of Britain's most wanted men had found themselves walking up the forbidding stone steps to face their accusers and the wrath of the sentencing Judge. Dr Crippen, Lord Haw-Haw, the Krays and the Yorkshire Ripper. All had pleaded not guilty. All were convicted. Crippen and Haw-Haw to drop at the end of a rope, the Krays and the Ripper to pass their days as useless, ageing social parasites, knowing that only death would buy their release.

Whilst many of the Courtrooms were now housed in an adjacent more modern building, some major trials still took place in the more daunting original edifice, and it was in one of those old Courtrooms that Janet Kelly was busying herself with her customary cleaning duties. Emptying the barristers' water decanters, cleaning the drinking glasses, tipping the contents of the waste bins into her black bin liner bag and vacuuming the worn carpets. She loved cleaning this Courtroom when the actors had left the stage and she could be alone. The courts normally rose at four-fifteen and her shift started half an hour later, but she always arrived early and listened to the last few minutes of the day's proceedings in awe of the pomp, the colour, the ceremony, and the formality of the language of the lawyers and the Judge. Then, when they had all shuffled away, in between her vacuuming and dusting she would act her part. Sometimes she would be the Judge and, sitting in the enormous throne-like chair, she would sentence the wicked murderer to imprisonment for life, shouting out the words "Take him down" so that they echoed eerily around the walls before bouncing back to her, high up on the dais where she looked down on the empty stage. On other occasions she would be the condemned man, standing in the dock, holding the cold, iron bars and looking across the Courtroom at the fearsome figure of the Judge who would exercise his power of life and death.

The jury's retiring room was just off to the side of this Court, with one door leading directly into the Courtroom and another into a corridor which formed part of the labyrinth of passages and stairways deep within the old building. Janet imagined herself in the Foreman's seat at the jury's large boardroom table, with its twelve seats pushed carelessly back, frozen in time at the point at which they had reached their verdict of guilty, just before returning to Court. Collecting up the jury's discarded notes, sweet papers and doodlings from where they lay on the table and on the floor she returned into the Courtroom to throw them all into her black bin bag.

However, on her return into court with her handfuls of discarded papers, Janet realised that she was not alone. Standing in the front row of Counsel's Benches staring at the witness box, was a tall, elegant woman, dressed in a smart black suit which contrasted starkly with the blondeness of her swept back hair and clear, fair complexion. Startled by the cleaner's entrance from the side door, the woman turned abruptly and looked in Janet's direction, enabling Janet to see the full beauty of her face.

"Court's closed, love. Finishes at quarter past four. You shouldn't have been able to get in," she began.

"I asked the Security Man. He said it was OK for me to take a look in here for a couple of minutes," the woman answered politely. "I hope I'm not in your way. I'm a barrister and I start a case here next week and I've never been in this Courtroom before. I needed to see it, if you understand."

"You're a barrister, are you? I'd have loved a go at doing that," Janet replied. "But where I come from, you end up a cleaner or a waitress, I'm afraid."

"Am I in your way if I just stand here for a minute? Take in the atmosphere. Get my bearings," the woman enquired.

"No, luv. If Security said OK, that's fine by me. I'll get on with my cleaning. You get the feel of the place," Janet responded as she busied herself filling the black bag and wiping down the benches and desks with her yellow duster.

Naomi Nicholas knew that she needed to have a clear picture of this Courtroom in her mind before the case began. The only time she had been in the Old Bailey before was in the new modern annexe, which was clinical and sterile. Nothing could compare with the atmosphere of this formidable setting. Its grandeur and power were physical. You could touch them. The smell of the air came from another time, the colour of the wood panelling, the cruelty of the dock, the isolation of the witness box and the twelve empty seats to her right where the jurors would take their places at ten-thirty on the morning of the trial. Even now, standing alone in an empty theatre, her nerves were tingling, until her thoughts were interrupted by the cleaner's voice.

"I'm done in here now, Miss. I'll have to ask you to leave."

"Sorry. I didn't mean to stay this long. It's timeless. Like it has power of its own. I'll leave immediately. I hope I didn't keep you."

"No, not at all. I know just what you mean, Miss. I stand here sometimes, just like you. I can feel it too. I imagine all sorts of things."

"Like what?"

"Sometimes I imagine I'm the Judge. I don't mind telling you I've even sat in his chair. Sent 'em down," she laughed nervously, watching to see how the woman reacted to her indiscreet confession.

"What fun," Naomi laughed. Who else have you been?"

"Oh, I've been the Defendant and the witness. But my favourite is to be the barrister. Like you are in real life. It must be wonderful. Better than cleaning, anyway."

"What's your name?" asked Naomi.

"Janet."

"I'm Naomi. You said that where you came from you were bound to end up being a cleaner or a waitress."

"'fraid so."

"Well, that doesn't have to be right. I come from the same place as you. Not the same town, obviously. But the same place if you understand me."

"I understand you."

"My father was a miner. He hated me for wanting to do this job. When I finally got there he never forgave me."

"How did you make it then?" Janet asked, looking directly into the blue eyes of this intriguing woman, who was deliberately reminding her that they stood as equals.

"It's a long story. But you shouldn't think that you can't make the break. You're still very young. One day, somewhere along the line, you'll see a chance to do something else."

"I always wanted to be an actress. My dad laughs at me when I talk about it. Not unkindly, mind you, but he doesn't take me seriously. I tried once. The local Rep offered auditions and I went. Didn't get anywhere though," Janet confided, her mind wandering away from her yellow duster as she remembered the thrill of stepping out and reciting her lines.

"When I was at school I had a mistress," responded Naomi, quickly recognising the spark in the young girl's eyes. "Miss Wickham. She was my inspiration. I remember her words to this day."

"Tell me the words, Miss."

"In most people's lives, there would probably come a time when they might have to take a big chance and, if they missed it, they might regret it for ever," Naomi quoted. "And my chance came. And I took it. If you look hard enough your chance will also come."

"They were wise words."

"I realised later that they were Shakespeare's words. She was just putting Shakespeare into language that I would understand."

"What were the words that Shakespeare had used then?

"I think I can recite the lines, they're from Julius Caesar," Naomi replied.

"There is a tide in the affairs of men,
Which, taken at the flood, leads on to fortune;
Omitted, all the voyage of their life
Is bound in shallows, and in miseries.
On such a full sea are we now afloat;
And we must take the current when it serves,
Or lose our ventures."

The young cleaner had stood entranced as Naomi's strong voice reverberated around the Courtroom and spelled out the reminder that perhaps they both required at that time. With the right spirit, everything was possible. For a few seconds they looked at each other as the sound died away and the silence produced its own effect, bringing them back to the reality of vacuum cleaners for the one and a hard night's study for the other.

"I shall go home and look those lines up. Then I'll learn them. I never had a Miss Wickham but you've given me her words. Thank you, Miss. And good luck in your case. I'll look out for you."

Naomi smiled at the young girl and walked slowly away from Counsel's Bench, across the well of the Court and towards the door back into the foyer. Now, all was still, but soon a fierce battle would rage in this arena. She was under no illusions and had quickly realised that the Establishment wanted this Prosecution dead and buried. As she saw it, all the more reason to pursue victory. But there would be no prospect of any real support from the authorities behind her and, as the final thrust of steel to the heart, she well knew who was to be her opponent. After her father, Ronan Cadogan QC was probably the most loathsome man she had ever had the misfortune to meet, but unlike her father, he was cunning, stunningly clever and a master of strategy. But, far more frightening than any of those qualities, he was the complete warrior. Ironically, but for his bravery, her own career would not have survived. And now fate had decreed that she must meet him in battle. In truth, all the other characters would be reduced to bit-part players. This was single combat. Mortal combat. Against a warrior. That was why she had needed to taste the atmosphere of the arena. And, in so doing, Miss Wickham's words had lived again and been passed on to another generation.

Chapter 19

The latest and youngest recruit to the ranks of QC knew that Cadogan would relentlessly seek every advantage in the case, every edge that might present itself, however seemingly minor. That was how he worked. Physically terrifying, he pursued the psychological dominance, sometimes rendering his opponent helpless, like the rabbit in the dazzle of the headlights, as he had done so cruelly to his opponent in that unforgettable and dreadful case at Leeds which still gave Naomi nightmares. His entrance into Court on that occasion had been one of the most spectacular and dramatic that Naomi had ever witnessed and she had no doubt that, in one way or another, he would seek to unnerve her today. It was an absolute certainty that he would have found out who his opponent was going to be after the death of Curbishley and, once he had learned her name, he would have shaped at least part of his psychological strategy around what he knew about her which, regrettably, was too much for her own good. Such was his mastery of tactics that she knew he would not pull any of the same tricks that he had pulled in the earlier trial. Everything would be new but everything would represent danger to her.

Important though the case was, the time estimate for trial was only a week and so, with Jack's approval, she had booked a suite at their special hotel by the river for the duration of the case and Jack would join her later in the week, as soon as he had done his mid-week commentary on the match at Anfield. Showering before six, breakfasting in her room and dressing in the new brand new black Chanel suit with the tight skirt, she had been in the back of the taxi by eight, looking like a film star. Moreover, she had worn her highest heels, so that at a natural five foot ten she now stood over six feet tall, reducing Cadogan's height advantage as much as she possibly could. By getting to the Court early and donning her new Court coat and silk gown, she could be in place and composed before he even arrived, ready for the opening round which, knowing him as she did, was bound to start with some attempt to unnerve her and derail her case.

As she pushed open the door of the Robing Room she walked straight into the barrel chest of Ronan Cadogan, already dressed in his wig and gown. He must have somehow seen her arrival at the building and then stood just inside the Robing Room door, awaiting her entrance into the room in a position where she would immediately be confronted by his formidable bulk. He had achieved his first objective without uttering a word as, startled and disconcerted, she heard her own involuntary intake of breath at the shock of seeing him filling her vision. Even in her highest heels he towered above her. So psychologically imposing was his effect that he seemed to have become even bigger then she had remembered. It wasn't just the height, but the enormity of his shoulders and chest, with that large head and the sagging, heavy jowls.

As she instinctively stepped backwards, he made no move to stand aside or offer any basic courtesy, openly weighing up if she had changed very much in the year since they had last met, as those small, narrowed eyes condescendingly looked her up and down.

"The lamb to the slaughter," he declared in that Southern Irish lilt.

"Very biblical," she snapped back. "Perhaps you'd step aside from your staged position and let me get into the room."

"I see your charm is at the same base level as it was in that dreadful town where you were my Junior," he replied, slowly moving towards the large oak table where the barristers selfishly threw their bags, papers and books, leaving no room for anyone else's things. Her eye had fallen upon the expensive, top of the range wig tin in pride of place near the edge of the table with 'Ronan Cadogan QC' etched in extravagant gold lettering across its black top.

"You mean Leeds. My home," was her response as she swung her case on to the table, its bottom corner neatly catching the side of the Cadogan wig tin and sending it crashing to the floor, spilling its contents of collar studs, newly laundered spare bands and collars across the grubby floor.

"Oops-a-daisy," she exclaimed without apology, beginning to unzip the case and removing her carefully folded new Court coat and silk gown.

"Crude," Cadogan observed, gathering the now-soiled articles from the floor and putting them back in the tin. "As is to be expected. And you've dented the lid."

"You shouldn't leave it on the edge of the table," Naomi muttered dismissively. "Isn't there anything you want to say to me about the case? You usually try to raise some red herring at the beginning."

"Lennox's statement to Smail. It's inadmissible. Without it you haven't got a case."

"You're right. Without it I haven't got a case. But I'm not without it. I've got it. And it's admissible."

"I propose submitting to the Judge that it is inadmissible. Before the case starts. So you're warned," he stated. "See you in Court at ten thirty."

"As you know, the courtesy is to inform your opponent well ahead of the trial, if there is an important legal point. And to serve a Skeleton Argument on your opponent and the Judge," Naomi replied.

"I did send one to the Court for the Judge. Last week. Must have overlooked sending one to you. Like you said, 'oops-a-daisy'," came the response. "Speak to my Junior when he arrives, he'll give you a copy."

"Who is your Junior?" she asked.

"James Stapleton. Absolutely useless. I always seem to get landed with useless Juniors. Anyway, he'll give you a copy of my Skeleton Argument and the references for the precedents I'm relying on. There's a Law Library somewhere in the building. He's always here by ten twenty-five so you'll have a good five minutes."

"Is it written on electric blue paper?" Naomi enquired, referring to one of the strokes that Cadogan had so blatantly pulled in their Leeds trial. "Or does that come later?"

"You'll have to wait and see, my dear. No doubt all will become clear. You're a QC now. In with the big boys. You've got to be ready for anything. Off for a coffee. Leave you alone. Give you a chance to do your make-up. We're all a year or two older, aren't we?" he declared, making his way through the door and off to the Coffee Shop, laughing his cruel laugh as he disappeared along the corridor.

When she emerged from the Robing Room there was no sign of either her Junior, nor Stapleton, from whom she was anxious to obtain a copy of Cadogan's Skeleton Argument and the precedents he was intending to recite. After depositing all of her papers in Court she positioned herself in the Main Hallway, which gave her a good view of the only public entrance to the building, and waited to see who would arrive first. Surprisingly, it was Brockley, loaded down with a large box of case papers and an assistant who seemed to have been delegated to carry the even heavier files.

"Good morning, Miss Nicholas," Brockley panted breathlessly.

"Hello, Mr Brockley" she replied.

"Hope we're not late. We had a lot to carry. The Office has given me an agent for this trial, a speed typist so you'll get a full typed note. Mel, this is our QC, Miss Nicholas," he said, putting his box on the stone floor and nodding towards the male assistant. He was rather handsome, Naomi thought. Tall, thirtyish, black curly hair, dark brown intense eyes but an easy grin.

"How do you do, Miss," the assistant responded politely, "too overloaded to shake hands, I'm afraid. I'm Mel Coleman."

"Right," she said. "Well, if you two take the papers through to Court, I'll wait here and waylay the Defence Junior. There's some legal argument before we begin and the Defence have failed to send us a copy of their Skeleton Argument."

"Is that an oversight or deliberate?" asked Coleman with interest.

"Deliberate," she replied. "That's what we're up against. You do agency work for the Prosecution then, do you, Mel?" she asked.

"Now and then, Miss. I do more for Defence Solicitors. That pays a bit better as a matter of fact. Sit behind Counsel, keep a full note on my laptop, interview possible Defence witnesses, that kind of stuff," he replied. "Mind you, this is the first one I've done with a QC in it."

"This is Miss Nicholas's first case as a QC," volunteered Brockley.

"Bit daunting then, is it? Good job you got me behind you then," joked Coleman. "Jack of all trades, master of none, that's me."

"I think that's Mr Stapleton, just walked in," Brockley volunteered. "I've seen him around before. Fair hair, glasses, umbrella. Do you see him?"

"Yes. I'll go and grab the Skeleton then. See you two in Court," she responded, walking away to intercept Stapleton, who immediately extracted a copy of Cadogan's written argument from his brief, obviously embarrassed that Cadogan had not sent her a copy beforehand. Whilst he couldn't possibly tell her, he had not the slightest doubt that Byron Bloom, their solicitor, had told him earlier in the week that Cadogan had indicated that one had already been sent to the Prosecution.

Chapter 20

Mr Justice Maullin resplendent in his red robes with ermine collar trim, laid down his white gloves and the small bunch of flowers always carried by Judges at the Old Bailey on the first day of each session as a traditional memorial of the days when flowers were necessary to mask the foul smell floating up from the old Newgate cells and took his seat. Mr Justice Richard Freeman Maullin was one of the old school. Now in his last year before retirement, he had destroyed the career of many a youngster starting out at the Bar, with his intolerance of any error and his insistence on linguistic exactitude. Known within the profession as 'Mauling Maullin' his brain was like quicksilver, his literary knowledge prolific and with a reputation for demanding that barristers did the job properly or not at all.

Despite these fearsome characteristics, he had a wicked sense of humour, littering the Court proceedings with his terse one-liners and, if he took a liking to a barrister, more than capable of turning on the charm. Thus, amongst a small but select few, he enjoyed great popularity whilst, amongst the majority, he remained feared, disliked but respected. Ronan Cadogan QC did not number amongst the small but select few. Naomi believed that the contest in Court was not going to have a weak referee.

For his part, the Judge knew absolutely nothing about this new female silk. Renowned for making quick decisions he would soon form his judgement but, based on looks alone, he had already concluded that she had got off to a very satisfactory start.

"Mr Cadogan has informed me that he wishes to argue a preliminary point of Law. I would respectfully suggest that this should be done before we swear in a jury. Indeed, were he to succeed, the Prosecution would be left without a case at all, so it would appear sensible to argue the point and receive your Lordship's ruling prior to empanelling a jury," Naomi began.

"Going for the knock-out blow as soon as the bell rings, is he?" observed the Judge.

"But not before the bell rings, My Lord," interjected Cadogan, rising imperiously to his feet to confront Maullin and take the initiative away from his opponent, before she could slip in a little clue that he'd held back on sending her a copy of his complex and detailed argument. "I am ready to embark upon my argument. The Law Reports of the precedents upon which I rely have all been photocopied and attached to the Skeleton that I sent to Your Lordship's Court last week. May I begin?"

"Certainly. I take it that Miss Nicholas was furnished with the same material in good time?" Maullin queried, alive to one of the more elementary stunts that Cadogan was likely to have pulled.

"No doubt my opponent will have had ample time to consider my argument, My Lord," Cadogan assured the Judge, well knowing that Naomi Nicholas was too proud and too inherently decent to call 'foul' at the outset of the case. In Cadogan's opinion her innate sense of decency was one of her greatest weaknesses and he intended to take every advantage of it as the trial proceeded.

Twenty minutes later Cadogan concluded his argument that the statement dictated to the solicitor Martin Smail by Derek Lennox from his death bed should be excluded. Lennox, he argued, was a lifelong criminal, with axes to grind and mischief to make. No one could ever know the reasons he may lie. To permit an entire case to be constructed on his word, when the Defence would never have the chance to cross-examine him, was manifestly unfair and unjust.

As Cadogan sat down, Mike Myott began to get to his feet in an obvious state of anxiety. He had explained to the new Leader when they had met in Lancaster Chambers in conference that Curbishley had anticipated this argument and had entrusted his Junior with the task of replying to the argument as he had written an article on it and thoroughly researched it. Naomi had thanked him courteously and asked him to send her an outline of his argument, which he had duly done. Now, nervously, he expected to have to argue the point in Court but, as he rose, she turned and politely but firmly whispered to him. "I think I'll handle this after all," and, in a second, turned back and launched into her reply.

It took her less than ten minutes to dispose of Cadogan's points. The jury must be allowed to hear Lennox's voice.

Mr Justice Maullin had made two decisions with his customary speed. One, the statement was admissible. Two, he liked this girl. To the point. Forthright. "Swear in the Jury," he pronounced, smiling down sweetly in the direction of Naomi Nicholas.

Round One was over. But Naomi knew only too well that when Cadogan was in the ring, this was a fight that would go the distance, unless he knocked her out first. The trouble was that his knock-out blow was as likely to be a knife in the back as a straight right to the jaw.

Barford sat in the dock. Dark grey suit. Staring defiantly ahead. Naomi never looked at him. She had no idea what he looked like. That would come later. The public gallery was full. In the back row sat Janet Kelly. The Press Benches were overflowing. The jury panel filed into Court and twelve names were drawn at random. They each rose, holy book aloft, and swore before their God to reach a true verdict upon the evidence.

Sebastian Viney : Professional artist
Dorothy Lyall : Hairdresser
Diane Finney : Recruitment Consultant
Michael Willetts : Computer Programmer
Alan Grigg : Mechanic
Arthur Field : Retired
Melanie Denley : Receptionist
Gary Thomas : Unemployed
Hilary Shore : School Teacher
Bazra Chauhan : Project Leader
Penny Redmond : Unemployed
Stefan Villars : Unemployed

Prosecuting Counsel got to her feet to open the case for the Crown. The hacks scribbled, seeking the headline for tonight's edition and tomorrow's nationals. She gave it to them.

"Members of the jury, Lewis Barford is a hatchet man. A Mr Fixit for dark forces about which we all know very little. He ordered the death of a man. Like you might order a round of drinks. So inconsequential to him was the life of another, that five thousand pounds was his valuation. He knew a hitman. A ruthless mercenary. He hired him. He paid him. The hitman delivered. And Lewis Barford's motive? The victim was going to the Press. With a story that would not merely embarrass some of those in high places, but may, in its wake, bring down a Minister or worse. And so, Mr Fixit took matters into his own hands. The result? Cold-blooded execution."

As Naomi Nicholas warmed to her task, the early nerves of her first case as a QC rapidly subsiding, and with Mr Justice Maullin nodding in silent approval at the punchy performance, the British Airways 11.55 flight from Heathrow to Geneva soared above the great City of London.

The International Conference in the small Alpine town of Davos was due to last five days and the passenger in Seat 1A had decided to add a few days on top of that for a 'private engagement', as it was referred to in the Department. That would bring him back to the Home Office well after the verdict was in and, hopefully, assuming Barford was acquitted, with the dust already settling. Will Templar, yet again, was showing his true colours. The student radical turncoat. Running. Putting his body hundreds of miles away from the Front Line but, just like Barford had threatened, his ghost was sitting right next to Barford in the Old Bailey dock. With a rope round his neck, waiting to see if he dropped.

"Members of the jury," Naomi continued, "at the point of death Derek Lennox chose to speak a truth. A young man, Ibrahim El-Hoorie, had overheard two terrorists plotting to shoot down a plane and had told the Police. If El-Hoorie gave evidence then it was inevitable that the public would learn that this entire disaster could have been averted. So Barford, faced with El-Hoorie's threat to go to the Press, had him silenced. Permanently. For five thousand pounds. Handed over in a Betting Office in Leicester by Barford to Lennox. And Lennox, the hitman, did Barford's bidding. El-Hoorie was found in his lounge with his skull caved in. But Lennox was not only a man of violence. He was also a thief and stole jewellery that he found in the flat and El-Hoorie's private journal, in which was recorded his profound anger at the refusal of the Police to act on his report and to call him at Yasin's trial. Thus, Lennox learned the truth of why Barford had ordered the execution. Lennox placed the journal, the top and bottom notes of the five thousand pounds and a betting slip discarded by Barford in the Leicester Booking Shop in a Bank safety Deposit Box. Later Lennox was sent to prison for twelve years and then learned that he was about to die. He sent for his solicitor, Martin Smail who recorded Lennox's confession to the murder at the behest of Barford. When the contents of the safety box were examined both the ten pound notes and the betting slip were found to have Barford's fingerprints upon them. Indeed, Barford's fingerprints are literally all over this case. He pulled the executioner's strings. Barford will stand condemned by words from the grave."

Over a tasteless sandwich and a polystyrene cup of thin coffee Naomi discussed the afternoon's evidence with Mike Myott. It was necessary to call Smail for the Prosecution to prove how he had taken the statement from Lennox but she had certain misgivings about the Runcorn solicitor for he seemed too close to his client. He sounded shifty and her vibes seldom let her down. Moreover, Cadogan would have demanded that every last little fact about him and his dealings with Lennox be researched and, given the mass of administrative machinery that had been set in motion to destroy the case against Barford, it would surprise her if they had not come up with something useful about Smail or his knowledge of Lennox.

Myott was less pessimistic, assuring her that Lennox's account was substantially corroborated by the fingerprints on the money and the betting slip.

"Don't forget that Barford denied to the Police that he'd ever met Lennox in a Betting Shop. Those prints are dynamite. Cadogan has a major problem there. Even if Smail is a bit dodgy," he reminded her.

"Cadogan always finds an angle," she replied ominously. "And if there isn't one there to be found, then he invents one. He manages to do that even when he stands alone. In this case he's got half of the Home Office and National Security at his beck and call. By the way, sorry about stealing your thunder and dealing with the admissibility argument, after you'd done all that work on it. Though I have to admit that I never located the article that you said you had written on the subject."

"No. I submitted the article but it never actually got published. No problem. You did an excellent job. Anyway, I'm better at the academic article than I am on my feet, so I was actually rather relieved. Maullin has a pretty formidable reputation."

"True. And he won't be bullied by Cadogan. You've no idea how important that may prove to be. Whether he can actually avoid being outflanked or outwitted by Cadogan is another matter. He has to be watched like a hawk," warned Naomi.

In the witness box at The Old Bailey Martin Smail looked more like a Defendant than a solicitor. Overweight and red-faced, he was sweating copiously before Naomi had even got him to describe how he'd had the summons, via a Prison Hospital orderly called Crane, to travel to Durham as a matter of great urgency. By the time he came to the end of his story, after recording Lennox's statement and later opening the safety deposit box, his grubby handkerchief was soaked from wiping his forehead and shining pate.

"Seedy, sloppy, greasy and sweaty," she whispered as she sat down at the end of examining him in chief, turning round to address the words to Myott, who should have been sitting behind her, taking a full note and ready with a second opinion. But in her first examination-in-chief in silk, the Junior had sloped out of Court behind her back leaving Giles Brockley, the feeble representative of the Prosecuting Authorities, in his place with Mel Coleman squeezed in alongside him, taking a breather from his typing and gazing intensely at her with his deep brown eyes.

"It's hard to squeeze a slippery bar of soap, though," Brockley whispered back.

"Cadogan won't try to squeeze him. He'll spear him. Straight through the middle, mark my words. And where the hell is Myott?" she demanded.

"Some problem in his chambers, apparently. Someone brought a note in just as Smail went into the witness box. Said he'd be back later."

"Well, he'll miss some fireworks," she grunted as Cadogan moved effortlessly into top gear.

R v Lewis Barford
Transcript 14

Cadogan :
Do you remember the first time you represented Lennox when he was charged with attempted murder?

Smail :
Yes, he was acquitted.

Cadogan :
Even before he was charged did Lennox allege that the Police had planted evidence? And at trial was he able to prove that they had done just that?

Smail :
Yes.

Cadogan :
He set the Police up didn't he?

Smail :
Looking back on it, perhaps they set each other up.

Cadogan :
But that was how Lennox worked, wasn't it? He loved setting the authorities up. And then crowing about it. Like this statement he gave you from his deathbed. Did he tell you he was setting somebody in authority up on this occasion so he could crow from the grave?

Smail :
No. But conscience perhaps.

Cadogan :
Conscience? Conscience? In all the years that you knew Lennox did he ever express remorse for any of the crimes that he had committed?

Smail :
Not that I remember.

Cadogan :
The sentence he was serving at the time of his death? Twelve years for raping a schoolgirl. Did he express any regret in his deathbed repentance for that crime?

Smail :
No.

Cadogan :
Did you go up to Durham Prison from Runcorn out of the goodness of your heart or did you expect to be paid for your time and services?

Smail :
I couldn't know until I learned what Lennox wanted.

Cadogan :
Did you think he wanted to make a will? That the lifelong criminal serving twelve years might have some money he wished to bequeath?

Mr Justice Maullin :
Is that a serious question, Mr Cadogan or is it a cheap sarcastic gibe?

Cadogan :
Perhaps veering towards the sarcastic, My Lord. But not cheap. I would hope never to be cheap.

Mr Justice Maullin :
Ask your questions. Avoid gibes, cheap or otherwise.

Cadogan :
Did Lennox pay you anything then?

Smail :
Nothing.

Cadogan :
Did you try to sell the story?

Smail :
The information went to the Police. If the papers wanted to pay me for the story then I'm just as human as you are. Paid to relay a story. Like you.

Cadogan :
How much were you paid?

Mr Justice Maullin :
Of what relevance is the amount, Mr Cadogan? Do you have instructions from your client on this or are you just fishing?

Cadogan :
Mr Barford knows nothing about this. I am fishing. But in waters where I have a licence. If the witness accepted a large sum of money for the story it is capable of tainting the reliability of what passed between him and Lennox. Thus, I argue, it is relevant.

Mr Justice Maullin :
Very well. But straight to the point. Less of the ringcraft.

Cadogan :
How much?

Smail :
Ten thousand pounds for the story. Seventy five thousand if the full story got published and a hundred and fifty if there was a prosecution.

Cadogan :
Was that the maximum you might receive?

Smail :
No.

Cadogan :
Mr Smail. Please. Like his Lordship said. Straight to the point.
Less of the ringcraft.

Smail :
A quarter of a million if there was a conviction.

Cadogan :
So you've already hit a hundred and fifty and you've got a
further hundred thousand pounds riding on the verdict?

Smail :
In crude terms, yes. But, the real point is that the public learn
the truth.

Cadogan :
Mr Barford was an innocent dupe in all of this, I suggest.
Having an innocent connection. His role was falsely
exaggerated into a criminal role to produce a juicier story. Do
you know anything about that?

Smail :
Nothing.

Mr Justice Maullin :
Very well. We shall adjourn until ten thirty tomorrow morning.
I imagine that you will not be required again in the morning,
Mr Smail. The Court will now rise.

As the Court emptied, Naomi turned round to see if Myott had
returned, but he had not. Brockley and Coleman were still sitting
there like Tweedledum and Tweedledee.

"No sign of Myott?" she observed. "Good job we've got you then, Mel. When do I get the notes you've made of today's evidence?" she asked.

"Tomorrow morning. I'll print them out tonight. You said there would be some fireworks from Mr Cadogan," Coleman observed with a touch of admiration in his voice as he closed the lid on his laptop. "A quarter of a million pounds! More like dynamite if you ask me."

"You were impressed then, were you?" she asked with interest. These people who did agency work for solicitors were, like he'd said earlier, Jack of all trades, and therefore often useful gauges of how the ordinary juror would have viewed the evidence and the quality of the witnesses.

"Well, put it this way," he answered slowly, "he's dangerous. I wouldn't want to cross him. Physically or intellectually."

"A shrewd judgement," she said, nodding in agreement. "He's dangerous, all right. And ruthless, you'll see."

Chapter 21

Dinner alone in her hotel room. Always miserable to dine alone, away from home, even in a luxury suite in a Five Star Hotel. She spoke to Jack briefly on the telephone but it was still another couple of days before he'd be down in London. Case papers all over the desk, bed and floor. Tired. Then the phone rang.

"Naomi, it's Mike here. Mike Myott."

"Oh! You're still alive, are you? Haven't done a Curbishley?"

"Apologies for the absence. I'll explain. But I'm downstairs in the lobby. I've got someone with me. I'd like you to meet him. Can we come up? Better than sitting in the Bar or Public Lounge?"

"Who is it?"

"Saif El-Hoorie. Ibrahim's father."

"I don't want to meet him. I'm under enough pressure as it is. And certainly not in my Hotel suite. If it's something important then he can meet us at Court. In a conference room. With the feeble Brockley present."

"No. He doesn't want them knowing he's spoken to you. He's a very nice man. And I just thought you might get a bit more insight into what's been going on if you had a chat with him. He did lose his only son."

"What is this? The human angle. What's that got to do with our job?"

"As you see it, not much perhaps. But no one else gives a damn."

"Nice one, Mike. It's getting late. I'm a woman. Bit of emotional blackmail."

"Did it work?"

"Yes. Give me five minutes to tidy the place up a bit."

A small, neat mean. Expensive, conservative suit. White shirt, pale yellow silk tie. Black hair. Tidy, trimmed moustache. Highly educated. Cultured. Soft voice. Just a hint of an accent.

Saif El-Hoorie and Mike Myott sat on the deep-cushioned Chesterfield, while Naomi Nicholas lowered herself gingerly on to the uncomfortable wooden chair opposite. Her back ached and, besides, she did not want this meeting to have the feel of a cosy social chat.

"What can I do for you, Mr El-Hoorie?" she asked.

"Nothing, Miss Nicholas. I'm not here to ask anything of you."

"Mr El-Hoorie phoned me. He wanted to tell me that their flat had been bugged," volunteered Myott.

"That's no surprise. They're protecting their own. Firstly, they wanted to ensure that Ibrahim didn't tell anyone, not even his family. Later, they wanted to know if he was speaking at home of going to the Press," Naomi responded.

"Did you know they threatened my son that if he spoke out then we would all be deported?" asked the father.

"I know that they must have put him under enormous pressure," she replied.

"In the days before he was murdered we had telephone calls from people at The Home Office, telling us that our visas were being reviewed. We would have to be interviewed and may not be able to stay."

"Did they give their names?" Naomi asked.

"Never," Mr El-Hoorie replied. "Nearly twenty years my brother and I have had business interests in the UK. My son and daughter were educated here. Our home is here."

"They were trying to frighten your son off. That's how they operate. They abuse their power. They lie. I can't tell you how high up the ladder it goes. Whether it stops before it reaches Ministerial level we'll probably never know."

"Templar, you mean?" El-Hoorie queried.

"Templar. It may even go up as far as Denstone. All I can tell you is that my job is to confront Barford. He's the only one against whom we have any evidence. If he finds himself with his back to the wall as the trial proceeds, perhaps he'll decide to name a few names but they have deployed every resource to defend Barford. Like I said, they're protecting their own."

"Were you aware that Templar and Barford were contemporaries at Oxford?" asked El-Hoorie.

"No. I wasn't. But it doesn't matter, I'm afraid. For all your success, you won't understand how the British Establishment works. Barford comes from the gutter. Nose pressed to the window from the outside. Seeing the good life within. Craving it for himself. Templar was a Marxist. Claimed to despise privilege. In fact what he despised was that someone else had the privilege that he yearned. Then they start to construct their networks," Naomi explained. "It's very subtle."

"So the fact they knew each other long ago is of no use to you?"

"Not really. Except that they would have started the network building even earlier than I'd supposed. They probably hated each other. Probably still do. But they would each have recognised that their objectives were the same. Power and influence. And they could help each other attain them."

"And my son's information threatened that?"

"Yes."

"And now it's you against the Establishment. You and Mr Myott."

"Pretty much. But I do have one advantage, Mr El-Hoorie,"observed Naomi.

"What?"

"I also come from the gutter. If Barford goes into the witness box I'll know how to fight him."

"What do you mean by that?"

"I know what he's likely to do if he thinks he's losing the fight."

"What?"

"He'll sneak. Shift the blame elsewhere. The question will be whether he shifts the blame higher up the ladder or lower. I can't predict that."

"I'm glad you allowed me a few minutes, Miss Nicholas. Now I have spoken to you I know that you have not been put up just to lose the case. If I'm totally honest I did not get the same feeling about Mr. Curbishley."

"Did you meet him then?" asked Naomi.

"No. But if I may be allowed to say so, Mr Myott had expressed certain misgivings and I shared them."

"Mr Myott seems to have been quite busy, doesn't he? Naomi declared, looking directly at her Junior who appeared quite unabashed. "There's one further matter you should know before you leave, Mr El-Hoorie," she added.

"Yes?"

"I know how Barford's mind will work. I can identify the routes I believe he's likely to consider taking and prepare for them. But I cannot say the same about Ronan Cadogan. He's the best possible choice that the Defence could have made. It's hopeless trying to predict his tactics."

"I understand, Miss Nicholas," the dapper gentleman replied, rising from the Chesterfield and looking Naomi directly in the eye. "I am a private man, but I feel able to tell you that I grieve for my son every day and every night. I am slow to anger. But, even above my grief, the anger now prevails. I hate them. Their hypocrisy. Their all-consuming selfishness. I told Mr Myott I wanted to know that you were not one of them. That they could not buy you off. That is why I wanted to meet you."

"And your verdict?" she posed.

"My verdict is that you will fight. To the bitter end. With all of your strength. I can ask no more than that."

"Good night, Mr El-Hoorie," Naomi said softly, getting up and offering him her hand. Even though she was in flat shoes, he did not even come up to her shoulders and he seemed so fragile and damaged that she would have liked to hug him and seek to reassure him. But her job did not allow her to do that and, more significantly, if she acknowledged the truth to herself, she had precious little material with which to offer any reassurance.

"Perhaps you'd see yourself out of the hotel. I'd like a few words with Mr Myott about the case now he's here," she added.

"Of course," he responded, bowing and fleetingly kissing the outstretched hand, in a gesture that took Naomi completely by surprise. It was the act of a natural gentleman, offering her his trust. "Good night, Miss Nicholas, Mr Myott. I feel so much better for our meeting."

After his departure, Naomi did not resume her seat but stared down at Myott with a flash of anger in her eyes.

"Two things, Mike," she began. "Not throwing my weight around just because I'm now in silk, but I didn't take kindly to you disappearing from Court without a word this afternoon."

"I'm sorry. Someone in chambers needed to speak to me quite urgently. I did check that the agency guy would make a full note of the evidence. Didn't he do it?"

"Oh yes. I'll have a full note tomorrow. And printed out which will be easier to read than your writing. But that isn't the point. You're paid to be in Court from beginning to end. Instantaneous unexpected decisions may have to be made. Barristers don't behave like that, just disappearing. And your excuse is pathetic."

"Message received and understood. What's the second thing?"

"You should never have brought Mr El-Hoorie here. Of course you're sorry for him. But this is a tough business. It helps no one to expose me to that. You seem very unworldly about how to do this job. How did you manage to land this brief for yourself?"

"Bit of luck, I suppose. I'll try not to let you down again. Am I forgiven my indiscretions?"

"You're on probation," she replied. "Don't be late in the morning."

"No," he promised with a smile, walking towards the door. "One last question before I go? How was Smail when Cadogan had finished cross-examining him?"

"Speared. Straight through the middle. Like an insect speared on the scientist's slide. Waving its legs about in its death throes but unable to move its body a millimetre. You were lucky to have missed it. Good night."

Chapter 22

Snow had survived until early spring in Davos and the skiers were still in town bringing fun and noise to the restaurants and bars at night. The mountains were still white with the occasional flash of colour lower down the slopes where the meadow flowers were beginning to peep through the thinner patches of snow. During the afternoon session of the Conference, Will Templar had the pleasure of being seated next to the corpulent figure of the Belgian Minister of the Interior who, at the last EU conference in Vienna, had negotiated a hefty subsidy for those Belgian farmers who had suffered losses in the market place after the floods in the North. The British Government's tepid objections to the inequity it represented to British farmers, who had suffered far worse losses as a result of other misfortunes, had been brushed aside over the brandy and cigars and the Belgian had won Templar's admiration for his resolute and completely selfish negotiating skills.

Sycophancy towards the Continental Ministers, with their multi-lingualism, natural appreciation of fine wines and gourmet foods, was often a rewarding attitude for a British Minister to adopt. Over a dinner of fresh wild salmon at the Belgian's hotel up in the mountains over Davos Platz, they had chatted earnestly about the hordes of asylum seekers pounding headlong towards the English Channel ports. Of course, Britain was very prosperous, the Belgian had explained in his immaculate English, and had benefited significantly from various economic advantages emanating from the co-operation of its European partners, therefore morally Britain must be prepared to take a high percentage of these desperate people. Templar recognised the force of his counterpart's arguments and assured him that his own sympathy with the Belgian's view would be faithfully relayed to the very highest level of Government in London. The offer of the use of the Interior Minister's villa on the outskirts of Cannes had been most unexpected, Templar assured him, but none the less an example of generosity and friendship which he could not possibly decline. Parting with warm handshakes after several brandies apiece, Templar had been taken down in the private funicular railway owned by the Hotel to the street below, where a car and driver awaited him for the short journey back to his equally lavish accommodation in Davos Dorf. London and the Old Bailey seemed so far away and, with just a touch of a following wind, he could hang on to the treasured trappings of power, wealth and influence which were now in his blood.

Within ten minutes of his return to his room, whilst relaxing in his soft, royal blue bath robe, a Remy Martin in one hand and one of the Belgian's Havana cigars in the other, he received the expected telephone call on his mobile phone, which he had already placed on the nearby marble topped table.

"Hello," he announced, "is this my daily report?"

"It is," came the curt reply in that distinctive metallic voice.

"And the report from the Home Front is encouraging, I hope?"

"Everything appears satisfactory. The attempt to achieve an early bath was unsuccessful, but that had been fully predicted. RC seems to be running on all four cylinders. The opposition is presently muted. She appears a little nervous according to the report given to me."

"Excellent news, excellent news. Still on course for a finish within a week, I trust?" asked Templar.

"The word is that it will probably just about stretch into a second working week, but all should be done and dusted before your return. Is the Conference going well?"

"Very demanding. Heavy workload. Little time for relaxation but most fulfilling."

"One little cloud on the horizon," the authoritative voice observed. "The referee is prepared to take RC on, I'm told. Could do without that, you know? Do you have any influence in that direction?"

"No. We were let down there, I'm afraid. Did try. But the one we wanted is under very close scrutiny at present. We had to take whichever one the rota produced. But RC is dealing with him I hope."

"Yes. Few minor skirmishes but nothing he didn't handle. Do you want a similar report, tomorrow," enquired the voice.

"Same time. Scrambled as usual."

"Of course," snapped back the voice before immediately disconnecting.

There was little room for the niceties when the Security Services were involved, thought Templar, pouring himself another glass of Remy before turning in for the night.

Looking through the French windows the sky was filled with millions of bright stars, sparkling in the cold, clear night air of Alpine Switzerland. This really was the kind of lifestyle he had always been cut out for, he reflected to himself with some satisfaction. Hard work and skill had got him here and no one was going to take it away from him, he assured himself. Once Barford was acquitted and the flurry of news had died with the acquittal, he'd have to apply his mind to moving Barford sideways. The debt would be too large to keep him at close quarters. Holidays used to be spent at Blackpool and Weston. This summer he would be in Cannes, by the side of the pool at Henri's villa. Worth cultivating Henri, he concluded, as he drained the last of the Remy from the cut-glass tumbler. Denstone hated what was happening at the Bailey. His control had come under threat. And one thing was for sure in this Government. You couldn't trust Denstone. A couple more years in the Department. Then a peerage and a European Ministerial position perhaps. The Gravy Train. They were even more corrupt than our lot.

Chapter 23

"My Lord, I propose playing to the jury the audio tape of Mr. Lennox's confession and statement," Naomi informed the Judge on the resumption of the proceedings the next morning before the jury were brought back into Court.

"Pure theatre My Lord," Cadogan barked back immediately. "It is customary for Counsel to read the statement. Strip away the emotion. The voice of a dying man is emotive and may mask rather than expose the truth. Sympathy, however natural, may influence the jury to believe a falsity. I submit that this statement should be read by Counsel. Dispassionately. No theatre. No voice from the grave."

"I had no idea you were so sensitive, Mr Cadogan," intoned Mr. Justice Maullin in a voice oozing with insincerity. "I suspect that you and the jury are robust enough to handle it fairly. The tape will be played. Bring in the jury."

The accent was thick and the voice was thin and weak but with the volume of the speakers turned up high, no juror failed to hear Derek Lennox make his final bid for revenge against the system.

R v Lewis Barford
Transcript 22

"My name's Derek Lennox. I'll speak for a few minutes. Then take a rest. I'm forty-four. Never married. No children. I'm in Durham Prison for rape. The Doctor's told me I'm fucked. Brain tumour. No cure. I know I'll be dead within a few weeks. I'm terrified of dying. I'm alone. No family. No religion. And I know I've been bad."

[Tape stopped. Rest : 10 minutes]

"I met Lewis Barford best part of ten years ago in Sierra Leone. Did a spell as a mercenary. Did a couple of jobs for his

147

lot and then I got out the bloody place. Back in the UK I saw him again. Did a little job. Then, around a couple of years ago he wanted a fella topped. Five grand. Gave me the cash in a bookie's. Leicester way. Address in London. Code to the basement lock. I said "You're a mean bastard. A topping's worth more than five." He said "You'll nick plenty on top. Your call." I asked him why he wanted the kid taken out. Said he'd upset some geezer. Big time. Less I knew the better."

[Tape stopped. Rest : 15 minutes]

"Did the job the next night. Young kid. Iron bar. One smack. He never knew what hit him. Nice drum. Poked around. Nicked a few bob, couple of rings. One bedroom had a locked drawer. Inside was like a thick diary. Leather and gold. Spur of the moment thing I'spose, nicking that. Next day went back North. Flogged the rings but read the diary. I knew that Barford was a cunning bastard. That's why I picked up a betting slip in the bookies. I forgot to mention this earlier. We'd put bets on to look the part. I lifted Barford's out the bin after he'd gone. Insurance as I saw it. Then I read the kid's story. It's in the box in the Preston Bank. You'll read it. A fucking cover-up. I still had the wad – the five grand. Put the top and bottom notes in the box with the betting slip and the book. You'll see them."

[Tape stopped. Rest : 10 minutes]

"The kid heard those Arabs in Manchester plotting. Shot down the plane. He'd warned the cops who could've stopped it but they done fuck all. Bastards warned him to keep his mouth shut or else. It's all in the fucking diary. Took him to a hospital where he picked one of the Arabs out. The trial of one of 'em was about to start. Now the kid was threatening to blow the whistle, so high and mighty Barford had him taken out. Save his Government pals."

Sitting bolt upright in the dock Lewis Barford listened to the hard Glaswegian accent rebounding around the Old Bailey walls. Lennox had spoken in short sharp bursts, his desperate, laboured breathing filling the gaps in the narrative with a horror of its own. Hitherto Barford had only read the transcript. When you listened to the eerie voice speaking from the beyond, it had a force of its own. And the bastard had lied through his fucking teeth. To the bitter end. Even in death.

Barford could remember the exact words he'd used in that filthy bookies.

'A man I know wants a message delivering. You put the fear of God into this creep. And I mean the fear of God. You terrify the little bastard. But you control the violence. You can slap him about a bit but we don't need any GBH. No need to go as far as you did with the Austrian. You get my meaning? No tools. My man just wants him terrified. Told to keep his mouth shut.'

Barford fought hard to retain his self-control. Lennox was a psychopathic liar. His lies could spell a life sentence. It was all well and good for Cadogan to tell him how to play it, but his neck wasn't on the line. And not even Cadogan could cross-examine a corpse. Sweat was pouring down his back. He'd nearly lost control. Some of the jury were looking at him. They were believing that lying Scottish bastard. Calm. Quiet, deep breaths. Better. The failing voice was still droning on but it was nearing the end now.

"For five grand. To save their fucking skins. That's it, Martin. I'm knackered. It's all in the box. If the money or the slip's got his prints on then he's fucked. Either way, you've still got the story for the newspaper boys. The bastards had him hushed . . . "

"Very distressing, we'll give the jury a break," Mr. Justice Maullin declared, thereby ensuring that the full impact of Lennox's telling words could be digested by the jury over a cup of coffee in their room.

"The pathologist who examined the body of the victim is the next witness, so you have very demanding duties today, members of the

149

jury," the Judge continued. "Very demanding, but it has to be done," he added, rising to his feet and smiling directly down at the irritated face of Cadogan who was staring straight back. Maullin could read the message in the balloon over Cadogan's head as clearly as if it was in flashing neon. *"I know just what you're up to, you old bastard, but lets's see who has the last laugh, shall we?"*

Dr Skelton had been a Home Office Pathologist for more years than he cared to remember and had delved into the innards of hundreds of corpses whose unfortunate owners, by one means or another, had met an unnatural death. Explaining to the jury in detail, via the skilled and selective questions of Naomi Nicholas, the mechanics of death occasioned by trauma to the cranium, Dr Skelton went through the routine in the witness box with which, over the years, he had become so accustomed. As the body had not been discovered until the afternoon when the victim's parents had returned home, he could not precisely identify the time of the killing, but it was within a time bracket of twelve to eighteen hours prior to discovery that the attack must have occurred.

This confirmed Lennox's assertion as to timetable and timing and brought the Prosecution's questioning to an end.

As Cadogan embarked upon the cross-examination, Dr Skelton's mind returned to his constant theme. These lawyers never had to face the harsh realities, he found himself musing, as Cadogan's painstaking questioning continued, much to the obvious irritation of the Judge who pointed out repeatedly that the detailed mechanics of death seemed to have little bearing on whether Barford had given the orders or not. The lawyers don't actually see the liver split in two by the lout's boot, or the heart sliced open by the robber's blade or the child's thorax crushed by the wheels of the drunken driver. They just see pieces of paper. So many times when being cross-examined by defending barristers he had yearned to shout out "Face the realities. If your client hadn't stamped on an unconscious victim half a dozen times then the victim would still be alive." But he never did. And now this Defence Counsel was busy seeking to identify how many blows had been struck to the victim's head. Did it really matter if it was one, two, three or four?

R v Lewis Barford
Transcript 32

Mr Justice Maullin :
I do insist, Mr Cadogan, that you come to the point.

Cadogan :
I am directly on the point, My Lord.

Mr Justice Maullin :
It had escaped my notice.

Cadogan :
Reference has been made to an iron bar being used. Is what you found consistent with such a weapon?

Dr Skelton :
Yes.

Cadogan :
Miss Nicholas never asked you whether in your opinion these fractures were the result of one blow or more than one blow. But your report contains a clear opinion on this, doesn't it?

Dr Skelton :
Yes. At least two blows, probably three.

Cadogan :
On the tape Lennox says "Iron bar. One smack." *That must have been a complete lie, mustn't it?*

Mr Justice Maullin :
Mr Cadogan. Whether Lennox was lying or mistaken cannot be a question for the pathologist.

Cadogan :

So sorry, My Lord. Dr Skelton, let me rephrase the question. Your findings would suggest that either Lennox was a liar, or in the process of murdering a defenceless young man, Lennox forgot whether he hit him once, twice or thrice or with his iron bar?

Dr Skelton :

That's not for me to answer.

Mr Justice Maullin :

Of course it isn't, Dr Skelton. We all know that. Including Mr. Cadogan who will now please sit down.

Cadogan :

Thank you, Dr Skelton. I do hope that I kept to the point, My Lord.

* * *

The afternoon was spent calling the various police officers who had handled the enquiry into El-Hoorie's death, making absolutely no progress, as Cadogan pointed out to the jury ad nauseam, until the day that they had received the information from Smail about Lennox's statement.

By ten past four Mr Justice Maullin had suffered enough of Cadogan's tactics and called a halt to the proceedings until the following morning and the jury went home, still hearing Lennox's words echoing from the beyond, but not quite as sure that his statement told the whole truth as they had been when Counsel for the Prosecution had opened the case to them yesterday.

Whilst Myott had been in attendance all day in Court after his disappearing act on the previous afternoon, Giles Brockley had not put in an appearance at all. Naomi could not help but resent the absence of back-up support that she was receiving in this case although Mel, the agent, had arrived at Court even earlier than she had, delivering her a full typed copy of yesterday's evidence and seemingly taking a close interest in the trial. Myott seemed to have struck up a good relationship with him, which certainly had not been the case with Brockley, whose input had started at zero and gone downwards ever since.

"Mr Cadogan's getting up the Judge's nose big time," was Mel's post-match summary, as he helped Naomi and Myott out of Court with their papers.

"Milking it. Taking too bloody long to get the point," said Myott.

"But he got there in the end, didn't he" Naomi declared. "He's shown that an important part of Lennox's account cannot be relied on."

"But not the most important part. The five grand. Let's see how he deals with that," Mel responded.

Chapter 24

"Morality," Chief Superintendent Ray Leadbetter spat the word out aloud as he slammed the phone down angrily, even though he was alone in the small, spartan office that had been especially selected just up the road from Dartford Police Station.

"Morality," he repeated. "They wouldn't recognise it if it hit them between the fucking eyes."

"It's a positive ID," the authoritative voice had just intoned down the phone. "We knew they'd try and pull something while the trial's going on. We'll have an address for you very soon. You know what to do."

"What if he doesn't play ball? What then?" Leadbetter asked.

"He'll play ball when it's his neck that's on the line. His type always does. Selfish survival. He'll send others on the Martyr's Mission to meet the Great Prophet but when it's his turn he'll sell out. He's got no morality."

That's when Leadbetter had abruptly brought the call to an end. It was the sheer hypocrisy of it. In one breath, under the guise of National Security, they ordered innocent civilians taken out so as to protect their jobs and, in the next breath they accused terrorists of having no morality. Anyway, unwelcome as the call had been, at least it hadn't been the dreaded call that he was required to give evidence in the trial at the Old Bailey. So far Barford seemed to be toeing the party line, but whether he would maintain that position to the end was anybody's guess. The latest report was that there was only a remote chance that anyone would need Leadbetter to be called, although it appeared that getting information from Barford's self-opiniated QC was proving difficult, if not impossible.

Sitting in a cold, empty room except for the desk, phone and specially-prepared chair with its manacles for wrists and ankles, he found himself posing the eternal question. What on earth was the point of it all?

Everybody knew it was a dirty business. He'd made some tough decisions in his time and got some wrong, but he had maintained some awareness that his role affected the safety of the public. This lot in Government and on the fringes, like Barford, weren't really interested in saving lives. They spent their time and energies controlling the outflow of information so that their jobs and their public image remained intact. And then they talked about morality. And what would happen if ever they got him in the witness box at the Old Bailey? Could he trust them then?

At that moment his phone rang again and he snatched up the receiver, now glad of the interruption from deeply worrying thoughts of the Old Bailey and the tactics and subterfuge being played out in that daunting arena.

"We've got the address," barked the voice.

"That was quick, wasn't it?" Leadbetter responded.

"We had a double trail. One crew with the suspect, the other on the Hackney cleric. They both came together. Ten minutes ago. Boothroyd Street, Hackney. We've got cars at each end of the street, so get yourself up here pronto."

"OK. We're on our way."

Intelligence over the last few weeks had been depressingly consistent. A terrorist attack, almost certainly in the Greater London area, specifically designed to coincide with the Barford trial at the Old Bailey, so as to underline their unshaken resolve and capacity to strike at will, whilst simultaneously demonstrating their contempt towards the due process of law. Target unknown.

Fifty-five minutes later, Leadbetter's driver brought the Range Rover to a halt twenty yards behind the surveillance vehicle at the north end of Boothroyd Street and Leadbetter eased his long thin frame out of the passenger seat and slipped quickly into the back seat of the surveillance vehicle, whose door had opened on his approach.

"Stinks like a back street curry house in here," was his opening gambit to the two undercover officers occupying the front seats. "Chicken vindaloo for breakfast now, is it?"

"We've been following the bastard since last night, Sir," answered the older of the two indignantly, turning round from his position in the front passenger seat. "He's changed cars three times. You grab what you can to eat whenever you can in this game."

"Where is he?" demanded Leadbetter.

"Number forty-seven," the officer in the driver's seat replied immediately. Halfway down the street on the right. We think he's on the first floor, back room. Cleric's gone. Only stayed a few minutes. Team yellow are following him, but only to let us know if it looks like he's heading back here. Orders were to leave him out."

"With someone of his calibre there'll be at least two guards. Front and back. Almost certainly armed," Leadbetter observed.

"Yes, Sir," replied the driver. "But our man is probably sleeping. He's been on the go all night. They've no idea we're about. Less than five seconds to get in. We've been told to ask you to stay in the car with us. Then to take over as soon as they've got control."

"No surprises, there," grunted Leadbetter. "The bastards want to keep me alive a bit longer. Possible witness box duties. Anyway, let's do it. And as soon as you've got him I want to be called in. Immediately. I take over from that point. Action."

Six minutes and thirty seconds later he was picking his way over the green front door of Number 47 Boothroyd Street as it lay, smashed and splintered on the linoleum floor of the hallway. Officers in their bulletproof vests and helmets stood aside on the cramped stairway as he climbed to the first floor and entered the back bedroom. Two dark-skinned youths were lying motionless face down on the floor, handcuffed, terrified and irrelevant.

"Get them out of here. You know where to take them," Leadbetter growled to the roomful of armed officers at large. "You'll get your orders what to do with them when we've checked who they are." As the two youths were dragged to their feet, Leadbetter turned towards the man lying on the bed with the barrel of an AK rifle pushed under his chin, distorting still further the puckered, ridged scarring down the left side of the neck.

"He's the one I want," he added. "Abdelkarim Mohammed. Give me the rifle," he demanded, before slamming the butt straight into the genitals of the helpless Arab. "Welcome back to London, Professor."

Back in the drab Dartford room, Abdelkarim Mohammed, now barefoot and cold, was manacled by both hands and feet to the steel chair on the opposite side of Leadbetter's desk. His bloated face with the distinctive flat nose was pale under the Eastern skin. Leadbetter's blow with the rifle had made him vomit, the dull pain still lingering in the groin and his head ached.

"We need to know the target. Place. Time. Means. The longer you take to tell us, the more you suffer," Leadbetter began. "Given the grief you've caused, I hope you hold out because I want to make you suffer some serious pain," he added. "Your choice."

"Easy choice. Go fuck yourself," came the immediate reply.

"Excellent," Leadbetter responded, picking up the phone. "Music to my ears. Sergeant, send Lativsky straight up," he barked down the phone.

As soon as he mentioned the name Lativsky, an involuntary tremor passed visibly through Mohammed's body and he stiffened in his seat.

Within a few seconds the door opened. A dark, swarthy man walked in, neither speaking nor acknowledging either of the other two men. Twenty-five, only medium height but powerful chest, barn door shoulders, khaki shirtsleeves rolled up to reveal large powerful, dark-haired forearms and a face hewn out of granite. His brown eyes were fixed unwaveringly on Abdelkarim Mohammed in a cold stare, eyeball to eyeball, that Mohammed could not sustain, his chin dropping to his chest and his eyes avoiding those of the other man.

"You two know each other, I believe," observed Leadbetter quietly. "Colonel Eli Lativsky, now with Mossad. You knew him when he was still on active service with the Israeli Army. That's when he put the bullets in your neck and stomach."

Lativsky positioned himself directly in front of Abdelkarim Mohammed, pushing his face into the face of the manacled Arab.

"I have permission from the British to take you back to Jerusalem. Tonight. We have places on a Hercules out of Brize Norton to Akrotiri and the Israeli Air Force will take over from there. Mossad will interrogate you. Then there will be a military trial. In secret. You'll be executed in the barracks. Under my command. I can promise you a slow death, with plenty of time for reflection."

"You see, Mohammed, the Israelis want you very badly," Leadbetter observed. "I have Ministerial authority to let them take you. We would welcome your execution. And you know as well as I

157

that Mossad will give you a death to remember. But you have something we want. Full details of the planned attack here in England in the next few days. You can bargain. But you only get one chance."

"What's the deal?" breathed Abdelkarim Mohammed, still unable to look the Israeli Colonel directly in the face.

"I told you. Place. Time. Means," replied Leadbetter.

"I wish time to think," the Arab spat back at Leadbetter.

"You get no time. It's now or never. And one chance. The Colonel wants you back in the Holy Land so that they can put you to death like the vermin that you are. You know their methods. You'll die a lingering, excruciating death at the hands of the Jews. That's after they've interrogated you and softened you up. The worst fate you could ever imagine," Leadbetter explained.

"And if I tell?" enquired the Arab, his voice shaking despite himself. Every Arab Freedom Fighter knew falling into the hands of the Mossad was worse than death itself.

"If you talk, then as soon as we have your brainwashed lackeys under lock and key, you'll be flown to Stuttgart. You owe them three life sentences. You'll be locked up in a German gaol for life. Colonel Lativsky and I both hope that you choose the Mossad. The Hercules leaves at nine tonight. Arrives at Akrotiri before dawn. The Israelis'll have you in Jerusalem for a late breakfast. Your balls will have been chopped off by lunchtime. A tasty little starter for what follows."

"I need time."

The sudden crack split the air. Lativsky was wearing heavy, army issue, studded boots and, without warning, he brought his right foot down in a vicious stamp on Mohammed's bare left foot, smashing numerous small bones in the foot and causing the Arab to scream in terror and pain, but unable to move an inch because of the manacles.

"I told you," said Leadbetter, "no time," although even he was shocked by the suddenness and brutality of the act.

Tears were now running down Abdelkarim Mohammed's face. His screams had subsided to desperate whimpers. It was so easy to plot the death of unarmed, unsuspecting civilians. Pretending it was a military action. Promoting the self-delusion that the civilians had a chance, that they were to blame in some way for the deprived circumstances of the brothers. So magnificent to send the mindless martyrs to their glorious deaths. But how different when it was him. How different when he was up against ruthless military men.

"The Tube," he spluttered. "Lancaster Gate Station. Tomorrow evening. Rush hour. Two brothers. They have been at the safe house since this morning and will remain there 'til I arrive. 92 Enson Street, Southall. The explosives are there."

"I told you that you only had one chance. If we find that you're lying . . . "

Leadbetter began."I'm not lying," Abdelkarim Mohammed muttered.

"No. I don't think you are. It's just as you predicted, Colonel," Leadbetter observed. "A hero with the lives of others and a coward where his own life is at stake. Once we've got his minions under lock and key he's all yours. The transport to Brize Norton is all set up."

"But you promised Germany," screamed Abdelkarim Mohammed hysterically, straining desperately at the steel bands around his wrists and ankles, his foot burning in agony from Lativsky's boot.

"Never believe the British," breathed Lativsky softly, "We learned that the hard way in 1948. But don't worry, Israel never breaks its promises."

Chapter 25

Meanwhile, at the Old Bailey Cadogan had spent most of the morning trying to persuade a resolute Mr Justice Maullin that the fingerprint on the bottom ten pound note from Lennox's box should not be admitted in evidence as it had only seven ridge characteristics which matched those of the little finger of the right hand of Lewis Barford. The Prosecution had called their fingerprint expert, Angela Dale, who was adamant that even with as few as five ridge characteristics she would be prepared to call a match. Cadogan had called Michael Ostler, a highly respected expert with considerably more experience than Ms Dale and Ostler expressed serious reservations about the reliability of comparisons made on the basis of seven ridge characteristics. He was adamant that five remained unacceptable for the purpose of a criminal trial and, in his opinion, so did seven. The Judge was untroubled. All of the fingerprint evidence was ruled admissible.

* * *

"Well so far, Naomi, the formidable Cadogan has lost all the battles. We have to be encouraged," chuckled Myott over his cardboard sandwich in the tacky Courthouse Coffee Shop."

"He couldn't care less about losing the battles, so long as he wins the war. Sooner or later he'll launch his Exocet," she replied. "The more the Judge does him down, the more devastating will be his response. The only question is when."

"And what?" added Myott.

"But from this morning's exchanges it seems that not even Cadogan can challenge the fingerprints on the top note and the Betting Slip," she observed.

"Then why did he spend most of the morning trying to exclude the fingerprint evidence on the bottom note if he's going to admit that Barford's prints are on the other note and the Betting Slip?" Myott asked.

"To achieve the very objective he has achieved. You and I sitting here, halfway through the trial, without the slightest idea what he's up to. He hasn't put a case. He hasn't really disclosed his Defence. Just a few meaningless words. We don't know which way he's going to jump. That's precisely how he operates," she replied knowingly. "Losing a few battles with the Judge while he waits with his finger on the trigger of a secret missile. Mark my words, the stage is set for a Cadogan ambush."

"Perhaps this afternoon, in front of the jury, he will challenge that the fingerprints are Barford's," suggested Myott.

"No. I can't see that now. But keep watching him like a hawk. I suspect that the Exocet will be launched when Barford gives evidence," Naomi replied. "Tomorrow morning is the most likely ambush time."

"Don't you think that we are worrying too much about Cadogan? Surely he can only be as good as the instructions he gets from Barford?" Myott asked.

"I'm afraid that you have no idea. His client and his instructions are just distractions. He takes a given set of facts and he sets about manipulating them into a scenario which undermines the Prosecution case. He manipulates words, the witnesses, the jury and his opponent. Whether we recognise it or not, he is engaged in manipulating us. I've watched him doing it when I was his Junior. He only needs one opening. One topic," she explained.

"And from what you're saying he also manipulates his own client," Myott observed.

"Undoubtedly. What you hear Barford say from the witness box will be neither the truth, nor what his original line of defence may have been. Cadogan will have had an input which dramatically improves Barford's chances of acquittal and is not what Barford originally intended to say," Naomi responded. "And he never completely breaks the rules. Jack says he plays most of the game offside, but at the crucial moment when he nets the winner, he's just squeaked back into an on-side position."

"Who is Jack?" Myott asked.

"The man I almost live with. He used to be a footballer. Now he commentates, writes articles and so on. He met Cadogan in Leeds. They hated each other on sight."

"Not Jack Farnham?" enquired Myott.

"Yes, that's him," she replied with a note of pride in her voice.

"He does the Saturday night show on cable. Gets at the truth. Now I know why," declared Myott laughing. "You've trained him."

"You don't train Jack. He's his own man. Anyway, you'll probably meet him. He's coming down to London tomorrow morning and hopefully he'll meet me here at lunchtime. Come on. Break over. Time to get ready for the matinee performance."

Angela Dale gave her evidence in front of the jury with the utmost care. There was nothing more disconcerting for an expert witness than to stand in the witness box under the scrutiny of not only the Judge, the barristers and the jury, but also the expert for the other side, who sat behind his team, pencil poised, eagerly awaiting the slightest slip or the tiniest over-statement. But by the time Prosecuting Counsel had adduced all of the fingerprint evidence, Michael Ostler had precious little additional ammunition to provide Cadogan with. Her evidence had been fair, balanced and absolutely accurate, except he remained more circumspect about the certainty level of the seven ridge print.

R v Lewis Barford
Transcript 48

Cadogan :
Ms Dale, is it your evidence that the fingerprints of Mr. Barford are on the top ten pound note, the bottom ten pound note and the betting slip.

Dale :
Yes. That is what I said.

Cadogan :
And on the bottom note and the top note did you identify prints that must have come from Lennox?

Dale :
Yes.

Cadogan :

Did you also find a print on the bottom note which was not that of Lennox or Mr Barford? The print of an unknown person? With sixteen characteristics?

Dale :

Yes. So capable of certain identification by fingerprint if we knew who that person was. And the same finger or thumb of the same unknown person as on the bottom note with twenty clear characteristics.

Cadogan :

Turning now to the Betting Slip. Did you find several fingerprints, all of which undoubtedly come from Mr Barford?

Dale :

Yes. I can tell you which fingers if you wish.

Cadogan :

Not necessary. Thank you so much, Ms Dale.

Mr. Justice Maullin :

Is that it Mr Cadogan?

Cadogan :

Yes, My Lord. As you put it – that is "it".

Mr Justice Maullin :

You mean that you are not challenging any of this evidence?

Cadogan :

Challenging, My Lord? Challenging? Fingerprint evidence is very powerful evidence.

Mr Justice Maullin :

Mr Cadogan. You understand my question. Are you disputing

this witness's expert testimony that your client's fingerprints are on both of these notes and on the Betting Slip? The jury and I are entitled to know.

Cadogan :
My Lord, if I dispute evidence on behalf of my client, then I can assure Your Lordship that neither you, nor the jury, will be in any doubt that I have challenged it.

Mr Justice Maullin :
So the answer to my question is 'No.'

Cadogan :
The answer is 'No.' No challenge. No dispute. Accepted. I go further. In due course to be relied upon by the Defence. Thank you, My Lord for allowing me to make matters so clear.

The handwriting expert gave evidence that the handwriting on the Betting Slip was an exact match for the writing in the letter recovered from Barford's briefcase at the Police Station addressed to his Bank Manager. In the expert's opinion the Betting Slip and the letter were the work of the same hand. Cadogan asked no questions.

Naomi then read to the jury short extracts from Ibrahim El-Hoorie's diary expressing his anger at the Manchester Police, his dealings with the Police who interviewed him later and his identification of Abdelkarim Mohammed by photograph and Fahid Yassin at the hospital. The last entry, in the days immediately preceding Yassin's trial, expressed his fury at being informed he was not required as a witness. "I know their reason," read the journal, "but I shall not be silenced. I'll go to the Press."

Finally, the interviewing police officer was called to read the transcript of the Police interview of Barford, in which he had admitted knowing Lennox in Sierra Leone, but had denied ever seeing him since returning to Britain and had never met him in a Betting Shop in Leicester. Cadogan asked no questions.

"That concludes the case for the Prosecution" announced Naomi Nicholas at five minutes past four.

"Thank you," the Judge responded.

"Yes, Mr Cadogan. Now it is the turn of the Defence."

"My Lord," began Cadogan. "Only a few minutes of Court time remains today. I would be grateful to start the Defence case tomorrow morning."

"But we wasted so much time listening to fingerprint evidence that was not, in the end, challenged, Mr Cadogan. I really do think we should make a start on your case."

"If your Lordship insists."

"I do."

"Very well, My Lord. I call Lewis Barford to give evidence."

With a lot of unnecessary clanging of keys, the door at the side of the dock was unlocked and a heavyset Senior Prison Officer led the way to the witness box, followed by the upright, defiant figure of the Defendant. The dark sultry looks lent his expression a look of great intensity and the jaw was solid and firm.

R v Lewis Barford
Transcript 61

Barford :
I'm Lewis Barford. I was born Norman Barford but I hated the name. I re-named myself Lewis and have been known as Lewis ever since.

Cadogan :
Where were you brought up?

Barford :
Huyton, Liverpool. Grim Council Estate. I'm from the bottom of the heap.

Cadogan :
Where did you go to school?

Barford :
The local comp. I detested it. None of the kids had any ambition.
They didn't work. They didn't want to break out of the mould.

Cadogan :
What mould?

Barford :
Leaving school. Going on the dole. Thieving.

Cadogan :
What did you want?

Barford :
To work and to succeed. So I buckled down. Swotted. Took the
flak off the other kids. Got three 'A's and got a place at Oxford.
Merton. Unheard of on our estate. But I'd escaped. Read
politics, philosophy and economics.

Cadogan :
My Lord, it is nearly twenty past four. Would it now be
possible to adjourn until tomorrow?

Mr Justice Maullin :
You consider that you've played out time with a brisk canter
through the biography, do you Mr. Cadogan?

Cadogan :
Just some useful background material, My Lord. Tomorrow I
shall move on to other territory.

Mr Justice Maullin :
Very well. Tomorrow morning. I cannot resume this case until
eleven o'clock. I have some other matters in chambers of an
important nature, which must be heard as a matter of urgency.
Eleven o'clock tomorrow.

Waving his enormous hand at the papers spread out on the Bench in front of him, Cadogan turned round to his hapless Junior and barked his commands.

"Bring all my papers to the Conference Room along the corridor, Stapleton."

"Right, I'll meet you in the Conference Room in a few minutes. Do we need the solicitor to join us there?" Stapleton replied obediently.

"No. Just you and me," Cadogan answered. "Cosy chat time," he added ominously.

Five minutes later, the two barristers sat together in the cramped Conference Room, their wigs tossed carelessly on the table-top, which was engraved with the initials and crude offerings of Defendants who had passed this way before. Cadogan's papers, neatly collected by the Junior sat in a pile, tied with pink tape, alongside the discarded wigs.

"The bastard made you call Barford for ten minutes this afternoon just to be bloody awkward," Stapleton muttered.

"Of course he did. That's all part of Maullin's game. Make life as difficult as possible for me. He's not a fan. I'm not one of the favoured few. Perfect. Just how I like it. And he's well ahead on points at the moment," Cadogan replied.

"Does that matter?"

"Most certainly. Let the bugger think he's winning. Complacency. Then he doesn't see it coming," Cadogan answered. "But you haven't done much to earn your corn yet, have you?" he continued sharply.

"I've done whatever you asked," replied Stapleton uncomfortably, looking about him as he spoke. Cadogan, even seated, seemed to fill the room and dominate him by his sheer size.

"How many times have you been led by a QC before this case?"

"Quite a few. Not by you, obviously. But I've got a good practice. This is my ninth year in chambers."

"Good," snapped Cadogan, "Then you'll know the three Golden Rules about being led.

"I'm not sure that I do, actually," came the nervous response.

"Number one. Never offer an opinion unless asked for one. Number two, hold the client's hand, thereby reducing the Leader's contact with the offending classes to the barest minimum."

"Yes, understood."

"And most important of all," pronounced Cadogan loudly, leaning forward in his chair so that his face was only a few inches away from the startled features of his Junior, who had never come across such a domineering, terrifying figure as this in all his nine years at the Bar. "Number three. If the Leader tells you to keep your mouth shut about something, then you keep it firmly shut. Do I make myself clear, Stapleton?"

"Well, no. Not really," Stapleton answered gingerly. "That hasn't arisen, as far as I can remember."

"No, of course it hasn't. Not yet," snapped Cadogan impatiently. "That's why we're having our cosy chat at this particular time. It's about to happen, do you see?"

"I do now, yes."

"And the question arises of whether you have the gumption to abide by the Rule. Can you keep your mouth shut? I had a Junior once who broke this Rule."

"And what happened to him?" Stapleton asked in subdued tone.

"He never got another case with a QC. Was never led again," Cadogan answered. "And his application for any appointment was blocked. He's hardly got a practice left. Was an able fellow as well. But I think you've got my drift, Stapleton, haven't you?"

"Absolutely. You can count on me," the worried Junior assured his Leader.

"Good. So I have your word that the instruction I'm about to give you will be carried out and then never spoken of again. Ever," insisted Cadogan.

"So long as it's not illegal, yes. I must be entitled to draw the line at that," Stapleton responded.

"Not illegal."

"Right. What do you want me to do?"

"Some time tomorrow morning, before the Court sits, I want you to give our solicitor a message."

"Byron Bloom, you mean?" asked Stapleton.

"Of course. How many solicitors do we have in this case, for goodness sake? Yes. Byron Bloom, the five hundred pounds an hour man."

"And what is the message?" Stapleton asked, now agog with the intrigue.

"This is the message. I want you to imprint it in your brain verbatim. *'Cadogan says Barford will be OK so long as she doesn't call Leadbetter,'* Cadogan announced, enunciating every syllable as he spoke. "Do you think that it's within your power to remember that?"

"Yes. *'Cadogan says Barford will be OK so long as she doesn't call Leadbetter,'* Stapleton repeated faithfully.

"Very good," observed Cadogan condescendingly. "Now you really are beginning to earn your fee."

"But I don't understand," Stapleton declared. "Why can't you simply tell Byron Bloom that yourself, if that's what you think?"

"You're not paid to understand, Stapleton. Your job is to follow orders. Your understanding is an irrelevance," was the dismissive response.

"But Nicholas can't call this fellow Leadbetter now. She's closed her case. We're half way through the Defence case. Barford is in the box," Stapleton persisted.

"Have you never heard of the Prosecution calling evidence in rebuttal, Stapleton? In your nine years at the Bar have you never come across rebuttal evidence?" Cadogan snapped aggressively. "That's the point."

"I see. Yes, I see that now. But it still doesn't answer my question. Why can't you tell Bloom that Barford will be OK so long as Nicholas doesn't call Leadbetter. Surely you can explain that much to me," Stapleton insisted.

"Because it isn't Bloom who I want to hear the message. I couldn't give a fig about Bloom," Cadogan replied enigmatically. "You are to recite that message to Bloom in circumstances where that weird Junior, Myott, is in a position to hear you. I don't care where. The mens' lavatories, the Robing Room, the Coffee Shop, the corridor. You say your line, loud and clear to Bloom, making sure that Myott hears."

"But he'll tell . . . " began Stapleton.

"Just shut up and listen. I haven't finished. You make sure Myott hears. But you make equally sure that he thinks that you don't know he's heard. You do it where you aren't visible to him. Round a corner. Hidden from view by a locker in the Robing Room, different section of the lavatories. He thinks he's inadvertently eavesdropped on you and Bloom and you don't know he's heard. Now, do you follow?

"Oh yes. I follow now, all right. You're bluffing them."

"No. No. I'm applying a strategy. Prosecuting Counsel should not act on snatches of private conversation they may pick up inadvertently from their opponents. Most improper. We can count on Myott's sense of propriety, I'm sure," Cadogan declared.

"You know he'll tell Nicholas. It's a bluff," Stapleton repeated.

"I never liked that word. So hard to distinguish a bluff from a double bluff sometimes as well. Now, do you understand your orders? Cadogan demanded.

"Yes. May be a bit difficult to engineer, but I'll do it," he assured the Leader.

"And repeat the third Golden Rule," commanded the QC.

"If the Leader tells you to keep your mouth shut about something, then you keep it firmly shut," was Stapleton's immediate and fluent response.

"You're getting there, Stapleton. Do your stuff properly tomorrow and who knows where it may lead. Conference over. Bring my papers up to the QC's Robing Room. Time to go home."

Chapter 26

All the other Courts were sitting at half past ten so that, by twenty past, the Robing Room was empty. Since receiving Cadogan's bizarre and disturbing command the evening before, Stapleton had been contemplating the best means of achieving the objective, finding himself torn between the appealing intrigue of the situation on the one hand and genuine distaste at the obvious attempted deception on the other. In a perverse sense, Cadogan had been right. In strict ethical terms, if Prosecuting Counsel inadvertently heard a confidential aside passed between Defence Counsel and the Defence Solicitor, then he should put it straight out of his head and pretend that he'd never heard it. But, of course, this was the real world and the chances of Myott keeping it to himself were remote. But what kind of barrister actually set up a sting like this? And a QC at that.

Principles of honour, loyalty and decency that had governed the profession over the centuries, were now being eroded by the acts of the few. But to receive instructions from one of the best QCs in London to pull a stunt like this had still shocked Stapleton and he wondered, when push came to shove, if he would really go through with it.

Fate sometimes plays a strange hand. The Robing Room had several little alcoves, with writing tables for last-minute work to be done, tucked away in the corners and behind some of the lockers. On each morning of the trial, when Stapleton had gone into there he had glimpsed Myott seated in the alcove at the far end, beavering away on his laptop at a feverish rate. On this particular morning Byron Bloom had been anxiously awaiting Stapleton's arrival, hovering in the corridor outside the Robing Room door, to raise a query over the costs of keeping Ostler at Court, even though the expert's participation in the fingerprint evidence aspect of the case seemed to have passed.

"Morning, Mr Stapleton," said Bloom as Stapleton loomed into view. "Sorry to attack you as soon as you arrive, but Mr Ostler is downstairs, getting very anxious. He wants to know if he really should remain. Apparently, Mr Cadogan has told him that he is not to leave the trial under any circumstances until Mr Cadogan himself says so."

"Well there's your answer then, Mr Bloom, he'll just have to stay. Do you fancy upsetting Cadogan, because I can assure you that I don't?"

"No, I certainly don't. But Mr Ostler wondered if perhaps Mr Cadogan had just forgotten to release him. He thought his part was over now. And if he's just been forgotten, then he's worried he won't be paid for the extra time he's here."

"Do you think that Cadogan forgets anything? I very much doubt it. He must stay until Cadogan releases him. There'll be a reason. Tell him to stop worrying," replied Stapleton. "And while you're here," he added, opening the Robing Room door, "just pop into the room a minute. I want to check the client's instructions with you on a particular point. I'll need to get my notebook from my locker, come in."

Stapleton's heart was beating fast as Bloom proceeded through the door ahead of him. There was no one to be seen, but Stapleton could hear the noise of the fast fingers tapping on the keyboard, coming from the far alcove which Myott always used. He'd made his decision. He wouldn't look to see if Myott was there. He'd recite his line and then leave. If Myott was there, so be it. If he wasn't, then he'd done his best. When Cadogan asked, as surely he would, then Stapleton would assure him that he'd done it and that Myott must have heard. No one could control whether Myott passed it on to Nicholas or not, so Cadogan would have no means of establishing whether Myott had heard but played the white man, or never actually heard at all.

Opening his locker noisily he pulled the blue Counsel's notebook from out of the pile of papers before loudly announcing; "Yes, Mr. Bloom, here it is. We couldn't remember one of the Eastern European postings. He went to Warsaw and Helsinki. Where was the other one, Mr Bloom?"

"Bucharest," Bloom replied immediately. "Is that all it was? Doesn't seem to matter much to me."

Stapleton strained his ears. Myott must have realised it was them. That's why he had deliberately repeated Bloom's name. The tapping had stopped. The bugger was listening.

"Oh, everything matters to Cadogan, Mr Bloom. Every single fact," he continued, his voice now rising in volume. "It's going well, you know. Very well. In fact, Cadogan says Barford will be OK so long as she doesn't call Leadbetter."

There. He'd done it. The tapping fingers were still silent. Myott must have been sitting there transfixed. Drinking it in. Time to get out. Bloom was responding. "Is that what he says? Really? Well . . . "

"Come on, Mr Bloom, I'm going to buy you a cup of coffee before I get changed," Stapleton interrupted, taking the solicitor by the arm and ushering him briskly out of the room before he could undermine the good work. "I'd forgotten we've got an extra half-hour this morning."

Turning left out of the door towards the Coffee Shop the two men walked to the end of the corridor. Just as they were about to turn right and head up the stairs, Stapleton deftly dropped his Counsel's notebook and stooped to pick it up. His timing had been immaculate for, as he took the slyest of peeps out of the corner of his eye, he saw the figure of Myott darting out of the Robing Room and scurrying along the corridor in the opposite direction, towards the Conference Room where Stapleton knew Nicholas always went to do her early morning preparation. Myott was taking the good news from Ghent to Aix.

Chapter 27

R v Lewis Barford
Transcript 62

Cadogan :
What did you after coming down from Oxford?

Barford :
I'd received an approach. In my final term. From a Government Department. Took some more exams. Went to some interviews. After a year in London I was sent to Warsaw. Then Bucharest. Helsinki. Back to London and then seconded to Sierra Leone. Ostensibly as a mercenary. In reality I was ordered to protect British interests out there. As best as I could.

Cadogan :
Is that where you met Derek Lennox?

Barford :
Yes. He was out there as a mercenary. There were various Brigades. Colonel Merle paid in diamonds and US dollars. That appealed to Lennox and others like him. We used him on the odd operation, but he deserted after a few months. Fairly typical. They came. Earned some good money. Then disappeared into the Central African fleshpots and blew it all. Sometimes they reappeared and did another few months. Lennox never did.

Cadogan :
How well did you get to know him?

Barford :
As well as an Officer gets to know a foot soldier. There was a distance, but I had no problem with him.

Cadogan :
Did you know he had a number of criminal convictions?

Barford :
I knew he'd done time. But you have to realise nearly all of them had. This was a Brigade of Mercenaries. He'd talked to me about being in prison. Made no secret of it. Said he'd done a long stretch in Belmarsh. Been in a serious fight and the other guy had come off worst.

Cadogan :
Did that disturb you?

Barford :
Of course not. Any white man working as a mercenary in Central Africa in those days had a past. Most of them had convictions for violence.

Cadogan :
You didn't.

Barford :
I was living a false life. I was there in the employ of the British Government. I had to be able to survive in the company of these men. A Liverpool council estate and Oxford University. HMG didn't have many like that on the books.

Cadogan :
Did you eventually return to Britain?

Barford :
Yes. My attachment had been under the auspices of a section of the Foreign Office. On my return I was offered an Adviser position, attached to the same Department. Later, in a similar capacity, I was transferred to the Home Office. In security. Advising on safety of Officials. Security ramifications of some political decisions. That kind of stuff.

Cadogan :

After your return to Britain had you ever met Lennox again?

Barford :

Not until the meeting that has led to me facing this Prosecution.

Cadogan :

How many times in total did you meet him after your return from Sierra Leone.

Barford :

Just the once. In the Betting Shop in Leicester. Like he said on the tape we listened to.

Cadogan :

In interview did the Police ask you if you had ever met up with Lennox again after your return from Sierra Leone and did you lie to them and deny it?

Barford :

Most certainly I did. Lennox was accusing me of hiring him to commit murder. It was rubbish. As soon as the Police read out Lennox's allegations against me, I realised immediately what had happened. I'd been used as a messenger. By National Security. Or Special Branch. It's often impossible to know who they're working for. But I knew how they operated. Whoever had used me would deny having had any contact with me. I'd be left isolated. But Lennox was now dead. I didn't know the Law. I didn't know you could read out a dead man's statement in Court. Let him accuse you from the grave where he can never be questioned. I'd committed no offence. Lennox was dead. Special Branch would lie. It was my word against a dead man's tale. I lied.

Cadogan :

Explain how you had come to be used as a messenger.

Barford :

I'd received a message. By email. It can't be recovered because the software is especially designed for security purposes. They self-destruct. It said that there was a serious risk of information being published which could affect a terrorist trial due to start here at the Old Bailey.

Cadogan :

Whose trial?

Barford :

It didn't actually say. But I was told later that it was the trial of Fahid Yasin. But I knew which trial anyway. It was big news. It was the Manchester Airport attack.

Cadogan :

Who sent the email?

Barford :

As I said earlier, it's often hard to distinguish which specific agency a particular individual is really working for. But it was likely that Special Branch were involved somewhere along the line. I was instructed to attend a meeting. A secret meeting. At a high level.

Cadogan :

With whom?

Barford :

The original message gave no name. It just carried the code to satisfy me it was genuine and involved a high level official. I responded that morning. Obviously, I agreed to attend. That kind of stuff was part of my job. I OK'd the various protocol conditions of secrecy and waited to hear a time and a place.

Cadogan :

Did you hear?

Barford :

Within the hour. I was directed to attend the following evening at a location which would be telephoned through to me late afternoon the next day. That call came. No name given. Time, location and directions to a canal barge. A narrow boat. Off Dingle Lane on the outskirts of Ashford. I can't remember the precise time now. But late.

Cadogan :

Could you find your way to the exact location on the canal now?

Barford :

Easily. I have done. After I was charged I drove back there to see if the boat was still there. I thought it might be useful. 'the Medici'. Given what I know now, they'd probably put a false name on it for the meeting. Of course, it had gone. No big surprise. I was dealing with professionals. Masters of survival. And the meeting was a long time ago.

Cadogan :

Did you go to this meeting alone or with someone?

Barford :

Alone.

Cadogan :

Did you tell anyone that you were going?

Barford :

Of course not. It's important to understand that all of these jobs work on the same principle. You only tell anyone anything if you really have to. I wasn't in danger. The security codes were all genuine. It was an exercise in protecting some information.

Cadogan :

Was anyone on the barge when you arrived?

Barford :
Just one man. I'd never met him before. Nor since.

Cadogan :
Were there ever more than just the two of you there?

Barford :
Never.

Cadogan :
Did the man say who he was?

Barford :
Special Branch. They have code words. He knew them. He said the terrorist trial was imminent. They'd received information that there was a diary. It could compromise the trial. He emphasised that it had no bearing at all on the guilt or the innocence of the man on trial. But he said if it got out, the publicity generated might prevent the trial even taking place. He wanted the diary. It was in a private London address.

Cadogan :
Why didn't he use Special Branch personnel to obtain it?

Barford :
Because it would have to be stolen. They didn't want to run the slightest risk. They wanted it stolen by a pukka thief. A thief who was a skilled burglar. Most unlikely to get caught and able to keep his mouth shut if he was caught.

Cadogan :
Why would Special Branch come to you? They would come across enough burglars, wouldn't they?

Barford :
No. Oddly enough, in practice they wouldn't. Too far down the criminal

pecking order for them to have dealings with. But that wasn't the point. They wanted a body that had no possible link to them at all.

Cadogan :
Why would they expect you to be able to help?

Barford :
Because at the very top of National Security they would have seen my file. They knew the type that had joined Colonel Merle's Brigade. And they were right. I could have found four or five men who would have qualified. He asked if I knew any candidates. I told him I did. But whether they were available was another question. This kind of flotsam could be anywhere in the world or in gaol. I was to find out immediately if there was one available to do a job. If so, I was to set up a meeting. Under no circumstances was I to give any clue as to what the job was. Not the slightest hint. Except of course that it was highly illegal. I had to phone the Special Branch Officer with a name before the meeting. No doubt so that they could check the man out on their files. He gave me a twenty-four hour number.

Cadogan :
What did you do?

Barford :
Went back home. Checked my personal records. I had a phone number for the man I thought most suitable. I found out he was in prison. Lennox was my second choice.

Cadogan :
How did you locate him?

Barford :
With surprising ease. I accessed Home Office Prison Release files. He'd come out on license not that long ago. Condition of residence at a hostel in Nottingham. I spoke to him the next morning. Arranged

to meet him at the Betting Office in Leicester the next day. Then I immediately informed the man from the barge.

Cadogan :
What did he say?

Barford :
He said I was to keep the appointment in Leicester. Satisfy myself that Lennox was still up to scratch. Still physically capable. Mentally alert. Lots of his type turn into alcoholics.

Cadogan :
And if Lennox passed muster?

Barford :
Tell him I knew nothing about the job. But I could make a phone call. There and then on my mobile. Once I'd got through I was to hand the phone to Lennox. He'd be given all the necessary details. Then he was to hand the phone back to me. The Special Branch man would then tell me whether the job was on or off. If it was on I was to pay up front.

Cadogan :
And if it wasn't on?

Barford :
I was to walk out.

Cadogan :
How would you pay?

Barford :
On the barge he'd told me they'd pay £5000.

Cadogan :
How was this money to reach you to hand over to the burglar?

Barford :

He had the money with him. On the barge. In an envelope. He threw it on the table. I took it out. A wad of tenners. That was it. I met Lennox in Leicester. Made the call. Same number. Same guy. Passed the phone over to Lennox. I placed that bet while Lennox was talking on the phone. Make things look normal.

Cadogan :

Did Lennox hand you the phone back when he'd finished?

Barford :

Yes. I spoke to the same man again and he confirmed that the job was on. I could give Lennox the money, but make clear to Lennox that it wasn't worth the candle for him to cut and run. The job had to be done. When he'd got the diary he had to burn it.

Cadogan :

Did you make all of that clear?

Barford :

Oh yes. In language Lennox well understood. And I gave him the five grand.

Cadogan :

Is it therefore any surprise that your fingerprints are on those notes and the betting slip?

Barford :
Of course not.

Cadogan :
How do you describe your role?

Barford :
I was a messenger. The message was to steal a diary. Full stop.

Cadogan :

In his deathbed confession, Lennox claimed you gave him the instructions to commit the offence of murder. True or untrue?

Barford :

Untrue.

Cadogan :

Lennox further alleged that you gave him details of the London address and the code to the lock of the basement car park of that building. True or untrue?

Barford :

Completely untrue.

Cadogan :

He alleges you gave him £5000 to murder and he complained that it should have been more.

Barford :

Untrue.

Cadogan :

Did you have any idea at all that the mission Lennox was embarking upon was a mission to murder?

Barford :

Absolutely not. I understood he had to break into a private address to steal a diary or something like that. Unattractive of course, but with real security justification. No question of any violence of any kind.

Cadogan :

From all that you know now can you say who it was who gave Lennox instructions to kill?

Barford :

Of course. It's now as plain as a pikestaff. The man on the barge.

Cadogan :

You have said that the man you met on the barge gave you a telephone number to contact him on.

Barford :

Yes.

Cadogan :

And you had phoned to confirm that you'd found someone. Was the man you spoke to on the phone the same man that you had met on the barge?

Barford :

Undoubtedly.

Cadogan :

Then you phoned again from the Leicester Betting Shop?

Barford :

Yes.

Cadogan :

Same number?

Barford :

Yes. Same number. Same man.

Cadogan :

Then you handed the phone to Lennox, placed your bet, and then took the phone back off Lennox?

Barford :

Yes. Same man again.

Cadogan :
Please describe him.

Barford :
Six three. Maybe six four. Stooped. Just short of forty, I'd say. Dark hair. Dark complexion. Poor teeth, I remember that, crooked.

Cadogan :
One final question, Mr Barford. The man you met on the barge and spoke to on the phone. Did he give you a name?

Barford :
Oh yes. Chief Superintendent Ray Leadbetter.

Cadogan :
Thank you, Mr Barford. I have no more questions of you.

Mr Justice Maullin :
Miss Nicholas, it's slightly early for lunch, but it is a convenient point to break off. Your cross-examination will start at two o' clock. The Court is adjourned until then.

As the Judge withdrew from Court, Naomi turned round and smiled at Myott before whispering :

"There you have it, Mike. A virtuoso performance. Music by Cadogan. Words by Cadogan. Conducted by Cadogan. What you eavesdropped begins to take shape. 'The Leadbetter-duped-me Defence'. Vintage Cadogan."

"I'm glad it's you that's got to cross-examine him and not me," Myott answered back. "He makes it all sound so bloody plausible."

"But he's lying. And lying hard. And this is one area of the case that Cadogan can't control. Cross-examination of his client. This is when even Cadogan is vulnerable," she responded, picking up her notebook to review her notes of Barford's evidence-in-chief over lunch, before sweeping out of Court with Myott following in her wake and Brockley and Mel behind Myott.

185

Cadogan had lingered, trying to pick up what passed between his two opponents, but Naomi was too smart for that. As soon as they had left the Courtroom he instantly turned to Stapleton, who stood anxiously awaiting the inevitable question :

"Well, snapped his Leader. Did you earn your corn?"

"Without a doubt. And Myott immediately hurried off to the Conference Room where she works before Court," came the obedient reply.

"Excellent," observed Cadogan. "She's a QC now. They pay her to make the big decisions. What fun this all is. Look after my papers over lunch, Stapleton, I don't want there to be any risk of someone taking a peek at them," he added as he wandered away towards the door.

Wandering nonchalantly through the doors into the Main Hall, he gave the impression of a man who didn't have a care in the world. Standing to his right were his two opponents plus Brockley and Mel together with the strong, imposing figure of Jack Farnham, who had obviously arrived in the building just as Naomi and Myott were emerging from the Courtroom.

"It's football's yesterday man, isn't it?" he called across. "Our paths haven't crossed since Leeds."

"Still as charming as ever then, Cadogan?" Jack replied. "I'd hate to think that you'd improved with age."

"Elland Road, wasn't it? Leeds and Bayern Munich, if I remember correctly," Cadogan observed, walking over to the group.

"Yes. You were doing a spot of pimping for one of your German pals," answered Jack, referring to the confrontation that had occurred in the Directors' Bar, when Cadogan had encouraged a drunken German to make a play for Naomi.

"Well, she'll be easier to sell now she's got QC after her name, won't she?" sniped Cadogan. "So glad to see you're still together. Must dash."

"What was all that about then?" exclaimed Mel incredulously, as the enormous figure disappeared slowly in the direction of the Coffee Shop.

"There's a history there," replied Naomi angrily. "Forget him. Let me introduce you all to Jack Farnham. Jack, this is my Junior, Mike

Myott, Giles Brockley from the DPP's Office and Mel Coleman who gets every word down on his laptop for me."

"How do you do, Mike, Giles, Mel," said Jack, shaking hands with each of them in turn. "I hope you're all protecting Naomi from the Wicked Giant."

"She's well able to look after herself. She doesn't need us," replied Myott.

"I'm afraid that I've got work to do Jack, and the Judge is resuming at two," Naomi interjected. "I can't stop for lunch. We're faced with a critical decision. I'll try to defer making it until tomorrow morning because I'd value your opinion on it, but I might have to make it this afternoon. And I've got to check my notes before I cross-examine Barford."

"Fine. See you back at the hotel this evening. We can discuss it then if you haven't been forced to decide this afternoon," Jack replied.

"Why don't you take Mike for a coffee and have a chat for a bit," Naomi suggested. "I need some time on my own. Come and join me in half an hour, Mike. I want your view on this. You can fill Jack in on what you told me you'd overheard this morning."

"Is it OK if Mel and I disappear and have some lunch then?" enquired Brockley.

"Of course," replied Naomi. "See you this afternoon."

Half an hour later, when Myott rejoined her in the Conference Room, Naomi had her shoes off, her feet on the table, her brow furrowed in concentration and her eyes tightly closed.

"So do we try to call Leadbetter in rebuttal or not?" Myott began.

"Cadogan has been ominously restrained so far," she replied quietly. "There's no way he'll finish this case without trying to pull a fast one. It's the nature of the beast. This could well be it."

"I tell you, Naomi, neither Stapleton nor Bloom had the slightest idea I was there. The Robing Room was deserted. I'd been in there for an hour before they walked in. Neither of them came anywhere near that end of the room. They couldn't have seen me," he insisted.

"Have you worked in that alcove before during the trial?"

"Yes. But I don't believe that Stapleton has ever noticed me there and Bloom hasn't been in the Robing Room at all before this morning."

"It still bears all the hallmarks of a Cadogan ploy. Designed to incite me to call Leadbetter. It smells like a bluff, it feels like a bluff," she declared, opening her eyes and staring intently at her Junior before adding the killer question. "Or is it a double bluff?"

"What exactly do you mean?"

"We'll have to take a look at the Law governing the Prosecution calling evidence in rebuttal after a Defendant has given evidence. But, given that Barford has already intimated that Leadbetter is the true culprit, Cadogan may conclude that I'm bound to ask the Judge for leave to call Leadbetter in rebuttal, so that the jury can hear Leadbetter say it's nonsense."

"Yes, I follow you so far."

"Well, if that is Cadogan's conclusion and he genuinely is frightened of us calling Leadbetter, then he would try to get a message to me that he doesn't want him called. He knows I will think that he really wants the exact opposite of what he says."

"You mean Cadogan believes that by saying he is frightened of you calling Leadbetter, you will think that he really does want him called. And therefore you won't call him."

"Yes. The double bluff. He's that bloody cunning, I can assure you."

"It's pretty subtle stuff to base a defence on. Where his client goes down for life if he gets it wrong."

"The higher the stakes, the more he enjoys running the risk. We'll have to see what I get out of Barford in cross-examination on the topic of Leadbetter. Then I need time to think. Come on, it's five to two."

Chapter 28

R v Lewis Barford
Transcript 63

Nicholas :
Mr Barford, you have travelled from the hard streets of a Huyton council estate to the edges of Government?

Barford :
In a sense I have.

Nicholas :
Via Oxford, Warsaw, Bucharest, Helsinki and Sierra Leone. And you have lived amongst, indeed led, hard and sometimes desperate men?

Barford :
I have.

Nicholas :
Leading them whilst at the same time deceiving them? You were not a genuine mercenary, were you? You were a Government plant? Hoping to protect British mineral rights and British plunder. You weren't there for the reasons that you pretended to your men, were you?

Barford :
No.

Nicholas :
At other times you've lived amongst scholars and in more recent years have you spent most of your working life with high level Department Officials? Going as high as Ministerial level?

Barford :
Yes.

Nicholas :
But despite this extensive, sometimes tough, often high-level experience, is it your claim that you were duped?

Barford :
I was used.

Nicholas :
So is it your defence that Lennox, a Scottish itinerant, a thug and a thief, had the capacity to deceive you, a man with the experiences I have just summarised, into thinking he was up to a spot of domestic burglary, when, in fact, you had just connected him to a murder mission?

Barford :
I was duped, as you call it, at a higher level. All Lennox had to do was take the money and leave. He did deceive me by saying nothing to me. But he was good at saying nothing. That's why I chose him for the burglary.

Nicholas :
Lennox did not deceive you at all, did he? He complained that a topping was worth more than five grand, calling you a mean bastard?

Barford :
That's how he spoke. But it had nothing to do with payment for a murder.

Nicholas :
Was he complaining that five grand was mean for a burglary, then?

Barford :
Presumably.

Nicholas :
Did you think five thousand pounds was the going rate for a burglary?

Barford :
I had no idea.

Nicholas :
You knew it was cheap for a murder though, didn't you?

Barford :
I had no idea.

Nicholas :
But I suggest that you knew your man. It was £5000 plus some valuables of the burglar's choosing. That's why you said "You'll nick plenty on top," isn't that right?

Barford :
I never said that.

Nicholas :
You knew Lennox. Your account is that you chose him on behalf of the authorities to carry out a sensitive burglary. From all that you knew of him, did you expect him to steal only the diary?

Barford :
Probably not. He was a cunning man. But the chances of him being caught were almost zero. And if he was caught he was unlikely to talk.

Nicholas :
Do you say that, once he had stolen the diary, he could be trusted to destroy it?

Barford :
Yes. He'd got his £5000. Plus whatever else he may have stolen. I would have expected him to destroy it, if that was the instruction.

Nicholas :
Is not the truth that you had no idea that there was a diary? This mission had nothing to do with a diary. It was a mission to kill. The existence of the diary only became known after Lennox's deathbed confession.

Barford :
Untrue.

Nicholas :
I put it to you that the diary had nothing to do with this mission. You knew nothing about any diary at that time. You were hiring a hit man.

Barford :
No.

Nicholas :
So you claim that Lennox lent himself to the deceit and that Leadbetter set it up?

Barford :
Yes.

Nicholas :
You said in evidence that when the Police read out Lennox's confessions you then realised what had happened? So why didn't you tell the Police the truth?

Barford :
I explained. I was dealing with high level subterfuge. They would deny meeting me.

Nicholas :
Why do you say 'they'?

Barford :
That is figurative. I mean the representative at that level. Leadbetter.

Nicholas :
So?

Barford :
So I saw it as my word against a dead man's. You heard what I said about that earlier.

Nicholas :
Did lying come easily to your lips in those circumstances?

Barford :
No. I found it most distasteful. And I recognise that it was a mistake.

Nicholas :
You're still lying now, aren't you?

Barford :
No.

Nicholas :
What operations had Lennox carried out for you in Sierra Leone?

Barford :
He was involved in an incident on the Guinea border. A rebel had caused some damage in a village there. We sent Lennox in to arrest him and there was some kind of struggle. The rebel escaped. Lennox made it back to our camp.

Nicholas :
Was the rebel ever heard of again?

Barford :
I think we heard some time later that he'd been killed by a mercenary group further south.

Nicholas :
You think?

Barford :

It's ten years ago. Communications were bad at the time anyway.

Nicholas :

Are you telling us the truth?

Barford :

Of course.

Nicholas :

It wouldn't be the case that in Sierra Leone you learned that Lennox was capable of extreme violence and would have no compunction about killing? Indeed, he relished violence? And that is why you recruited him? A man of violence for a mission of violence?

Barford :

Untrue.

Nicholas :

Going back to the barge. I asked you earlier about Ministerial contact. Did you tell any Minister that you were having this meeting?

Barford :

No.

Nicholas :

Did you tell any Minister after the meeting that it had taken place?

Barford :

I do not recollect doing so prior to my arrest, no.

Nicholas :

Is there a record that can be checked to verify that?

Barford :

You'd have to ask the Home Office.

Nicholas :
I'm asking you.

Barford :
I'm not aware of any such record.

Nicholas :
If you, as a Political Adviser, were approving a burglary of private premises, albeit for purposes of safeguarding an important criminal trial, would you not, in turn, require the approval of the Minister?

Barford :
Debatable.

Nicholas :
So if the burglar had been caught red-handed and had said "Lewis Barford, attached to the Home Office, put me up to this," what would you expect your Minister to say to you?

Barford :
He'd be furious.

Nicholas :
Unless he had given you his authority to act in any such way as you thought fit?

Barford :
Yes.

Nicholas :
Then he would have to resign wouldn't he?

Barford :
I can't answer that?

Nicholas :

Why not? If a Minister gave you authority to use any means, including burglary of an innocent man's home, to achieve a security objective, and that got into the public domain, is that not unequivocally a resigning matter?

Barford :

Probably.

Nicholas :

You're a Political Adviser. Who better to ask?

Barford :

The Minister himself.

Nicholas :

I suggest that you are unable to call the Minister to give evidence. Because if he says he was aware that you were authorising burglary he would have to resign. On the other hand, I suggest that if you were authorising burglary you would have sought approval. And, on your present account you didn't seek approval for burglary, did you?

Barford :

No.

Nicholas :

So the Minister can't help you? Or can he?

Barford :

Speculative nonsense.

Nicholas :

Weren't you on good terms with the Minister? Not only a professional relationship but also long-standing friends?

Barford :
We did not socialise together.

Nicholas :
Weren't you contemporaries at Oxford?

Barford :
So what?

Nicholas :
I suggest that you knew him very well. I suggest that if you were engaged in a plan, for security purposes, to have a diary stolen, you would have consulted him.

Barford :
That isn't how it worked.

Nicholas :
On your version you were recommending a burglar?

Barford :
In crude terms. Yes.

Nicholas :
On your version Leadbetter must have been looking for a murderer?

Barford :
Yes. Unknown to me, though.

Nicholas :
But how could it be that in seeking a recommendation from you for a burglar, you managed to come up with a man who would murder?

Barford :
I don't know.

Nicholas :

On your version the only contact between Leadbetter and Lennox was one short conversation on your phone in the Leicester Betting Shop?

Barford :

Yes.

Nicholas :

About, as you understood it, five thousand pounds to steal a diary?

Barford :

Yes.

Nicholas :

Are you suggesting that in that short call, a man you had recommended for burglary, was persuaded to murder?

Barford :

He must have been.

Nicholas :

It must have been an inspired choice by you then, to pick a burglar who, at the drop of a hat, agrees to murder?

Barford :

I knew nothing of a plan to murder. As to Lennox's propensity for violence you must remember a number of the men in Central Africa were capable of violence. The pool from which I can draw for security purposes is murky. Murky characters. Stealing. Violence.

Nicholas :

And out of the murky waters, on the hook at the end of your line, came Derek Lennox?

Barford :

Yes. But I, in turn, had been hooked by Leadbetter.

Nicholas :

Who you now say must have issued the directive to kill?

Barford :

Correct.

Nicholas :

Then what possible reason could exist for Lennox, on his deathbed, to allege that you were the man who gave him the instructions to murder?

Barford :

I've asked myself that very question many times. That question is at the heart of this case.

Nicholas :

By doing that, didn't Lennox ensure that the man who you say really gave him instructions to kill, namely Leadbetter, would never be caught?

Barford :

Probably.

Nicholas :

And, in letting the real culprit escape, Lennox put you at risk of a conviction for conspiracy to murder? You, a man who had nothing to do with murder at all?

Barford :

Yes. I've thought hard about that aspect of it. You need to understand how a man like Lennox thinks. He was not seeking redemption as he faced death. This was an embittered man seeking his final revenge. Striking back at the system. I never mentioned Leadbetter's name to Lennox. Leadbetter wouldn't have given Lennox his name in that call. Lennox only had my name. He needed a name to blame.

Nicholas :

Why does any of that make him falsely accuse you?

Barford :

Without a name for the man on the phone, I was the perfect choice. I represented what Lennox despised. Not only did he see me as part of authority, part of the system, he knew that, like him, I came from the gutter. But I'd made it. I'd joined "them". Lennox's self-justification for a life of failure was that he'd come from the gutter. My success destroyed his excuse. If his dying words sent me to prison, he'd feel that he'd won in the end.

Nicholas :

Did you read the copy of Ibrahim El-Hoorie's Journal that was sent to the Defence?

Barford :

I did. Mr Cadogan and Mr Bloom explained only small parts of it were admissible.

Nicholas :

El-Hoorie mentioned Leadbetter's name in that diary, didn't he?

Barford :

Yes. He was one of the officers who'd had dealings with El-Hoorie.

Nicholas :

So Lennox did have a name. Leadbetter?

Barford :

Yes, but in a different context. Taking a statement off El-Hoorie. Showing him Yassin. That name in that context was worthless to Lennox. He wouldn't have known that Leadbetter was the man to whom he spoke on the phone.

Nicholas :

But the name wasn't worthless to you, was it?

Barford :
No. Because I knew the full story.

Nicholas :
Haven't you chosen Leadbetter's name because you knew he was involved in the overall enquiry at a high level?

Barford :
No. I met him about this matter. On the barge, as I've explained.

Nicholas :
I suggest that you recruited Lennox specifically to kill because you knew, through sources that have nothing to do with Leadbetter, that there was a real risk of El-Hoorie going to the Press with a story that would do grave damage to the authorities.

Barford :
My source for everything that I learned about this including references to the Press was Leadbetter. And only Leadbetter.

Nicholas :
Yet you never breathed a word about Leadbetter from beginning to end of your Police interview?

Barford :
I didn't.

Nicholas :
I suggest you didn't because you hadn't invented that line of defence at that stage. You've invented it at a later stage, haven't you? Or has someone else invented it for you?

Barford :
It's not invented by anyone. It's the truth.

Nicholas :

You had many means at your disposal to access the files on Leadbetter? You are attached to the Home Office. Leadbetter's name was in El-Hoorie's diary. You could look Leadbetter's files up without difficulty and see photographs. That's how you are able to give an accurate description of him.

Barford :

I knew because I met him. On a barge.

Nicholas :

Why didn't you ask to see the Police again and tell them what you now claim Leadbetter did?

Barford :

The Police doing a number on one of their own? Do me a favour.

Nicholas :

You hired a hit man.

Barford :

Untrue.

Mr Justice Maullin :

Do you have any re-examination, Mr Cadogan?

Cadogan :

Yes, My Lord. Just one question. Mr Barford, you were asked if you were aware of the risk of revelations to the Press. Did you have a specific part of the Press in mind?

Barford :

A very specific part. I believed that Leadbetter had reason to be concerned about a particular journalist. This journalist enjoys a "publish and be damned reputation." A trial could easily be compromised by him. He is known as "The Molecule Man".

Mr Justice Maullin :

Members of the jury. There is a matter I wish to raise with Counsel which need not concern you.

[Jury leave Court]

Mr Justice Maullin :

Miss Nicholas, would I be right in anticipating that you may wish to raise the question of calling evidence in rebuttal?

Nicholas :

Yes. I wish to consider whether or not I am going to ask Your Lordship for leave to call certain evidence in rebuttal. Evidence which may challenge the Defendant's account that Leadbetter was behind this crime.

Mr Justice Maullin :

Yes, as I thought. But do I infer from your answer that you have not yet made up your mind?

Nicholas :

Correct, My Lord. As Your Lordship knows we do have a Witness Statement from Chief Superintendent Leadbetter. It formed no part of the Prosecution evidence against Barford. It was in the papers as Unused Material. The Defence have a copy. It simply sets out Leadbetter's dealings with El-Hoorie on the night that the plane was shot down.

Mr Justice Maullin :

Does it state whether Leadbetter had any dealings with El-Hoorie other than in the hours immediately after the terrorist attack?

Nicholas :

It does. He had no further dealings. He states that shortly prior to trial, when El-Hoorie learned that he was not going to be called as a witness in the Yassin trial, Leadbetter was informed of El-Hoorie's disquiet, but that is all.

Mr Justice Maullin :

I see. Does Leadbetter state that he had ever met Barford?

Nicholas :

He makes no reference to meeting Barford anywhere, let alone on a barge. The Defendant's allegations against Leadbetter, raised now as the cornerstone of his defence to the charge, have only surfaced since he went into the witness box. I wish to consider whether to ask for leave to call Leadbetter.

Mr Justice Maullin :

I understand. A perfectly reasonable position in the circumstances. No doubt Mr. Cadogan has a view about all of this.

Cadogan :

Yes, My Lord, I do. This decision should be made now. It is only just after half past three. My learned friend for the Crown should be obliged to make her mind up now and the case should move on accordingly.

Mr Justice Maullin :

Do I take it that if Miss Nicholas applies for leave to call Leadbetter in rebuttal then you will be objecting to her application?

Cadogan :

With respect, My Lord, I cannot be invited to answer a hypothetical question. Your Lordship may nevertheless conclude that I am unlikely to be enthusiastic about evidence being called at this stage which may damage my client's case.

Mr Justice Maullin :

I am of a mind to rise for the day. Miss Nicholas may announce her position in the morning.

Cadogan :

Yesterday, at five minutes past four, Your Lordship insisted that I proceed to call my client into the witness box, despite my request to wait until the morning. Today, at three thirty-five, Your Lordship is allowing the Prosecution to defer their position until tomorrow. I respectfully submit that the same approach should apply to both sides. Miss Nicholas should announce her position now. We have over forty minutes of sitting time left.

Mr Justice Maullin :
I am against you, Mr Cadogan. Miss Nicholas's decision is a difficult one and has only emerged today. Your analogy is without merit. The jury will be told that the case has been adjourned until ten thirty tomorrow.

Chapter 29

"Mr Brockley, Mike, I'd like to see you both in the Conference Room immediately. Mel, this is a confidential matter, so I'm afraid you'll have to excuse us," announced Leading Counsel for the Crown.

"Right, Miss Nicholas," Coleman replied. Mr Myott has kindly offered to buy me a quick drink before I go home, so I'll wait in the Main Hall."

Five minutes later she sat at the battered table with the two men opposite her. Whilst she would eventually come to her own decision, both Junior Counsel and her instructing solicitor had a right to express an opinion and now was the time.

"Very well, Mr Brockley. You've seen the contents of Leadbetter's statement. Do we have any information or any reason to fear that a Chief Superintendent in Special Branch has lied in that statement?" she began.

"Not that I'm aware of, Miss Nicholas. On the face of the statement he had little if anything to say that had any bearing on Barford's position," the young solicitor replied nervously.

"Right. The decision whether I apply to call Leadbetter is ultimately mine. However, I believe that every member of the team has a right to express their view. Are you in favour or against the application to call Leadbetter, Mr. Brockley?"

Now shifting uncomfortably in his seat, Brockley looked down at the ground. Naomi had realised from the moment she'd met him that he was a complete wimp, obviously put up by the Prosecution to do as he was told from above and provide her with no help.

"I'm not sure on this one," he eventually mumbled. "Not sure at all."

"Have a go," she urged.

"Fifty-fifty. Fifty-fifty," he answered, unable to look her in the eye.

"And you, Mike?" she asked, turning away from the weakling.

"As you know, Naomi, I've reason to believe that Cadogan is extremely worried that you may apply to call Leadbetter. If you call Leadbetter and he is believed then Barford's defence is destroyed. We've no reason to suppose that Leadbetter is a liar. I believe in going for the jugular. Go for it," came Myott's response.

Naomi eyes were fixed on Myott as he delivered his judgement on the question and, when she spoke, her tone revealed her surprise at his decisiveness.

"No messing with you, is there, Mike, no messing at all?" she began. "OK. I'll meet you both in this room in the morning. I'll be here from eight-thirty onwards. Here's what we'll do. Mr Brockley, do you have a notebook handy?" she enquired.

"Yes," he replied, scrabbling in his thin briefcase.

"Write this down then please. You are to arrange for Chief Superintendent Leadbetter to be here at eight-thirty tomorrow morning. You can speak to him. As Counsel we should not. You will show him a copy of his statement and invite him to read it through with care. You will then ask him these questions. I shall dictate them so that there's no room for error. Are you ready?"

"Yes."

"One. Is that statement true?

Two, does he have anything to add to it which may have any bearing on the case against Barford?

Three, has he ever met Barford on a barge?

Four, has he ever met Barford at all?

Five, did he instruct Barford to find a man to steal a diary?

Six, did he ever speak to a man called Lennox?

Seven, did he ever speak to anyone and give them instructions to kill El-Hoorie?

Have you got all of that down?"

"Just about."

"You'll meet me here in this room as soon as you have the answers. I'll have made a decision in principle, subject to the answers you obtain. Do you understand?"

"I do."

"Thank you, Mr Brockley. I just want a quick word with Mr Myott. There's no need for you to stay."

"Good afternoon, Miss," Brockley mumbled as he hurriedly stuffed the notebook back in his otherwise empty briefcase and left the room. He didn't like this one little bit. His instructions from above had been to do as little as possible. They'd given her an assistant to type the notes of evidence for her every day. What more did she want? Now she was making heavy demands. Tomorrow promised to be a very difficult day."

"I have one question for you, Mike, before we go," she said.

"You're going to ask me what I made of Cadogan's evasive reply to the Judge's question about whether he would object to you trying to call Leadbetter, aren't you," he stated.

"No. I'm not. I'm asking you what work were you doing in the Robing Room that kept you so busy in that alcove for an hour before you eavesdropped on Stapleton and Bloom this morning?" came the unexpected enquiry from Naomi, studying him carefully as she awaited his answer.

There was a pause before he replied. "Checking yesterday's notes. Jotting down a few ideas for cross examination of Barford. That kind of thing."

"You didn't offer me any ideas you'd had though, did you?"

"No. They weren't very good ideas, that's why. You'd thought of lots of angles in cross-examining him that had never even occurred to me," he answered, smiling uneasily, as her intense scrutiny of his face continued.

But she didn't smile back.

Chapter 30

Back in the sittingroom of their suite there was a note for her on the coffee table in which Jack said he was downstairs in the Symphony Bar having a drink with Ben Railey and they would wait for her to join them. Ten minutes in the power shower, with steaming hot water blasting down on her, quickly washed away the mental and physical grime of doing business with Cadogan all day. At least with Cadogan she knew that he would fight dirty. More puzzling was the true position of her Junior and, to a lesser extent, Brockley. The Establishment's obvious lack of enthusiasm to secure the conviction of Barford probably explained the pitiful Brockley being offered as a feeble representative of the Prosecuting Authorities whilst pretending to be helpful by providing her with a note-taker and dogsbody in the form of Coleman, but she found the role of Myott far more enigmatic. Something about him didn't ring true and she found herself wondering whether he had truly overheard any conversation between Stapleton and Bloom. It all seemed so convenient and Cadogan's sphere of influence was extensive. Often when he had spoken to her Myott had imitated the voices of people he was describing, with no mean degree of skill but somehow, as a barrister, he appeared lightweight. Paradoxically, in the discussion at the end of the day, Myott had been strong in his opinion and absolutely decisive.

With her blonde hair now loose and free, sporting a new sky-blue lace blouse that Jack hadn't seen before and designer jeans with knife edge creases, she set off for the bar. Ben Railey made his money as a comedian in the Clubs. Cheeky-faced, outrageously rude, very loud and extremely funny. But, above all else in this life, he was an Everton supporter, which is how he had met Jack many years ago. According to Jack, he had been a moderately good player himself and might have made it professionally in the lower divisions but, in the end, the money available on the Night Clubs circuit had lured him away from the game. Late nights, heavy drinking sessions and years of performing in smoke-filled rooms, had taken their toll and he was now overweight and podgy, but as loveable as ever.

"I hear you're a Quality Controller now," had been his opening gambit on seeing her as she walked into the crowded bar, turning heads as she approached the corner table, occupied by the two men.

"No, Ben. QC means Queen's Counsel, as you well know," she answered, as he kissed her noisily and enthusiastically on both cheeks. He was a very physical person which was one of the reasons why there were already four ex-Mrs Raileys and no current model.

"Jack tells me you're performing at the Bailey," he continued in his broad Scouse accent, while Jack ordered a fresh round of drinks.

"I'm thinking of taking your job up," he continued without pausing for breath. "Then I'll be known as Railey of the Bailey. Ma wanted to call me Diz, you know. Then I'd have been Diz Railey of the Bailey," he bellowed. One of Ben's uncontrollable faults was that, funny though he was, he couldn't stop himself laughing at his own jokes. Often, he was laughing so hard at the joke he had just told, that he couldn't finish the one he had moved on to.

Over the years, Jack had learned just to sit back and let Ben perform his act. There would be a barrage of jokes, all of which resulted in Ben dissolving helplessly in laughter and then, quite suddenly, he would take a break. The length of the break depended on his mood, his alcohol level and the current state of his love-life. Sometimes the break lasted five minutes, sometimes an hour, but seldom longer. It was during these breaks that Jack and Ben would talk football and there was, quite simply, nothing that Ben did not know about Everton Football Club.

"Ben's one of my guests on the show on Saturday," Jack explained. "It's the Everton-Liverpool derby that day. We've just been talking it through."

"Liverpool offered Cinderella a trial. She turned 'em down though, didn't think she'd get to the ball," he roared, rolling back into his chair in delight "Have you done any cases up in Liverpool, sweetheart? A jury of scousers. So long as you were defending you couldn't lose, could you? Except your wig. They'd pinch that off you while you weren't looking," he chuckled.

"How did you get on in Court?" asked Jack.

"Long story. We'll talk over dinner. Are you joining us for dinner, Ben?"

"Can't darling. Got to dash. Send my regards to the old Judge," he added, knocking back the newly-arrived whisky in one hit whilst easing his portly figure out of the chair at the same time. "It's not fair, Naomi, ninety-nine per cent of lawyers give the rest a bad name," he shouted as he negotiated his slightly unsteady way across the room, still laughing hilariously at his own joke as he disappeared through the door.

"A breath of fresh air. Lifted my spirits in five minutes flat," Naomi remarked. "Did Myott tell you the dilemma?"

"Yes. Part of it anyway. I can't say I took to him. Gregarious. Pleasant on the surface. But I got the impression he wasn't all he seemed."

"Odd you should say that. I even found myself wondering if he'd really heard what he claimed. Anyway, do I try to call Leadbetter or not? I might as well get your verdict now. Otherwise we'll spoil dinner talking about it."

"From the facts Myott gave me I'd look at it this way. Make your decision exclusively on the merits of what Leadbetter can do for the Prosecution case. Forget what Myott said he heard. Assuming you have no reason to believe what Barford alleges against Leadbetter, then he'll destroy the Defence case."

"I won't know until the morning exactly what Leadbetter says or if he's backing off in any way. If he isn't, then I'm inclined to give it a shot."

"There used to be a couple of Managers who often named a team omitting their best players. Wanted us to spend all week planning our tactics on a false basis. Half an hour before kick-off the best players were back in the team. A week's planning out the window. No game plan. So we learned. Never base your plan on what the opposition says. Base it on your own strengths. Same here, if you ask me."

"Your football analogies have a habit of working out. I'll call him, subject to bad news in the morning. Let's eat and talk about anything other than lawyers. Like Ben said, it's the ninety-nine per cent that give the rest a bad name," she laughed.

Having Jack at her side gave her such confidence. His unassuming strength was her greatest support. For the rest of the evening and night Cadogan, Myott, Barford were despatched to another planet while she and Jack Farnham dined together and then wandered slowly, arm in arm, through a small riverside park where once, Hungarian magic had filled the air.

Chapter 31

Tomorrow was the last day of the Davos Conference. The wind had abruptly switched direction this morning, bringing noticeably warmer air from the South. Soon the snow would have disappeared entirely from the lower slopes and the season would change. Rebirth. Fresh hopes and aspirations. If only this wretched trial would finish and the dust could start to settle. His private engagement would take him to Lucerne tomorrow evening and then a flight home on Thursday. The daily reports indicated that it should finish by Tuesday at the latest. Wednesday's papers would be better avoided and then, by Thursday, the fresh hopes. Move on. In the meanwhile, Lucerne promised some light relief.

He'd met Bill Wedderley, as he then was, at Merton. Committed Trotskyite. They'd marched together several times. Templar could remember the first time as clearly as if it had happened yesterday. The Government was intending to introduce more stringent immigration controls so Wedderley had arranged eight coachloads of protesters from Oxford alone. Down to London. Along the Mall and up to Whitehall with Wedderley at the head of the March and Templar on his shoulder, screaming abuse at the Police and spitting venom in the direction of the House of Commons. Later, under cover of darkness, Wedderley had put a brick through the windscreen of a Police van before scurrying away into the night. Templar had observed this particular episode from his usual discreet and cowardly distance, but had ensured that he had been the first to congratulate Wedderley on the achievement.

Now, here they were, forty years on. Templar was a Minister of State and Wedderley, after years of incredible fortune in industry, had somehow inveigled his way into the Chairmanship of one of the largest communications companies in the country. Under his aegis, the profits had slumped, the shareholders had been impoverished, the customers had been fleeced and the Directors' salaries and pensions had soared into the stratosphere. Hanging on to his job with a resolve as formidable as that he'd shown when he was decrying capitalism, his wealth had mushroomed until, eventually last year, accepting that all good things must come to an end, he'd trousered a ten million pound golden handshake and retired to Lucerne with the peerage that Denstone had bestowed upon him in exchange for donations to the Party. So Will Templar was to be the house guest of Lord and Lady Wedderley in their nine-bedroomed, ten-bathroomed mansion overlooking the eastern edge of the lake. It promised to be an excellent few days. Hypocrites United.

Right on time the mobile rang. Daily Report time.

"Yes," Templar said.

"Rather an uncomfortable day, I'm afraid," the metallic voice declared ominously. "She did him a considerable amount of damage."

"Did he hold the line?" asked the Minister. "No ship-jumping?"

"No. But she pushed him hard on his contact with you. Very hard as a matter of fact. Oxford. Resigning matter if you knew. Unable to call you. All that kind of stuff," reported the detached, cold voice.

"Damn. Worse than I feared. But he resisted, you say?" Templar responded, his voice low and subdued. They'd taught him that when you were badly shaken if you forced the voice down half an octave and spoke quietly, then the tremor was more easily controlled. Deep breaths. Terrified at what might be coming next.

"He did the best he could in the circumstances. But there's a twist. Seems she may call the tall, thin one. All kinds of games being played by RC. Referee called foul. But the bottom line is that she's showing interest in the tall, thin one making a guest appearance."

"You will use all means at your disposal to prevent that, do you understand?" exploded the Minister, forgetting the lessons in voice control, as the tone bordered on panic. "We don't know which way he'll jump if the net closes. You stop him."

"I have no control over RC. He's doing what he's paid for. Trying to win. She's making more of a fist of it than we were led to believe."

"Tomorrow morning you'll speak to those behind her. The message is that under no circumstances does she call him. We can't have the same confidence in him as we do in someone who comes from my Department.

It's not up for negotiation," barked Templar, the sweat now running freely down his face, as his eyes darted left and right and that cursed tic in his left cheek started up again.

214

"I'll do what I can, but these affairs develop a momentum of their own, you know," came the reply.

"I demand more than that. I demand that you take control. Deal with it," he shouted.

"I'll go there in the morning. Speak to who I can. Got to be careful."

"I've seen the Press Reports. Could have been worse. Off the front pages in most. Except for the bastard. His report has been front page all week," Templar remarked.

"Yes. But restrained. He's waiting for the final outcome before he really lets fly."

"Exactly. Everything depends on the final outcome. If it goes our way then the evidence will have been shown to be unreliable. The spinners will be able to handle that. It's if it goes the other way that spells disaster. That's why you take control. She doesn't call him," declared Templar, his voice getting increasingly agitated.

"I have got your message. I'll go. I didn't want to, but it'll have more impact if I'm right there."

"Call me. With the right result," the Home Secretary snapped, breaking the connection.

Chapter 32

Crammed into the packed carriage of the Central Line, his thin, plastic briefcase clutched to his puny chest, Giles Brockley contemplated his lot. How he detested the Law and, most of all, the people in it. He'd never wanted to be a Solicitor but his domineering father had put the pressure on and, somehow, he'd survived the exams and articles, only to find that his unimpressive CV and even more unimpressive persona, weren't attracting any job offers until this opening in the Great Prosecuting Department appeared. Slotted into some mystical hierarchical scheme that he would never understand, answerable to commands despatched by internal email and faceless superiors, he found himself sitting behind Counsel in Courts far from home, doing precisely nothing, save making up the numbers.

Then, they'd allocated him to the Barford case, with instructions over the phone from an unidentified voice way on high, to let it run its course to inevitable acquittal and to do nothing to make that result less likely. The last piece of the jigsaw had fitted neatly in when he met that old duffer Curbishley, who they'd instructed to lead for the Prosecution. This was plainly a case they were determined to lose for all kinds of political reasons in which Brockley had precisely no interest at all. Let them get on with it. But the new QC wasn't wearing it and, to make matters worse, she was actually involving him in the process, even asking for his opinion on such an important matter as whether or not to call a witness. No way was he getting involved. The sooner this morning was over the better, and he intended to keep his head down as low as possible.

By twenty past eight he was ensconced with Chief Superintendent Leadbetter in a CPS Room on the very top floor of the building, far away from the main thoroughfares and Courtrooms. Leadbetter had peered down at the weak face, accepted the limp handshake and jumped immediately to the right conclusion as to why this specimen had been put up for the job. The prospect of going into the witness box in this case appalled Leadbetter for he knew that telling the whole truth could only be catstrophic. The summons to attend had come like a bolt from the blue because the last he'd heard was that the Prosecution case had closed and that Barford had given evidence. The time when he might have been called had well passed and yet, last night, the phone had rung and the directive had been issued to attend.

"Why am I here?" he demanded aggressively. "I understood the Prosecution had closed their case."

"They're talking about calling you in rebuttal," Brockley replied, scrabbling in his briefcase for the piece of paper on which he'd written Naomi Nicholas's questions last night. "To rebut Barford's evidence."

"To rebut what specific details of Barford's evidence?"

"Well, he blames you. Said you met on a barge. You wanted a diary stolen, gave him £5000 to pay the thief. Then, on the phone, you must have told the man he found to do a murder, because Barford says he certainly didn't," Brockley explained hesitantly.

"That's the bastard's defence now is it? All down to me?" Leadbetter spat out.

"So you can see why they're talking about calling you in rebuttal, can't you?"

"Oh yes. It all becomes very clear now," he answered.

"I've got these questions here," Brockley continued, brandishing the piece of paper. "You've got to reread the statement you made. I've got that in here somewhere," he added, fumbling inside his briefcase again. "Yea, here it is. Read through that carefully. Then answer the questions."

Leadbetter sat himself down in the far corner of the room and slowly went through his earlier statement, then read it through again and then picked up and perused the written questions. Eventually he spoke :

"I've read all of that. You can have it all back."

"OK. Let me ask the questions and write down your answers. I'll give them to Counsel and they'll decide whether to call you."

"What if I don't want to answer them? What if I don't want to give evidence? What then?" Leadbetter snapped.

"I'd have to ask. I don't know. But surely you can answer the questions. They seemed pretty straightforward. Let's try anyway."

"Is the statement true?" Brockley began.

"Yes"

"Do you have anything to add to it which may have any bearing on the case against Barford?"

"Yes. He's a lying bastard."

"Have you ever met Barford on a barge?

"No."

"Have you ever met Barford at all?

"No."

"Did you instruct Barford to find a man to steal a diary?"

"No."

"Did you ever speak to a man called Lennox?"

"No."

"Did you ever speak to anyone and give them instructions to kill El-Hoorie?"

"Never."

"Thank you. I'll report to Counsel. If you'd stay up here it may be better," Brockley replied, gathering up his briefcase and papers before heading for the door.

"You tell the bloody lawyers I don't want to go near that witness box. What Barford did is his problem. I don't want to know."

Looking at his watch it was still only a quarter to nine, so he'd done his part rather efficiently he thought as he got the lift down to the floor where he'd arranged to meet Prosecuting Counsel. In the Conference Room she was alone, seated at the table, poring over her papers.

"I've got the answers for you," he declared immediately, handing her the piece of paper.

"Thank you," she replied, taking the sheet, reading from it and then announcing her decision. "Right. You may inform the Chief Superintendent that I shall be applying to call him to give evidence. You can also tell him that I expect my application to be successful so he'd better prepare himself for battle."

"He's not keen, I can tell you. He particularly said to tell you that he doesn't want to go near that witness box. He said what Barford did is his problem. He didn't want to know."

"I shouldn't think he does. But I'm trying to win the case. My decision is made. You'd best go tell him," she declared emphatically.

Setting off along the long corridor towards the lift, to take him back up to the top floor, a figure suddenly appeared, as if from nowhere, stepping straight into Brockley's path, causing him to stop abruptly.

"Are you Giles Brockley?" the silver-haired, slender figure barked.

"Yes" came the startled reply.

"We need to talk. I'm from one of the Security and Anti-Terrorist Units. Just step into one of these rooms for a moment, will you," the man announced, taking Brockley quite firmly by the arm and steering him into a small room off the corridor, which he had obviously commandeered, for his hat and coat were lying on the table.

Closing the door behind him he stood ramrod-straight, staring directly into Brockley's face.

"Is Leadbetter here?" he barked.

"He is, yes. But I really would like to know who you are. You could put me in a very awkward position," responded Brockley.

"I'm a Commander. In National Security. That's all you need to know. Question. Is she calling Leadbetter?" the Commander demanded to know.

Brockley found himself completely disconcerted. The stare was relentless and yet Brockley could not actually see the eyes under the lizard-like lids.

"Yes, she is," he obediently answered. "She's just made the decision."

"Right, Brockley," the almost metallic voice responded. "You get back in there and tell her to unmake it. Leadbetter does not give evidence."

"She won't change her mind. I've watched her. She's thought it through. Weighed it up. Without a very powerful reason she won't move," Brockley replied.

"There is a powerful reason. Me. I'm telling her not to call him. My instructions come from a very high place indeed. You tell her that. You tell her that this direction comes from the very top of Government. Have you understood me now, Brockley?"

"I understand. I'll tell her. But I doubt it'll make any difference," Brockley answered.

"Then you'd better make sure it does make a difference", he snarled. "That's your job. Now go and do it."

Scurrying out of the room and back down the corridor, he bumped into Mel Coleman, who was looking for Leading Counsel to give her the printed copy of yesterday's evidence.

"Got a bit of a crisis on, Mel. I'll give her the notes. You take yourself off for a coffee and meet me in Court at the kick-off," he mumbled hurriedly before continuing down the corridor.

Naomi Nicholas was still at the same table, reading over her notes as Brockley burst through the door. Myott had now joined her and was sitting in the corner of the room, with a text book open on his knee, no doubt researching the Law on rebuttal evidence.

"Sorry, Miss Nicholas," Brockley began, panting out of nervous reaction, rather than the speed of his retreat from the Commander.

"I think we'd better forget about calling Leadbetter."

"What are you talking about?" she asked.

"I've just been told that the authorities don't want him called."

"What is that supposed to mean?"

"There is a direction from the very top that you should not call him. The very top of Government. That's how it was just put to me," Brockley declared.

"By whom?"

"A man from an Anti-Terrorist Unit. Security. Intelligence. I don't know. Said he was a Commander. But a man with a message from the very top."

"Where is this man?"

"Here in the building. Obviously it's considered appropriate for me, as your instructing solicitor, to deliver the message. And I've delivered it."

"Who is said to be behind this message?" she asked.

"The top. The very top. That's what he kept repeating. Tell her this is a decision from the very top. Top of Government. As powerful a reason as she can get. No Leadbetter. That's it. Don't call him, Miss Nicholas. I'm giving you those instructions."

"I make my decisions on the merits of the case. Logic. The state of the evidence. Not ten minutes ago you were standing in this room informing me that Leadbetter stood by his statement and that Barford's defence was a tissue of lies. And that Leadbetter can say that from the witness box. Has any of that changed?"

"No."

"Right. I call him. Tell your Commander he has no status in this decision. Your instructions are based on a misconception of our relationship, Mr Brockley. I'm calling him. I suggest you report back. Immediately," she ordered. "Unless you've anything to say, Mike."

"Yes, I have as a matter of fact. I'd tell this Commander to go stuff himself. You can tell him I said that if you like. You can tell him that's a direction from the very bottom," Myott said.

Brockley bolted out of the room and back down the corridor. The Commander was standing at the door of the other room, now in his hat and coat, the brim of the hat worn low so as to lend the whole appearance an even more sinister aspect.

"Come inside and shut the door," he ordered, removing his hat and throwing it on to the table. "Have you done it?"

"It's like I predicted," he breathed. "She won't budge."

"Did you tell her precisely what I said. You didn't dilute it?"

"No."

"What was her exact response?"

"She said that her decision was based on logic, the state of the evidence and the assurance that Leadbetter's evidence would show that Barford was a liar. That's why she was going to call him," Brockley repeated.

"Anything else?"

Hesitating before replying, Brockley responded :

"She also said that you had no status in her decision. I can't do any more. I instructed her to do as you said. She won't listen."

Grabbing his hat and marching to the door, the Commander threw it open in anger and stormed out of the room, his eyes narrowed and lips tightened. As he stepped into the corridor he was immediately confronted by Naomi Nicholas and Mike Myott, who had deliberately positioned themselves directly outside the door. Her eyes locked on the corrupt image of power, absorbing every detail as he glared back. This was a face that she would not forget.

Chapter 33

R v Lewis Barford
Transcript 64

Nicholas :
My Lord, the jury have been kept out of Court as I wish to apply for leave to call Chief Superintendent Leadbetter. We could not reasonably foresee that the Defendant was going to claim that the true culprit was Leadbetter. Unless Leadbetter is called to contradict Barford's allegations, then the jury are cheated of crucial evidence to which they are plainly entitled. It is in the interests of justice.

Mr Justice Maullin :
Thank you. Now Mr Cadogan, this is your opportunity to argue that I should not allow this witness to be called. The argument that you must meet is that Miss Nicholas claims that the interests of justice demand that Leadbetter should be called before the jury.

Cadogan :
The interests of justice, My Lord. A fine phrase. A lofty aspiration. The whole objective of the Criminal Trial. If Your Lordship and Miss Nicholas are convinced that calling Leadbetter is in the interests of justice then it would be churlish of me to resist. Indeed, it is a privilege to be part of process that seeks such an ideal. Let justice be done. Let Leadbetter testify.

Mr Justice Maullin :
I see, Mr Cadogan. You had another agenda after all.

Cadogan :
As Your Lordship pleases.

Mr Justice Maullin :
Miss Nicholas, apparently your application is unresisted. Leadbetter

will be called. In the light of the words we have both just listened to from Mr Cadogan's lips the real question is whether Leadbetter is going to turn out to be a witness for the Prosecution or for the Defence. Send for the jury.

As the usher opened the side door to the Court and called the jury back into their places, Naomi turned round to Myott, her face white with worry and self-chastisement.

"We've been completely shafted. We fell for it, hook, line and sinker. So did Maullin. Now you'll see Cadogan at his worst. At some point in the next few minutes the rabbit is going to come out of the hat. You may have no doubt about that at all. The bastard's shafted us."

In turn, Myott turned round to Brockley and Coleman seated in the row behind him. "Cadogan bluffed us all right," he breathed in Brockley's direction, "he really wanted us to call Leadbetter. But then you had the squeeze put on you this morning to stop us calling him. Who's on whose side?"

Brockley shook his head in puzzlement while Coleman sat and listened intently, waiting for the next development.

* * *

As the tall figure of Chief Superintendent Ray Leadbetter made his reluctant way across the well of the Court towards the loneliness of the witness box, Naomi Nicholas felt as if all the strength had drained from her body. Her every instinct had told her that Cadogan would seek victory by a deceit somewhere along the line. It had all seemed so convenient that Myott had overheard that deadly snatch of conversation between Stapleton and the Defence Solicitor and her suspicions had been aroused from the outset. In a way that is what made it worse, for she had let herself walk into his trap with her eyes wide open. When Cadogan had declared those dreaded words *'then it would be churlish of me to resist. Let Leadbetter testify'*, she had thought that she might pass out. Now, as a QC, prosecuting a high-profile murder conspiracy at the Old Bailey, she had just called into the witness box the Defence's secret weapon.

Where did Myott really fit into all of this, she found herself asking. There was something that didn't ring true about him. Had he really overheard that conversation at all? With her mind in turmoil as Leadbetter took the oath, she allowed herself a quick sideways glance at her dreaded opponent at the far end of the Bench. His huge body was angled towards her, staring intently at her, as if he somehow knew that, at that very instant, she would feel compelled to look into his face, like the rabbit transfixed in the headlights of the car bearing down on it, bringing death. As their eyes met he spoke, his voice carrying easily to her along the Bench and probably beyond for, in his moment of triumph, he wanted the Judge to hear.

"And yet thou art thine own executioner," he smugly proclaimed.

"You have misquoted your pronouns," the Judge's voice snapped sharply at Cadogan.

"Deliberately, My Lord," grunted Cadogan, without rising to his feet, savouring the fact that neither the Judge nor the Prosecution had any idea of the identity of the other fingerprint on the envelope and the ten pound note whereas he did.

"And we would be better served without any further asides," the Judge added, now recognising the deliberately misquoted words of John Donne *'And yet I am my own executioner'* was Cadogan's cry of triumph at leading Nicholas into what was plainly a trap. Mr. Justice Maullin was furious with himself, for he, too, had encouraged her to call Leadbetter. Cadogan may have outwitted them both. Moreover, as the officer was taking the oath, the Judge observed with foreboding that the man did indeed have crooked teeth, just as Barford had asserted in evidence. On such little things could cases turn, he reflected ominously.

R v Lewis Barford
Transcript 65

Nicholas :
Were you involved in any aspect of the terrorist attack at Manchester airport?

Leadbetter :

Yes. On the night of the attack I was directed to interview El-Hoorie to see if he could identify the two men he'd apparently heard plotting earlier in the day. I took him to a terrorist incident de-briefing location and interviewed him. Later he was taken to a secure hospital where Yassin was being treated for his injuries. I never saw him after that.

Nicholas :

Was he given any indication in your presence as to whether or not he may be required as a witness in any later trial?

Leadbetter :

Not specifically. He was told that this was a major and sensitive enquiry. He wasn't to discuss what had happened. In terrorism cases we have a lot of interests to protect. The old adage really, careless talk can cost lives. We told him we'd be in touch when we knew a trial date.

Nicholas :

Was the decision taken that he should not be called as a witness?

Leadbetter :

Apparently. Those kind of decisions are part-legal, part-Police, part-Security. It was obvious that there was no need to call him. The evidence against Yassin was overwhelming. We didn't need El-Ibrahim.

Nicholas :

Was El-Hoorie informed that he wouldn't be called at Yassin's trial?

Leadbetter :

Yes. Again, someone within the administrative side of our department would have told him that. Apparently, he was angry. Sometimes potential witnesses in cases attracting a lot of publicity are delighted to learn that they won't be required to give evidence. Sometimes, they feel frustrated. There was nothing surprising or unusual in El-Hoorie's reaction.

Nicholas :

Did you learn that he intimated that he might go to the Press about this?

Leadbetter :

Yes. Again, this was not an unusual reaction.

Nicholas :

Was any specific newspaper or journalist mentioned?

Leadbetter :

Not at that stage, as far as I can recall.

Nicholas :

Did you make a written statement setting out these facts?

Leadbetter :

I did.

Nicholas :

Have you ever met Lewis Barford, the man you see in the dock?

Leadbetter :

Not that I can ever remember.

Nicholas :

Did you meet him on a barge?

Leadbetter :

No.

Nicholas :

Did you instruct him to recruit a man to steal a diary belonging to Ibrahim El-Hoorie?

Leadbetter :

Absolutely not.

Nicholas :
Have you ever spoken to a man called Derek Lennox?

Leadbetter :
No.

Nicholas :
Did you instruct Lennox, or did you instruct anybody, to kill Ibrahim El-Hoorie?

Leadbetter :
Of course not.

Nicholas :
Thank you, Chief Superintendent. I have no other questions for you.

R v Lewis Barford
Transcript 66

Cadogan :
Do you smile a lot?

Leadbetter :
What kind of question is that?

Cadogan :
Your teeth are crooked aren't they?

Leadbetter :
You can judge for yourself.

Cadogan :
I have. Unless Barford had met you, how else could he know that you had crooked teeth?

Leadbetter :

In his world, they can get access to any file they want. There'll be lots of photos of me in the files.

Cadogan :

How would you describe the relationship between Advisers to Government Departments, like Mr Barford, and your unit within Special Branch?

Leadbetter :

Are you looking for a full and frank answer, Sir?

Cadogan :

Of course.

Leadbetter :

Mutual loathing.

Cadogan :

Frank indeed, Chief Superintendent.

Leadbetter :

They're brought in to spin. Hatchet men with experience in the field. With a brain. Ruthless. And liars. I can't get any franker than that, Sir.

Cadogan :

Just the kind of man to find a criminal to do a job for you?

Leadbetter :

No.

Cadogan :

By the time that you interviewed El-Hoorie on the night of the atrocity, did you have a clear understanding that El-Hoorie had heard two terrorists plotting and then actually seen them with his own eyes and given detailed descriptions of them?

Leadbetter :
Yes.

Cadogan :
Did you know that Yasin, who was alive and in hospital, fitted one of these descriptions and the dead terrorist did not fit the other?

Leadbetter :
Yes.

Cadogan :
Did you realise that the second man at the Café must therefore still be at large?

Leadbetter :
Of course. I found out it was Abdelkarim Mohammed.

Cadogan :
Did you therefore appreciate that the only witness that you had to give evidence against Abdelkarim Mohammed was El-Hoorie?

Leadbetter :
Possibly. We might have turned up other evidence if we'd managed to arrest Mohammed.

Cadogan :
When you took El-Hoorie to the place you described earlier as "a terrorist incident de-briefing location" did you show him any photographs of Abdelkarim Mohammed and let him identify Yasin, disregarding all the rules about identification procedures?

Leadbetter :
Lawyers' points, sir. I was trying to catch murderers. Out in the real world. Thirty-one people were dead. I wanted to know exactly who I was looking for. Not what questions some barrister might ask me about identification procedures.

Cadogan :

It isn't the position is it, that you were deliberately flouting all rules governing Identification of Suspects, so that El-Hoorie would be hopelessly compromised as a potential witness if this came to trial? So that lawyers would say that El-Hoorie's evidence was inadmissible because you broke all of the rules?

Leadbetter :

No. That isn't the position.

Cadogan :

As Yassin's trial approached, and you heard that El-Hoorie was angry at learning he was not to be called as a witness, were you concerned?

Leadbetter :

Why should I be?

Cadogan :

Because he could blow the whistle on the criminal negligence of the Manchester Police and the suppression of that negligence.

Leadbetter :

Who are you saying suppressed it?

Cadogan :

You.

Leadbetter :

Untrue.

Cadogan :

You were desperate to keep El-Hoorie quiet, I suggest. Using threats of one kind or another over the months prior to Yassin's trial. And then, you learned, didn't you, that El-Hoorie was threatening back? Threatening to go to the Press.

Leadbetter :
That was not an uncommon reaction.

Cadogan :
But this wasn't a common case, was it? Information that would have damaged public confidence in the whole security Administration was at risk of becoming public. That's why you went to a higher level of the Executive, isn't it?

Leadbetter :
Untrue.

Cadogan :
And you telephoned a number available to you for contacting an Adviser in the capacity of a man like Barford so that he could find a rough, tough, no questions-asked criminal to do your dirty work?

Leadbetter :
Rubbish.

Cadogan :
And you met Barford on a barge named Medici, moored on a canal near Ashford and I suggest that you fed him a lie about wanting to recover El-Hoorie's diary, when in truth you intended to use that criminal to commit murder, anticipating that the type of man Barford would locate would be rough, ruthless and criminally versatile.

Leadbetter :
That story is the invention of your client. He's trying to save his own skin.

Cadogan :
And you handed £5000 to Barford on the barge.

Leadbetter :
I did no such thing.

Cadogan :
You had put the money in a grubby envelope.

Leadbetter :
Lies.

Cadogan :
You threw the envelope down on to the chart table.

Leadbetter :
Lies.

Cadogan :
You did this at the time you were telling Barford that the diary should be recovered as it may, and I quote the expression that I suggest you used, 'compromise the forthcoming trial'.

Leadbetter :
This is fiction.

Cadogan :
You implied that expression included revelations to the Press, indeed to a particular journalist who writes under the pseudonym 'The Molecule Man'.

Leadbetter :
Untrue.

Cadogan :
So, in summary, you deny ever meeting Barford, ever producing an envelope, ever handing Barford £5000 and ever mentioning to him 'The Molecule Man'.

Leadbetter :
Correct.

Cadogan :

Thank you, Chief Superintendent. Just before I finish I wonder if I could trouble you to look at this item. It is sealed in a tamper-proof transparent bag so that it can be seen and handled, yet not actually touched. No doubt you are familiar with this type of secure packaging, to prevent contamination by fingerprints and the like?

Leadbetter :

Yes. I'll look. What is it?

Cadogan :

You'll recognise it immediately, I suggest. It's the very envelope that you threw down on the chart table on the barge. Take a good look. Please take your time, I've no doubt His Lordship will allow you all the time that you need. In the interests of justice.

Leadbetter :

I've looked. As far as I know I've never seen it before. It's just an old blank envelope.

Cadogan :

Not quite blank. If you turn the package over so that you're looking through the transparent packaging at the back of the envelope, you'll see there's writing on it. In black biro. Your writing, I suggest.

Leadbetter :

[Silence]

Cadogan :

Is it your writing?

Leadbetter :

[Silence]

Cadogan :

Does it look like your writing?

Leadbetter :
Vaguely. That means nothing.

Cadogan :
Is it in black ink on a white envelope?

Leadbetter :
Yes.

Cadogan :
Perhaps you'd be good enough to read out the writing to the Judge and the jury. They haven't seen this before.

Leadbetter :
There's only three words.

Cadogan :
Read them out.

Leadbetter :
[Silence]

Cadogan :
Read them out I said.

Leadbetter :
'The Molecule Man'.

Cadogan :
You had written those words on that envelope. That was the name of the journalist El-Hoorie was going to. You told Barford to find a burglar for you for £5000. The £5000 was in that envelope.

Leadbetter :
None of that is true.

Cadogan :

We have in Court two ten pound notes recovered from Lennox's Safety Deposit Box. He stated they were the top and bottom notes of the wad of £5000 handed over to him by Barford in Leicester.

Leadbetter :

Yes?

Cadogan :

On each of those notes is an unidentified fingerprint. The same unknown finger has touched each of those notes. Could it be your print?

Leadbetter :

No.

Cadogan :

That envelope can be tested for fingerprints. We have experts in Court. It's been sealed in that bag since Barford brought it into my chambers with his instructions. If we were to have it tested, could it have your prints on it?

Nicholas :

My Lord, I object. The Defendant never gave evidence about this envelope. We do not know where it came from. My learned friend's assertion that Barford brought it into his chambers does not provide any evidential foundation. My learned friend cannot give evidence.

Mr. Justice Maullin :

That is quite right. Where is the evidence that lays the foundation for this aspect of your cross-examination, Mr Cadogan?

Cadogan :

It is to be found in the evidence given by the Defendant, My Lord. It is in re-examination. I quote Barford's answer in re-examination :

" . . . I believed that Leadbetter had reason to be concerned about a particular journalist. This journalist enjoys a "publish and be damned reputation." A trial could easily be compromised by him. That's the message Leadbetter communicated to me all right, that's the message I took away from that barge. In black and white."

Has Your Lordship found the note. Hard to be clearer. A message taken away from the barge in black and white.

Mr Justice Maullin :
Mr Cadogan, I find this most unsatisfactory, most distasteful. The answer makes no mention of an envelope recovered by Barford from Leadbetter. It suggests an implied message.

Cadogan :
In black and white, My Lord? Implied? In black and white? A contradiction in terms, I would suggest. A linguistic inexactitude.

Mr Justice Maullin :
You are bordering on the impertinent, Mr Cadogan. My reputation for linguistic exactitude is well known.

Cadogan :
Precisely my point, My Lord. May I also quote the next answer in re-examination, My Lord :

"In a sense I had a name. He writes anonymously. He is known as 'The Molecule Man'"

White envelope, black ink. From Leadbetter. A message. Taken away from the barge. The Molecule Man. A perfectly adequate foundation for my questioning, My Lord. Particularly bearing in mind that, at the time of adducing that evidence from my client, Leadbetter was not a witness that the Prosecution intended to call. If they had called Leadbetter initially, instead of at the end in rebuttal, then I would have put the envelope to Leadbetter earlier.

Mr Justice Maullin :

You should have asked your client to produce the envelope while he was in the witness box. Detailing how he came to be in possession of it in clear, unambiguous terms. So that Miss Nicholas could cross-examine your client upon it.

Cadogan :

With respect, My Lord, I argue to the contrary. Leadbetter was not at that stage a witness for the Prosecution. If he had been called during the Prosecution case, at the proper time instead of in rebuttal, I would have put the envelope to him and suggested Barford took it away from the barge.

Mr Justice Maullin :

What do you wish to say about all of this, Miss Nicholas?

Nicholas :

My Lord, I find it hard to restrain my outrage. The Defence have sought to spring an ambush upon us. Deliberately and cynically. My learned friend must have had his instructions from his client about this envelope long before the trial began. It was his duty to ask the straight questions of his client about it in-chief. Then I would have cross-examined Barford about it in detail. I would have had the envelope forensically examined overnight. Instead, stealthily, he has, in his inimitable way, provoked the Prosecution into calling Leadbetter in rebuttal, so that he could spring the trap.

Mr Justice Maullin :

Mr Cadogan. When did you first receive instructions about the envelope?

Cadogan :

During my second conference in chambers with my client. My Junior and Mr Bloom were also in attendance, of course.

Mr Justice Maullin :

I agree with all of your submissions, Miss Nicholas. But I am faced with the dilemma of how to deal with the matter. I think I see a solution. It's Friday. If you ask for forensic examination of the envelope to be done over the weekend, I shall authorise it.

Mr Justice Maullin :
Is there anything you wish to say, Mr Cadogan?

Cadogan :
I shall welcome any forensic examination of the envelope and comparison with the prints on the ten pound notes.

Mr Justice Maullin :
Very well. Continue with your questions.

Cadogan :
Do you still deny any knowledge of that envelope?

Leadbetter :
As far as I can remember.

Cadogan :
Is there any possibility that your fingerprints could be on the ten pound notes?

Leadbetter :
I suppose in the course of ordinary circulation.

Cadogan :
Behind me sits Mr Ostler. An expert in fingerprinting. He has remained here for this very purpose. The Prosecution have access to the services of Ms Dale, also a highly qualified expert in fingerprinting. Are you prepared to allow your fingerprints to be taken and compared to any found on the envelope and to those found on the ten pound notes? The work can be done over the weekend.

Leadbetter :
[Silence]

Mr Justice Maullin :
Chief Superintendent, it would appear appropriate that you should consent. Are you reluctant?

Leadbetter :
I'm very suspicious of what tactics may be deployed, My Lord.

Mr Justice Maullin :
I have the power to ensure that there is no risk of error in the procedure. I shall infer consent from your silence. Right. Members of the jury, you will have an early day for reasons that are obvious to you. I shall discuss with Counsel the precise mechanics of how this forensic examination is to be conducted. You need not remain for that. Be back at ten-thirty on Monday morning. You may withdraw.

Chapter 34

As the black chauffeur-driven Mercedes cruised past the still-medieval, yet gently modernised, town of Lucerne and out along the Lake, the Home Secretary stared out of the window across the water towards the hill on the far side of the Eastern shore, where the imposing Wedderley mansion was located. 'A pearl in the world's most beautiful oyster', was how Alexandre Dumas had one described this magical town, but Templar found it impossible to put the news from the Home Front out of his mind. Being away from England softened the reality of the drama that was being played out back in the Old Bailey, but the telephoned report today had sent a chill down his spine. For a few seconds he had started to vent his fury on the Commander, raging at his inability to exert proper control, but the response from that quarter had been immediate and crushing.

"Panic does not become a Government Minister," the Commander had interrupted in that detached but authoritative voice. "A cool head. Restraint. No ranting. Otherwise I go straight to Denstone."

Now that Leadbetter was actually in the witness box, who knows where it may lead. The news that the envelope was to be forensically examined for fingerprints had terrified him for, try as he may, he could not remember whether or not he had touched it himself. He had no trouble in reconstructing the desperate scene on that barge in his own mind and he could even picture Leadbetter pulling the envelope from his pocket and throwing it onto the chart table so that it fell face-up right beneath Templar's gaze. But he still couldn't remember if he touched it. His own words echoed round his head for he specifically recollected what he had said as he had stared in horror at the grubby envelope lying there, inanimate but threatening. *"The Molecule Man"*, he had declared. *"Terminally dangerous"*. Only the proceedings on Monday morning would reveal whether, in his shock, he had handled it. In any event, although his fingerprints were on record, it was unlikely that either of the QCs would see any reason to apply for their release for comparison purposes. It was Leadbetter's prints that really mattered.

Anyway, once that buffoon Curbishley had dropped dead, it had proved impossible to influence either his successor or Cadogan. Neither of them seemed able to fight the case on any alternative agenda and simply pursued victory at all costs. Monday morning threatened to be explosive and only the acquittal of Barford could save Templar's job. The Commander's threat of going above his head and reporting the full facts to Denstone was terrifying, although it was a miracle that neither Denstone nor his odious Rottweiler PR man had not yet been in direct contact. On the other hand, if the Commander went to Denstone he could hardly tell him the whole truth for he could not possibly afford to admit that he had been on the barge. Would Leadbetter ever let the Commander down? Templar simply had no way of knowing.

As the Mercedes approached the gated entrance to the long driveway winding up the hill, the wrought iron gates effortlessly slid open and the saloon eased its way up the tree-lined drive, passing the Spanish-style stucco garages with bays for fifteen limousines and on towards the front courtyard, where the centrepiece was an enormous Baroque fountain and cascading waterfall. Templar could see that the extensive grounds had been specially designed with exotic foliage and fruit-bearing grove trees. An English manservant had helped the Home Secretary from the car, directing another underling to take the Minister's Gucci suitcases to the Renoir guesthouse beyond the Southern Terrace. All of the guest-houses were dotted around the grounds and were named after Old Masters, the only condition being that Wedderley would only use the name of an artist whose work he actually owned. Connected to the main house by walkways and trails, Templar strolled casually behind the porter past the horse barns and tennis courts and the separate media room where, apart from the stereo equipment, juke box, televisions and electric piano, Wedderley had installed his own thirty-seater home cinema.

After soaking in the antique sandblasted solid marble bath and spending five minutes in the walk-in steam room with Italian tiled seating, Templar had donned a cream linen jacket, tailored pink shirt, plum-coloured velvet trousers and his latest pair of hand-made loafers before walking back along the trail, into the main house through the open veranda doors which led into one of the magnificent reception rooms. All the rooms at the back of the house had wrap-round patios providing panoramic views over the pool and spa, out across the lake, which was now shimmering in the early evening twilight and beyond to Mount Rigi and the other white topped Alps in the middle distance. The porter had announced that Lord Wedderley was awaiting him in the library and Templar had wandered appreciatively through more of the reception rooms with their works of art on the walls, hardwood floors, vaulted ceilings and marble fireplaces, before espying the open door of the black walnut panelled library where Wedderley was seated at his desk perusing some papers.

The two men had warmly embraced, reminisced awhile over a glass or two of Glenfiddich, before departing for a private viewing at the Rosengart Collection and Picasso Museum, which Wedderley had specially arranged. As Templar gazed in awe at the works of the Classic Modernists such as Chagall, Utrillo, Matisse and Vuillard, the sheer power of wealth and purchasable culture had served to heighten his determination to stay in office. The former placard-carrying Trotskyite now wielded his chequebook with the same single-mindedness that he had used to put a brick through the windscreen of a Police van.

Afterwards they had been driven through the central streets, past the multitude of houses with colourfully painted gables and numerous Renaissance fountains, emerging from the town by the Chapel Bridge with its thirteenth-century, octagonal water tower before heading towards Tribschen, where Richard Wagner had resided over a century ago. Wedderley was a well-received and frequent diner at Les Levres Rouges, a tiny, exclusive French restaurant hidden away in the narrow streets behind the old Wagner residence and where Lady Wedderley was due to join them for dinner after a shopping trip to Bern with the wife of the Chairman of the German National Bank, whose headquarters had been moved to Lucerne last year. Tina Rowbottom, as she been known in a former life, had been a minor journalist with the *Guardian* before she had met Bill Wedderley in the Bar at a Labour Party Conference in a Bournemouth Hotel. Having both imbibed several glasses too many of the endless, free supply of liquor that the Party Organisers always ensured were made available on such occasions to the journalists and businessmen in attendance, the two of them had lurched into the lift together and ended up in drunken embrace in Wedderley's room with a sea view. Morning sobriety had brought about a mutual recognition that each could be of considerable political, social and financial benefit to the other and thereafter, in joint relentless pursuit of the wealth, privilege and elitism that they each publicly decried, they had double-talked their way to the opulence of a peerage and their estate on the hillside overlooking Lake Lucerne.

Templar had studiously avoided raising the topic of his massive problem back home, but it would have been impossible for the Wedderleys not to have heard or read about the trial and his potential involvement in it, so sooner or later the topic was bound to be raised. In any event, just as the crème brulee arrived, his second mobile phone, the one he was never allowed to turn off, vibrated ominously in the pocket of his plum-coloured trousers.

"Templar," he announced, gesturing his apology to the Wedderleys at this unfortunate intrusion.

"This is Downing Street," a nondescript female voice declared. "I am about to put the Prime Minister through. Are you in a location where you are able to take the call without being overheard?"

"No. I'll step outside. Please wait a moment before putting the call through," he replied, his heart pounding with alarm, as the call arrived that he had been dreading ever since this wretched affair had reared its ugly head. How typical of Denstone to wait until late on a Friday night before striking, he thought to himself as he excused himself from the table and walked out into the street. It was cold now and the breeze off the lake sliced instantly through his thin jacket, making him shiver, yet his brow was sweating and those early waves of an impending panic attack were ebbing and flowing in his brain.

"I'm alone now," he announced down the phone, noticing that his hand was actually shaking.

"Very well, sir. Hold the line," said the telephonist.

"This is the Prime Minister. Can you hear me, Will?" asked the voice.

Secreted in a narrow street, in an ancient Swiss canton, the deadly tone of Roger Denstone reached across the Channel and across Europe before it enveloped Templar, bringing with it the next chapter in this endless nightmare.

"Yes, Prime Minister. I left the Davos Conference this morning. Very constructive indeed. I shall be working on my report over the weekend and it will be with you by Tuesday afternoon. I'll have it sent to Zurich and they can use the Diplomatic Bag from there," Templar recited, seeking to convey the impression that he imagined that was what must lie behind Denstone's call.

"Better still, you can bring it with you on Monday, when you return," Denstone responded immediately, making it clear that this was nothing less than a direct summons to return to London.

"I'd arranged a private visit after the Conference. First time off for several months. I'm expected to stay until Thursday. I'm the guest of Lord and Lady Wedderley. From our conversation at dinner there may well be a further significant contribution to Party Funds before the summer. It may not assist if I leave early," Templar urged desperately.

"Your Office and your name are echoing along the corridors of the Old Bailey. I don't like it. And I won't have you cowering in some Swiss schloss until it's all over. You'll get the British Airways Zurich to Heathrow flight at six-thirty Monday morning," Denstone directed. "There's to be no debate about it."

Seething with resentment, yet terrified to resist, Templar recognised that the command would have to be obeyed, but the frustration burned deep within. No-one had been more ruthless or manipulative than Denstone in his relentless pursuit of the ultimate prize. As Minister of Europe he had curried, bought and sold favours which, when his predecessor had suddenly fallen from grace, he had called in, then recruiting Templar to run his campaign, so as to ensure support from the left of the Party.

Templar had seen at first hand the double-dealing, the false sympathy that a Prime Minister should have to resign over an affair, whilst, behind the scenes Denstone had twisted the knife in the wound. Acknowledging at the time that he could never prove it, Templar had the gravest of suspicions that the initial leak to the Press had come not, as was widely circulated, from the Prime Minister's mistress, but from the intricate, precision engineering of Denstone himself.

Late on the night of Denstone's victory, the two men had sat alone in the living room of the Belgravia house lent to them by Roderick Stirling to be used as headquarters for their campaign. Sharing a bottle of Chivas Regal they had both become inebriated by the contents of the bottle and by the sense of absolute power that they had just achieved. In an unguarded moment Templar had suggested to Denstone that he was behind the first anonymous leak of the affair to the *Daily Mail*. In an instant, Denstone had thrown off the effects of the liquor and shown Templar a flash of the vicious temper that lurked beneath the surface. Almost threatening him physically, Denstone had emphatically denied the charge and promised Templar that if he ever repeated a similar accusation then he would find himself destroyed. Retreating with all the skill of the coward that he truly was, Templar insisted that it had just been a poor joke, fuelled by drink, and would never be repeated.

The next morning, the announcement had been released that Templar had been appointed as Home Secretary. The following month, one of Roderick Stirling's construction companies had been awarded the massive, lucrative contract for re-development of a section of the old docklands, funded by public finances. Denstone knew exactly how to operate in this high-powered, seedy world of the stick and the carrot and favours done and favours owed. If Denstone smelled big trouble was brewing for the Government, or even perhaps for his own position, the first essential would be to have a scapegoat set up for the early sacrifice. Such a creature needed to be at hand and on the spot so that when the dagger thrust was made, the public would not perceive the execution to have been made to an absentee, behind his back. Such a thrust had to have the appearance of being to the heart not in the back.

Denstone's carefully chosen words conveyed this message loud and clear and Templar knew that his fate now lay absolutely in the hands of some Defence Barrister in the Old Bailey. Only if Cadogan achieved Barford's acquittal was there any chance of Templar surviving. That had to be the theme that he deployed in his dealings with Denstone. All of these thoughts raced through his mind as

Denstone delivered the command to return to London and, immediately, Templar sought to lay the foundations of his escape route.

"Very well, Prime Minister. I shall, of course, do as you suggest. My reports do indicate however that the matters being raised at the Old Bailey are liberally sprinkled with fantasy and fiction. Barford's acquittal should make it clear that mischief-makers are at work," he replied.

"You'll have leaks prepared for release as soon as the jury goes out. You'll say nothing publicly until the verdict's returned," Denstone directed. "If it's guilty, then you'll report to me, wherever I am and I'll make all necessary decisions. If it's not guilty, then there'll be Press releases, backed up by Department Records, that none of this was the work of your Department. It was an attempted cover-up by a corrupt few of the Manchester Police, at a low level. You'll assure the public that no efforts will be spared in identifying them, if that is humanly possible."

"I understand the approach. I'll attend to it all personally. I'll draft the releases myself," Templar assured him emphatically.

"That's the last thing I want," the Prime Minister growled back. "I'll instruct my man to draft them. He'll deliver them to you in person on Monday afternoon. You'd better hope that you get to use them. The alternative, in the event of a conviction, will lead to a re-shuffle. I'm sure you understand my meaning."

"It won't come to that. This case is littered with deceit. Barford knows how to handle himself. The Defence QC is well on top of events," Templar insisted.

"Barford's not your problem. From the information I have, which comes from the highest source, you've got three problems. The Judge, Leadbetter and this new QC who prosecutes. You'd better say your prayers," said Denstone ominously. "Send my regards to Wedderley. Tell him the contribution is deeply appreciated. Enjoy your weekend."

Breathing the cold night air deep into his lungs, Templar could sense the proximity of the massive lake below and taste the biting purity of the nearby range of mountains, towering above. But one feeling outweighed even the effects of these mighty natural wonders. Fear. It inhabited every fibre of his being.

Chapter 35

Back in London the next evening, Naomi was allowing herself a precious night off from preparing for the final stages of the trial, and had accompanied Jack to the television studios to watch his programme from the wings, after which they were going to take dinner at The Caprice with Ben Railey and the producer. Spending half an hour in the Green Room with Jack and the guests had been a re-assuring experience, revealing that even the most experienced performers still suffered from nerves, which had provided her with some comfort. Ben had arrived very late, with only a few minutes to go before the programme went out. Sporting a sickly yellow Versace shirt, which the technicians were unsuccessfully advising didn't work on the TV screen, he puffed and panted his way to the bar. Then, proclaiming that he'd only got one clean shirt to last him all weekend, he had slumped into an armchair in the corner of the room, full whisky glass in hand, and entered one of his brief quiet periods, plainly settling his nerves. Another guest was the latest French Manager to descend upon the English Premier League; suave, cultured and so debonair as to despatch into history, the aggressive, bullying, shouting image of the old-school Football Manager.

As the time neared for them to take up their positions to go on-air live, the atmosphere became tense and Naomi could see the effects of the rising adrenalin on all of the participants and the behind-camera team. As the final seconds to count-down arrived, the true professionalism surfaced. Each of them became calm and composed. The private face turned into the public face. Jack smiled confidently. Ben Railey started cracking his jokes and then the producer counted them in. Three, two, one. Camera on Jack. Looking so handsome on the monitors. Action.

"Tonight," Jack began, his voice completely under control, his manner easy and relaxed, "my first guest is a man who dreamed of playing for Everton, but ended up playing for laughs . . ."

"Is there a difference, then?" Ben interrupted across the introduction.

"Now, rendering my introduction obsolete, it's my great pleasure to welcome Ben Railey. He's only just arrived, cutting it very fine, having attended today's Merseyside Derby."

"Yea, came by train. Had to get off at every station and buy me ticket to the next stop."

"Why didn't you buy one ticket for the whole trip?" Jack asked, setting him up for the punch line.

"'Cos me Doctor advised me not to make long journeys," came Ben's instant response, throwing his head back as he bellowed at his own joke.

"I think we'd better move on quickly to your report on the game at Goodison?" Jack suggested.

"Everton won two-nothing" Ben replied. "One-sided match. Liverpool were lucky to get nothing. Two goals from the new Boy Wonder. Not a great match, to be honest."

"Is Goodison Park as exciting for you as it always has been?"

"Well, I don't get excited as easy as I used to, not since the fourth Mrs Railey left me for an older man," Ben answered, dissolving into fits of laughter and struggling to get his breath in time to snap out the next one-liner that was bursting to escape from his brain. "But it's always good to go back to Liverpool, see the old Mersey running through the City. Mind you if it walked, it'd get mugged," he added, now rocking back on his seat in glee.

"Was it a sell-out crowd?"

"Not quite," he replied, his breathing now back under some kind of control. "Since the Judges've been stopped from sending burglars down, the gates have dropped, you know."

"Why's that?"

"Professional duty. Have to go nicking on Saturday afternoon now as well. Used to be burglars' half-day so you could get to the match," Ben replied knowingly, his cheeky expression indicating that he had inside information on this Liverpudlian social nicety.

"You live in the stockbroker belt now, Ben. That's a long way from the cobbled Northern back streets where you were brought up."

"No. I don't live in no stockbroker belt, mate. I live in the suspender belt. Unless your face fits, they hang you out to dry."

"And does your face fit?"

"In Esher?" Ben responded noisily. "What do you think? When they see me mowing me lawn, they think I'm doing Community Service."

"I know that you had a trial with Everton and Manchester City. Do you regret that you didn't quite make it into the ranks of professional football?" Jack enquired.

"I regret not having the Ferrari that goes with the job, but I've lasted longer on the stage than I would have on the field. I've still got my knees. You know all about that, injuries finished your career," said Ben, his face momentarily screwed up in concentration as he gave a straight answer, whilst, at the same time, his brain was busy sorting out the next quip.

"But I have my memories," Jack smiled.

"Don't we all, mate? I have me memories of me first relationship. Tracey Gillespie at Vulcan Street Primary. She had nice knees, an'all," Ben giggled, raising his eyebrows at the camera, his face now glistening red under the make-up as his part of the show came to an end.

"Enjoyed having you on the show. My thanks to Ben Railey."

Back in the Green Room, Naomi was now watching on an alternative set of monitors and was still laughing at Ben Railey's one-liners when he walked in and joined her, his yellow shirt looking damp and rumpled, but his face creased in smiles.

"Laugh and the world laughs with you; weep and you weep alone" she said as he helped himself to another generous measure of the television company's best malted whisky.

"For the sad old earth must borrow its mirth, but has trouble enough of its own", he retorted. "I know me poetry Naomi, I'm not as dumb as I look. Behind every comic's face lies unseen sadness. We're actors. Just like you when you put that wig on. Waiting for the applause."

"And what happens when there isn't any applause?" she asked.

"You move on to the next venue. The next theatre at the end of the pier for me. The next case for you. And you try all over again."

"This is my first case as a QC," she explained. "High-profile. High stakes. Dirty dealings. Formidable opponent. I need the victory. I need the applause," she found herself saying to this odd character who traded in laughs, but somehow seemed to understand exactly what she meant.

The cheeky face was studying her with great care and she returned his steady gaze, eager to hear his response. This time he was not smiling nor offering his natural comedy, for he knew only too well what it was like to face humiliation on the empty stage. They were travellers on the same road.

"You look at that jury like you're looking at me, luv. Tell'em the tale. Fix 'em with those captivating blue eyes of yours and make that voice carry 'em away. Convince 'em that you know he did it and you can bloody prove it. You let 'em have it with both barrels. You show 'em that you're a fighter. Then you'll hear the applause, my girl."

"Thank you, Ben. Inspiration sometimes come from unexpected quarters," she said.

"From the mouth of a clown, you mean?"

"Some clowns have wisdom," she replied. "Wisdom gained from standing alone on the stage, listening to the deafening silence. Roll on Monday morning."

Chapter 36

R v Lewis Barford
Transcript 68

Mr Justice Maullin :
Have the forensic tests been completed over the weekend?

Cadogan :
They have, My Lord. The experts agree. I shall now continue cross-examining Chief Superintendent Leadbetter. Chief Superintendent, have you been informed of the results of the fingerprint examinations conducted over the weekend?

Leadbetter :
No. No one has spoken to me at all.

Cadogan :
The results show that on the ten-pound note, said by Lennox to have been on the top of the bundle, there appears a print from your right index finger. And on the bottom note, your right middle finger has left its mark. Do you wish to offer any explanation?

Leadbetter :
[Silence]

Cadogan :
Do you have any explanation other than that you handled the money in preparing the bundle and giving it to Barford?

Leadbetter :
[Silence]

Cadogan :
Turning to the envelope. Your right thumb print. Any explanation offered?

Leadbetter :
[Silence]

Cadogan :
This is your last chance, Chief Superintendent. Either you explain or I sit down with your silence telling its own story. Namely that you have lied. The truth being exactly as I put to you on Friday.

Leadbetter :
[Silence]

Mr Justice Maullin :
Mr Cadogan seems to have left the matter there, Miss Nicholas. Did you have any questions in re-examination?

Nicholas :
Oh yes, My Lord. I do. Chief Superintendent, you have just been told by Mr Cadogan that you had been given your last chance to offer an explanation for this fingerprint evidence.

Leadbetter :
Yes.

Nicholas :
Well, Mr Cadogan was wrong. It wasn't your last chance. Your last chance is now. Your fingerprints were found on that money and on that envelope. Barford says the instruction to murder is down to you. Do you now want to tell the jury what really happened?

Leadbetter :
[Silence]

Nicholas :
Well, that was your last . . .

Leadbetter :

I do intend to answer. I've tried to respect the fact that national security was involved. I've tried to protect Government interests. I must now abandon those principles. I've put myself last. Barford has put himself first. I take risks. I've always honoured the Service. Last week, while you were safe in Court, I was arresting a dangerous, armed terrorist connected with this plot. Now I'm forced to dishonour my position.

Nicholas :

What happened between you and Barford?

Leadbetter :

We did meet on a barge. Just like he said. The place, the name of the barge, late at night, all just as he says.

Nicholas :

And?

Leadbetter :

Barford was not alone.

Nicholas :

Who was with him?

Leadbetter :

The Home Secretary. Mr Templar. I told them El-Hoorie was threatening to tell his story to the Molecule Man. I did produce that envelope with the name. It's my writing. I'd noted it when I was told by one of my men that El-Hoorie was serious.

Nicholas :

Did either of them make any reply?

Leadbetter :

Templar saw the name. I remember his exact words. "Terminally dangerous. The Molecule Man. Terminally dangerous." That's what he said. Then Barford took over. Told Templar to leave. Wait outside in the car. Demanded an undertaking that none of us ever spoke of this meeting again. It hadn't happened. Templar agreed. That's why I lied earlier. I was instructed to. By a Minister of State. What am I supposed to do?

Nicholas :
Did the Home Secretary leave?

Leadbetter :
Yes.

Nicholas :
What did Barford say?

Leadbetter :
He said there were only three alternatives. The threat of violence. Actual violence. Fatal violence. I said I would not contemplate either actual violence or fatal violence. Under any circumstances. Barford said that choice is nothing to do with you. "I make those decisions," he said. I had to meet him the next evening at Brockwell Park Lake. Give him £5000. Never speak of either meeting again. None of this had ever happened. I did as he ordered. I've never seen nor spoken to him again.

Nicholas :
Did you ever speak to a man on the phone and order him to murder El-Hoorie?

Leadbetter :
There was no phone conversation. Barford has made it up. Barford contacted Lennox, who I never knew or had even heard of, until this case. Whatever instructions Lennox received – they came from Barford.

Nicholas :
When you were on the barge you have said that the Home Secretary accompanied Barford. Did anyone accompany you?

Leadbetter :
Absolutely not.

Nicholas :
So there were only three of you?

Leadbetter :
*To begin with. Then Barford told the Home Secretary to leave.
And he did as he was told. Then there were just the two of us.*

Nicholas :
Have you now told the whole truth?

Leadbetter :
The whole truth. No holds barred.

Mr Justice Maullin :
*Members of the jury, you have now heard all of the evidence
in the case. You will soon hear the final speeches of Counsel.
I shall adjourn for an hour to give them time to finalise their
arguments. After their speeches, I will sum the case up to you.
I will summarise the evidence and direct you on the Law. You
will retire to consider your verdict mid-morning tomorrow.
The Court will now rise for one hour.*

It was as dramatic a piece of evidence as Naomi could ever
remember. Picking up her notes to take with her, she turned to speak
to Myott. He wasn't there. Brockley and Coleman sat there, unable
to offer any explanation on Myott's behalf. Yet again, at a critical
stage, he had disappeared from Court without a word. Her eyes
angrily scoured the Courtroom for him, even looking high up into
the Public Gallery, which was full to the rafters, but there was no
sign of Myott anywhere, although there were three faces that she did
immediately recognise.

Sitting in the front row and smiling down at her was Jack
Farnham. Half a dozen rows further back was Janet, the girl she'd

met who worked as a cleaner at the Courts, still sitting transfixed, recovering from the gripping tension of what she had just observed. And right at the back, invisible to the jury and most of those below, surreptitiously slipping out of the shadows, was a lean, silver-haired man, his face like thunder with hollow cheeks, reptilian features, sunken eyes and those lizard-like lids.

Chapter 37

Her first closing address to a jury as a QC was probably the best speech she had ever made in her entire career at the Bar. As her eyes travelled slowly along the two rows of six, she let her gaze lock on to each juror in turn, making that person, for that instant, believe that only he or she was of real importance in the quest for justice. Her expression and her tone communicated to the jury that only she and they mattered in this trial, sharing together the secret truth. For the hour that she addressed the jury, even Cadogan was reduced temporarily to an irrelevance and, to her own surprise, the primary driving force behind her words and energy was not the pursuit of justice, but that chubby little Liverpool comic in his crumpled yellow shirt. As the power of her performance dominated one of the most famous Courtrooms in the land, pressing for the conviction of Barford and the public denouncement of the insidious and savage corruption which he represented, it was Ben Railey's words that she could hear resounding within her own head.

"You look at that jury like you're looking at me, luv. Tell'em the tale. Fix 'em with those captivating blue eyes of yours and make that voice carry 'em away. Convince 'em that you know he did it and you can bloody prove it. You let 'em have it with both barrels. You show 'em that you're a fighter. Then you'll hear the applause, my girl."

It had always been her habit to make a note of the names of the jurors when they took their oath at the outset of the trial and, accordingly, the first page of her notebook invariably started with a list of the twelve names drawn at random from the Jury panel. As she came towards the end of her speech, her notebook stood open at that first page and, in her final words it felt as if she was somehow able to convey her message to each individual by name :

Sebastian Viney : *Professional artist*
Dorothy Lyall : *Hairdresser*

Diane Finney : Recruitment Consultant
Michael Willetts : Computer Programmer
Alan Grigg : Mechanic
Arthur Field : Retired
Melanie Denley : Receptionist
Gary Thomas : Unemployed
Hilary Shore : School Teacher
Bazra Chauhan : Project Leader
Penny Redmond : Unemployed
Stefan Villars : Unemployed

"You stand as a buffer between the powers of the State and the freedom of the individual. A young man was callously executed so that a grotesque truth might be concealed. So that the jobs and reputations of powerful people might be protected at the cost of an innocent human life. So that the relatives of the thirty-one victims on that ill-fated aeroplane might never know that their loved ones could have been spared, if the Police response had not been so criminally inept. You now have the unique chance to strike back on behalf of the thirty-one and those who are left to grieve for them. You now have the unique chance to strike back at a cynical, cruel act of corrupt suppression, orchestrated by the hatchet man in the dock to keep the truth from the public, for fear of the political backlash it might provoke. This is your chance. Your turn. Your duty."

Naomi Nicholas QC had spoken. The jury had listened. Spellbound.

* * *

Unfortunately, Naomi did make one mistake that day by walking into the QCs' Robing Room at exactly the same time as Ronan Cadogan was in there alone, admiringly adjusting his ancient wig in the mirror, before going back into Court to make his address to the jury.

"Good to see the old 'freedom of the individual' theme is still being trotted out," he volunteered sarcastically. "I thought that hackneyed *cri de coeur* had died with the old King. Very touching to hear it again after so long."

"You don't really think your cheap little jibe will get through to me, do you? she replied.

"Cheap?" he retorted. "Please, my dear. Call me anything you like, but not cheap. My instructing solicitor would doubtless confirm that cheap is not an appropriate word to apply to me."

"You may charge your clients a fortune, Ronan, but your values are still cheap. And your cheap little tricks haven't been lost on Maullin, either. He's got your number, all right."

"We do have a spiteful tongue today, my dear. Never mind, you very graciously called Leadbetter for me, aided and abetted by your admirer, Mr. Justice Maullin, the King of linguistic exactitude," Cadogan laughed.

"And no doubt aided and abetted by your Junior setting out to deceive my Junior by another of your subterfuges," Naomi barked at him, her eyes flashing with contempt.

"Like I said to you on the first day, you're in with the big boys now. Anything goes."

"Victory at any price. Nothing changes with you, does it?" she snapped, her face and tone of voice revealing her utter contempt for him, as he continued to busy himself in the mirror.

"To the victors belong the spoils of the enemy," came his immediate retort. Please excuse me, my dear, the old wig's on straight and it's time for me to head for Court. I have a case to win, you know. Now it's my chance, my turn, my duty. Very appropriate words of yours, I thought. Now watch me make you eat them."

As soon as he left the Robing Room, Naomi slumped into one of the chairs in the corner. Never had she met such an insufferable and arrogant man. Yet, at the same time, for all of his dirty tricks, his conceit and his contempt for others, he was dangerous beyond measure. His physical and intellectual power combined so as to overwhelm his opponent and completely dominate the thinking of a jury. Even after the recent exchange of just a few acid words with him, she felt exhausted. By force of logic and cruel wit he immediately gained the ascendancy in any confrontation, but the characteristic that she feared most was his natural fighting spirit. From head to toe he was a fearless warrior. In this case, Maullin had not given him one inch, yet

Cadogan had soldiered on undaunted. And now, in the next couple of hours in the crucible of the Courtroom below, he would stand alone and subject the jury to the full force of his crushing power. Much as she despised him, she feared him more. A warrior who had hardly ever lost a case since he took silk so many years ago. The deadliest of opponents.

On her way back downstairs to Court she espied Myott, leaning on the wall of the stairwell, speaking quietly into his mobile phone. As soon as he became aware of her approach he abruptly terminated the call and fell in alongside her as she descended the stairs.

"AWOL again, Mike. Missing probably the most significant evidence in the case. It's a good job I've got Mel and his laptop or I'd have big gaps in the notes of some important answers given when I'm on my feet," Naomi declared, making no attempt to disguise the irritation in her voice.

"I know. Sorry. I had to make an urgent call. I was only gone for a few minutes. Mel told me what happened with Leadbetter," he inadequately replied.

"It's hardly the point that you learned what happened. You're paid to be there when it's said. You have a knack of disappearing at crucial times. I'm not impressed, I have to say," she said.

"I was there for your speech though. Dynamite. You had them hooked. Probably as powerful a speech as I've ever heard."

"Flattery will get you everywhere, I suppose," she responded, reluctantly smiling at his cheek. "But if you want to hear real power, then listen to Cadogan this afternoon. Horrible man, but as an orator he's something special."

Taking their seats in Counsels' row, a poignant quiet descended upon the arena as the expectation of Cadogan's speech filled the air. In magnificent style he opened with a barrage of cannon fire.

"On the combined words of a dead rapist and a self-confessed perjurer, the Prosecution contend that you can be certain of guilt. Lennox, the career criminal, the man who rented out his brutality in Sierra Leone and unleashed his savagery on a schoolgirl back in England. Leadbetter, whose evidence on any analysis is a litany of brazen lies on oath. A heady concoction. The thug and the deceiver. The mercenary and the corrupt.

Lewis Barford has been put up as the scapegoat. That's just how the faceless men of Special Branch and the Intelligence Services direct their subordinates to operate. Everything done at arm's length, with the dupe at the end of the line acting in ignorance of what is really intended. You may rest assured that in some dark corner of London skulks a sinister Establishment creature, watching every twist and turn of this trial, assessing who can be relied upon and who cannot."

This heavy artillery barrage was followed by the precision marksmanship of the trained sniper, picking off each allegation against his client and leaving it mortally wounded on the ground. Naomi squirmed uncomfortably in her seat as his sights moved from target to target, never missing, because his skill ensured that he selected only those targets that he could completely destroy. At a quarter past four, with impeccable timing, he reached his crescendo, that powerful Irish voice booming out the innocence of his client, whilst his awesome presence completely overwhelmed the thinking processes of the jury. By the time that he concluded, with a thundering proclamation of his client's innocence, the jury had been bludgeoned into submission. Where Naomi had captivated them, Cadogan now dominated them by sheer force of personality.

Tomorrow morning the Judge would sum the case up and by noon the jury would be considering their verdict. The end game was near.

Chapter 38

Wearing a navy blue woollen hat pulled low across his forehead and sporting a mid-grey Adidas tracksuit with barely-used black running shoes, he was completely unrecognisable as he jogged at snail's pace across Chelsea Bridge in the darkness of the night. As he approached the mid-point of the Bridge he could see that the other man was already there, leaning casually on the stone parapet, wrapped in a heavy Crombie overcoat and wide-brimmed hat.

Unathletic, unfit and living in fear, the jogger panted to a halt alongside the slender, elderly man who stared out along the rippling surface of the black river, making no attempt to acknowledge the figure who had just joined him. "We've reached the point of no return," the jogger began breathlessly. "We can't afford to leave anything to chance."

"You mean you've reached the point of no return, Home Secretary. I was not named in Court. You were. There were only three men on that barge, not four," barked the older man, in a voice that did not seem to come from within his body.

"Leadbetter lied. We both know you were there. If Barford is convicted we both fall. Denstone's axe is poised. He won't just take off one head. He'll need a sacrifice from your lot," Templar said, now leaning on the parapet alongside the older man, the sweat on his pallid face drying rapidly in the breeze off the water.

"He's got that already. Leadbetter's finished whatever the verdict."

"Leadbetter isn't enough. In the context of this fiasco he's a foot soldier. Denstone will take out the top men. The Chief Constable of Manchester. Me. And you, Commander," Templar announced emphatically, aware that the tic in his left cheek had started up again.

"He doesn't know I was there. Leadbetter will never give him my name. We still retain a modicum of loyalty in our Service," the Commander retorted angrily.

"But I know you were there."

"He won't believe you. You will have been discredited by the verdict."

"Wrong. He already knows. I told him this evening. He believes me. If I go, then you go. If Barford walks, we both survive. My prints weren't on that envelope so it would only be Leadbetter's word that I was there. So acquittal spells survival. That's where Denstone stands. Like I said, we've reached the point of no return."

"You're a bastard, Templar," the Commander snarled, turning aggressively to face the Home Secretary. In the eerie light Templar caught a glimpse of the small, sharp teeth within the dry, thin lipped mouth and saw the biblical snake striking at its prey from the beneath the rock. "But I can forgive you that. It's the fact that you're such a coward that I can't stomach," the metallic voice continued.

"You'd lost control of this disaster long before the barge," Templar snapped back. "You failed to re-establish control when Curbishley dropped dead and you blew it when you tried to stop that woman from calling Leadbetter. Abusing me doesn't absolve you from the consequences of those failures."

"I recognise the stench of fear, Templar. It's rank. Even out here in the open air. But I don't doubt that you will have done everything you can to put my head on the block alongside yours," came the acid reply.

"So let's be constructive. You operate at the highest level of National Security and Intelligence. You wield great power. You can move in. Strike. And move out. Invisible. But deadly," Templar urged, his voice becoming increasingly animated and his eyes darting to left and right.

"Move in? Move in where?"

"Think about it. You'll work it out. That's why you're a Commander. Time I got back home. Got out of this ridiculous gear," replied Templar, turning to go back the way he had come. Pausing for a moment, he then asked, "Have you worked it out yet?"

The lizard-like lids were almost closed, displaying the dry scales upon the surface of the flaky skin. The nose was narrow and pinched and the lips were totally bloodless. The long head was moving slowly around on the shoulders and, beneath the coat, the upper body was beginning to shake. Templar stared in horrified fascination at this grotesque apparition, waiting for it to speak. But the sound that emerged was thin, distant and high-pitched, like a child's cry from the grave. It took Templar a few seconds to understand what was happening, before the full realisation hit him. The Commander had worked it out. The Commander was laughing.

Chapter 39

Mr. Justice Maullin, barely disguising his profound distaste at Cadogan's tactics, summed up a six-day trial in one hour and twenty-five minutes in a masterpiece of conciseness. At last all of the actors had played their parts, recited their lines and were about to withdraw from the stage. It would be for the jury to bring the final curtain down.

The sombre-looking jurors followed each other out of the jury box and through the door to their right, where their spartan jury retiring room awaited them. The oblong table. Twelve hard, straight-backed chairs. Twelve paper cups and six decanters of tepid water. The notice on the wall directing them that the Law would never allow them to reveal the content of their discussions within the hallowed sanctuary of the retiring room. The pile of foolscap paper in the middle of the table for note taking. The tired menu listing the variety of sandwiches they could order through the jury bailiff for their lunch. The crude tools of justice.

On that night Arsenal were at home to Newcastle United and Jack Farnham was covering the match for his newspaper. Consequently, he had been able to stay down in London, lend Naomi some moral support and attend parts of the trial, although he had missed the Judge's summing up. Shortly after the jury's retirement he had arrived at the Old Bailey, tracked Naomi down in the coffee shop and suggested that at one o'clock they might walk down to El Guerrero Valiente, a tapas bar just off the main road, to escape the tension of the Courthouse for an hour.

As one o'clock neared Mike Myott wandered into the coffee shop, already changed into his ordinary collar and tie, and invited himself along to the Wine Bar with them. Like most of the hostelries in that part of the City at lunch time there was hardly a spare seat, but as the trio walked in a couple of rather scruffy youths were just vacating their table and Myott deftly manoeuvred himself into one of the seats to claim the table. One of the youths turned to look at him on his way out and acknowledged him with a wave of the hand. "Nice one, Mike," he laughed as he made his way to the door and disappeared from view.

"Friend of yours?" Jack enquired.

"No. I often have a drink in The Nailer's Arms round the corner from here. It's not far from my chambers. He goes in there. He's a runner for one of the papers. Chats to anyone," Myott replied. "Were you in Court for Cadogan's speech?" he continued.

"I deliberately chose not to be there," Jack answered. "He's not exactly my cup of dry Martini. Naomi said it was powerful stuff, though."

"It was out of the top drawer. But, if I can spare Naomi's blushes, it was no better than hers. She was dynamite," Myott responded.

Jack caught the waitress's eye and ordered a bottle of Rioja and a plate of sandwiches while Naomi chatted to Myott about the virtues of the Judge's summing up. Their order promptly arrived and, as Myott enthusiastically attacked the roast beef sandwiches, Jack asked him about his practice.

"I enjoy doing research papers. Particularly on the rules governing the admissibility of evidence."

"But what kind of cases have you done in Court, as opposed to research?" Jack asked.

"Anything that comes my way. Bit of Crime, bit of Civil," Myott answered as he reached across for yet another of the sandwiches. "Can I ask a personal question?" he added, neatly changing the subject.

"You can ask," Jack replied with a twinkle in his eye, "but I may not answer. Is it about football?"

"No, not directly anyway. I just wondered how you two met. A footballer and a barrister. How did your paths cross?"

Jack and Naomi looked at each other, as they both recalled the cruel circumstances which had led to their meeting. Naomi was about to tell Myott to mind his own business, but Jack seemed quite prepared to answer.

"My wife was killed by a drunk driver. Naomi prosecuted him. That's how we first met," Jack explained.

"Oh, I'm sorry" said Myott, "I had no idea that . . . "

"Don't be sorry. It's not a secret. It happened. We bumped into each other some time later when the pain was healing. So I started to learn a little bit about barristers and Naomi started to learn a lot about football," Jack responded.

"And on that subject, are you covering the match tonight?" Myott enquired.

"Yes. I'm doing a newspaper report, not a commentary. I have to be at the ground before five so I'll have to leave the Old Bailey by four o'clock."

"I'm an Arsenal supporter," said Myott in a perfect imitation of the famous French Manager of the team. "I have spent thirty million pounds on building the finest team in Europe," he continued, as Jack laughed in instant recognition of the impression.

"Not bad at all. Can you do anyone else?" asked Jack.

"Oh, yes. I can do most of the Premier Managers and half of the Cabinet," he replied in a stunning impression of the Prime Minister's voice. "I was involved in the Footlights Revues at Cambridge and I've never lost it," he continued in the exact tones of Ronan Cadogan. "I could do plenty more of Cadogan for you, now I've listened to him for a week."

"I think we'll pass on that one," insisted Naomi. "I've heard just about as much of that voice as I ever want to hear, thank you very much."

"I second that," Jack laughed. "But do you reckon there'll be a verdict before I have to leave?" Jack asked.

"Doubtful, in my opinion," Naomi volunteered. "I'd say there's an even money chance that they won't reach a verdict today. We'll probably all be back again tomorrow, forced to endure another day in the same building as Cadogan."

"You despise him, Naomi," Myott interjected. "I've seen the way that you look at him. No doubt you've got good reason. But I have to tell you that something he said in his speech yesterday really struck a chord with me."

"What?" Naomi asked with some interest.

"When he said *'You may rest assured that in some dark corner of London skulks a sinister Establishment creature, watching every twist and turn of this trial, assessing who can be relied upon and who cannot'*. I think you and I know who that is. We actually saw him at the end of last week."

"The man with a reptile's face," Naomi responded immediately. "Venturing out into the sunlight to put the pressure on Brockley to stop us calling Leadbetter."

"One and the same," Myott declared.

"Surely you can't be surprised that there are shadowy figures in the background of a case like this?" Jack queried. "Political intrigue oozes out of every pore of this story."

"No. It's not surprise, Jack. It's the fact that Naomi and I saw him. Someone felt it necessary to exert so much pressure on us not to call Leadbetter, that the man from the shadows was forced to venture out into the sunlight," Myott explained.

"But the impetus to call Leadbetter came from Cadogan. So it wouldn't seem that Cadogan and the mystery man were singing from the same hymn sheet, would it?" suggested Naomi.

"I'd disagree with that," Myott replied firmly. "I suspect that Cadogan had a hymn sheet but ignored it. Played it his own way. Took his own course without ever bothering to inform the power brokers."

"The only course that Cadogan will ever follow is the course that he believes will lead to victory. Whoever gets trampled on is an irrelevance. He knew from his instructions that Leadbetter's prints were highly likely to be on that envelope, or the money, or both. In fact, I suspect he knew for sure. So he went for it. He's ruthless," Naomi declared with conviction.

"A fearless warrior," laughed Myott as he drained his glass. "That's the name of this Bar, you know. 'El Guerrero Valiente' – the Fearless Warrior."

"So Spanish is another of your hidden talents is it?" Jack grinned, gesturing to the waitress for their bill.

"I'm bi-lingual. My Spanish is fluent. We all have our hidden talents. Mel Coleman speaks fluent German, for example. In fact he is German, his middle name is Ulrich, but he's lived here most of his life. My mother is Spanish, although she's spent most of the last twenty years in England and America. She writes in Spanish," said Myott as they all got up to leave the table.

"What does she write?" asked Naomi, somewhat intrigued at this revelation by her oddball Junior.

"Books about injustice. Mainly about injustice in Spanish society. Before and after Franco. But any injustice. She's had eight books published," he announced with some pride in his voice.

"Well," said Jack, "Let's get back to Court and see some justice done. A Guilty verdict before four o'clock so that I'm there to see it."

As the trio wandered slowly back towards the Old Bailey, the lowering clouds began to spit rain, the narrow pavement became a sea of umbrellas and the noise of the traffic changed as car tyres skimmed through the surface water. Outside the Courts TV cameramen had set up their equipment under golf umbrellas, whilst the crews huddled in the main doorway of the Court as the rain grew heavier.

"The vultures are gathering," Jack grunted in Naomi's direction, as they hurried up the steps and into the shelter of the building. "See you in the Coffee Shop when you've changed."

Dirty plates and discarded paper cups littered the tabletops, whilst small pools of spilt drinks lay on many of the red, plastic seats. The Coffee Shop was completely deserted, save for the tiny oriental woman behind the counter, scowling at the desolate scene where she spent most of her daylight hours. When Naomi arrived in her robes, Jack bought two coffees, smiling at the unfortunate soul, but her job left no room for smiles. There was no sign of Myott and so Jack and Naomi sat alone, watching the world outside grow darker as the heavy rain settled in for the rest of the day, and felt their mood follow the pattern of the weather. By quarter to four Jack was becoming restless. The relentless rain meant taxis would be hard to find and there was always a lot of work to be done before the kick-off. The two or three pre-match hours in the Bars, the VIP Lounges and the Press Box invariably threw up material for the article, which could be threaded into the match narrative and provide the extra edge that editors always expected their writers to unearth.

"Go on, Jack. I can see you want to get off to the match. Besides, there's not much prospect of them reaching a verdict in the next three quarters of an hour," volunteered Naomi.

"If you really don't mind, I will shoot off. I'm bound to be back at the hotel late, so don't wait up for me," he replied, looking at his watch anxiously, before kissing her gently on the cheek and hurrying away.

Sitting around waiting for things to happen just didn't suit Jack's temperament, Naomi thought to herself, as she levered herself slowly out of the uncomfortable seat. There had hardly been a customer in the place while she and Jack had whiled away the time that afternoon and the oriental woman was now sitting on a high stool, staring emptily into space until half past four arrived and she could escape.

Outside in the Main Hall there was little sign of activity. A few people were seated on the wooden benches and the odd Court Official could be seen wandering about. The whole atmosphere was lethargic and bored, for it was obvious to everyone that the jury would not return with their verdict today. Naomi headed towards the stairs, intending to spend the last few minutes of the day in the Robing Room before the Judge summoned them back into Court to adjourn the proceedings until tomorrow. Over the years she had tried to learn to switch her mind off during the long hours, and sometimes days, of a jury retirement. But the nervous tension was inescapable and, in reality, in most cases, her mental energies were directed towards willing the jury to find in her favour. There was no avoiding the importance of this case to her career. High-profile. First case as a QC. The Old Bailey. Her name had already been splashed all over the front pages of the national newspapers at the beginning of the trial and, once the verdict had been reached, it would be there again. The public would thereafter automatically associate her name with success or failure, according to the verdict in this one case. A defeat at this level would not look good on her professional record, whereas a victory would probably make her one of the most sought-after silks in the country. Besides, Barford deserved to be convicted. Whilst she had no doubt that the judicial proceedings had not unearthed anything like the whole truth, she was sure that Barford was a ruthless hatchet man, well capable of giving the orders to kill and, whether he actually had or hadn't done so in this case, there would be other people whose lives he had destroyed along the way. The notion of rough justice was always a source of comfort to the criminal barrister. And then there was Cadogan. The prospect of inflicting defeat on that insufferable bully was the most powerful incentive of all.

"Naomi, Naomi," a voice rang out excitedly from above.

Looking up she saw Myott, leaning over the bannisters from two floors above and shouting down into the stairwell.

"They're back. There's a verdict," he cried, now running down the stairs to join her.

"How do you read it?" he panted as he caught up with her and they both descended the stairs together and headed back towards the Main Hall.

"I don't read it," she replied, her mouth now dry and her heart pounding as the final moments of high drama approached. Battling to appear calm, she deliberately slowed her walk, demanding of herself that she remained composed. As they reached the Hall, the tranquil, bored scene of a few minutes earlier had undergone a complete transformation. People had appeared from nowhere and there was an animated throng of reporters, members of the public, barristers and Court Officials clamouring to get into the Court. A hubbub of noise filled the high-ceilinged Hall as the moment of truth neared.

Suddenly, the crowd parted and there was just a second or two of awed silence, as the enormous figure of Cadogan strode imperiously through the middle, his Junior in his wake. Naomi was still on the steps and able to observe the whole scene and, whilst she could not see Cadogan's face, she had no doubt that his expression would reveal how he relished these desperate moments of tension. He thrived on them. They fed his ego. Supreme self-confidence. And, with hardly an exception, his record in silk justified such self-confidence. Could this be the case that broke his run. The case that dented his insufferable arrogance. How she craved victory. She wanted to wound him. The crowd's expectant chattering and buzzing had now resumed again and she and Myott were carried forward on the surge of bodies, momentarily crushed tightly together as they reached the double doors of the Courtroom and then they were through and back into the arena. Standing on the sand. Gladiator against gladiator. The ultimate confrontation. In a few minutes either she or Cadogan would taste the elation of victory, whilst the other would lie face down in the sand, vanquished. How she prayed to be the victor.

Suddenly, there was a loud banging on the side door of the dais as the usher heralded the approach of Mr Justice Maullin. A silence descended in an instant upon the crowd. Scarlet robes, ermine and white wig strode through the door and Mr Justice Maullin, his face set and grim, bowed perfunctorily in Counsel's direction before taking his seat. A clanking of heavy keys and turning locks presaged the arrival

271

of Barford in the dock. Neither Cadogan nor Naomi turned to look at him as he took up his position, still standing, between the four burly prison officers who flanked him on either side. But theirs were the only eyes that did not look. Stapleton looked. Myott stared, transfixed. Coleman's eyes were riveted on him. The packed public gallery upstairs, the dozens of Reporters in the Press Seats close to the well of the Court, strained their necks to see the face of the prisoner in the dock, the man who was prepared to kill so that Establishment figures might hang on to their jobs and salvage their prestige at any price. But Lewis Barford denied them their pound of flesh. He stood tall, his face resolute. He had spent a youth on the streets of a Liverpool Council Estate, he had actually killed in the Arctic and he'd seen the savagery of death, African-style, in Sierra Leone. Calling upon the steel that had seen him through those extremes, he determined that this sea of white-faced ghouls, gathering like the *tricoteurs* at the guillotine, would see not one sign of fear, nor sense one whimper of distress. Jaw set, shoulders back, hands at his side, he stood to attention and awaited the opening of the door through which the jury would emerge.

In they marched. Twelve solemn faces. Mostly with heads down. None looking at the Defendant. Barristers' folk lore had always been that a jury never looked into the face of a prisoner they were about to convict. All eyes, including those of Naomi Nicholas, Ronan Cadogan and even the Judge, had now switched to study those twelve worried faces, desperately seeking some clue as to what their verdict would be.

As the last juror took her place, the Clerk of the Court, a rather plump, middle-aged woman, looking slightly ridiculous in her wig which was unable to sit properly on top of her heavily lacquered hair, rose to her feet to begin the final rites.

R v Lewis Barford
Transcript 76

"Will the Foreman please rise," the Clerk declared.

Arthur Field rose to his feet. He was the oldest member of the jury. For thirty-one years he had worked in the Finance Department of one of the old Borough Councils. It had been a lifetime achieving nothing. He had produced nothing. He had added nothing to society. He had watched, year by year, as the profligate, ill-directed spending of the Council had frittered away the community's precious resources, realising that he could exert no influence over the culture of waste that dominated Local Government. And so, whilst still a young man, he had just given up. Ensuring that he never put his job at risk, never asked the wrong questions, he pushed his pen, and later his computer mouse, from nine until five and then went home to the same house and the same wife, counting the days until he could take retirement at the earliest possible opportunity. Now, he was Foreman of a jury in a major trial at the Old Bailey. Not because he had wanted to be. But because none of the other eleven had wanted the job. He had simply proved to be the weakest of the twelve and so had been coerced into acceptance. Still not yet sixty but looking nearer seventy he was bald, bespectacled, small, thin and, above all, the epitomy of insignificance. He had been born to be insignificant. And now, for the next sixty seconds, he was probably the most important person in the country.

"Mr Foreman, will you please answer my first question either 'yes' or 'no'. Have the jury reached a verdict on which you are all agreed?"

"Yes, My Lord," came Field's surprisingly loud response. Having not wanted the job, this instant of celebrity had suddenly developed its own macabre appeal.

"On the charge of Conspiracy to murder do you find the Defendant 'Guilty' or 'Not Guilty.'"

"Not Guilty, My Lord," Field replied.

"You find the Defendant 'Not Guilty' and that is the verdict of you all?"

"It is, My Lord."

Pandemonium broke out in the Press Seats as the reporters, in a frenzy, raced for the doors, frantically pressing the buttons on their mobile phones, which they had already been clutching in their sweaty hands out of sight of the Judge. Mr Justice Maullin was an old hand. It was easier to wait a minute, let them all get out of Court, and then seek to restore some dignity to the proceedings. Just shouting at them would make not the slightest difference as they engaged in their feeding frenzy. The rest of the public gallery upstairs had remained remarkably well-behaved, but the Judge's steely eyes were fixed on Ronan Cadogan, casually leaning back in his seat, those massive arms stretched out along the back of the Bench and his face gloating, looking around the Court as if he was some famed classical actor taking his bow at the end of yet another fine performance. As Cadogan's sweep came full circle, his eyes met those of the Judge and he held them there, the half-smile instantly disappearing to be replaced by an expression of triumphant defiance. Maullin hated him and Cadogan knew it and relished it. Significantly, it was Maullin who looked away first, averting his gaze in the direction of Naomi Nicholas.

In his judgement, she had done nothing wrong. A breathtaking re-examination of Leadbetter, a brilliant closing speech and never allowing Cadogan to steamroller her or bully her. She had not deserved to lose and her lovely face was now sad to behold. The colour had drained away and her head was down, staring disconsolately at her closed notebook. From his lofty position, Mr. Justice Maullin could see that her hands were shaking.

Gradually, as the last reporter pushed his way out of the door, order returned to the Courtroom and Cadogan rose arrogantly to his feet.

"May Lewis Barford be discharged from the dock, My Lord?"

In the midst of the noise and bustle following the verdict, little attention seemed to have been paid to Barford, who had displayed not the slightest of emotions. Simply resuming his seat, without any invitation to do so from the Judge, he had stared straight ahead, expressionless, awaiting his release from the dock.

"Let him be discharged," announced the Judge.

One of the Prison Officers unlocked the door of the dock and Barford walked out. He looked at no one but marched, like a soldier, towards the exit doors of the Court, the noise of his heavy footsteps echoing around the Court.

"Please wait, Mr Barford," Cadogan shouted towards the disappearing figure as he reached the doors. "I intend to apply for Costs."

Barford stopped and turned, looking back on the bloodied sand of the arena where the battle had been fought, seeing the wigs and gowns, the pomp and trappings of the rotten society of which he was part. Within the dramatic atmosphere he could now sense the wall of frustration and disappointment that the quarry had escaped and his heart was filled with abject contempt for them all and for the system as a whole. Strangely, his eyes lingered longest on Naomi Nicholas. She had undoubtedly believed that he had given Lennox instructions to kill and had fought with everything that she'd got. Ironically, of all the major players in the game, she was the only one for whom he'd had even a modicum of respect. He recognised where she came from. When you escape from the gutter you instinctively recognise someone who has travelled the same road. Now she sat with her head down, bowed and defeated while Cadogan, her Nemesis and his Saviour, barked out his command that Barford should remain, while he applied for costs and added the final public humiliation to Naomi Nicholas's position. Barford knew which one of the two he preferred.

Cadogan was still looking at him, as was the Judge, awaiting him to return to a seat within the Court, so that the costs application might be pursued. Barford stared back at him and then at the Judge.

"Stuff your bloody Costs," he declared, turning on his heel and striding out of the doors into the Main Hallway and out of sight. Mr Justice Maullin was too wise to have him dragged back and threatened with contempt proceedings. It was over.

"I do apply for a Defendant's Costs Order, My Lord, despite the Defendant's observation."

"Why?" snapped Mr Justice Maullin.

"Because he has been acquitted, My Lord. He is Not Guilty. An acquitted Defendant is entitled to his costs."

"Unless his own behaviour has brought the Prosecution upon himself," came the Judge's retort. "The evidence before me, as given by your own client on oath, is that he was a key figure in a conspiracy to burgle someone's home to steal a diary. Even though the jury, for such reasons as they see fit, have acquitted him of conspiracy to murder, in my judgement his own admitted actions have played a significant part in his prosecution. Your application for costs is refused. Sit down, Mr Cadogan, you've said enough. Members of the jury," the Judge continued, now rising from his chair and flouncing towards the door, "you can go."

Slowly, the Court began to empty. Cadogan busied himself for a moment or two, gathering up his papers, tying them up with the pink ribbon that traditionally bound a Brief for the Defence. "Stapleton," he barked. "Kindly take all of these papers and my lectern up to the Robing Room. I'll instruct my clerk to come and collect them in the morning."

"Thank you for your services, Mr Cadogan," the solicitor Bloom announced from his position alongside Stapleton, as they awaited the big man's departure.

"A pleasure, Mr Bloom. Most enjoyable way to spend a few days," he replied loud enough to ensure that Naomi, still motionless in her seat, could hear. Moving his vast bulk along Counsels' row he went directly up to her. "I'll have to ask you to let me out, my dear," he declared with overtly false courtesy.

"You could have gone out the other way," she replied crossly, as she stood up and stepped out of the row to let him pass.

"No, I couldn't, because I wanted a quiet little word in your ear before I left," he replied as he passed close by her.

"I don't really think I want to hear," she replied, now physically nearer to him than she had been at any previous stage in the trial, so that the ugly jowls were almost directly at her eye-level and she was able to see how the heavy flesh hung over the edge of his starched wing collar. Everything about him was so huge, except for the eyes, which seemed to reduce in size when he spoke, in direct proportion to the venom of his words.

"Just this," he continued, ignoring her expressed lack of interest. "A little word of advice. A Golden Rule for Silks."

"I really don't want any advice from you, thank you very much," she answered, resuming her seat and turning away from him.

"The bitterness of defeat," he sighed. "An emotion with which I am singularly unfamiliar. Anyway, here's the advice. Never, but never, listen to your Junior. It's a recipe for disaster."

"I take that as an admission that you set Myott up in the Robing Room to provoke me into calling Leadbetter," she replied. "If so, I can tell you that your deceit played no part in my decision."

"Take it however you like. Anyway, you've lost your first case in silk. Let's hope that someone gives you another chance. It can only get worse," he replied, as he moved away. As he neared the doors she heard him starting to laugh. A horrible, mirthless sound starting from deep within his belly and bursting out of the barrel chest. The cruellest of sounds. Cadogan was crowing.

Chapter 40

Case papers lay scattered carelessly across the desk in front of her. Everyone had gone. There was not a sign of Myott. His brief had been taken away. Brockley and Coleman had disappeared. The Public Gallery was deserted and the Court Officials had scurried off home. Twenty minutes ago, this Courtroom had been the focus of attention of half the country and a spectacular scene had been played out to a packed audience. Now, there was no sound. The arena was deserted. The panelled walls had absorbed another piece of human drama into their varnish. Naomi sat alone, head in hands and, temporarily, beaten. When that insignificant little man had risen as the jury's foreman, her vibes had told her all was not well and when he announced the verdict, she had felt her strength ebb away. It was a desperate defeat. Cadogan had humiliated her but, slowly, the immediate shock subsided and her strength began to return.

Somehow she was going to have to face the world. Looking at her watch it was now nearly quarter past five. All the reporters and the crowds would be gone. As she started to collect up her papers, the drone of a vacuum cleaner could be heard from the room off to the right of the Court where the jury's room was situated and, a moment or two later, it grew louder as the cleaner worked her way into the main Courtroom itself, pushing her vacuum cleaner with one hand and clutching a bundle of odd pieces of paper in the other. It was Janet Kelly and, as she loomed into view, she espied Naomi, tying up her brief and about to depart.

The young cleaner's face broke into a smile as soon as she saw her and she immediately turned off her vacuum cleaner, placing her bundle of papers on the desk whilst looking for the black bag into which they would go with the rest of the rubbish of the day.

"I'm so sorry you lost," she exclaimed. "I came nearly every day to listen to you. I heard your final speech. You were marvellous."

"But I lost," Naomi replied, her voice still flat and down.

"There's losing and there's losing, isn't there, Miss. The case was lost. But that had nothing to do with your performance. In a way, you won, 'cos you were the better barrister. That big man was horrible, he was," Janet answered.

"Horrible, but a winner nevertheless. Still, thank you for your vote of confidence. It helps."

"I'm only saying what everyone else in the Public gallery was saying. Lots of the same people came every day, you know. They all says the same. That Miss Nicholas, she's brilliant, they said. You can trust her. You can't trust that big one."

"Well, you are making me feel better already. I'm glad we met again," Naomi answered, beginning to smile for the first time since the verdict.

"Not as glad as I am that we met in the first place, Miss. I learned those lines. Those lines you recited. I went home and learned them. Then I phoned our local amateur dramatic society. Got an audition and they've given me a part. Tilburina. I'm going to be Tilburina," she proclaimed with great excitement. That's all down to you, that is."

"Tilburina. 'The Critic' by Sheridan. Have I got the right one?" asked Naomi.

"That's the one. It's a good part. Who knows where it may lead. All because I met you and learned those lines."

"Let's hear them, then," demanded Naomi enthusiastically. "I'm entitled to the first public performance. Off you go. Stand on the Judge's dais and pretend that this is your theatre, packed to the rafters."

The young girl put down the black dustbin bag and, without protest, strode confidently up the short flight of stairs and took up her position on the raised platform alongside the Judge's empty throne-like seat.

"Right, here I go. Julius Caesar. Act Four."

"There is a tide in the affairs of men,
Which, taken at the flood, leads on to fortune;
Omitted, all the voyage of their life
Is bound in shallows, and in miseries.
On such a full sea are we now afloat;
And we must take the current when it serves,
Or lose our ventures."

This time it was Naomi's turn to stand entranced as the strong voice of the young cleaner echoed around the Courtroom, lifting Naomi's spirits from the depths they had so recently plumbed and, in the silence that followed, she realised that Janet was right. She had not lost the case. No other barrister could have done it better. She had not made any mistakes. Calling Leadbetter had been the right decision, made for the right reasons. In inspiring Janet to look for a better life, Janet had, in turn, reminded her that she was an outstanding barrister, from an impoverished home in a Nottingham mining village who had risen to the rank of QC on sheer merit. She had nothing to be ashamed of.

"It's no wonder you got the part with a performance like that," she finally announced to the delighted face staring down at her.

"Thank you, Miss. I'm so excited. Rehearsals start this weekend. When we do the real thing I'd love you to come. Do you think you might?" she asked as she came back down the stairs to return to the vacuum cleaner, the discarded papers and the black bag.

"It's a promise. I'll write my chambers telephone number down for you. You phone when you know the date and I'll be there for sure. But only if you stop calling me Miss, for goodness sake. You know my name. Naomi. Not Miss. Not Miss Nicholas. Naomi. Have you got that?" she laughed.

"Right, Naomi," Janet giggled. "Here, write your number on this scrap piece of paper," she declared, picking up the top piece from the pile of papers she had brought through into the Courtroom with her. "I'll put it in my diary when I get . . . " The girl's voice tailed away as she walked over towards Naomi to hand her the piece of paper. She stood, staring at it in surprise. "Oh, my goodness," she exclaimed. "Just look at that. Just look at that."

Naomi took the foolscap paper from the girl's hand and saw, staring straight back at her, a pencil portrait of her own face adorned by her barrister's wig. It was so skilful that it had accurately captured not only every tiny detail, but also the light in her face when she smiled. It was drawn at a slight angle and she knew immediately that the expression on her face was the expression that the jury would have seen at close quarters as she addressed them in her final speech.

"Where did you get this from?" she demanded to know.

"It's the rubbish from the jury's retiring room. I have to collect it all up. Put it in my black dustbin bag and take it down to the basement. It gets incinerated 'cos it's private. Jury room stuff has to be burned. So one of them jurors must have drawn you. It's brilliant."

"It is," Naomi agreed. "But you'll have to put it in your bag and have it incinerated. You'd get us both the sack if anyone knew you'd given to me."

"Are you going to tell then, Naomi? 'Cos I'm not. Come on. You keep it. Put it in your scrapbook. It's too good just to chuck out," Janet insisted, pushing the rest of the rubbish into the bag. Got to get on with my cleaning now. Just write me your number down on one of your pieces of paper this time, though," she laughed.

Naomi opened her Counsel's notebook, tore out a clean piece of paper, wrote down her name and number and thrust it into the girl's hand.

"I'll keep the picture and show it to Jack. He's my boyfriend. Then I'll decide whether to keep it or burn it," she declared. "But it's our secret, isn't it? We could get each other into a lot of trouble."

"What piece of paper is that, then?" Janet giggled. "I don't know nothing about any piece of paper. See you at the play. Make sure you come."

"I'll be there," Naomi assured her, as the girl switched on the vacuum cleaner and carried on with her work. She put the portrait on top of her brief and set off for the Robing Room. When she got there it was not, as she had expected, deserted. She had no doubt that Cadogan would long since have departed, but she was not expecting to see anyone at all in there at this late hour. However, sitting at one of the desks, beavering away on his laptop computer, sat Mike Myott.

"Naomi," he exclaimed as she came in and put her papers down on the desk. "I hope you didn't mind me waiting for you but I didn't want to interrupt you while you were sitting alone in Court. I guessed that you needed a bit of time to yourself."

"Just felt a bit depressed, for a while, I have to admit. Much better now, though," she replied as she removed her wig, robes and bands and put her suit jacket on.

"I just wanted to thank you. You did a fantastic job. I didn't want you to think that any of this was your fault. And I felt badly about the Leadbetter business."

"No. I've thought it through. Calling Leadbetter was the right decision. It wasn't just because of Cadogan's foul play. The decision was made for the right reasons. And, given what you'd heard, it could hardly be expected that you wouldn't tell me. But thanks for staying to say what you said," she replied, looking into the earnest face opposite.

"I meant it. You handled the case brilliantly."

"Thanks," she mumbled, looking around the room at the same time. "I don't know what has become of my suitcase," she announced, disappearing around the lockers and starting to open some of them.

There were eight rows of lockers in that section of the Robing Room and it took her a couple of minutes to go through them all until eventually, she found it pushed behind the locker furthest away. Throughout those couple of minutes, Myott had been out of sight, making no attempt to help her locate it. When she walked back to the desk he was staring at the pencil portrait of her on top of her brief.

"That's a pretty impressive piece of work," he proclaimed. "Who drew it?"

"None of your damned business," she snapped back, angry both with herself for leaving it on top of the brief and with him for looking at it.

"I see," he replied, rather icily. "Right, I'll be on my way, then."

"A friend of mine. Came to watch some of the trial. He knows me very well. That's why it's so good. He gave it me here yesterday and I put it in my notebook, that's all," she lied, putting it inside her notebook and packing everything away into her case.

"OK. Well, I hope I get to be led by you again," he said, zipping up his laptop carrying case. "If ever anyone asks me who to recommend to lead in a criminal case your name will be top of my list. Goodbye."

"Goodbye," she replied, as he hurried away.

Chapter 41

Arsenal beat Newcastle United by four goals to one under the floodlights. It never stopped raining for the entirety of the match. Jack got one pre-match interview with the celebrated manager of the Newcastle team, but failed to obtain any post-match interviews at all. Newcastle were keen to get back on to their coach for the long journey North and the Arsenal contingent seemed more interested in heading home on such a foul night than hanging round feeding the journalists a few lines for the morning editions. In the Press Box, Jack had filed his report down the line by ten-thirty and had accepted the offer of a lift back to the hotel from the *Sun*'s jovial football correspondent immediately afterwards. The awful news from the Old Bailey had come through on the wire and he had tried to phone Naomi before the kick-off, but her mobile had been switched off and the hotel said that she hadn't got back there yet. At least tomorrow they could head back home to Leeds and he'd have a couple of days with her to help her weather the storm.

When he let himself into the suite, her robes were thrown across the back of one of the armchairs, her brief was standing on the coffee table and she was lying fully clothed on the bed, fast asleep. Gently shaking her arm he woke her up, and, as her eyes opened and saw his kind face looking down on her, she reached out, took his hand and smiled.

"I'm OK," she said, swinging her long legs off the bed. "I'm dealing with it. Was it a good match?"

"So, so," he answered. "But your news is more important. They must have come back immediately after I left."

"Pretty soon after you went. It was absolutely awful. Cadogan was quite ghastly. The Judge tried to slap him down but you could hear him crowing all the way down Fleet Street."

"I had to wake you up. You're still dressed," Jack explained apologetically. "Otherwise I'd have let you sleep. Things may seem a bit better in the morning."

"Better?" she declared, walking over to the fridge alongside the minibar and extracting an opened bottle of Pinot Grigio. "My name'll be splashed all over the front pages as a loser. Do you want a glass of this?"

Nodding his acceptance, Jack sunk into the large sofa and patted the cushion beside him. "Come and sit down. Get it off your chest," he said.

Putting the two glasses on the coffee table she sat down next to him and rested her head on his broad shoulder. "I'm not indulging myself in any self-pity," she declared defiantly. "I came out of Court, walked all the way back to the hotel, stopping in two pubs en route before buying that bottle of wine from the shop on the corner. I've drunk half of it and I'm ready to tough this one out. That isn't to say that tomorrow's going to be easy when the papers come out."

"Of course it isn't. When I had a bad game and we lost I hated reading the papers next day. And when I had a good game and we lost I hated reading them just as much. You had a good game, Naomi, but you lost. It happens. Move on. Next match. Next case."

"I sat in Court afterwards and thought it through. I know I did the case pretty well. So I'll come to terms with it. I've refused to put the TV News on, but it'll be hard to avoid the papers tomorrow. Once that's over I'll cope," she told him. "Oh, by the way, when I was in Court afterwards the cleaner came in. She had the waste paper from the jury room which she has to have incinerated. But there was an absolutely brilliant drawing of me. Pass me my notebook off the table and I'll show you."

Jack leaned over and picked up the blue foolscap notebook from the coffee table and handed it to her with her glass of wine.

"There it is," she announced, sitting up and extracting it from within her notebook before giving it to him. "It's strictly against the rules that I've got it. But it was so exceptional that I kept it. It would cost the girl her job if anyone found out and would be pretty dangerous for me as well. I should have told her to take it with the rest of the stuff."

"But it is pretty special," Jack responded, studying every line of the drawing with great care. "Look, can you see in the bottom right hand corner, there are two initials. I can just make them out. S.V. Do you see?"

"You're right," she agreed, immediately thumbing through her notebook. "Yes, here's my note of the jury's names. Number one was Sebastian Viney. He must be a professional artist. I really shouldn't have it but I'm reluctant to destroy it, what do you think?"

"I'm not too troubled about keeping the picture of you, Naomi, but have you looked at the other side?" Jack asked with some concern in his voice.

"No. I never thought to look. Why? Is there something there?" she enquired anxiously.

"Look for yourself," he replied, handing it over.

"Oh, my God," she exclaimed in horror as another face stared out at her, drawn with the same accuracy and skill as the picture of her. A lean, elderly face, hollow cheeks and sunken eyes with lizard-like lids. The reptile. The corrupt image of power who had used Brockley to threaten her not to call Leadbetter and whom she'd seen at the back of the upstairs gallery after her speech, but invisible to the jury. How could Sebastian Viney have ever seen this man at all, let alone seen him for long enough to draw a portrait of this detail and quality?

"Who is it? Do you recognise him?" demanded Jack impatiently.

"Oh, yes. He's the man who tried to stop me calling Leadbetter. He took Brockley into a room and put the frighteners on him. He's either from the Intelligence Services or from the Government. I saw him coming out of the room. We glared at each other. He's haunted this case. But it's worse than that, Jack. There's some writing. Read it," she insisted, handing the paper back. Read it out loud."

"It's not that easy to read. The writing is very small. Hang on, I think it says 'Guilty' he began.

"And then?"

"Do we do as The National Security man says?"

"Bloody Hell" cried Naomi. "Bloody Hell. We're sitting on a piece of dynamite. I can't believe it. He's got in there and nobbled them. In the middle of the Old Bailey. I just can't believe this is happening."

"You've got to destroy this immediately, Naomi. Now. Put a match to it" Jack declared emphatically.

"But I won the case. I beat that bastard Cadogan. That reptile nobbled them. It's obvious," she cried.

"Of course it's obvious," he replied. "But if you give this to the Police you'll have to admit that you received a piece of paper from the secrecy of the jury room. Not only will the cleaner be sacked. Not only will you be disbarred. But you'll both be prosecuted for breaking the Law. It's one thing keeping a picture, but it's quite another to keep and read vital details of the jury's secret deliberations."

"You're probably right. The price of trying to get at this creature is to sacrifice my own future," she agreed, her voice now shaking as she spoke.

"Has anyone else seen this?" Jack enquired anxiously.

"Janet, the cleaner. But she only looked at the side with my picture on. Same as me."

"Anyone else?" he insisted.

"Yes. Mike Myott. He was in the Robing Room when I eventually went up there. It was on top of my brief."

"Which side up?"

"My portrait side."

"Are you sure about that?"

"Positive," she replied, straining to recollect every last detail. "He passed some comment about it. Asked me who drew it and I got shirty with him for prying."

"What did you say?"

"I lied. Something like a friend of mine had drawn it. He'd come to watch some of the trial and given it me yesterday."

"Did he believe you?"

"I can't see why not."

"Did he look at the other side?"

"No. Absolutely not. As soon as he mentioned it I put it straight into my notebook. Just where it was when I pulled it out to show you a minute ago."

"So he had no chance to see the other side?"

Naomi paused for a long time before answering. "Yes. He had the chance. I couldn't find my suitcase. Had to look around for it. I was out of sight of him and the piece of paper. He could've looked then, but I very much doubt it. He never said anything more about it."

286

"OK. We destroy it. Now. If anyone ever asks, you say that there was a piece of paper with a picture of you on it, left in Court after the trial. You took it upstairs to the Robing Room, got changed, tore it into a thousand pieces and left. That's it. You did look briefly at the portrait of you, thought it was harmless but nevertheless felt it was prudent to destroy it, as you weren't sure exactly where it had come from. Have you got that?"

"I've got it."

"Do you agree? Because once we make this decision we're stuck with it forever?"

"Perhaps we should sleep on it," she said hesitatingly.

"No. We make a decision. You don't know who you're dealing with. As long as that piece of paper exists you're vulnerable."

"You mean a juror could spill the beans?" she asked.

"I view that as most unlikely. Once those jurors reversed their verdict as a result of whatever this individual said to them, then they were stuck with that decision for good. They had their chance. They blew it when they acquitted Barford. Now they can never speak out without putting themselves at all kinds of risk. But he knows you saw him."

"So?"

"He knows you realised it was him putting the pressure on. He's dangerous. I don't want you in possession of anything that he might want."

"OK. You've convinced me. I can never give this to the authorities without jeopardising my own position. Barford won't be prosecuted for the same offence twice and the chances of ever getting that reptile into a criminal dock are non-existent anyway. We burn it. There's a book of matches on the mantelpiece."

Jack stood up, moved the green, metal waste bin nearer the sofa before collecting the flimsy book of matches from the mantelpiece. Holding the paper over the bin he struck a match.

"Last chance. Yes or no?" he said dramatically.

"Yes," came the eventual reply.

Slowly the small flame curled up the from the bottom of the white sheet of paper, as he tentatively held it by the corner between his thumb and index finger, when she suddenly jumped to her feet, snatched it from his hand, threw it on to the floor and quickly dropped her heavy brief from the coffee table on top of it, immediately extinguishing the flame.

"I can't let you do it," she gasped. "I just can't let you do it".

With a deeply troubled expression on his face Jack knelt down, lifted the heavy brief up and surveyed the deadly piece of paper beneath, which still displayed its enigmatic portraits of a beautiful woman and a reptile.

"It's survived" he announced. "Only the corner is burned. The pictures are intact and so are the notes. Why did you stop me?"

"Because it's so important and because it's too late at night to make a final decision," she answered.

"Or is it because you beat the bastard?" came Jack's biting riposte, as he placed the salvaged paper on the table and they both stood staring at it in unwilling fascination.

"Do you think my vanity outweighs all other considerations then?"

"All I know is that as long as that piece of paper exists you are at risk," Jack responded emphatically. "But the decision must be yours."

"The time for a decision is tomorrow. In the cold light of day. Not in haste. Not in panic. Not late at night. Leave it there. On the table. We'll talk about it in the morning," she replied. "Now it's bedtime. I'm tired out."

"Ashes to ashes," he said. "That's the solution in my opinion. But we'll see how you feel about it tomorrow. Let's get some sleep."

Chapter 42

It was after midnight when the two calls came in. Templar had been guest of honour at a civic reception in the Mansion House and had not returned home until nearly half past eleven. Throwing his dinner suit on to the sofa for the valet to attend to in the morning, he had slipped into the mid-grey Adidas tracksuit and black running shoes, poured himself a large Remy Martin, settled into the comfortable armchair in front of the gas log-effect fire in the study and ruefully reflected on the day's events. The Commander had come through in the end. Barford would be dispensed with. The jury's verdict had shown Leadbetter to be a liar. He would be sacked and paid off. Tomorrow's papers would be a rough ride, but the emphatic denials had already been leaked. A formal statement would follow and then Templar had been invited to accompany the European delegates to the two-day conference in Edinburgh. By the time he returned to London it would all be yesterday's news.

Denstone's call came first.

"Just one more mistake, Will. That's all it will take," had been Denstone's opening gambit.

"There won't be any further mistakes, Prime Minister. You have my word on that," came the sycophantic response.

"Your word?" Denstone replied sharply. "We both know that your word is worthless. This matter has been all about your skin, not your word."

"I understand, Prime Minister."

"You can tell the other individual that he's survived as well. But you're both on a final warning."

"I'll pass the message on."

"Of course you will. Good night."

The Commander's call had followed almost immediately.

"Are you ready?" enquired the metallic voice.

"Give me ten minutes," Templar replied, breaking the connection.

He slowly finished the brandy, taking his time, letting the bastard sweat it out. Then, collecting the navy blue woollen hat from the hall table, he pulled it down low over his head and set out into the night air, at his snail's pace. The sinister figure was in the identical position on the bridge as last night, but this time Templar had his confidence back. The crisis had passed.

"Has he phoned?" barked the Commander anxiously.

"Yes. Two minutes before you did, as a matter of fact," came the reply, as Templar stooped, pretending to be occupied with his laces.

"And?" snapped the Commander impatiently.

"My position is secure," declared Templar, as he straightened up and looked into the drawn, bloodless face.

"And?"

"Is there any risk of any of the jury talking?" the Home Secretary enquired anxiously, deliberately ignoring the Commander's question.

"Absolutely none. Getting in and out was far from easy. I wasn't seen. Fortunately, it's a labyrinth back there. The bailiff sits at the far end of the corridor. But the jury's silence is assured. I had the National Security Document. It convinced them. And I petrified them."

"Excellent."

"So? How much longer do you intend to play games?"

"You called me a coward last night. I didn't like that. I'd appreciate an apology," Templar demanded.

The head shot forward like a snake striking. The face came right up to Templar's so he could see the horrible, white skin, forcing Templar instinctively to step backwards, until he was pressed right up against the stonework of the bridge and could retreat no further. "Don't mess with me, Templar. I know too much. Your ministerial cars and grace and favours are safe. What about me?" he hissed.

"All right. All right. You've survived. We've both survived. Final warnings have been issued. That's the message," Templar breathed. "I'd be grateful if you allowed me some room," he added.

"We shan't need to meet or talk again, then," the Commander said, now visibly relaxing.

"No," replied Templar, turning away. "It's over. A couple of rough days in the paper. Denials leaked already. It's over. Finished."

And he jogged silently away into the night leaving the Commander on the bridge. Alone.

Chapter 43

Neither Jack nor Naomi slept very well that night and at seven o'clock Jack got up, took a shower and dressed. Naomi sat up in bed watching him, reflecting on the events of yesterday whilst the piece of paper sat menacingly on the coffee table, as yet unmentioned by either of them, as if by ignoring it some extraneous event would make the dreaded decision for them.

"Let's go down to breakfast and then get an early train home," Jack suggested.

"Fine by me," she smiled, her long, blonde hair dishevelled by the night. "On condition that we don't buy any morning newspapers. Today will be the worst day."

"Agreed. But with one exception. I must get a copy of the national my report is in. Back page reading only, I promise," he said. "I'll go and do that while you shower and I'll come back up for you in a quarter of an hour."

"OK," she replied, jumping out of bed, as Jack set off for the lift.

Ten minutes later, when she emerged from the bathroom wrapped in one of the hotel's bright blue, fluffy towels, Jack was already sitting in the armchair. Ashen-faced. The newspaper lay on the coffee table alongside the sheet of paper with the burned corner.

"Before you read it," he began, with a tremor in his voice, "you have to know that this is nothing to do with me. Nothing. I saw the headline on the News Stand. I realised we had to know exactly what it said."

In silence she reached out for the newspaper, her hand still damp and her hair dripping water on to the newsprint. The headline alone forced her to sit down and then, word by dangerous word, she read the article in a state of disbelief.

BARFORD ACQUITTAL LETS GOVERNMENT OFF HOOK

Questions over verdict. Was it a fix?

Crime Correspondent : 'The Molecule Man'

After a sensational trial at The Old Bailey, Lewis Barford yesterday walked free at the hands of a jury about whom the Molecule Man raises serious questions. Charged with conspiring to murder a young Arab who intended to blow the whistle on attempts by the authorities to suppress information about the Manchester Airbus atrocity, Barford was maintaining absolute silence as he sped away from the famous old Court in a limousine with blacked-out windows.

Naomi Nicholas QC, prosecuting, alleged that Barford had recruited a mercenary to carry out the contract killing for the sum of £5000. Derek Lennox, who had operated under Barford's command in the bloody uprisings in Sierra Leone, had claimed from his prison deathbed that Barford had met him in a Betting Office in Leicester where the deal was struck. Whilst Barford admitted an agreement to steal a diary, he adamantly denied any instructions to use violence. By their verdict, the jury would seem to have believed him, but the Molecule Man is not so sure. At the heart of the case lay the role of Chief Superintendent Leadbetter whose evidence, in most unusual circumstances, was called by the Prosecution after the close of the Defence case. Exposed as a liar by fingerprint evidence dramatically demanded by Ronan Cadogan QC, defending, Leadbetter subsequently stated that in a clandestine meeting between Barford, the Home Secretary and himself on a canal barge, the young Arab was intending to give his story to the Molecule Man. In the course of a stunning re-examination of Leadbetter by Miss Nicholas, despite his earlier lies, there emerged a compelling tale of Barford's involvement. Yet the jury acquitted. The Molecule Man has followed this trial closely and learned of sinister attempts from high places to keep Leadbetter out of the witness box. Even more disturbing, last night, the Molecule Man was given reason to suspect, from a most reliable source, that the jury probably wanted to convict. What stopped them? Or, more accurately perhaps, who stopped them? No one in authority will ever answer that question. But readers may be assured that the Molecule Man will not shrink from continuing to ask the awkward questions.

"It's all right, Jack," she breathed softly. I know it's not you. You were with me all night and I hardly slept. Besides, I would believe you anyway."

"So who is it?" asked Jack. "Who has told this reporter that the jury may have been nobbled?"

"There are sixteen candidates," she replied with surprising calm.

"I can see that the jury count for twelve of those," Jack responded immediately. "So who are the other four?"

"You're right about the jury. I firmly believe that we can discount them for the reasons that you gave last night. The other four are you and me . . . " she began.

"Both discounted," interrupted Jack immediately.

"So we're left with Janet Kelly, the cleaner," Naomi continued, "but I know for a fact that she never saw the other side of the piece of paper. She only saw the picture of me. So she goes."

"Leaving?" asked Jack breathlessly.

"Myott" she declared. "Mike Myott. My bloody Junior."

"You mean that Myott must have seen the other side of the piece of paper and given that information to the Molecule Man?"

"No, Jack. I don't mean that. I don't mean that at all?" she replied angrily.

"Then, what do you mean?" he demanded impatiently.

"I mean that Myott is the Molecule Man," she replied, staring intently at him to gauge his reaction.

There was a long pause before he answered. "Lunchtime in 'El Guerrero Valiente.' He knew that runner for the papers. The fellow whose table we took. And he never gave proper answers about his practice."

"He hasn't got much of a practice, has he?" she replied. "He is a barrister. I even had doubts about that at one stage so I checked in The Bar Directory. In a third rate set of London chambers. Does some written work occasionally for the legal periodicals. Although he did claim to have had an article about 'Dying Declarations' published, when in fact he hadn't. But his practice is just a smokescreen. He's a journalist."

"You can't be sure."

"His mother is a writer. About injustice. Think about it," she insisted.

"From what you say he certainly had the opportunity to look on the other side of the piece of paper last night while you were trying to find your suitcase," Jack reasoned.

"More than enough time. And then I got ratty with him when he commented on the portrait. So, if he'd looked on the other side, he'd know why I'd turned nasty. To make it worse, I then lied. That's when he knew that he'd struck gold."

"I'm a journalist now, Naomi. I see them and I mix with them. They're curious by nature. If he's a journalist and he saw that portrait of you, then it's a pound to a penny he'd have picked it up and looked on the other side. Just like I did when you showed it to me last night."

"I'm pretty convinced. Look how he brought Mr El-Hoorie to see me that night. Here in the hotel," she said. "That was a journalist at work, not a barrister."

"There's some evidence it's him, I agree, but it still remains unlikely."

"It all fits though, doesn't it? The way he kept on disappearing. Always at times when there was a chance that there might be a reference to the Molecule Man during the trial. Particularly, when Smail was in the witness box and when I re-examined Leadbetter. That was inexcusable for a Junior," she said.

"Why is that significant?" Jack asked. "I don't follow."

"Because he was paying some scant regard to the rules about being a barrister. If, in truth, he is a journalist reporting on this case, then he should never have been appearing as Counsel in the case. Here 'The Molecule Man' actually had dealings with Smail, so Myott absented himself from Court. He was probably nervous that Leadbetter might also mention the name, so he cleared off. At least he could say that he never let anything he knew about the case from his contacts as a journalist have any influence on the trial."

"But it's still completely against the rules, surely?"

"Of course it is. Absolutely. He broke the rules."

"So you think that he leads a double-life?"

"I'm getting surer by the minute," she answered.

"There is one other fact we've overlooked," Jack added. "The Molecule Man. MM. Mike Myott. His initials."

"He's certainly cute enough," she agreed. "Anyway. The acid test. I phone up his newspaper. Ask to speak to 'The Molecule Man'. Or ask him to phone me back. I give a false name. Then, as soon as I hear the voice I'll know."

Jack paused for a while before replying. "If it's him I don't think that will work."

"Why not?"

"Firstly, because I doubt that he takes any incoming calls personally. The fact that someone's called for him will be relayed to him. He'll only call them back after checking and re-checking. He'll be wise to people using false names. Anonymity is everything to him. He'll have a very effective filtering system set up," Jack explained.

"You said 'firstly'. Is there another reason as well, then?" she asked.

"Yes. Myott is an extremely talented impressionist. In the bar he put on the voices of the Arsenal Manager, the Prime Minister and Cadogan within a minute. All done to perfection," Jack explained.

"So?"

"So, if he really is leading a double-life, using the true Myott voice when he's being a barrister . . . "

" . . . he's going to use a different voice for his alter ego," Naomi said, completing his sentence for him.

"Of course."

"OK. Plan B. I demand he comes round to the hotel immediately. With you by my side. We confront him."

"Where are you intending to go with this? You personally can't report him because any enquiry instigated by you, in your name, will risk exposing the fact that you were in possession of a piece of paper from the jury room," Jack reasoned.

"I need to know if my damned Junior was this Molecule Man, Jack. I'll decide how to deal with it when I know if it was him. At the moment tt seems perfectly obvious to me that it was, but I want to have it out with him."

"OK, I'll go along with that. You're entitled to know. But if it isn't him, then we leave it. This case has got to come to an end for you. And the sooner the better. If it is him, we threaten to expose him, unless he agrees never to refer to the case again in his paper."

"Of course it's him," she insisted, reaching for her notebook. "I've got his number in here. I agree with your plan. I do need to put this nightmare of a case behind me, but not until we've sorted the double-dealing bastard out. Here it is," she exclaimed, immediately dialling the number.

Jack watched her intently as the call rang out, observing the fury and determination in her eyes as she sat on the sofa, still wrapped only in the bath towel, her hair tumbling down across her lovely face. He had no doubt that if they got Myott in the room then, between them, they'd break him down.

"Mike. This is Naomi," she snapped. "I need to talk to you as a matter of urgency. In person. Face to face. You know my room number. Get yourself over here as soon as you pick up this message. If I haven't heard from you by ten o'clock, I'll come looking for you. Starting with your chambers. I'm warning you not to ignore this message."

"Does he normally keep his phone switched on?" asked Jack.

"Oh, yes. As soon as we come out of Court his hand goes for his phone. Switches it on. Checks his messages. Makes his calls. I've watched him doing it for over a week," she replied angrily. "Just like the bloody journalist he undoubtedly is."

"Get yourself dressed then," suggested Jack. "We'll need to be on our mettle. I'll order some breakfast to be sent up while we wait. We go into battle on full stomachs. Eggs and bacon. OK by you?"

"Not enough. Eggs, bacon, sausage, tomato and mushrooms," she replied, picking up the piece of paper and slipping it inside her Counsel's notebook. "But that's just a starter. We're having Myott for the main course."

* * *

The knock on the door came at just before nine. Dressed in a lime green linen jacket, open-necked check shirt and jeans, he looked very different from how Naomi had seen him before. His long face appeared even longer, because he was not wearing the rimless glasses, which he had always worn, nor had he bothered to shave.

"I came straight over," he began. "You sounded so angry."

"Don't you really need glasses then?" she barked at him.

"What on earth is the relevance of that? he asked. "I've got contacts on if you really want to know."

"Come in," she replied. "Jack and I have a very serious issue to discuss with you. We'll try to keep it civilised."

"Do you want a coffee?" Jack asked, pointing to the breakfast tray and the large vacuum jug upon it.

"No. I don't," Myott answered, lowering himself into the armchair immediately beneath the picture window that looked out over the river. "I want to know what I'm meant to have done to upset Naomi like this. It wasn't my fault we lost the case, any more than it was Naomi's."

"Have you seen the article?" demanded Naomi, as Jack positioned the two hard-backed dining chairs opposite Myott, so that he and Naomi encircled him when they sat down.

"Yes"

"And?"

"He's a journalist. And a damned good one at that. He's looking for the extra ingredient. He's got no firm evidence that the jury were nobbled, but he's got the courage to raise the question. Anyway, he gave you a good write-up," Myott replied.

"I want some straight answers, Mike. Listen to this," Naomi continued, picking the newspaper article up from the table and reading from it :

'The Molecule Man was given reason to suspect, from a most reliable source, that the jury probably wanted to convict. What stopped them? Or, more accurately perhaps, who stopped them?'

What possible source does he have to make that allegation?

"How am I meant to know?" Myott protested. "What exactly are you suggesting?"

"I'll come to what I'm suggesting in a minute. But listen to this quote :

'The Molecule Man has followed this trial closely and learned of sinister attempts from high places to keep Leadbetter out of the witness box.'

Hardly anyone knew about that. But you knew," she declared, leaning forward in her chair and pointing her finger at him.

"Other people knew. Brockley knew. I've no doubt you told Jack. So why am I under attack?" he answered indignantly. "I don't like this one little bit."

Jack got up from his chair and slowly poured himself a cup of coffee while Naomi continued her barrage of questions. Returning to his chair, he interrupted. "I've got a few questions for you," he said. "Like why did you keep on disappearing during the trial at times when the witness was likely to refer to the Molecule Man?"

"Because things came up in chambers and at home," he insisted. "And besides, let's be honest here, Naomi didn't need me that badly. My real role would have been to keep a note of the evidence when she was on her feet, but about the only useful thing Brockley did was to get Mel in and he kept a verbatim note on his laptop. I didn't matter."

"Do you share the same ideology as your mother, a perpetual quest for justice?" Jack enquired, carefully watching Myott's reaction to this line of attack.

"My mother? How does my mother fit into all of this, for goodness sake?" he replied angrily.

"Pursuit of the truth, perhaps," Jack continued. "But here's the key question. In the Robing Room, after the verdict, when Naomi was looking for her suitcase, you looked at that pencil portrait of her, didn't you?"

"I did. It was pretty impressive. Done by a professional artist, I'd say. I asked her who drew it and she said a friend of hers."

"Carry on," demanded Jack.

"What do you mean, carry on?"

"You know exactly what I mean. Did you look at the other side of the paper?" Jack snapped aggressively, fixing Myott with an unwavering stare.

There was a long silence, during which Myott was shifting uncomfortably in his seat, reluctant to look either of them in the eye.

"Well? We're waiting for an answer," Naomi barked at him, still unable to provoke any response from him.

"Your silence provides the answer, doesn't it?" Jack finally said.

"I was shocked," Myott spluttered. "Naomi had got cross when I mentioned the picture at all. Then, because I did see the other side, I knew she was lying about a friend drawing it. I didn't know what to do. So I left. I was out of my depth."

"Did you realise the ramifications of what you'd seen on the other side?" Naomi asked.

"Of course I did. That dreadful character we saw come out of the room with Brockley must have somehow frightened the jury off. They were going to convict. But you were so aggressive. Then you lied. I didn't know how to deal with it."

"So what did you do? Take the story off to the Press? Or are you the Press?" Jack growled at him.

"I was worried by what I'd seen, so I went to the pub and had a few drinks."

"To meet one of the runners from a national newspaper perhaps?" Jack continued in the same tone.

"No. To meet Mel Coleman, as a matter of fact. I'd arranged to see him in "The Bat and Wicket" round the back of St Paul's. He'd worked hard during the case, been interested in it, seemed to be a decent guy. I said I'd buy him a drink. In the circumstances I was glad of the company."

Jack and Naomi looked at each other immediately. For a long time no one in the room spoke. Gradually, Myott's expression changed and he put his head in his hands. Then, in a nervous voice, he whispered.

"You don't have to ask. I did tell him. I was shocked by what I'd seen on the piece of paper. I knew from your attitude and your lie, Naomi, that you wouldn't talk to me about it."

"So you told a solicitor's agent? A dogsbody?" Naomi exclaimed in horror. "Who probably gets paid a pittance. You supplied him with confidential material, which he could sell to the papers for thousands?"

"I didn't think. I was upset. A couple of drinks. He kept wanting to talk about the case. I'm sorry. I told him it was never to be repeated."

"And what did he say when you told him?" asked Jack, his face screwed up in intense concentration.

"Kept asking questions. More and more questions."

"And did you tell him that you recognised the face drawn on the other side?" Naomi demanded.

"It just tumbled out. He kept saying not to worry about it. I told him I reckoned that was the guy who'd put the squeeze on us not to call Leadbetter," he admitted, shaking his head as he spoke.

"So you told him everything," Jack concluded.

"Probably," Myott mumbled.

"And no doubt, as soon as you parted, he was on the phone to the Press. And who did he contact? The bloody Molecule Man," Naomi declared in disgust. "Thanks, Mike. For being so dumb."

"But I suspect that there's still one mistake in your reasoning, Naomi" Jack said slowly and quietly.

"What?" she asked.

"Do you remember in 'El Guerrero Valiente' yesterday lunchtime? You, Mike and me," he continued, in the same deliberate delivery, as if he was thinking aloud.

"Yes."

"Mike told us he spoke fluent Spanish."

"Yes."

"Mike told us his mother was Spanish."

"Yes."

"And then he told us that Mel spoke fluent German. Actually was German."

"You've completely lost me," Naomi said. "What's his nationality got to do with any of this?"

There was a sharp intake of breath from Myott, who had been staring transfixed at Jack, as Jack's careful analysis had unfolded.

"It's not his nationality, Naomi," Jack continued. "It's his name. Mike told us, in the bar, his middle name was Ulrich."

"So?" she replied, still bemused.

"You're a brilliant barrister, Naomi, but you've never been much good at crosswords, have you? Anagrams," Jack explained. "Mel Ulrich Coleman. Mel U Coleman. Work it out."

"Oh, my God," she shouted out as the letters rearranged themselves in her mind. "I don't believe it. *Molecule Man*. His name is an anagram of *Molecule Man*. Mel U Coleman is *The Molecule Man*."

"You're nearly right," Jack nodded. "Except for one thing. There won't be any Mel U Coleman. It's his smokescreen. The name he's used when he's decided to surface to get the inside story. In fact, Mel Coleman won't exist. I would guess that it's the Molecule Man's sense of humour to choose that name. We'll check, but I suspect that we'll find that no one's ever heard of him."

"I can check immediately. It will only take one phone call," interrupted Myott, immediately reaching inside his jacket pocket for his mobile phone and hitting a pre-set button."

"Giles Brockley? Mike Myott here," he said a few seconds later when the call was answered. "I've got a question for you, Giles. About Mel Coleman? How did you get him? Which agency?"

After a minute he broke the connection.

"The Lexical Legal Services Agency based in Fulham. They phoned Brockley not long before the trial," he reported back. "Told him they did a lot of work for Defence solicitors but wanted to attract some Prosecution work," he continued. They'd let him have one of the brightest ones on their books, touch typist, willing, polite, the works. And, if Brockley was impressed with the service and used them again, then, as a special introductory offer, there'd be no charge for their services for this trial. They'd pay Coleman themselves."

"So get Directory Enquiries on your mobile, Mike, and get the number for The Lexical Legal Services Agency in Fulham," demanded Naomi.

"There won't be any such number, nor any such company," Jack assured her. "But try just in case."

Two minutes later Myott put his phone down. "No such name. No such company. No Lexical anything, anywhere in London, nor anywhere in the country."

"He's shafted us. Cadogan style," Naomi declared in anger.

"And he got his story," Myott said.

"But we're all losers, including him," Jack replied. "Barford walked and the mystery man with the reptile's face will disappear back under his stone. And, most importantly from the Molecule Man's point of view, Templar will survive. The acquittal saved Templar. That's who he will have wanted to bring down. A Cabinet Minister."

"But he still can, surely," Myott insisted. All we have to do is send him the piece of paper. Anonymously. He'll know it's from us. There's no way he'll breach that anonymity. He'll publish it. You can't doubt his courage. Then Templar will fall."

"We can't do that," Naomi replied.

"Why not?" demanded Myott. "That way, the culprit at the top of the ladder will fall."

"I told you, we can't do it," she repeated.

"But because we now know who the Molecule Man is, and because he will know the source of the piece of paper and will never reveal it was us, we're safe. We can bring Templar down and probably the Commander as well."

"Don't you listen, Mike. We can't do it," Naomi insisted.

"But then everyone will know that, in truth, you beat Cadogan," Myott continued unabated. "You beat him."

"We can't do it," she repeated sadly, looking across at Jack. "We burned the paper. The ashes are still in the bin. I'll give you them as a souvenir."

"Forgive me, Naomi," declared Myott hesitantly after a long pause, "but I don't believe you. I've watched you carefully over the last week or so. You're as shrewd as they come. And you've got a will of iron. There's no way you would have destroyed that evidence. What's more, you're a woman."

"What the hell has that got to do with it?" she snapped.

"Plenty," Myott declared. "Firstly, you're testing my reaction. Seeing where I really stand. That's exactly how a woman would think."

"And secondly?" she asked.

"Secondly, that piece of paper proves you outgunned the best criminal barrister in the country. A man you detest. No woman could allow herself to destroy that proof."

"Female vanity. Is that what you're implying?" she asked.

"In a word, yes."

Naomi and Jack looked at each other for a few seconds before Naomi's face gradually softened and, despite herself, she began to laugh, followed quickly by a relieved chuckle from Myott, until Jack, remaining stony-faced, brought them sharply back to the dilemma.

"If we give it to him, then he'll publish the whole document. Naomi's picture will be all over the front page of his paper. She'll be under suspicion. How can we be sure that The Molecule Man will never disclose his source?"

"Let me get a message to him through the paper," Myott urged. "I'll demand that he phones me as a matter of urgency. When I speak to him, I'll tell him that we've worked out who he is and we're prepared to expose him. On the other hand, if we have a cast iron guarantee that he'll never disclose his sources, we'll send him the original of the piece of paper and he can use it as he sees fit. The portrait of Naomi proves nothing against her. Everyone knows she was Prosecuting Counsel and was seen by the jury throughout the trial."

Jack was watching Myott with great care, observing how he seemed to fluctuate from nervousness to decisiveness. Now, he was seeking to take complete control, call the shots and assert his will over all the other players.

"What's driving you on here?" Jack demanded to know. "You're so keen to give the Molecule Man even more bullets to fire at Templar and the Establishment, yet you show little interest in the fact that Barford walked. Given that we believe that the jury really thought Barford was guilty, I can't fathom exactly where you're coming from."

"You've put your finger on the irony of the whole situation, Jack," came Myott's measured response. "I've found myself thinking about this ever since Leadbetter went into the witness box. I read the notes of his evidence again last night. I don't believe Barford did tell Lennox to kill El-Hoorie. It was a hush job, backed up by some muscle. Do you remember Leadbetter's evidence, Naomi? Barford telling him that there were only three alternatives. The threat of violence. Actual violence. Fatal violence."

"Very clearly," she replied, nodding her head.

"The only evidence that the order was to do fatal violence, rather than just knock him about a bit, came from Lennox. None of them have told the whole truth. Not Barford, nor Leadbetter, and certainly not Lennox," Myott said.

"And what a final gesture from a career psychopath," Jack volunteered, starting to find the argument compelling. "Striking back at everyone from the grave. The last laugh. The Establishment left in tatters. Barford inside for life. I must admit that five thousand pounds to commit a murder always sounded a bit on the cheap side."

"But much more like the going rate for putting the frighteners on someone," added Myott. "And, like I said, they all lied. Leadbetter eventually told part of the truth when he said that Templar was on that barge, but that wasn't the whole story."

"You mean he was still lying when he claimed there were only three of them there? I was less than convinced about that myself," Naomi interrupted.

"Of course. Leadbetter and Barford went to that barge with their superiors. Barford had Templar with him, as Leadbetter finally admitted, and no doubt the Commander was with Leadbetter, but no-one ever implicated him," Myott asserted confidently.

"It makes sense," Jack agreed.

"Exactly. In the final analysis, the Commander could be relied upon to find a way out of the mess. To save Barford and thereby save Templar," Myott reasoned. "But none of that even begins to prove that Barford gave the order to kill, as opposed to dishing out a bit of the rough stuff. The jury's final verdict, coerced though it was, probably turned out to be right."

"So you suggest that we make a copy of the document. You contact the Molecule Man's newspaper. You leave a message that he must get in touch with you urgently. You extract the guarantees. You make it clear that it's Templar's head we're after. And then you give him the original sheet of paper. Is that the plan?" Jack asked.

"Only if that is a unanimous decision," Myott replied. "But that plan would certainly win my vote."

"And I'm persuaded. A journalist of that quality would never go back on those guarantees. Naomi would be safe," announced Jack, as both men turned to look expectantly at Naomi.

"Then we have a verdict," she declared without hesitation. "Unanimous. Now we'll really see what the Molecule Man is made of."

Chapter 44

It had been a dreadful morning. Accusing eyes staring into his back. Vicious whispers in the corridors of the House. Animated conversations stopping dead as he walked into the room. Sniggers of contempt from the Opposition in the Bar at lunchtime. But, despite all of this, he had survived.

The Molecule Man's attack in the newspaper was long on innuendo and short on proof. If he could just ride out the next few days the story would start to subside. Once off the front pages it could be dismissed by the Downing Street spinners as journalistic froth. The culture of this Government was denial of accountability; no Minster resigned unless there was a smoking gun. And then, as he stood alone getting some fresh air on the lower terrace, his mobile phone had rung and the final walk to his execution began.

"Is that the Home Secretary?" demanded the voice urgently.

"Who is calling?" Templar responded anxiously.

"This is the Molecule Man," came the immediate reply, sending a shudder down Templar's backbone.

"Who gave you this number?" Templar barked, trying to retain some note of authority in his trembling voice.

"Let's not waste time with that, Home Secretary. Like you said on the barge, I can be terminally dangerous so I suggest you hear me out."

"What do you want? You've got one minute," Templar answered, hurriedly walking over to the far corner of the terrace which was deserted and well out of earshot of any the Members.

"I'm giving you a choice, Home Secretary," the voice ominously intoned. "We've got two headlines prepared for the morning edition. You're about to tell me which one we run with."

"Do you realise that you're within an inch of threatening a Minister of State?" spluttered Templar. "I can get your call traced. I can force you out into the open."

"Spare me the righteous indignation. By this time tomorrow at the latest, you won't be a Minister of State. Not even you will be able to cling on to office."

"This is preposterous. I refuse to listen . . . "

"Forget the protests. Here are the choices. Headline one. Home Secretary Resigns. Ill health and anxiety cited as reasons. Headline two. Home Secretary To Be Sacked. Evidence of involvement in Jury Nobbling sent to Scotland Yard. Do I get my message across?"

"What evidence?" Templar spat venomously.

"In my hand. At the moment. A document recovered from the jury room."

"A forgery, no doubt."

"No way. If necessary the jury will have to be interviewed by the Police. Not a forgery, I can assure you. Anyway, at the end of this call, you'll give me a fax number and I'll send you a copy."

"You're committing a criminal offence by having material from a jury room," Templar declared defiantly.

"I can live with that," the Molecule Man said. "This document has two drawings on it. One is the Prosecuting QC. The other is a portrait of your man. The fixer. The Intelligence Services Commander you sent in to nobble them. That's the only time they could ever have seen him. They were going to convict. Your man. He stopped them. We're ready to have him confronted as well. Depends on your decision. It's your head we want."

"You're a low grade hack. Working for a sensationalist rag. You're trying it on, making it up. Bluffing. All your allegations are emphatically denied. I've no more to say to you," Templar shouted angrily, his voice growing increasingly shrill, as terror eroded his self-control.

"As I said, this is your choice. When you check the jurors' names and occupations you will doubtless find that one of them is a skilled artist. His initials are on the document, so he'll be the first to be interviewed after we go to press. On the other hand, if you just want to resign on the grounds of ill-health and avoid the investigation, then, for my own reasons, I'm prepared to settle for that. Your choice. Do I send you the fax or do I send it straight to the Yard?" the merciless voice demanded.

"Very well. Send it to me then. I'm prepared to look. 0208 448 6731. It's my home fax. Send it at four o'clock. I'm looking out of a sense of duty, not because there's a word of truth in your allegations."

"Of course, Home Secretary. Just duty. Public duty and principle. Your guiding lights, no doubt. I'll give you one hour exactly after receipt of the fax. Then I'll phone you at five. You'll give me a decision. Otherwise I fax a copy to Scotland Yard and go to press with the full story."

"Your story is a fiction and you're a liar," Templar declared, still desperately struggling to sound convincing.

"Really?" came the sharp reply. "And I suppose you also claim that you didn't instruct your man to try to spike Leadbetter. Stop him going into the witness box. That's a lie as well, is it?"

"It's all lies. A tissue of lies," the faltering voice responded weakly.

"You were right about one thing though, Home Secretary, I'll give you that," the journalist said.

"What?"

"I am terminally dangerous. I took that as a great compliment. And now we've reached the end game. We'll speak at five," he laughed, putting the phone down.

As the connection was broken, Templar sank on to an iron bench in the corner of the terrace alongside the immaculately tended flower beds. His face was white as death, the paleness accentuated by the white strands of hair, worn too long in a vain attempt to disguise the ravages of the years. The fear and self-disgust that he felt in the pit of his stomach were now plainly visible in the haunted, darting eyes.

There was no one left to whom he could turn. Barford was gone. Denstone would destroy him. If they interviewed the Commander he would certainly take Templar down with him. He was finished. All the sacrifices of principle, the abandonment of sacred beliefs in pursuit of power were now destined to end in disgrace or worse. Tears ran down his cheeks as he wallowed in self-pity. That despicable hack had taken him apart. Molecule by molecule.

Chapter 45

Six long months had passed since the sudden and unexpected resignation of the Home Secretary on the grounds of ill health. Jack Farnham's live television programme was top of the cable ratings and Naomi's practice in silk was flourishing. Today she had travelled across the Pennines by train to represent a young man at Liverpool Crown Court who was charged with killing his own mother. Matricide. The rarest of crimes.

Attracting all the big-name journalists from the tabloids.

Arriving at Lime Street Station with its tired, outdated glass canopy of a roof, Naomi had hurried to the underground station and boarded the dirty, grubby tube to James Street where the Crown Court was situated. City of thieves, she had thought to herself as she observed the shifty faces of the scruffy people on board, their eyes forever flickering this way and that, as if in constant pursuit of the next victim. Clutching her own bag tightly to her chest, she reflected on the misery of the youth she was about to represent and the squalor of the society in which he had been brought up, but kept finding her thoughts distracted by one face in particular at the far end of the carriage, which seemed to be staring at her, but quickly turning away whenever she looked in his direction. As the train pulled into James Street Station, the figure scurried off the train and disappeared rapidly along the platform towards the clanking iron lift that transported the passengers back up to street level. The heavy doors were just closing as she reached the lift but the bored male operator, espying the approach of an attractive female, held the lift back for her and, as he cranked the ancient doors shut, she found herself standing in a small knot of people, directly alongside the man from the train and their eyes directly met.

"I suppose you hoped that I'd never see you again," she said calmly.

"No, Miss Nicholas, to the contrary," he smiled.

"I'd like a word. Upstairs, if you don't mind. In private," she snapped.

As the lift heaved its cargo out of the bowels of the city and into the mean street above, they stood in silence until, on the steps of the station, exposed to the thin, cold wind blowing in off the Mersey, she confronted him.

"You tricked your way into the Defence team, picked up privileged and confidential information, and used me," she announced in a cold fury, her eyes flashing with anger as she spoke.

"It's not true, Miss Nicholas. I knew that you'd suspect me, but it isn't true," he earnestly insisted.

"I don't even know your proper name," she continued, her fury unabated and ignoring his protestations of innocence.

"It's Mel. Melvin. Melvin Andrew Coleman. They called me 'Mac' at school. That's my real name."

"Melvin Andrew Coleman," she repeated mockingly. "Myott said that you'd told him that your middle name was Ulrich. The 'U' was to complete the anagram. Mel U. Coleman. You're the Molecule Man."

"You've got it all wrong, Miss. I am exactly what I said. A solicitor's agent. That's my job."

"And I suppose you'll be telling me next that the Lexical Legal Services Agency actually exists as well," she snapped.

"Lexical Legal Services? I've never heard of them. I work for Bosworth's. Their offices are in Walthamstow. Look, here's my card," he assured her, producing his wallet and extracting a business card from within. "My name's on it. Who told you I worked for Lexical Legal Services?"

"Myott," she answered, a note of doubt now creeping into her voice.

"Ah," he smiled, knowingly. "And have you seen or heard from Myott since Templar resigned?"

"No, I haven't."

"Have you heard anyone say that he'd been seen in Court, doing a case anywhere?"

"No, I haven't."

"And who suggested that my middle name was Ulrich?" he asked

"Myott," she whispered. "He said you were German."

"Did you check me out with Giles Brockley after the case and the newspaper article?" he asked.

"No" she answered quietly.

"Did anyone?" he persisted.

"Yes. Myott."

"I think you've got your answers, Miss Nicholas. Things are seldom as they seem, are they? I must get off or I'll be late," he said politely. "Very nice to see you again. Nothing is more elusive than the truth."

"One last question," she exclaimed, putting her hand on his arm to hold him back. *"Konnen Sie die Wahrheit sagen?"*

"I beg your pardon," he laughed. "I thought they spoke Scouse in Liverpool. What language is that you've broken into?"

"I think you know only too well," she said. "It means *'can you speak the truth?'* Don't you speak any German?"

"Nicht ein Molekul, meine gute Freundin," he replied with a smile. *"Nicht ein Molekul."*